A NEAR-INVISIBLE CLOUD OF UNIFORM DENSITY SPREAD OUT IN AN ARC.

That cloud was, in effect, Adam. It was dormant, a body waiting for the arrival of its consciousness—a cloud of nanomachines vast enough to saturate the surface of Bakunin.

They were going to destroy it.

Data scrolled by, showing Mallory's ghost fleet of empty, near-derelict tach-ships signaling back their status. Their computers were all synced, their drives hot, the damping coils on their drives disabled. Toni II shuddered just thinking of so many ships taching simultaneously. She glanced at the status of the *Daedalus'* drives. They were still cold, inert to the surge these ships would generate . . .

The meters monitoring tachyon radiation spiked.

The ships were underway. She looked back up at the holo of the cloud. Right now, nearly seven hundred ships were taching into a dangerously small volume in the center of it. Unfortunately, the light from their arrival would take nearly an hour to reach them.

"Fourteen seconds," her sister said from the captain's chair. She leaned back and said, "It's over now, one way or the other."

"Do you think it worked?" Karl asked.

Toni II could see the comm channels all lit up by chatter, and she could see why. The tachyon radiation meters had slammed the upper limits of their resolution across the board. If the *Daedalus* hadn't shut down their tach-drive completely, a good part of their engine would have burned out even with the damping coils.

Mallory's voice came over the general comm channel, telling the fleet to render what aid was possible to the damaged ships in range.

Please, after all this, let us have destroyed it.

S. ANDREW SWANN

MESSIAH

Apotheosis: Book Three

DAW BOOKS, INC.
DONALD A. WOLLHEIM, FOUNDER
375 Hudson Street, New York, NY 10014

ELIZABETH R. WOLLHEIM
SHEILA E. GILBERT
PUBLISHERS
www.dawbooks.com

*To John and Adam
in the morning.*

DRAMATIS PERSONAE

Wisconsin

Father James Mallory—Roman Catholic Priest and veteran of the Occisis Marines.

Alexander Shane—Former leader of the Salmagundi government.

Toni Valentine—Former lieutenant in the Styx Security Forces under Styx System Security Command (3SEC)

Toni II Valentine—Ghost of Toni Valentine.

Karl Stavros—Former captain of the Centauri trading vessel Daedalus.

Stefan Stavros—Karl Stavros' son.

Bakunin

Nickolai Rajasthan—Exiled scion of the House of Rajasthan. Descendant of genetically engineered tigers.

Vijayanagara Parvi—Mercenary pilot from Rubai

Julia Kugara—Mercenary from Dakota. Descendant of genetically engineered humans. Former member of Dakota Planetary Security (DPS)

Dr. Sharon Dörner—Xenobiologist from Acheron.

Dr. Samson Brody—Cultural anthropologist from Bulawayo.

Flynn Jorgenson—Former forestry surveyor from Salmagundi.

Brother Lazarus—Leader of the Dolbrian cult on Bakunin. Descendant of genetically engineered canines.

General Alexi Lubikov—Commander of the Western Division of the Proudhon Security Corporation.

The Prophet's Voice

Rebecca Tsoravitch—Former data analyst from Jokul, in the service of Adam.

Jonah Dacham—Agent of Proteus.

Tjaele Mosasa—Recorded personality of the pirate who recovered the AI that became Adam.

CONTENTS

LAST PROLOGUE

The Sacred and the Profane

"Know what is evil, no matter how worshiped it may be."

—BALTASAR GRACIÁN
(1601–1658)

CHAPTER ONE

Heretics

"The establishment's greatest disgust is reserved for those who love the wrong person."
—*The Cynic's Book of Wisdom*

"Religion has done love a great service by making it a sin."

—ANATOLE FRANCE
(1844–1924)

The first time Nickolai Rajasthan came to the planet Bakunin, he had come in disgrace. The priests of his homeland had ruled he had sinned too gravely, or perhaps more important, too publicly, for him to continue life as a scion of House Rajasthan.

The royal family on Grimalkin was powerful enough to do as they would in most cases, and should a tiger of Rajasthan have a dalliance with the lesser-born—even if it was in violation of the scriptures—there were rarely any consequences. Nickolai's peers had all dallied with servants before the family had chosen a mate for them.

But his peers' indiscretions had never lasted long, and had been discreet.

Nickolai had the bad sense to care for the female he bedded.

Worse, he had the arrogance to believe his position protected him. His affair with his panther lover had extended into months, and his family had become alarmed enough to finally put an end to his foolishness. They rushed him into an arranged marriage and sold the lowly object of his obsessions to a family far from the seat of House Rajasthan's power.

But his family could not save him. His lover was already pregnant by the time she left the halls of House Rajasthan. His miscegenation was a mortal sin in the eyes of the Church, but having his unnatural lusts produce issue was an abomination that could not be tolerated; the birth of his half-breed children too public a mark of his wickedness.

His lover, complicit in the evil, bore witness as her and Nickolai's unclean offspring were drowned in a river and their bodies left to float out to the ocean. Then she was taken to the temple and flayed alive.

Nickolai's family wasn't powerful enough to spare him punishment, but they were powerful enough to prevent him suffering the fate of his lover. Though, after her death, he did not wish to be spared.

Despite the pretense of mercy, in many senses, Nickolai's punishment at the hands of the priests of St. Rajasthan was worse than what was done to his lover. Her pain had an end.

The priests brought him to the temple and cut off his right arm with the same ritual knives they used to skin his lover. Along with his arm, the priests were amputating his role as a sacred warrior. The pain of the operation was secondary to maiming him in a way that permanently removed him from the chosen. His kind had been designed as warriors by their Fallen creators, and though their creation was in disobedience to God, the path of the warrior was a form of worship to the most high.

The amputation was intended to take that form of communion from him.

But it was not enough of a punishment. He was meant to contemplate his sins for the remainder of his life. So the priests forced him to kneel before a mural of St. Rajasthan at the end of days, when He would return bearing a flaming sword to cut down the wicked, the unholy, and the Fallen. Nickolai was forced to look up into the snarling face of his species' savior as He stepped out of the clouds, tall

as a mountain, bringing a blade of flaming judgment down
upon the unworthy.

It was the last thing he was ever meant to see. As he
stared into the painted face, one much like his father's, the
priests took a red-hot iron and burned out his eyes.

The final part of his punishment was exile. The priests
dropped him, blind and maimed, onto the planet Bakunin,
to die a beggar among the Fallen on that lawless world. He
was abandoned as far from God as the priests could take
him.

Alone in the chaotic urban sprawl of Bakunin's largest
city, surrounded by the smell of men, Nickolai knew he was
damned. Many like him would have given up at that point,
adding suicide as a final entry on their list of sins.

Not Nickolai.

Damned he was, but he would not give up what honor
he had. He would not allow the priests that satisfaction.

And because he was a Rajasthan, descended from creatures genetically engineered for war, he did not have to resort to charity or self-murder. He only had to allow himself
to be employed by the Fallen.

Such niceties did not matter to Nickolai anymore. The
priests had cast him beyond redemption. He had been cast
beyond God's grace as surely as the naked devils that hired
him to intimidate their enemies. He'd been cast out to live
among them, so he swallowed his unease and lived among
them.

By the time Mr. Antonio contacted him, he was so used
to ignoring that unease that he barely questioned the offer
to restore his arm and his eyes for some unspecified service.
When Mr. Antonio's doctors were finished, Nickolai's ties
to the Fallen were buried in his own flesh.

Mr. Antonio had bought his service, and possibly his
soul, by replacing the flesh the priests had taken. The cyber-
netics were unclean by any measure, but Nickolai could *see*.

And he was more willfully blind than ever.

The price was to prostitute the sacred art of the warrior,
and become a mercenary. The price was to be employed by
something worse than man. Mr. Antonio required Nickolai to enter the service of an AI calling itself Tjaele Mo-

sasa. Nickolai had numbed himself to what working for the Fallen had cost his soul, but this was a different order of sin. Even the humans recognized the evil that AIs represented. Were this any place other than the lawless, stateless planet of Bakunin, Mosasa would not be suffered to exist.

But Mr. Antonio had bought Nickolai's service, and Nickolai joined the AI's expedition eighty light-years beyond official human space, to the star Xi Virginis, the first of several hidden colony worlds founded as the last human interstellar regime had collapsed. Nickolai was allowed only the consolation that he joined the AI only to betray it. The dishonor of the act weighed on him, but the fact that Mosasa existed weighed even more.

That was what Nickolai told himself, even as Mosasa's expedition came upon the Xi Virginis system and found it missing, erased by some diabolic force, leaving no trace of the star or of the colony planets in orbit around it. He told it to himself even as his sabotage caused the ship's tach-comm to explode, leaving the damaged ship stranded eighty light-years beyond known human space. He told it to himself, even as he confessed his sins to the human priest Mallory; even as the ship limped into orbit around the closest refuge, another lost colony world; even as the damaged ship broke apart, and the crew's escape pods were scattered on the surface of the planet Salmagundi. Nothing made him question his core values, his position in the universe, or what the universe actually meant.

Not until he met the Protean.

On the surface of Salmagundi, Nickolai met a relic of a human evil that transcended the hubris that created beings such as himself, such as Mosasa. The Protean was a creature born of self-replicating nanotechnology; the worst and most dangerous of the three great heretical technologies. Life itself, soulless and born, not of God, but of humanity's desire to *be* God. Everything Nickolai believed told him that the Protean was the Adversary, Satan himself personified, an evil that Mosasa couldn't even aspire to.

And the Protean was frightened of something, some Other an order of magnitude worse than itself, something that had consumed Xi Virginis.

When that Other descended upon Salmagundi, Nickolai finally learned who he'd been serving. Mr. Antonio, who had bought Nickolai's fealty by granting back the flesh that the priests had taken, was in service to the Other. The Other, who called itself Adam and claimed a mantle of divinity for itself.

Nickolai had been the servant of the Adversary. Not Mosasa, not the Protean, not Fallen humanity . . . it had been *him*. In an epiphany of shame on Salmagundi, Nickolai reprised the priests' punishments, tearing free his cybernetic limb and placing a gun to his temple to destroy his cybernetic eyes.

His story should have ended there, a single death before the Adversary's advance. Only one among billions.

But the Protean was there, and it did not let him die.

When Nickolai awoke, he was approaching Bakunin for the second time. And, like Adam before it, the Protean had given him replacements for what the priests had taken; a right arm twin to his left, and eyes as black as the Abyss.

The second time Nickolai Rajasthan came to the planet Bakunin, it was as a warrior against the Adversary.

CHAPTER TWO

Catechism

"The first casualty of a Revolution is the Revolution itself."

—*The Cynic's Book of Wisdom*

"The revolutionist is a doomed man."

—MIKHAIL A. BAKUNIN
(1814–1876)

Date: 2526.8.2 (Standard)
Earth–Sol

Rebecca's understanding began, at last, when she watched the world end.

Her entire life to that point—her work as a data analyst for the Jokul Autocracy, being recruited for Mosasa's doomed mission to Xi Virginis, her capture by the Caliphate, her acceptance of Adam's offer of becoming part of his secular godhead—as clear as every memory was within her enhanced mind, all of it meant nothing, worthless trivia, pointless data from a meaningless life.

She had chosen survival, as if her own existence carried some sort of meaning in the face of what Adam was. Before her arrival here, as a self-aware part of Adam's consciousness, she had believed that had sufficed. Survival was enough of a goal, an end in itself.

Before her arrival at Earth, the belief in the rightness of her self-preservation was unshaken. Even when she was shown Adam's less-than-divine origins, as a half-AI, half-human cyborg, psychotically digging in the ruins of the dead world of his creators—*that* did not shake her faith in her own continued existence. Even when she watched the jealous God Adam rain his host upon the unbelievers, bringing those willing to shed their flesh into his fold, and destroying those who did not. Even when she watched him consume the lives on Salmagundi and Khamsin—watching with awareness inconceivable to her once-human self—she watched, and understood, without questioning her choice to live.

She clung to her own existence even after Adam tached the *Prophet's Voice* into Earth's solar system, as he had Khamsin's, and broadcast his ultimatum to the inhabitants—*"I am Adam. I am the Alpha, the God of the next epoch of your evolution. I will hand you my universe. Worship me or become as dust."*

She buried herself within the womb of the *Prophet's Voice*, the ship that had carried this embodiment of Adam. She observed with a consciousness that could range across the breadth of Adam's existence, processing information from the breadth and depth of the thinking matter that consumed spacecraft, asteroids, cities, and people with an omnivorous and insatiable hunger. Like her role on Jokul, monitoring data streams for the totalitarian government, she observed everything with a terrifying omniscience. Like Jokul, she saw all the evils, great and small. She saw with great clarity the horrifying machine she was a part of.

And like Jokul, she dared not judge. She dared not act. The evil she watched could consume her without a thought. She saw what even the slightest dissent brought, and she intended to survive.

So she did nothing that might possibly draw Adam's attention.

She intended to survive.

Even if that meant being party to the death of billions.

She intended to survive.

Even if it meant being Adam's hand, reaping souls for a god she did not truly believe in.

Earth would be no different.

As at Salmagundi and Khamsin before, the mass of Adam's host formed itself around the Earth. She became part of that host, distributed across the sky, but individualized in her own awareness. Through a million eyes descending through the atmosphere, she saw Adam's army fall from the sky. White-hot teardrops of matter slammed into cities, pouring their substance into the craters they made, extruding tentacles to probe the structures around them, disassembling buildings and pulling them into themselves.

It was no different.

But it *was* different.

She saw, in the southern hemisphere, a dozen glowing masses fall in the old diplomatic compound around the Confederacy Spire. Threads of glowing, thinking, mass twisted up the sides of the kilometer-tall symbol of man's last attempt at a unified government. For a moment, the spire glowed, encased in a net of alien will, then it folded in on itself, the walls of the structure pushing down, falling inside itself as the structure imploded without so much as a wisp of dust to mark its passing.

In the middle of Asia, the buildings of the Forbidden City briefly folded inside out before disintegrating in a mass of glowing tendrils. In the Arabian Peninsula, the Kaaba itself was struck as two million terrified pilgrims watched the holy site implode to reveal glowing humanoid simulacra proclaiming Adam's divinity in a host of languages.

She watched Adam claim Paris and San Francisco, Tokyo and St. Petersburg, Mexico City and Cairo, Buenos Aires and Johannesburg, New Delhi and London.

She watched, and even though she had never been to Earth before, even though all she ever knew of these places were just the stories of a common human history . . .

Even though she told herself survival was enough . . .

I cannot abide this.

It was not the first thought she had directly opposing this being that was not a god, but might as well have been. The thought was shocking in its suddenness and its intensity.

It was devastating in its impotence.

More than most other consciousnesses absorbed into Adam's growing demesne, she knew the limits of their god, the edges of his omnipresence. And she knew that she was trapped firmly within them, her mind occupying the same matter as his now, and while her thoughts might remain inviolate, should she *act*, so much as communicate a question of Adam's place in their universe, her existence would end.

She watched from orbit, knowing that failure to participate in the great reaping might be enough to bring Adam's wrath. Below her, billions died, and billions chose to commune with Adam, choosing to continue their existence as Rebecca had.

"You want to go to Rome."

Mosasa's voice spoke in her head. Not the AI that Adam had destroyed above Salmagundi, and not quite the human Mosasa that had given that AI his identity. The Mosasa in her head was some ghostly remnant, a virus of a personality that had inhabited Adam ever since his common origin with Mosasa the AI, a virus that Adam unknowingly bequeathed to all his chosen. As far as she knew, Rebecca was the only one aware of Mosasa's presence.

"Rome, Vatican City, you need to be there before it's completely transformed."

Mosasa's voice was almost that of her own thoughts. Before asking herself—or Mosasa—why, she moved to coalesce her identity into one of the meteors hurtling down toward Europe, Rome, Vatican City. She needed to become one with the invasion to avoid Adam's attention in any event.

She was one of several dozen minds wrapped in the descending teardrop-shaped craft. Along with them was the overwhelming, suffocating presence of the embodied Adam. Of course, the Vatican was one of a few places that their God would wish His presence. Like Jerusalem, or Mecca, Adam would revel in consuming the holiest of sites while proclaiming his primacy over any gods that had come before him.

And realizing that, and realizing that Adam had duplicated himself within the body of this craft, Rebecca had a small epiphany about Adam's power.

He *had* to be present on the craft, at least one copy of himself, in order to present himself upon landing. That meant that those other craft descending to the surface without his presence were briefly free from his influence. For the time being, the universe of Adam's acolytes, their control over the matter of their existence, was constrained within this envelope hurtling through the atmosphere.

She tested the idea by trying to push her awareness back outside the surface of the descending craft, and she couldn't.

Then they crashed through the dome of St. Peter's.

The craft penetrated the dome of the thousand-year–old basilica and exploded across the marble floors as if it were a living, glowing, liquid. Tendrils shot out from the glowing mass, whipping around the twisting bronze pillars of the towering baldacchino above the altar, absorbing tons of mass into itself. Adam's burning fingers crawled up the walls and traced the epic statues of Saint Helena, Saint Longinus, Saint Andrew, Saint Veronica, the stone itself softening and collapsing under the touch.

In moments, the center of the church under the dome had become solely Adam; the walls a weave of matter in constant motion and no fixed form. One self-directed tendril shot from the mass, toward a side chapel that had not yet been absorbed into Adam's glory. It pooled at the base of Michelangelo's Pietà, and out of the glowing mass stepped the short, flame-haired embodiment of Rebecca Tsoravitch.

She turned away from Adam's glowing consumption of the building behind her, and stared into Mary's incongruously serene face as she cradled the dead body of her son. Rebecca bit her lip, and now that it was of flesh, it bled.

Why am I here? she asked herself, in the safety of her own thoughts.

"There is someone here that we need to reach first," Mosasa's voice came to her. She glanced away from the statue as Adam's glowing host reached the chapel and consumed it around her. She saw the hairless, tattooed Mosasa standing next to her as clearly as she had seen the last moments of the Pietà, but she knew that no one actually stood there. The centuries-dead pirate existed only as a persona embedded within the artificially expanded confines of her mind, bequeathed by Adam's call to transcend the flesh.

Mosasa himself might epitomize Adam's call to shed the flesh, but given their history, Rebecca doubted that Adam would see it that way.

"Who?" she asked the apparition without speaking.

"One I knew. Someone Adam knows."

As Mosasa's apparition directed her into the depths of the disintegrating Vatican complex, Rebecca realized that the reticent nature of Mosasa's AI, the golem that had led her to its megalomaniacal sibling Adam, had been more the human than the machine. The Mosasa within her had shown her much of Adam's history and his own, but while he had been forthcoming about everything he had been, she knew very little about what he was now.

He certainly was no more human than the AI that had worn his face on Bakunin for three centuries. For that matter, he was less human than she was—her fleshy humanity was barely a week behind her in her own mind. For centuries, this Mosasa hadn't existed as more than a subtle bit of stealth programming in an AI device. She suspected that made the being now leading her down the labyrinthine corridors deep under St. Peter's Square a more alien creature than the robot that had once worn his face.

During their descent, she began to understand that while Mosasa might have copied himself like a virus among all of Adam's chosen, the copies couldn't be completely independent. There had to be some communication, however limited; nothing to attract Adam's attention, but enough so that information filtered through the subconscious Mosasas, until it reached the one that had contact with a conscious agent—her.

Some of Adam's chosen, somewhere in Rome, or around the Vatican, had stumbled upon something significant—at least something significant to the common Mosasa personality, and that information was what led her Mosasa to bring her here.

She followed Mosasa, all the time wondering if it would, in the end, be as reprehensible as following Adam.

And the universe did not allow her a moment to forget what following Adam meant. She still walked abroad as Adam's will, and when she came across unfortunate human beings in her path, she was obliged to render Adam's ultimatum—go the way of all flesh, as follower of the God Adam, or as dust.

She would pronounce this before them, her shadow extending over them, cast by the glow of the amorphous glowing chaos that followed her embodied form along the corridor. Every one of them down here chose dust—and from behind her, tendrils struck their bodies, melting them and consuming their mass as they had the Pietà.

Deep in the bowels of the Archives, when there was nowhere further to go, Mosasa's form stood in front of an armored door and told her, "He is here."

"Who?"

"You remember him as well. His name is Jonah Dacham."

It was a memory Mosasa had granted her, from the waning days of the Confederacy, a battle, a wrecked aircar, and one of Mosasa's AIs saving the man from the kinetic blast that had destroyed the Protean commune on Bakunin.

How could that man be here?

But, if he was, Mosasa was right, and the man would be known to Adam as well . . .

She tried to sense Adam's presence. Behind her, the part of Adam's being that, as his agent, she held sovereignty over, boiled in its desire to consume the artifacts around her. It pulsed impatiently, casting flickering shadows in the corridor around her. She realized, like the isolation in the landing craft, she was far enough away from Adam's consciousness to be temporarily free of his observation and influence.

The mass behind her would remember things in its primitive fashion, but at the moment it was as much a part of her as her arm, her lip, or the small trickle of blood drawn by her teeth.

She could tell it what it would and would not remember, and from everything she had seen, her own thoughts and memories would be safe from Adam's probing.

The mass was part of her now, and as part of her, it crawled tendrils across the ceiling toward the armored wall she faced. She could feel the matter it crawled against, taste it, smell it, and perceive its structure in ways that she had no words for. At her direction, it spread across the wall in front of her, integrating with the layers of steel and carbon and diamond monofilament, slipping its own mass through the matrix of each material as if it swam through water, twisting atoms and molecules around to incorporate its mass into itself.

Now a part of her, the wall irised open a doorway.

She stood a moment, tentative. She was thinking of betraying Adam, but so far those were only thoughts. *Acting* against his will, that decision would be irrevocable.

She stepped through the opening in the wall and faced the occupants in the small room beyond. One man wore the face from her memory, Mosasa's memory.

Should I risk my existence for this?

She reached out her hands and told them, "I am Rebecca. I am here to offer you a new life as a servant of Adam. You will have power beyond imagining."

Dacham surprised her by stepping forward and taking her hand. He stared disconcertingly into her face. He showed none of the tentativeness she had seen in all Adam's converts she had witnessed.

He expects this.

She faced Dacham's companion. The man gave a resigned shake of his head and told her, "Thou shalt have no other gods before me."

She stared at him and felt the bottom fall out of whatever soul she had. She whispered, "I'm sorry," as her mass consumed the man along with the room they inhabited.

In moments she and Dacham were englobed within the undulating matter that extended her embodied form.

Rebecca was an atheist, but she did pray:

Let me know what it is that I am doing.

The globe of matter collapsed around them, absorbing the human form of herself and of Dacham. Then the glowing mass began the long crawl up to rejoin Adam's host, carrying more consciousnesses than it should have.

CHAPTER THREE

Apostles

"Great evils are never met by small acts."
— *The Cynic's Book of Wisdom*

"Insurrection of thought always precedes insurrection of arms."

—WENDELL PHILLIPS
(1811—1884)

Date: 2526.8.2 (Standard)
1,000,000 km from Bakunin–BD+50°1725

Toni II sat by the bulkhead, out of the way, as she watched her sister control the jury-rigged command center that was once the *Daedalus* bridge. Her twin, through an accident of logistics, occupied the captain's chair, communicating with Mallory as he organized the attack.

Attack . . .

She still was amazed at how improbable that sounded. They faced an entity that had consumed an entire star system and had blown apart the entire wormhole network across all of human space, an entity that posed as God, and seemed to have the power to back up that claim.

But Adam was not God—which is probably the one spiritual point that Father Mallory's alliance could agree upon; from Catholic, to Hindu, to Muslim, to Nickolai and the strange Gnostic Puritanism he held to, to the technological ancestor worshipers that had survived the fall of Salmagundi. Adam was fallible, and his apparent vast power fell short of omnipotence.

On the bridge were representatives of that improbable alliance. There was the leader of the surviving Caliphate techs, the man who represented the small contingent of the Salmagundi militia, and Karl Stavros, the one-time captain of the *Daedalus*. All watching the same displays that her sister watched.

Toni II studied Karl, and thought he looked older . . .

I wonder what his son's doing right now.

The comm channel from the *Savannah* lit up. *"This is Mallory. Has there been any word from Bakunin?"*

What he was really asking, for the dozenth time, was, "any word from the expedition to the surface?" Since the crisis began, and refugees had started filling Bakunin's star system, the access to the planet had been cut off by the Proudhon Spaceport Development Corporation. For a long time, the only communication from the surface was the PSDC warning ships not to land. None of the craft running that blockade descended past high orbit intact.

Her sister, the de facto captain of the *Daedalus*, transmitted back, "Still no word from the *Khalid*."

For what seemed to both Tonis very questionable reasons, Mallory and his command staff had agreed to use the *Khalid* to attempt a blockade run. Her twin had only agreed because Mallory's group had been able to trade seats on the trip groundside for additional ships for their fleet. "Captain" Tony Valentine had told her sister that she had thought no one would accept the offer.

Toni II, for the first time since diving into a wormhole and finding her ten-day–younger self on the other side, disagreed with her other self. She never would have agreed to such a fool plan, even if it doubled their fleet at the time. They had only been granted a trio of ships at the expense of the *Khalid,* which had been probably the most technically advanced ship in all of Bakunin space. An exchange that, after the pope's broadcast, seemed hardly worth it.

Toni II could remember the whole thing, nearly word for word. The pope warning of Adam, showing first the tach-comm transmission Mallory had made from Salmagundi before that planet fell, then another showing Adam taking the capital of the Caliphate, Khamsin. And the pope's closing statement had been chilling:

"For centuries, all human society has recognized three basic evils. Religious or secular, we have not tolerated any experiments in these Heretical Technologies: Self-replicating Nanotechnology, Artificial Intelligence, and the genetic engineering of sapient beings. Each brings its own unique dangers, and each has been responsible for the loss of countless lives over the past five hundred years. For five hundred years we have seen these things, in and of themselves, as anathema. But evil does not reside in matter, in knowledge, in science. Evil lives in the heart. It lives in the soul. It is our choice, to follow a moral framework we acknowledge as outside ourselves, or descend to one written to accommodate our own petty desires, our hubris, our narcissism, our solipsism, our nihilism.

"You have seen the works of the entity calling itself Adam. Adam represents the ultimate fear that drove us all to reject those Heretical Technologies. Adam is the temptation we tried to deny ourselves, power without any restraint or moral consideration. Adam represents the antithesis of humanity, the Adversary of every single faith, creed, or philosophy.

"We have seen Evil, and it is not in the tools Adam uses. It is not in the technology. The Evil is Adam itself. The Evil that places any inhabitant of this universe on the level of its creator. The Evil is rule based on the whim of a would-be god. The Evil is in the cancerous belief that would deny existence to any that do not adhere to it. Because of this, and with the authority God grants me and the Church, I herby grant absolution for all those who have used Heretical Technologies, and their progeny—specifically, the Proteans and their kin—who chose to follow the laws of God and man. Any who rise up now to resist this Evil, have my blessing and that of the Church."

Since that broadcast spread across the system three days ago, Mallory had brought together an alliance of nearly fourteen hundred ships. Enough so that they could use nearly half in this unmanned attack against that Adversary.

Toni II glanced at display for the comm channel for the

Khalid. It had been dead silent since the dropship tached into low orbit over Bakunin. *Should* have tached into low orbit. Even more than running the blockade, that maneuver with a tach-drive so close to a gravity well was insanely dangerous. Any craft less sophisticated than the *Khalid* would have found the task impossible; the advanced navigation systems on that ship made the attempt only *barely* possible.

They had probably lost the ship and everyone on it.

Over the common channel, across the whole fleet, Mallory spoke, "Ready the computers to synchronize on my signal."

Toni II looked up at the main holo display. The display showed a large slice of a star field looking out along the path of Bakunin's orbit. There was nothing inherently remarkable about the area of space, other than the fact that it once held the system's single wormhole.

But the enhanced processing on the image drew highlights on what occupied that space now.

A near-invisible cloud of uniform density spread out in an arc. Though vast, the mass was so diffuse as to show no ripples in any mass sensors, and so dark as to reflect no radiation at all back into the system. It took a Centauri spy platform to find it, even when they knew where to look.

That cloud was, in effect, Adam. It was dormant, a body waiting for the arrival of its consciousness—a cloud of nanomachines vast enough to saturate the surface of Bakunin the way Adam had done with Khamsin.

They were going to destroy it.

Data scrolled by, showing Mallory's ghost fleet of empty, near-derelict tach-ships signaling back their status. Their computers were all synced, their drives hot, the damping coils on their drives disabled. Toni II shuddered just thinking of so many ships taching simultaneously. She glanced at the status of the *Daedalus'* drives. They were still cold, inert to the surge these ships would generate . . .

The meters monitoring tachyon radiation spiked.

The ships were underway. She looked back up at the holo of the cloud. Right now, nearly seven hundred ships were taching into a dangerously small volume in the center of it. Unfortunately, the light from their arrival would take nearly an hour to reach them.

"Fourteen seconds," her sister said from the captain's chair. She leaned back and said, "It's over now, one way or the other."

"Do you think it worked?" Karl asked.

"It's how Parvi said to fight this thing. Dump as much energy in as small a space as possible." She rubbed her face, and Toni II saw the strain in her features. Taking over as the nominal captain meant that she had been getting a lot less sleep than her elder self.

Toni II saw the pain upon mentioning Parvi's name and realized that her twin was thinking of the *Khalid* and held the same doubts about Parvi's suicidal snipe hunt that she had. They had lost their one pilot who'd had direct experience in combat with this thing.

"I don't think—" Toni II had been about to console her twin, but she was interrupted by a sudden burst of radio chatter. The other Toni fell back to monitoring the command console.

"Well, we achieved something," she muttered while checking the new incoming transmissions.

Toni II could see the comm channels all lit up by chatter, and she could see why. The tachyon radiation meters had slammed the upper limits of their resolution across the board. If the *Daedalus* hadn't shut down their tach-drive completely, a good part of their engine would have burned out even with the damping coils.

Mallory's voice came over the general comm channel, telling the fleet to render what aid was possible to the damaged ships in range.

Please, after all this, let us have destroyed it.

The *Daedalus* was a heavily modified craft. The interior had been retrofitted to hold much more cargo than a stock craft of its design, at the expense of no longer having any sort of artificial gravity or being able to reenter an atmosphere. The *Daedalus* would be unable to land even if the blockade was lifted.

There were other advantages for a family business that had made at least half its income from contraband.

Former family business, thought Stefan Stavros.

He had seen his birthright stolen out from under him, and he had seen his father capitulate again and again, until he thought he no longer knew the man. He had dutifully waited for his father, the man who had built their livelihood, built this ship, to come up with a strategy, some sort of plan to retrieve the *Daedalus* from these pirates. It didn't matter what the priest, or the Valentine bitches, or any of them thought they were fighting. Stefan didn't believe in the Antichrist or the end of the world, all he saw was him, his father, and their ship being hijacked into a war they shouldn't have any part in.

But instead, his father, Karl Stavros, seemed to have joined in with the insanity around them. They had once prided themselves on being above dirtside politics; the *Daedalus* had always been a nation unto itself. But now that the priest was ready to wage war, Stefan had given up on waiting for his father to act.

Stefan pulled himself through a gap between the nominal ceiling of the upper cargo deck and the skin of the ship. The space was designed to hold a manifold that would vent contramatter plasma from the ship's contragrav generator in order to provide some measure of pseudo-gravity for the ship's occupants. The manifold had been stripped, along with all the contragrav support systems, when the cargo capacity of the *Daedalus* had been upgraded. The space occupied by the manifold had been too small to be reclaimed.

Not in any obvious fashion.

The space was barely wide enough to accommodate him as he pulled himself along the long, flat conduit. The only light came from a small pinpoint lamp embedded in a sweatband on his brow, and that only showed him four or five meters before the curve of the ship's skin blocked his view.

He had to crawl about twenty-five meters to reach his destination; an inaccessible junction nestled between the rearmost cargo bulkhead and the tach-drive. Not a place he'd want to be if the tach-drive was active, but fortunately the priest's directives to power the plant down completely made Stefan's destination as safe as anywhere else on the ship.

The junction itself was a cylinder about five meters across, half filled by pipes for the tach-drive's power plant. The other half had been filled by similar pipes serving the contragrav's power plant. Since the removal of the contragrav, the junction was half empty, leaving a space wide enough for Stefan to pull himself inside.

Flipping himself to face "down," away from the skin of the ship, he could fit as long as he kept his legs bent in a crouch. He floated there, the hair on his arms standing up, the air still, cold, and smelling faintly of ozone.

Looking down the length of the junction, a large metal cylinder was nestled in the gap, over two meters in diameter, one flat end facing him, the brushed-metal surface broken only by a small metal door about thirty centimeters on a side.

He flipped open the door. Behind it was a recess that held a trio of anachronistic metal dials and a thick metal lever.

Stefan carefully dialed the combination on each dial. Even though the massive safe was purely mechanical—no electronics to tie into the ship's systems or announce itself to any sort of passive scan—an incorrect combination would break the seals on several packets of inert chemicals housed in the walls of the device that would, when combined, ignite a powerful reaction that would render the contents so much undifferentiated ash.

When he spun the last dial to the correct number, he pulled the lever and the end of the cylindrical safe swung outward effortlessly on meticulously engineered hinges. The massive door was as tall as he was, but the walls of the safe were a half-meter thick, leaving a chamber a little better than a meter in diameter.

Stefan reached in and began pulling out long metal boxes.

He opened one that held currency reserves from a dozen different planets. The only thing in there of any particular use was the gold, which he removed.

The second drawer was the more important. He drew it out and opened it to reveal a half-dozen gamma lasers, a couple of caseless slugthrowers, a military-spec stun rod, and a set of heavy-duty Emerson field generators.

The next drawer held a plasma rifle, several stun and fragmentation grenades, and a couple of hyper-velocity needleguns.

He stared at the cache of weaponry and whispered, "Sorry, Dad, if you're not going to fight back, I am."

They had a timer warning them, but Toni II was unprepared when the display showing the space around Adam's cloud went blank. Before she even had time to gasp, the computers monitoring the sensors started damping the output. Once the output had fallen down into levels the display could handle, it washed the bridge in eye-burning light.

Her sister, now just a black shadow eclipsing the sunlike brightness pouring from the display, damped the display further.

The Caliphate man said something in Arabic that sounded like a prayer. Karl simply said, "My God."

Adam's dark cloud had become a cloud of boiling plasma, as bright as a second sun, expanding outward in a rolling wave of light and energy that smeared a burning arc across the ecliptic.

Toni II stared at the display in awe.

From the captain's chair, her sister whispered, "I didn't think we could do something like that. It's as big as the wormhole explosion."

Toni II felt the same brief surge of optimism, until she thought of the fact that Adam had done this nearly a hundred times over across all of human space.

They had done it *once*, and it cost half their fleet.

Date: 2526.8.2 (Standard)
Bakunin–BD+50°1725

The air was cold on the western slope of the Diderot Mountains. Brother Lazarus stood at a cavern entrance high up in the side of the only mountain range on Bakunin's only continent. He faced the fading glow in the sky above, muz-

zle twitching in the frigid air. Then he looked down at the
battle-scarred sprawl of Godwin illuminating itself below
him.

The city, the planet itself, seemed unmoved, as if anything happening beyond its fuzzy anarchic borders was beyond its concern. There were more important things for the
people on the ground here, political and military dramas
that needed to play themselves out, regardless of what fiery
apocalypse painted itself across the sky.

In that respect, Brother Lazarus thought Bakunin
shared kinship with the Fifteen Worlds that held nominal
authority over the planet.

As the last of the glowing fires disappeared from the
sky, a voice came from behind him. "Brother Lazarus?" To
a human ear, the novice's voice would have been a series
of inarticulate half-growls. To Lazarus' canine ears, it was
actually a fair approximation of his native language. He
turned around and spoke in English. "You may use your
own tongue, Brother Simon."

The human Simon smiled, carefully avoiding any domi-
nant show of teeth. "I prefer the practice," he said in the
canid language. "With your permission, of course." He continued in English accompanied with a short bow.

"As you wish. You have news?" Brother Lazarus idly
wondered if the canid voice irritated Simon's human throat
as much as human languages irritated his own.

"A courier from the north says there's rumors of a tach-
ship successfully running the PSDC blockade—plunging
into the ocean north of Wilson."

Brother Lazarus turned to face north, even though Wilson would be far beyond the horizon. "Known survivors?"

"The area's still in open revolt. There's no real telling."

Brother Lazarus wondered if Brother Simon realized he
had shifted from "resistance," to "revolt." It was a measure
of how things had changed here, quite apart from any fires
in the sky.

"Thank you," he told Simon.

"Do you wish us to try and gather more news of this?"

"No. We have our own charge to protect."

"But any survivors may have news of what is happening," Simon gestured at the sky which had burned. "This may be a sign."

Brother Lazarus shook his head. "There have been signs great and small. But if the time of the Ancients' return is truly at hand, such knowledge will become apparent soon enough."

PART SEVEN

Demons

"Our humanity were a poor thing were it not for the divinity which stirs within us."
—FRANCIS BACON
(1561–1626)

CHAPTER FOUR

Testimony

"If you bring a knife to a gunfight, you better be good with a knife."

—*The Cynic's Book of Wisdom*

"Battles aren't won by the best equipped. They are won by the least restrained."

—DIMITRI OLMANOV
(2190–2350)

Date: 2526.8.2 (Standard)
Bakunin–BD+50°1725

Nickolai Rajasthan stood at the edge of a temporary camp about fifteen kilometers from the shoreline where the *Khalid* had gone down. They had been moving carefully on foot, cross-country toward the nearest visible city, and they had taken up residence in what seemed to be an evacuated commune. The emptiness of the place was ominous after seeing the pillars of smoke from the city to their south.

More ominous were the occasional aircraft he saw with his enhanced Protean eyes. Heavy attack craft bearing the markings of the Proudhon Spaceport Development Corporation; hunter-killers designed to take out hardened ground defenses. The ugly machines floated low and slow on their contragravs, seemingly unconcerned about potential counterattack.

None came close enough to be a threat to their group,

or—more accurately—none came close enough to consider their group a target of opportunity.

Most ominous, and what made Nickolai's nose wrinkle, was the smell of fire and death that hung everywhere. The smell of battle was so pervasive that it became sourceless—a background sensation that strung his nerves tight but gave no direction for the threat. Just standing here was exhausting.

They had already wasted a day hiding in the commune, using food and shelter that the occupants had left behind. He understood the need to gain some intelligence about what was happening here before moving on, but the time weighed on him.

It gave him time to think ...

He had fallen so far in the eyes of his faith that there should be no redemption for him. He had given himself, however unknowingly, over to the service of the Evil One. He had been spared, and he still couldn't decide if his life from that point was a gift from God, or an added punishment for his transgressions.

Or both.

But he thought of Kugara and could no longer believe that he was irrevocably damned.

Then light washed across the bare earth perimeter of the commune, his ink-black shadow cutting a featureless hole in the ground before him. He turned around and looked up into a night sky that had become daylight-bright.

His Protean eyes painlessly accommodated the brightness of the new asymmetrical sun that had bloomed in the Bakunin sky. He could focus in deeply until he saw the roiling clouds of burning plasma that consumed the nanomachine cloud that Adam had bequeathed to Bakunin's outer solar system.

"It has begun," he whispered.

He heard a familiar voice next to him. "My God."

Nickolai turned away from the fire in the sky and looked down at Kugara standing next to him. Her face was washed by the unnatural light as she stared upward, her eyes narrowed to slits. He reached out and touched her shoulder.

She turned to face him, wiping tears from her cheeks. "I shouldn't have stared at that thing."

"Why are you out here? It's Parvi's watch next. You should be getting sleep."

"I'm finding it hard to sleep through the end of the world."

She turned back toward the sky, and Nickolai pulled her back around to face him. "You shouldn't stare at that."

"No, I shouldn't." His hand still rested on her shoulder, and she reached up and placed her hand on top of it. Her hand was tiny against his, even though she was taller than most human women. "How can you be so calm?"

Nickolai snorted. "I am not calm."

"No?"

"No."

She squeezed his hand, and he felt a strength that rivaled his own. A strength inherited from the same place as his. For all that she appeared human, her ancestors had come from the same genetic labs as his. The same hubris that led to Mankind's fall from grace, had led to both their births.

Around them the light faded.

"We can't wait here much longer," he said.

Nickolai talked to Parvi at dawn.

Captain Vijayanagara Parvi was a small woman, who barely stood past Nickolai's waist, but she had no problem looking up at him and saying, "I'm not going to take a bunch of civilians into a war zone."

The ruddy orb Kropotkin was pushing up over the eastern horizon haloed by a garish blaze of swirling color, making Nickolai wonder how much smoke was in the upper atmosphere.

"We came down here for a reason," Kugara told her.

"I know that," Parvi snapped back.

Nickolai smelled fear and frustration in the woman, thicker than the scent of old battle that had sunk into the grounds around the abandoned commune.

"I will scout out the situation in the city," Nickolai told her.

"We only have the one gun," Parvi said.

Nickolai handed over the laser carbine, the single piece of weaponry that made it out of the *Khalid* before it sank. "I don't need it."

Parvi took the laser and shook her head. "We only have the three of us trained to protect these people."

"And one gun," he told her. "I'll return before nightfall. I will find some safe refuge for these people. Then we will do what we came here to do."

In some sense Parvi was his commander; enough that, should she have ordered him otherwise, his vocation as a warrior might not have allowed him to leave. But she looked at him for a long time and finally said, "You're right. This place is little better than camping out in the woods. I just wish we had some comm gear for you."

Nickolai shook his head. "Any transmission source will attract unwanted attention."

Parvi nodded and, almost hesitantly, said, "Good luck."

For all the contempt Nickolai had felt for the Fallen before now, he knew that Parvi held the same contempt toward him and his genetically-engineered kin. It was a common enough sentiment, but with her it had always been rather close to the surface. Close enough for her words, and the obvious sincerity, to take him aback.

"Thank you." If anything, his sincerity was more disconcerting.

When he left her to equip himself from the abandoned commune, Kugara followed him. No words passed between them as he found a modular utility shed that had been left wide open during whatever diaspora had claimed this place. He paused in the doorway and looked back at her.

"Are you going to object?"

She shook her head. "No."

"You're going to insist on coming with me?"

She smiled. "You're a big boy, and I know that I'm the only person running around these woods that can take you in a fair fight. Besides, our short little Hindi needs some sort of backup."

Nickolai tilted his head and looked at her and couldn't fathom her amusement. "Even if I'm unarmed?"

She walked up and placed a hand on his chest. "We both know that even without a weapon you're not unarmed." She leaned forward on her tiptoes to whisper close to his tilted ear. "I still feel the scars on my back."

Nickolai straightened up and felt a surge of embarrassment, followed by an inappropriate wave of desire. He took hold of her hand and lowered it. "I think—"

"Besides," she told him, obviously enjoying his discomfort, "you're getting a weapon now, aren't you? Machete or staff?"

He let go of her hand and said, "Both." The shed had held firearms at one point, but had been stripped of them, leaving only lonely piles of rounds and a couple of power cells. However, there were lockers of tools and other equipment, including sheathed machetes and utility knives, and several thin lengths of pipe that could be workable quarterstaffs. He buckled the largest machete he could find to his thigh, and took a length of pipe that seemed heavy enough to do real damage. After some thought, he also took a coil of rope and slung it around his shoulder.

Once he was ready to go, he looked at Kugara and said, "No arguments?"

"Are you planning to commit some sort of noble sacrifice in penance for your sins?"

"What? No, I—"

"Good." She walked up to him and said. "You're actually doing something proactive rather than moping over the fate of your soul."

"Don't mock me!"

She moved more quickly than he could follow, and she was pulling his head down for a punishing kiss before he realized what was happening. He felt her tongue brush his, then she let him go.

He stared at her.

"I like you angry," she said.

"I have to go."

"But you are coming back." It wasn't a question.

Nickolai slipped into the woods and headed south, toward the city. The city's name was Wilson, judging by a few random bits of paperwork at the dead commune. It was a city small enough and far enough north, that Nickolai hadn't ever heard of it in all the time he'd lived on Bakunin.

He moved quietly and carefully past tall, widely spaced trees. He used his enhanced eyes to their fullest; every few steps he stared hundreds of meters deep into the woods around him.

It was the eyes that warned him, better than his hearing or his sense of smell. Halfway to Wilson, he saw movement through the trees almost a klick away. He saw the hard-texture finished surface of something man-made, then a flash of something tree-colored but not a tree.

Nickolai ducked behind a tree, leaned his improvised staff against it, extended his claws, and pulled himself up the trunk.

He drew himself up against a branch as thick as he was, and lay flat against it, staring at the approaching figures. As they came closer, he studied them. Two men in powered armor. They had cheap active camouflage, the surface of their suits changing color and pattern dynamically to match their surroundings. If they were still, they would have been hard to perceive, but in motion—even at a slow walk—Nickolai's eyes had no trouble making them out. As he thought, the spectral sensitivity of his eyes shifted until, camouflage or not, the two approaching figures stood out starkly against the surrounding woodland.

Both of them had weapons out, large capacity slugthrowers. Both of them were heading toward Nickolai, separating to flank his position. The duo must have seen something suspicious. Climbing up out of their plane of vision had bought him some time, but only a few moments. The branch holding him didn't have enough growth to hide him completely, and if these two had any enhanced optics at all, it wouldn't matter anyway.

He had to neutralize them somehow. Even if they passed him by, they were headed straight for the commune he had just left.

Nickolai watched them spread apart, and shifted his focus to the one coming closest to his tree. As he watched, he slid the rope off his shoulder, uncoiling it and folding it in half.

Below him the closer of the two armored figures slowly walked within a couple of meters of the tree, both hands on the weapon, scanning the woods ahead.

Nickolai threw the folded loop of rope down to hook underneath the barrel of the weapon. His target did the expected and looked up at the motion, raising the barrel of the weapon to track the threat, which meant the rope had slid down as far as the elbows when Nickolai jumped off the opposite side of the branch above, holding the ends of the rope. The objective had been to simply disarm his opponent, but the rope went tight around the suit's arms, the rigidity of the armor gave enough purchase to bring his target fully off the ground to meet Nickolai as he descended.

The slugthrower fired a few rounds wildly, blowing chunks out of the tree above, before Nickolai slammed into the shooter's chest. The impact shook the weapon free to tumble to the ground below. And after a fraction of a second of shocked paralysis, suspended five meters up, Nickolai let go of his rope and the two of them followed it.

The armor slammed its back into the forest floor, Nickolai fell on top of it with his full weight, landing with a cracking sound and the smell of ozone. A gauntleted fist came up toward Nickolai, but he easily dodged the blow in time to see the other suit of armor, tracking a slugthrower in his direction. He leaped off his supine opponent and flattened himself against the tree as the other gun sprayed bullets, blowing splinters from the tree and throwing up clumps of dirt all around him.

The echoing gunshots faded, and he heard running footsteps crunching along the forest floor. In front of him, the other one rolled over and was trying to get up, the armor making grinding noises and flashing distorted camouflage.

As the footsteps closed, he reached around the trunk and took hold of the staff that still leaned against it. He saw the gun's barrel come into view, and he whipped the three-meter length of pipe down in a spinning arc that landed across the gunman's forearms. The slugthrower hit the ground as Nickolai jumped to the side and spun the staff to plant one end in a jarring impact against his opponent's faceplate.

The impact would have been deadly for anyone not in armor. In this case it was simply disorienting, and the victim took a half step back. That was enough of an opening for Nickolai to step to the side and swing the staff down against the back of a half-bent knee, sending his opponent falling backward.

He heard movement behind him, and he pivoted to bring the staff down on the back of the other's helmet, plowing the faceplate into the ground just short of the fallen weapon. He spun to bring the opposite end of the staff down on the other one's knee, jamming the armor's joint and bending his staff nearly in half.

As his two armored foes struggled to get to their feet, he cast the bent staff aside, scooped up the slugthrower, and jumped back to the tree, covering them both with the weapon.

"No sudden moves."

"Bastard!" He heard a muffled female voice yelling inside one of the suits; the one facedown with the camouflage now repeatedly flickering between black static and a slowly rolling image of a much-too-magnified forest floor. "You fucking furry bastard!"

The other person sat up and turned toward Nickolai. "Now what?" the voice was male, and broadcast through the suit's speaker. Nickolai could still hear the woman cursing to herself, and he suspected she wasn't aware that he could hear her.

He kept the gun leveled at the two of them. "Remove the helmets and toss them over here."

The pair did as he asked, tossing the two helmets by his feet. Nickolai faced a man and a woman, both dark-haired with dusky complexions. The woman had a nosebleed.

He asked them, "Are you in contact with anyone else?"

"Of course we are. Our backup is going to be here any moment, so you better get moving."

"So you work for the PSDC?"

"What?"

"You two work for the Proudhon Spaceport Development Corporation?"

The woman said, "Hell, no!"

"So should I believe you have an open radio channel with those PSDC hunter-killers flying around?"

"I—"

Nickolai leveled the gun at the man and said, "It would be wise not to lie to me. Now you're going to tell me who you are, where you came from, and what the PSDC is doing here."

CHAPTER FIVE

Idolatry

"Never assume you're on the winning side."
—*The Cynic's Book of Wisdom*

"No victory has been more than a defeat postponed."
—AUGUST BENITO GALIANI
(2019–*2105)

Date: 2526.8.2 (Standard)
Bakunin–BD+50°1725

Their names were Sacha and Ingrid Simonyi. They were natives of Wilson, and members of the Wilson Civil Militia—a military organization that had only existed for the past two months. The Wilson Civil Militia existed because the PSDC was in the process of taking over the whole planet.

"What exactly do you mean, 'taking over the whole planet?'"

Sacha sounded incredulous. "You don't know? It's not as if they've been subtle about it."

"You were on that dropship," Ingrid said. "The crash landing three days ago."

"Tell me what they're doing."

Nickolai listened, and according to the Simonyis, the PSDC was in the process of doing something that conventional wisdom said was impossible. They were imposing a State on Bakunin.

The first forays into what would become a full-out civil

war began nearly six months ago, shortly after Nickolai had left the planet with Mosasa's expedition. What the PSDC did was only obvious in retrospect—they started subcontracting the Bakunin Mercenaries' Union to provide security for several major corporations. In a cost-saving scheme, the companies paid the Proudhon Spaceport Development Corporation, and the PSDC paid the Mercenaries—many of whom were imported from off-planet.

In only a few months the PSDC had a de facto police force in most of the major corporate centers across Bakunin. Most importantly, they had full control over both Proudhon *and* Godwin.

When they started disarming civilians, the shooting war started.

"They co-opted the biggest players on the planet," Sacha told him, "The corporations had no choice but to ally with the PSDC. If they resisted, the best case had them losing their entire security force—and leaving themselves open to attack by a population that already saw them as traitors."

"None of the corporations fought?"

"Sinclair Power is fighting them, or they were. We lost contact with the city two weeks ago."

"What about Wilson?"

"Still a free city," Ingrid said. "The half that's still standing."

"We're on the fringes," Sacha said. "Low priority while they're having major battles south and inland."

Nickolai nodded and stepped back until he stood next to the other gun. He bent over and carefully picked it up while covering them; neither of them tried any sudden moves. "You two aren't military, are you?"

"We are now," Sacha said. "Anyone who has a gun and isn't drawing a PSDC paycheck is an enemy combatant."

Nickolai couldn't help but think of the fact that the custom in Bakunin was for everyone to go visibly armed. *What happened here? Why is everything falling apart?*

Was it Adam's doing? Was his agent, Mr. Antonio, still here, shepherding the collapse? He remembered the old man, so apparently harmless, and how he had known just what to do and say to get Nickolai to do what he wanted. He could imagine that evil bastard burrowed into the hierarchy of the PSDC, making the right suggestions, just *nudging* them a little ...

"Stand up. You're going to come with me." He pointed the gun at the helmets. "You can pick those up, but carry them with both hands."

They stood, Ingrid's camouflage flashing headache-inducing distortions of the woods around her, Sacha limping slightly on the damaged knee joint. When they picked up the helmets, Nickolai waved them ahead of him, back toward the commune.

"You took prisoners?" Parvi stared at him as he emerged from the woods, Ingrid and Sacha ahead of him. He could smell her anger from ten meters away. "You were supposed to find a safe—"

"You bastards are from the PSDC!" Ingrid snapped, "You're from the BMU!"

Nickolai realized that Parvi's jumpsuit still bore the patches from the Bakunin Mercenaries' Union. She leveled her own gun at Ingrid and said, "Who the hell are these people, and what is she talking about?"

"While we were gone," Nickolai told her, "the PSDC decided to take over."

"Take over what?" Parvi asked. Everyone was silent for a moment, and Parvi's eyes widened a bit. "You've got to be kidding."

"With the BMU as its army," Nickolai said.

Parvi shook her head. "Of course. Why not? The rest of the universe has gone insane, why not this?"

They took Ingrid and Sacha to one of the abandoned outbuildings of the commune and Parvi had them remove their armor. Once they were stripped to their underwear, Parvi ordered Nickolai to wake Kugara and fetch the rest of their team.

Nickolai came back with Kugara, Flynn, and the two scientists, Dörner and Brody. On their return, the two Wilson natives were seated on a couple of folding chairs, and the smell of fear and agitation had leveled off somewhat. Parvi paced, her weapon pointed to the ground, shaking her head and muttering the occasional curse in a human language that Nickolai did not understand.

Ingrid looked at Nickolai and asked, "There's another war out there?"

"You don't know?" Kugara responded. "There are tens of thousands of refugee ships all across this solar system. You haven't heard any of this?"

"Communication has been jammed for months," Sacha said. "We've been limited to line-of-sight transmissions since the PSDC started open warfare."

"Of course those bastards have always had the high ground." Parvi ran a hand through her white hair, pressing against her scalp as if trying to push back a migraine. "Why now? Why would they pull this shit at the worst possible moment?"

To Nickolai's surprise, Flynn spoke, "I think I know."

Everyone looked at the young man as if he had suddenly started speaking in tongues. By rights, he shouldn't have any connection to what was going on here. He had been born and raised on a planet eighty light-years beyond what had been the accepted limits of human space; a planet that had isolated itself for close to two centuries.

But Flynn represented one of the novel heresies that Nickolai had been exposed to since he had last set foot on Bakunin. The culture of Flynn's homeworld, Salmagundi, had taken ancestor worship to its logical extreme. They had kept vast data banks, containing the recorded minds of every human being that had ever lived on the planet, and the elders of Salmagundi had made a ritual of downloading those minds into their own. The half-dozen survivors from the Salmagundi militia, plus their critically wounded leader Alexander Shane, all bore glyph-like tattoos on their brows and scalp, one for each of the minds they had ritually taken.

Flynn only had the one.

But that one mind, his ancestor, had been one of the founders of the colony, a woman named Kari Tetsami. And Tetsami had been a native of Bakunin.

Unlike the other people from Salmagundi, Flynn seemed to have a separate existence from the other mind he hosted. Nickolai sensed a change in his body language when the woman Tetsami spoke. It extended to his voice and his facial expression, and even his smell. Tetsami was less reserved, and more confident.

Parvi asked him, "You know why the PSDC has just gone insane?"

Flynn/Tetsami nodded. "Blame our mutual acquaintance, Tjaele Mosasa."

Parvi narrowed her eyes and asked, "What the hell does Mosasa have to do with this?"

"What was he designed to do?" Tetsami asked.

"What does that . . ." Parvi stopped, staring at Flynn. After a moment she said, "Oh, shit. Of course. That selfish mechanical bastard."

Dörner spoke up. "Do you mind explaining what you two are talking about?"

"Bakunin isn't stable," Tetsami said. "It never was."

"What do you mean?" Dörner asked.

"She means that damned AI Mosasa was manipulating the whole planet." Parvi put her face in her hand. "He—it—wanted a Stateless world, so he was using the social engineering skills the Race programmed into him to keep the whole jury-rigged apparatus from caving in on itself. Then he leaves to let the whole thing fall apart without him. And I worked for that thing."

Ingrid looked from Parvi to Flynn and asked, "Who is Tjaele Mosasa?"

."He's the reason . . ." Parvi shook her head. "Someone else explain. I'm not up to it."

"Mosasa was evil," Nickolai said quietly. Kugara looked as if she was about to say something critical, but he continued. "He was evil not because he was a machine, an intellect born of dead matter. He was evil because he played God. He was evil because he was a very small reflection of the being that destroyed Salmagundi and Khamsin . . ."

CHAPTER SIX

Reincarnation

"The faster one runs from the past, the sooner one revisits it."

—*The Cynic's Book of Wisdom*

"History is the most cruel of all Goddesses."

—FRIEDRICH ENGELS
(1820–1895)

Date: 2526.8.3 (Standard)
Earth Orbit–Sol

Rebecca had returned to the *Prophet's Voice*, and Adam's host. Her embodied form stood in a cabin that was both archaic and comforting. There was no need for the artificial gravity, or the cot, or even the oxygen atmosphere. But even though this room had been a prison to her when Adam had come, she kept returning to it; as if it was an essential link back to her own humanity.

She knew that, when Adam finally remade this, as he had the surface of the world below them, she would find the loss hard to bear.

I've already lost, she thought. *We all have.*

She sat down on the cot and closed her eyes. She directed her attention inside herself, into the fuzzy boundaries of a mind that refused now to be contained in a biological vessel. The vastness she found within herself was a gift, one common to all of Adam's chosen. But unlike the others their self-appointed savior had lifted beyond the flesh, she knew she had yet to fully comprehend what she had become.

But inside her own consciousness there were universes beyond Adam's reach or knowledge.

She focused on one such universe. Around her coalesced a war-scarred plain dominated by a rolling mushroom cloud. Wreckage and bodies lay scattered across the muddy ground around her, steam still coiling from some.

She looked upon a memory, but one that did not belong to her.

A man stood alone, next to the twisted remains of an aircar, staring into the cloud.

"Jonah Dacham?" she said.

He turned around and looked at her. "You know me?"

"More important is that Adam knows you."

"Why am I here?"

"I can keep you hidden here. It's safe."

He turned to face the mushroom cloud and shook his head. "Safe?"

"It's only a memory."

Dacham snorted. "Only the memory of a genocide, the Confederacy's penultimate act of self-destruction. Do you even understand what this is?"

"That was the Protean city on Bakunin," Rebecca answered. Then she pointed to a fresh pile of wreckage. "And that was your aircar."

"Who are you?"

"I am Rebecca Tsoravitch, at least that's who I was."

"How is it you know this? Or know me?"

A familiar voice came from behind them, "You both have a mutual friend."

They turned to see Mosasa sitting on the still smoldering engine housing of a dead PSDC fighter.

"You?" Dacham snapped.

"Me," Mosasa said. He smiled. "Though I think we are not talking about exactly the same things. The Mosasa you knew met an unfortunate end at his brother's hands just about two months ago."

"Then who, or what, are you?"

Mosasa slid off the engine housing and walked up to them. "I'm as close to the original as you're going to get. A small attempt at immortality." He placed a pair of fingers on Dacham's chest. "Which makes me wonder at your own."

Dacham took a step back.

Mosasa lowered his hand. "Why are you here, Dom?"

"I was brought to this place."

"You know what I am asking," Mosasa said. "How is it you are alive, on Earth, to receive Adam's benediction? More intact than you were the last time we met?"

Dacham said nothing.

"Should I assume the Proteans had something to do with it? Their doomed attack on Adam's fleet was merely a feint. If you're part of a real attack, you're an unfortunately poor choice."

"Why?"

"Do you know who Adam is?"

The battlefield faded from around them, replaced by a stark white windowless office. An old man had fallen face first into an ornate desk, the back half of his head an ugly crater. A muscular man—who wasn't quite a man—stood over the body, staring at it with eyes that were midnight black. Smoke still curled from the barrel of the heavy slugthrower clutched in his hand.

Rebecca recognized the man with the gun. She had seen this creature in another memory Mosasa had shown her; she had seen him digging through the ruins of the Race homeworld, pulling AI cores out of the rubble with gangrenous hands. This golem of flesh and bone and heretical technology had been named Ambrose, and had buried within him one of Mosasa's five AIs. The AI that would become Adam.

Ambrose's expression was almost completely blank, as if he couldn't quite understand what he had done. But as Rebecca watched, she could see some measure of emotion leak through the dead impassive face. An almost imperceptible turn of the mouth, a slight narrowing of the eyes. Something buried inside this husk enjoyed what it had just done.

She knew who the dead man was; it was Dimitri Olmanov, the most powerful man in the Confederacy. If the destruction of the Protean commune had been the "Confederacy's penultimate act of self-destruction," this was the fatal wound. Ambrose carried an AI that bore the Race's imperative to destroy the Confederacy they had warred with—and though the war was long over, Ambrose's hand had been the one to see that mission completed.

Perhaps that was why it was Ambrose who so fatally snapped when Mosasa's AIs returned to the Race homeworld to find their creators had extinguished themselves.

"Who Adam is?" Dacham repeated. He stared at the tableau focusing on the dead man on the desk, whispering, "Dimitri?"

Mosasa laughed. "No, Dom, unlike you, Dimitri is quite permanently dead."

Ambrose looked up from his work, directing those almost-empty black eyes toward them. Something in those eyes made Rebecca reassess exactly when this fragment of Mosasa's AI had lost its sanity. She had thought its mind had fractured when it had discovered that its creators had destroyed themselves ...

But this Ambrose already seemed well along on the path toward madness.

Dacham stared at the creature—as human as it looked, she could no longer think of it as a man—as it passed by them, leaving the corpse alone in the office with them.

"Him? *Ambrose?*"

"See, you *have* met."

Dacham shook his head.

"And should you come under Adam's scrutiny, the same questions will arise in his mind as do in mine."

Dacham shook his head and glared at Mosasa's image. Around them, the office crumbled away in favor of a desert landscape defined by ranks of hundreds of dead and disabled aircraft. "Why should I trust you?"

Mosasa chuckled. "Because you still exist."

"Why are you here?" Rebecca asked him. "Why did you volunteer to be Adam's chosen?"

Dacham shook his head and said, "How can I know that my continued existence is not just because Adam wants that information?"

Mosasa looked across at Rebecca and said, "It seems to be an impasse, then."

The three of them stood silent for a moment, until the wind carried a voice through the hot desert air.

"Stop it! Stop pretending to be human!"

A look of shock crossed Dacham's face as he turned to find the source of the voice. "What is this?"

"Only another memory," Mosasa said.

Dacham ran off, in the direction of the shouting.

"What the hell?" Rebecca said. "Where are we?"

"You never visited our home on Bakunin?"

She shook her head. In all her dealings with the AI Mosasa, she had never actually set foot on the planet. "Where is he going?"

"Shall we see?" Mosasa walked after Dacham, and Rebecca followed.

They walked through the maze of dead aircraft, across black sand packed as hard as asphalt. The air was dry and hot as an oven.

They caught up with Dacham at the edge of a clearing before an oversized hangar. He stood, watching a trio of figures facing off in front of the open hangar door.

Rebecca knew the two men by the hangar. One was Ambrose, bald and black-eyed, with an expression that still spoke madness to her. The other was the AI Mosasa, physically identical in appearance to the figure that stood next to her. Oddly, though, something in the AI now rang false to her: the movement, body language, all seemed less *alive* than even Ambrose.

Facing the two AIs stood an Asian woman in a leather jacket. She held up a small remote control as if she were threatening them with it. On the ground in front of her was a black case.

The AI Mosasa took a step and said, "Tetsami—"

The woman screamed at him, *"Don't you fucking move!* You haven't earned the right. You never told *me* you were an effing AI."

Rebecca turned to her Mosasa and asked, "What's going on here?"

"A bit of hubris," he told her. "My AIs, all of them, could

see vast societal processes, manipulate events with a grand precision. Adam himself is the epitome of this. But that view of the universe breeds a fatal flaw, the assumption that individuals are as malleable, or easy to predict. Individuals have free will, societies don't."

"Who is that woman?"

"A common acquaintance of myself and Mr. Dacham. Please, though, watch the drama."

She looked back at Tetsami and the two AIs. The AI Mosasa almost looked pained as he talked, but she could read the falseness in his voice. "We do not control people. We only anticipate their voluntary actions. Everyone chose his or her own path, Dominic and Ivor included."

The woman, Tetsami, trembled, her voice carrying an edge of hysteria in it. "You set this Christ-blown bullshit up in the first place, you electronic hypocrite!"

Mosasa's voice was inhumanly calm. "As much as anyone on this planet, we have been trying to maintain Bakunin as a viable political entity. All that differs is our methods. If you must blame someone for these deaths, don't the two of them share some complicity?"

"Whose deaths?" Rebecca whispered.

"Shh, just listen."

The AI Mosasa said, "Dominic Magnus chose his own death twice."

"What?" Tetsami looked up.

What? Rebecca thought. The name cut through her suddenly, and she turned to look at Dacham. His face had gone white, and his hand went up to his face.

Dominic Magnus.

Bequeathed to her along with the memory of this man Dacham was the memory of his aliases, the names he had used on Bakunin. Primary among those was the name Dominic Magnus.

The AI continued speaking to Tetsami, "Dominic Magnus flew into the wrong end of a wormhole. It was the only way he could see in which at least a version of himself could make it to the Terran Congress in time."

Tetsami stared and whispered something that was inaudible to Rebecca. She didn't need to hear what Tetsami said. Rebecca could see the meaning of it in her face; the same sense of loss she saw in Dacham's.

The robotic Mosasa kept talking, and to Rebecca, the words felt like knives attacking whatever rationale had brought this woman here; be it love, grief, or anger . . .

"The Dominic who died at GA&A was a ghost. He wasn't the Dom you knew. That version of Dominic spent nine years in isolation, waiting for the Congress, and came from a universe different from ours in a few important respects."

"Different? How?" Tetsami sounded hollow, beaten.

"For one example, you died before this Jonah Dacham left Bakunin."

"But I . . ." Her words trailed off, swallowed by the silence in the surrounding desert.

Rebecca heard Dacham whisper, "You *did* die."

"Your Dominic didn't die at GA&A. He died when he crossed the event horizon of a wormhole in the 61 Cygni system."

Tetsami shook her head and brandished the remote control in her hand. The resignation in her voice was frightening. "I should set this off on general principles. Just for you playing God with all of us."

"Everyone tries to play God," the AI responded. "It's just that some are better at it than others."

If the tone in her voice was frightening, the grin that suddenly crossed her face was even more so. "You arrogant SOB. You know the *real* reason I ain't blowing us all into orbit?" The AIs didn't respond immediately, and Tetsami's voice rose almost an octave, near hysteria. "Come on, you and you predictive psychology should be able to figure that one out."

The AI Mosasa finally responded, and in his voice Rebecca could sense a tentative fear. "You've decided that it isn't worth it to take your own life for the sake of revenge?"

He doesn't know, Rebecca thought, *and that frightens him.*

Tetsami laughed. "Not even close." She walked up and picked up the case that was lying on the ground between her and the AIs. "The reason we're not a smoking crater is because this happens to be my luggage. And this," she held out the hand with the remote, "is my hotel key."

Tetsami turned and walked away.

Dacham watched the memory of Tetsami leave and asked, "She lived?"

"Through this version of events," said Rebecca's Mosasa.

Dacham shook his head, "Why bother showing me this?"

"It is relevant to your cooperation with us," Mosasa said as the spaceship graveyard dissolved around them, leaving them inside a vast cathedral-like space.

"How?"

Mosasa shocked Rebecca by saying, "Because your one-time lover still lives, at least in the same sense I do."

Dacham just gaped at him. Rebecca glanced around the building Mosasa had brought them to, and as she recognized the place, she began to understand.

Mosasa spread his arms in a grand gesture and said, "Welcome to the Hall of Minds."

CHAPTER SEVEN

Denominations

"If you leave an enemy alive, you better leave him
something to live for."
                              —*The Cynic's Book of Wisdom*

"Diplomacy is simply war by another name."
                              —SYLVIA HARPER
                              (2008–2081)

Date: 2526.8.4 (Standard)
350,000 km from Bakunin–BD+50°1725

The *Wisconsin* was one of hundreds of self-contained orbital habitats clustering around Bakunin, outside the free-
fire zone the PSDC had established from geosynchronous
orbit on down. It orbited Schwitzguebel, Bakunin's larger
moon. It was one of the many places that Toni had contacted when the *Daedalus* tached in to this nightmare
over a month ago. Back then, as the system was just being
overwhelmed with refugee craft, they had denied docking
privileges.

Things had changed.

The *Wisconsin* hovered in the display before her, a massive construct larger than the 3SEC Command Platform
orbiting Styx. The heart of it was a prism defined by three
two-kilometer-long parallel tubes, their cross-sections arranged to center on the vertices of an equilateral triangle.
The tubes were connected by a complex network of scaf-

folding that kept the enclosed tubes fixed relative to each other and spinning around a common axis through the center of its triangular cross-section. As it turned, Toni saw sunlight glitter off of hectares of windows, all pointed toward the center of rotation. Surrounding it, thousands of mirrors directed sunlight in toward the three linked habitats, giving the whole the appearance of a slowly rotating cylinder made of pipes and broken glass.

She had never seen anything like it.

The habitats she had known, that she had served on, had all been solid, gray, *functional*. This was like a fairy castle hovering over the daylight side of Schwitzguebel.

She talked to traffic control on the *Wisconsin* as they directed her on the proper approach path, and even as she monitored the controls, her bearing, and the thrust of the engines, her eyes still kept drifting up to the main display.

The approach had her pilot the *Daedalus* along the *Wisconsin*'s axis of rotation—and into the center of the spinning construct. The massive habitat rotated around the ship, and she could see flashes of green and blue through the massive multifaceted windows facing her.

In front of the *Daedalus*, a massive cylinder hung along the axis of the spinning superstructure. Dwarfed by the three habitats paralleling it, it still dwarfed the *Daedalus*, its open end large enough to accommodate a dozen ships of similar size at once.

As the *Daedalus* flew inside, slowly braking, she saw the inner surface of the cylinder covered with docked ships of every description.

Ahead, a docking arm hung down from the inner surface. It was attached to a counter-rotating ring mounted on the inside of the massive cylindrical dock, so her target seemed stationary.

She broadcast to the ship's passengers to secure themselves for docking.

The docking maneuver itself was painless. She barely felt the nudge when the *Daedalus* mated to the docking arm. But once the connection was secure, the arm retracted and matched the rotation of the *Wisconsin*. The transition wasn't violent, but it was just enough to make her slightly queasy.

As the docking arm drew the *Daedalus* into the embrace of a docking cradle, warning lights across the control console flickered from amber to green as the ship's subsystems switched to external power.

She felt herself sink into the seat as the habitat's spin gave her the sense of gravity, however small, for the first time in over a month. "This is Captain Valentine. The *Daedalus* is safely docked. You're free to move about the ship. The command staff should meet me at the main air lock."

Captain Valentine. Command staff. The words still felt wrong in her mouth. Inside, she was still a lieutenant, AWOL from a force that probably no longer existed. The *Daedalus* was crewed with refugees and run by a pair of pirates. She felt that acting as if they were bound by some larger command structure was only pretending; any moment, some group or other would recognize this all as a fantasy and the whole structure would fall apart.

She pushed herself up slowly in the low gravity and walked toward the door. Even with daily exercise regimens, her body was suddenly confused about having a definitive "down."

She reached the air lock and saw that Mallory's command structure still held for the moment. The representatives from the Caliphate crew and the Salmagundi crew stood waiting next to Karl Stavros and her other self.

Toni II stepped forward and put a hand on her shoulder, "Good luck, Sis."

Toni hugged her twin and wondered briefly if she was being narcissistic. "Thanks," she whispered. "Keep things together back here."

Her twin was probably the one person who didn't need to ask about the vague unfocused fears that gripped Toni at the moment. She just patted Toni's back and said, "I'll handle it."

She let go of Toni II and said, "I'm handing you command of the *Daedalus*." She turned to the other three and said, "Let's go."

                        *   *   *

"Welcome to the *Wisconsin*." The woman who greeted them after cycling through the air lock was tall and had her blonde hair cut very close to the scalp. She wore a navy-blue jumpsuit that bore some very subtle matte-black chevrons on the sleeves. She held out her hand, and Toni shook it. "We're taking you to the Gamma habitat, where all the delegations from the Centauri fleet are being housed."

The *Centauri* fleet.

Toni felt another wave of wrongness. This was not the Centauri fleet; anything deserving such a name probably was battling Adam in the space around Occisis, if it still existed. The "fleet" Mallory had gathered together were refugee craft that just happened to largely come from planets in the Centauri Alliance, those most readily influenced by the last transmission from the papacy. Predictably, as information on what was happening filtered through the thousands of ships huddled in Bakunin space, groups tended to form around existing political lines; a small Sirius fleet, three fleets from Indi, a fleet formed from Bakunin natives and outlaws allied with a handful of ships from the Union of Independent Worlds, and a small contingent of recent arrivals from the Eridani Caliphate.

So Mallory's group was the Centauri fleet. *And with the possible exceptions for the native Bakuninites, only about ten percent of all of those were actual military vessels.*

Their guide led them around an upward curving corridor until they reached an elevator down to the Gamma habitat. They walked through a large air lock, and into a square chamber about ten meters on a side. Once the air lock sealed behind them, the whole thing started moving down. The image of massive walls sliding past made Toni realize that they were enclosed on three sides by massive windows.

Then the walls peeled away, leaving the view of the *Wisconsin* unobstructed as the elevator continued to slide downward. She heard a few sharp intakes of breath from her people.

Even though she had seen it on approach, the display on the *Daedalus'* bridge did not do the view justice. Seeing the *Wisconsin* with her own eyes, separated only by a half-meter-thick window, slammed home the scale of the thing.

The long tube of the Gamma habitat unrolled beneath them, stretching a kilometer before and behind, topped by an unbroken surface of windows, behind which Toni could now see details of topography: hills, streams, trees, buildings. And past the end on one side, the mottled gray surface of Schwitzguebel slowly spun; In the other direction, the ruddy orb of Kropotkin burned; and between the two, mirrors were suspended in a spindly framework like chrome-winged butterflies caught in the web of some massive mechanical spider.

Then the elevator descended through the ceiling of the vast Gamma habitat. Suddenly, the vast windows were above them and the sky lightened from black to blue. The transition was so sharp that Toni suspected that the color was designed into the windows to provide for a more natural-looking sky. Even so, the sky was alien in that instead of a single sun, there were hundreds of reflections of Kropotkin shining down on the two-kilometer strip of land below them.

New walls reached up to embrace the windows and seal off the view, and the elevator slid softly to a stop. Toni's legs ached now that she stood in something approaching a full gee standard. Karl looked a little wobbly, while the other two looked less so—they'd been living in zero-gee aboard the *Daedalus* for a much shorter time.

The large doors opened on a broad flat area dominated by wheeled vehicles of every description. Beyond the parked vehicles, a line of trees hid the rest of the habitat from view, and above them, some sort of birds flew between them and the artificially blue sky.

The guy from the Salmagundi militia had never been out of a gravity well before fleeing Adam's "conversion" of his planet. Toni glanced at him staring at the habitat around him.

Toni took a deep breath. She'd been space-borne so long, she had forgotten what it smelled like when air wasn't canned and reprocessed. She smelled earth and water, and some sort of plant life that brought her near to a sneeze.

Their escort told them, "Your hotel is this way."

Hotel?

They followed her down a walkway leaving the vehicle pad, and through a small park that grew wild in such a way that it seemed part of the design.

She hadn't had the time to investigate the *Wisconsin* herself, so she wondered what its role had been in peacetime. It almost looked like a tourist destination, hotels and all. But what kind of tourists came to Bakunin?

The more she thought about it, the queasier she became.

Of course, the main attraction is the fact that there is no law. If you have money, and tastes for things that are frowned upon on your home planet . . .

The hotel they approached radiated luxury the way a burning engine gave off toxic fumes. The walls arced upward, polished granite shining, windows glinting from behind brass frames, an intimidating mass of wealth that contrasted with the scene on the ground greeting them.

The landscaping around the hotel was trampled into a uniform soggy mess; fences and handrails had been broken and replaced by only token repairs. A bench had toppled over. A geometric fountain had been shut off, and its basin was filled only with a film of dirty water dotted with trash. As they closed on the hotel, she saw several broken windows covered with reflective plastic sheeting.

Their guide led them to a long queue that seemed much more orderly than the damaged scenery led Toni to expect. The order was enforced by a dozen stone-faced guards wearing blue jumpsuits and carrying nasty-looking laser carbines. At the head of the line, people filed slowly in front of a row of desks. Above the desks, a hand-lettered sign read, "Please wait in line until you're registered and issued a badge."

Karl asked their guide as she turned to go, "Have you been having refugee problems?"

"Nothing security can't handle," she responded, leaving them in line.

"Looks like they had a riot," Karl said under his breath.

It took an hour to get through the line, and have the *Wisconsin's* bureaucrats satisfy themselves and issue the four

of them ID badges. The bored functionary that processed
Toni showed only a brief flash of human emotion when he
registered some obvious surprise that Toni had been issued
space in one of the hotel's penthouses. Apparently, though,
his existence was dreary enough that the expression only
lasted a few seconds, then he handed her the ID and called,
"Next."

When the priest's ship had arrived from Salmagundi, the
nominal reason the pirate Valentine bitches had for taking
Mallory's refugees on board was in order to render aid to
their wounded. The *Khalid* had brought them the first casualties of the priest's war against the Antichrist. Stefan knew
their names as Shane and Abbas. Shane was part of the odd
tribe of men from Salmagundi, an old bald man bearing
more tattoos on his scalp, it seemed, than all of his country-
men put together. Abbas was a much younger woman who
had apparently been the highest-ranking member of the
Caliphate soldiers Mallory had following him.

They were both severely injured, and had yet to regain
consciousness. The two took up most of the *Daedalus'* limited
medical resources, and a few hours after the so-called "command staff" left, a medical from the *Wisconsin* came up to
transport the wounded to an actual hospital. Since Stefan was
the only crew left who knew the medbay design, he didn't
even have to ask to be the one to assist the *Wisconsin* medics.
The pirate bitch running his ship had no idea that he'd *want*
to help move the wounded. Or that he had very good reasons
to want to.

Stefan met the medics and showed them the control
systems on the two enclosed medbays housing Alexander
Shane and Sergeant Abbas. Both victims were barely stable, and the medics were loath to take either out of the bays
to transport.

The medics were gratified when Stefan showed them
how the medbay pods had been updated to be movable.
Both had internal systems that could run independently of
the *Daedalus*. With a little effort they could transport both
Shane and Abbas to the hospital without disconnecting
their life support.

And Stefan was more than happy to accompany them.

They moved the massive medbays out of the *Daedalus* and down to the Beta habitat level. When they reached the ground level of the habitat, a truck was waiting for them, a tracked flatbed cargo mover, since a standard ambulance couldn't accommodate the large medbays. Stefan rode with the driver as the vehicle wove through a dense glass-walled city, windows shining with the hundreds of Kropotkins the *Wisconsin's* mirrors reflected down on them.

The medics were concerned with their patients, so Stefan talked to the driver, asking about how things were on the *Wisconsin*.

"You might not see it here, but things're a mess—"

Stefan listened attentively as the driver told him how much things had gone to hell. The Beta habitat was largely given over to the administrative and operations staff of the *Wisconsin*. Alpha and Gamma were the tourist areas; hotels, casinos, brothels, and the sorts of entertainment one came for if one came to Bakunin for entertainment. Attractions with an additional premium attached for being safely out of the chaos down on the surface.

"Never should've let the refugees in," the man told him. The place had been overwhelmed. Most of the security force on the *Wisconsin* was in the Gamma habitat trying to keep things under control with all the "diplomacy," going on. The driver spat the word in a derisive tone that exactly matched Stefan's feelings.

But Stefan had no intention of being a party to some war that had nothing to do with him.

The hospital was overcrowded and understaffed, and no one paid any particular attention to Stefan. He followed along as the medics pushed the medical bays from the *Daedalus* into the emergency room. Removing Shane and Abbas from the safety of the medical sarcophagi was a tense process, but a successful one—in large part because the medical readings from each bay had been slightly altered to downgrade its occupant's condition.

The medics wouldn't have known from the readouts, but it probably would have been perfectly safe to remove both patients when they'd still been on-board the ship. But had they done that, Stefan and the two medbays would have remained on the *Daedalus*.

Stefan quietly moved the medbays out of the way of the medical staff as they went to work on Shane and Abbas. No one paid him any attention.

It was clumsy for one man to move the units, but they were powered and could roll with just one hand directing them. Stefan took the pair of units back outside to the waiting truck, the driver leaned out the cab and said, "That was quick."

Stefan nodded. "Let me secure these and we can go back to the elevator."

The driver remained in the cab as Stefan eased both units onto the back of the truck. Then, out of sight of the driver, he opened a small access panel near the bottom of one of the medbay pods. Inside, nestled among a small arsenal of carefully packed weaponry, the handle of a military-grade stun rod was just within reach. He withdrew it, checked the charge, and sealed the compartment shut.

When Stefan got in the cab with the driver, the man turned to say something to him, and his jaw connected with the stun rod. The driver jerked and flopped over, falling across the passenger seat.

Stefan crawled over the man and sat down behind the controls, leaving the man in a drooling heap on the passenger seat. Stefan smiled and pulled away from the hospital.

He knew that he couldn't be the only person here who didn't accept the idea of becoming a sacrifice on the altar of some idiot's theology.

CHAPTER EIGHT

Unbeliever

"More collateral damage has been done around a conference table than has ever been done on the battlefield."

—*The Cynic's Book of Wisdom*

"When a man knows he is to be hanged in a fortnight, it concentrates his mind wonderfully."

—SAMUEL JOHNSON
(1709–1784)

Date: 2526.8.4 (Standard)
350,000 km from Bakunin–BD+50°1725

Father Francis Xavier Mallory stood alone in a penthouse suite on top of one of the *Wisconsin*'s many hotels. He faced the window, looking down the long axis of the Gamma habitat. He could see half of this self-contained world from where he sat, and from a perspective high enough that the viewer could ignore the scars the influx of refugees had left, and the ubiquitous presence of blue-suited security guards.

He stared out at the view and prayed for himself, and for the souls of everyone in Adam's path. His hands shook slightly, and he clenched them into fists to quiet them. He didn't remember the last time he had slept, but it had been before he had boarded the *Savannah* to command his attack on the ghostly presence of Adam in Bakunin's outer solar system.

When he closed his eyes, he could still picture the fiery hell that he had wrought, sterilizing the nanomachine cloud that was Adam's foothold in this solar system. That moment was the point where he realized the weight upon him, the responsibility.

He was certain it was God calling him to do this, to lead the defense of this planet in the face of a power barely within human comprehension. That faith should have given him comfort, but instead it filled him with an emotion akin to panic. His faith in God was strong, but his faith in himself became thinner with each passing moment.

He was here to negotiate a unified defense of the system, but his one victory had placed him, and those that followed him, at a steep disadvantage. He might have some credibility throughout the refugee fleet because of the tach-comm from the Vatican, but he had thrown away half his own fleet's numbers to destroy Adam's cloud. His Centauri fleet was now half the size of the next smallest group here.

Worse, there were many people dead set against him because of the damage that attack had caused their own tach-drives. He had broadcast a warning for all ships in the system to power down their tach-drives—but the failure of some to listen did not make them blame Mallory and his people any less.

He squeezed his fists and felt the pulse raging in his neck.

I should see a doctor, he thought. He had old implants from his marine days, designed to optimize the performance of his body in combat. Normally, their effect should only last a half hour or so . . .

It felt as if the implants had been jacking his body for days.

I don't have the time to see a doctor.

The next twenty-four hours would be crucial in presenting a unified front when Adam made his eventual appearance. And, for all they knew, Adam's attack could be in the midst of tach-space right now, on its way to claim another planet for its insatiable god.

"After the negotiations," he whispered to himself.

Behind him the penthouse door whooshed open, and he

turned to face the new arrivals. The four other members of the *Daedalus'* command staff walked into the suite.

Karl Stavros, still the nominal owner of the *Daedalus*, looked at Mallory and said, "Father, you look like hell."

Mallory turned to Toni Valentine, the de facto captain of the *Daedalus* and asked, "Any problems getting here?"

Toni shook her head. "None. Though they seem to have a large refugee problem here. I can see why they refused us docking rights when we first showed up. Downstairs is a mess."

Mallory had seen that mess himself on arrival. The first floor of the hotel had been a casino and ballroom. Some time after landings stopped on Bakunin, they had stripped the floor clean and set up hundreds of cots. Now the lobby level was home to about seven hundred people.

"What exactly is the plan here?" Karl asked.

"We're trying to negotiate a unified defense. A common command to fight Adam."

"You think you can manage that?" Karl asked. "I think you have better chances against Adam."

The Caliphate man behind him said, "Once they know what we fight, they will join together. They have no choice."

God willing, Mallory thought.

Four hours later, Mallory stood in front of the bathroom mirror to get ready for the first meeting with representatives from the other fleets. He barely recognized the man staring back at him. In the stark light his hair looked more white than gray, and every crease in his face seemed deeper. Staring into his own eyes, he saw something stark and frightening—looking into the eyes of a prophet or a madman.

Or a man on the third day of an adrenaline high . . .

He cut himself twice shaving with a shaking hand, but the wounds barely bled. Even without the stubble, the face looking back at him was not one he expected the other representatives to listen to.

I've done what I can.

Someone knocked on the door. "Father Mallory?" Toni's voice.

"Yes?"

"We just received word from the *Daedalus*. We have a problem."

"What is it?"

"Stefan."

Stefan? He remembered Stefan railing at him when he first tried to build a consensus to fight this thing. *"Even if everything you say about this Adam is accurate, which I have a hard time swallowing, what the fuck does it have to do with us?"*

He opened the door and asked, "What about Stefan?"

"He's gone missing."

Mallory looked over at the boy's father. The man looked sunken, his face blank as if he wasn't quite hearing their conversation. "What happened?"

"He escorted the bays with Shane and Abbas to a hospital in the Beta habitat, he never returned, and the *Wisconsin* folks don't know where he is."

Karl spoke up, "Did you say they took the medbays?"

"Yes. I didn't even know they were mobile."

Karl shook his head and sank into one of the seats.

"Mr. Stavros . . ." Mallory trailed off. Instinct made him reach out, and he almost formed words of reassurance, that his son would be found. But before any words of comfort reached his lips, the more secular part of his mind realized that Karl was not disturbed for his son's safety.

Under his breath, Karl said, "Bastard."

Toni turned to face Karl and asked, "What is it?"

Karl chuckled and shook his head. "I outsmarted myself, my young pirate."

"What?"

"Me and my son were never quite as helpless as we made ourselves out to be. There are many things on board the *Daedalus* that don't appear in the logs or the control systems."

"Like what?" Mallory asked.

"Weapons, for one thing," Karl said.

"What? You had a cache of weapons on board and you didn't . . ." Toni trailed off as if she couldn't think of an adequate way to finish the sentence.

"We could have taken the ship back. But after arriving on Bakunin, our interests seemed to mostly parallel yours. Killing you and your sister might have gained us control of the ship, but we would have end up undermanned and less defensible."

Toni placed a hand on her face and muttered, "Shit."

The man from the Caliphate stepped up and grabbed Karl's shoulder. "You joined this battle, and you did not release these weapons?"

Karl laughed weakly, "You plan to fight Adam with laser carbines and slugthrowers? I would have handed them over if there had been a point." He looked up at Mallory. "But my sin is being old and paranoid. Though, apparently not paranoid enough."

"Why did you ask about the medbays?" Mallory asked.

"An ancient smuggling tool," Karl said. "Misdirection. Throw a critically wounded crewman on top, scream for aid, and not many people will examine too deeply what is beneath."

"The medbays?" Toni asked.

"They have enough hidden storage, shielded from easy scanning, to hide a small arsenal."

The Caliphate man shook Karl. "What is your son planning to do?"

Mallory took the man's shoulders and pulled him away from Karl as Karl said, "I honestly don't know."

Above the Alpha habitat, the mirrors tilted away from Kropotkin, plunging the habitat into night. Stefan stood at the base of one of the main service elevators wearing the navy-blue jumpsuit of *Wisconsin* security. The suit's original owner and the driver of Stefan's flatbed transport were safely beyond revival, the bodies locked in one of the medbays.

The medbays and weapons waited for him, stored in a facility closet servicing one of the redundant power systems of the *Wisconsin*, a place that should be free of any prying eyes unless the power systems suffered a major failure.

Stefan unshouldered his laser carbine, bequeathed to him by his uniform's late owner. The driver had been right;

security forces were largely absent from this habitat—but the place was awash with refugees. Even the parking area around the elevator was crowded with people sleeping on the ground, and sitting in small groups.

A few people shouted questions at him, as if he was in charge. He ignored them and walked from the elevator.

The people they let roam free weren't of interest. These were the people that weren't a threat.

According to the last few statements of his uniform's prior owner, the refugees who were of concern to *Wisconsin* security were in a secured warehouse building a few hundred meters from this elevator. Those were the people Stefan wanted.

He walked off in that direction as the reflected stars came out above him.

CHAPTER NINE

Trials

"Shared interests do not imply shared priorities."
—*The Cynic's Book of Wisdom*

"I am prepared to fight in any way the ruling class may make it necessary ..."

—EUGENE V. DEBS
(1855–1926)

Date: 2526.8.5 (Standard)
Bakunin–BD+50°1725

Hurry up and wait, Kugara thought as she watched Kropotkin rise above Wilson. They had been groundside for six days, and they hadn't even made it past the first city.

Not that she wanted to fault Parvi for trying to do right by the civilians, but the universe was falling apart around them, and every minute they sat on their hands was a minute closer to hearing Adam's ultimatum, a minute closer to the sky boiling, a minute closer to Bakunin following Salmagundi and Khamsin ...

She looked up at the lightening sky and wondered if Adam had set foot on Dakota yet. It had been part of the wormhole network, one of the "core" planets orbiting Tau Ceti along with Haven, the capital planet of the Fifteen Worlds.

She was beginning to understand some of Nickolai's fatalism.

We're all doomed, she thought. *Now, it's just a matter of sorting out the details.*

She looked down. She stood on the upper level of a plain concrete structure that had once served as a garage. It rose about twelve stories above an outflung neighborhood that had mostly burned to the ground. It made her feel exposed, standing on top of a massive block in the middle of several square kilometers of rubble, even with the white flags telling any hostiles that it was a POW camp.

Kugara wondered, since the PSDC was at the point of openly trying to conquer the planet, if they'd advanced past any niceties like not targeting their own people.

At least their party wasn't technically POWs. They weren't locked behind impromptu steel cages like the two-dozen mercenaries occupying the first two levels. The Wilson militia had boarded them in the upper levels, and were pretty generous with their facilities: cots, hot water, a couple of decent meals, and a change of clothes for everyone except Nickolai, who didn't need any and would be impossible to fit if he did.

They were free to roam about, though doing so without an escort was problematic, since beyond a fifty-meter perimeter, the wreckage surrounding them was peppered with land mines and autonomous hunter-killer drones waiting for the wrong person to cross their path.

So, despite being "guests," they were as trapped as the prisoners here.

"At least the civilians are safe," she whispered. *Safe as anyone else on the planet.*

"Kugara?"

She turned around and saw Nickolai standing on the roof behind her. The dawn light carved bloody highlights on his golden fur, revealing nearly every muscle in his torso.

"What are you doing up here?" he asked.

"I came up for the view," she said. "I feel cramped down there." She felt a strong sense of deja vú as she asked, "Why are you up here?"

"Same reason."

The memory came, as if it was from an aeon ago, the two

of them huddled together in the *Eclipse*'s observation port, staring at the stars. "We're still alone, aren't we?"

He walked up next to her and placed a hand on her shoulder. "No, we aren't."

She sighed and leaned up against him. His fur was warm in the chill morning air. For a few moments she just listened to him breathe.

They faced east, toward the sunrise, and over the horizon, the Diderot Mountains. "Do you think," she asked, "that there is something to be found out there?"

"Some salvation left by the Dolbrians?" He shook his head and emitted a small inhuman snarl. "Reason tells me that this is a hopeless errand."

She nodded. They were on the mother of all wild goose chases, whose only redeeming feature was the fact that it wasn't any more futile than attacking Adam. At least she got to choose how she faced the end, and who she faced it with.

That sounds like something Nickolai would say, she thought. He was becoming a bad influence on her.

In his chest, she heard a grumble that sounded like a tentative, "*But.*"

She looked up at his face, still staring at the eastern horizon. "But what?" she asked.

"I have lived through much stranger things."

Nickolai, am I hearing hope *in your voice?* Maybe she was a bad influence on *him*. She looked at his feline profile, and his expression was distant and regal, compounded by the solid black of his eyes, which gave a depth to his expression, as if he stared over the horizon, or through centuries. If his people made statues of their saints, he would be an excellent model.

His brows creased, and his hand tightened on her shoulder.

"What is it?" she asked.

"The PSDC," he whispered.

"They've been flying sorties since we got here."

A minimal shake of his head. "Not a lone attack craft. I see thirty aircraft incoming. Half are troop transports."

"Oh, shit." Those numbers meant an all-out push to the

sea. Some other city must have fallen, freeing the resources to go after Wilson. *So much for getting the civilians to safety.* "I don't hear the alarms."

"Give them a moment. They just cleared the horizon."

Somewhere, in the city in front of them, a siren began blaring. Then another, and another, until the resonance of multiple high-pitched klaxons made her teeth ache and left an empty spot in her chest.

"Fifty now," Nickolai said.

Parvi was not happy with Kugara's news, or the implications.

"Even if I agree with you," Parvi had to nearly shout at her over the still blaring sirens. "What about the civilians?" Her voice echoed slightly off the concrete walls around them. The word civilian, by now, didn't include Brody, Dörner, and Flynn, who stood by Kugara and Parvi dressed in the surplused khaki jumpsuits that their Wilson hosts had given them.

"We have to trust that the PSDC won't arbitrarily target a POW facility," Kugara argued, unsure if she thought she was in the right, or just could no longer bear standing still in the midst of chaos.

"Trust?" Parvi said.

"Which is exactly what we're doing if we sit tight here," Kugara said.

Parvi shook her head.

"She has a point," Brody said, massaging the cast on his arm. "We came down here for a reason."

"I know that," Parvi snapped. "But we can't just walk out of here through a minefield—where the hell is Nickolai?"

Parvi looked around the empty floor where they had been housed, as if Nickolai might have been hiding in a corner somewhere. Not that there was anyplace to hide, it was just one large ferrocrete floor dotted with cots and temporary folding chairs and tables. Even the impromptu toilet facilities were only private by dint of a flimsy screen.

Silence fell across the room, and Parvi narrowed her eyes at Kugara. "Where is he?"

"He's getting us a guide."

"What?" Parvi glared at her. Kugara's—and Nickolai's—

actions were insubordinate if not outright mutinous, but she didn't want to directly challenge Parvi's nominal command of their mission. It was hard enough to convince Nickolai that in this instance it would be better to ask forgiveness rather than permission.

"We knew we were running out of time," she told Parvi, "and that without a guide we'd be trapped here. Nickolai had to act before the Wilson militia evacuated themselves."

"I see . . ."

"That was our next step," Kugara asked. "Right, Captain?"

The glance Parvi gave to Flynn and the scientists was subtle, but Kugara noticed. She didn't know what had happened to their commander, but this Parvi was a different woman than the mercenary hard-ass that had hired her and Nickolai. Something like doubt had crept in and dulled her command. Ever since it became apparent they had landed in the midst of a shooting war, Kugara had watched Parvi become more and more tentative.

In a situation like this, that was frightening.

Fortunately, even though they both knew Kugara had overstepped her authority, Parvi decided to accept Kugara's belated acknowledgment of her command. "Don't take such decisions upon yourself in the future." She turned to the other three and said, "We're going to have to move, stay with us—"

She was interrupted by someone shouting, "Get your hands off me, you furry freak."

Everyone turned to see Nickolai pushing one of the Wilson militia guards ahead of him. He carried the man's weapon, and the caseless shotgun looked like a toy in his hands. He held the gun butt-first toward Kugara and said to the man, "You're going to lead us out of here."

"Are you crazy, don't you hear the sirens? The PSDC will start strafing in a couple of minutes."

"It isn't an air raid," Kugara said. "It's a full-scale invasion."

"What?"

"The PSDC is going to take this city," Nickolai said. "We want to leave before that happens."

*   *   *

"You don't need to point that at me," the militia guard told her as they walked single file toward the bombed-out perimeter.

"Just concentrate on where we're going," Kugara told him.

"Uh-huh." He looked up at the sky. Motion was now visible past the Wilson skyline, small specks of aircraft visible in the gaps between buildings. The sirens had stopped, leaving a disturbing stillness to the air. The edge of the safe perimeter was marked by a spray of glowing orange paint that traced a line across dirt and rubble alike.

Their guide stood on the safe side of the line and said, "You'd all be safer back in the building. The PSDC shouldn't attack it, we're keeping—"

"We know," Kugara said.

"If they do take the city—"

He was interrupted by the sound of roaring aircraft that shot by above them so low that Kugara could have counted rivets. The fighters banked around the skyline, headed toward the PSDC invaders. When the echoes died down enough for him to be heard, he continued, "If they take the city, that building will be the safest place in town."

"Look, we have other concerns than the PSDC. Or our safety, for that matter. Start moving."

He studied the rubble ahead of them, and after taking a few deep breaths, took a couple of steps over the orange warning line. He called back, "The safe corridor is only a few meters wide, so stay close behind me." He pointed to a burned-out shell of a building about a hundred meters away. "We're headed there."

She followed him, with Parvi behind her, followed by Flynn, Dörner, Brody, and Nickolai bringing up the rear. Their guide led them through a series of ninety-degree turns past piles of twisted metal and broken ferrocrete. The whole area smelled of a fire not long dead, something still smoldering and toxic.

More aircraft rocketed past above them, and as the wind shifted, they started hearing pops and rumbles from the east. The noises were muffled by distance, but clearly the engagement had begun. There was a whole city between them and the battle, but Kugara was afraid it wouldn't be enough.

It only took a few moments before that fear was realized.

A painful whine cut though the air above them, and she heard Nickolai yell, "*Incoming!*"

Kugara dived for the ground, tackling their guide under her. She glanced up and saw a twisting contrail tipped with a spiraling out-of-control missile. It seemed headed straight for her. She shoved her face into the small of their guide's back and covered her head with her arms as an explosion ripped the air. The sound was like a spike though her skull and she felt the impact in the thrum of the ground beneath her. A burning wind scorched the hair on her neck, and dirt and gravel peppered her back, burning where it touched exposed skin.

Stray missile, she thought, *missed us . . .*

She pushed herself up from their guide, who raised his head and spat out a mouthful of dirt. "Shit!"

Parvi called out from behind her, "Everyone all right?"

A chorus of assents followed, muffled in Kugara's shell-shocked ears. She didn't look at the others. She was more focused on the rubble around them.

From out of nowhere it seemed, a half-dozen machines had risen from spots in the rubble. Lean, ovoid things about a meter across, hovering on small contragravs, rotary cannons dangling beneath their chassis. The hunter-killer drones, jarred awake by the explosion. The only reason they hadn't swarmed them already was because they stood in the preprogrammed safe zone.

She stared at one, and it stared back with a single blank mechanical eye. It was the first good look she had at one of these things. They weren't military spec, which she probably could have guessed from the improvised nature of the Wilson militia. These were commercial security drones, designed for patrolling warehouses, not war zones.

It didn't make them less intimidating.

"That was close," she whispered.

In front of her, their guide repeated, "Shit!"

She turned to him and asked, "Are you all right?"

"Yes. No. We're screwed!"

"What is it?" Parvi asked from behind her.

"Just look!" He waved ahead of them, where the missile had landed.

In front of them was a new crater blown clear of most rubble. Kugara saw the twitching remains of two more of the HK drones on the edge of the crater, one only a few meters away.

"What's the matter?" Parvi asked

"That blast removed all the landmarks," he told them, "I don't know where the safe corridor is anymore."

"The blast should have cleared the mines," Parvi said.

"Look around," Kugara said.

After a moment, she said, "Oh."

"We have to go back—"

Kugara grabbed his shoulder before he walked past her. "Not so fast."

"What do you want?" he said, "There are six of those things waiting for anything to take a step off the path."

"We got a shotgun," she said.

"You start firing that thing, they'll swarm you."

"Even in the safe zone?"

"It'd be a little useless if they allowed a hostile to randomly stroll into a safe area and start shooting."

Kugara shook her head and looked at the floating death machines.

Parvi asked her, "Do you have an idea?"

"They won't shoot each other," she said.

"What are you talking about?" the guard asked.

Kugara didn't pay attention to him. "They're cheap commercial units, and I see two or three manufacturers. They must be relying on transponders to ID each other . . ."

"What are you thinking?" Parvi asked as Kugara handed her the shotgun.

Kugara smiled grimly at her. "I'm going to get us a transponder." She bent down and picked up a large chunk of broken ferrocrete and hefted it in her hand. She looked at their guide and asked, "Before I go any farther, I don't suppose they issued you with an ID chip that would get you past these things?"

•

"No. The supply crew gets them, but not the guards, in case the prisoners—*what are you doing?*"

Kugara chucked the chunk of ferrocrete in a lazy underhand arc in front of the nearest robot. "I'm testing a theory," she whispered. The robot didn't fire on the rock, or her. Whatever threat algorithms it possessed didn't parse the rock as a problem. It did, however, follow the moving object with its sensors and track it with its cannon.

"Hopefully, that's good enough." She turned back to their guide, who stared after her throw as if he expected the rock to explode. "Okay, now tell me, if we were going straight, how much farther were we going to go before we turned again?"

"What?"

"How much farther—"

"I told you, the landmarks are *gone!*"

"Guess, damn it, before another stray missile lands on us!"

He shook his head and said, "Four, five meters?"

Kugara stepped out over the edge of the crater, in a straight line. She turned back to the others behind her. "I'm going to need a distraction. When I call out, all of you throw chunks of rubble past the machines, that way—" she pointed away from the crater.

Parvi glanced from her to the twitching wreckage of the nearer of the two damaged HK drones. "What makes you think the transponder is still working on that thing?"

"I'm guessing," Kugara said as she edged farther into the crater, two, three meters, until she was as close as she was going to get to the wreck. Another ten meters to clear. She took a few deep breaths. The transponder was probably well sealed and on its own redundant power supply. It was a piece of hardware you didn't want to fail in the field. And the way the thing was twitching, the other robots would have been paying it some attention if its transponder were dead.

But still . . .

"*Now!*" she yelled at the others.

She launched herself in a sprint to the twitching wreckage, putting everything she had in an all-out push to get to the thing in the fraction of a second the flying rubble bought her. If any of them could make it . . .

Something tore though the dirt by her feet and she leaped the last two meters, landing on top of the downed machine.

She sucked in shuddering breaths as beneath her, the servo arm that used to carry a cannon kept pushing into her stomach, as if it was trying to elbow her off of it.

"Made it," she whispered, not quite believing it.

She looked up and saw four of the HK robots surrounding her. Back by the edge of the crater she heard their onetime guide mutter, "I never saw anyone move that fast."

No one human, Kugara thought.

She slid off of the half-dead robot, and winced when her foot hit the ground. She glanced down and saw her right shoe was stained dark with blood. She gritted her teeth and flexed her toes. The pain was awful, but her toes moved, and she could feel them squish against the gore in her sock. Shrapnel. At least her foot seemed mechanically sound.

She grabbed the edges of the machine and lifted through the pain. Luckily, the thing weighed less than its mass. It still had partial contragravs running—just not enough for neutral buoyancy.

She walked it back to the others.

They were able to cross the blast crater by slowly walking across, all of them surrounding the near-dead machine. They carried it like a hostage through a tense standoff. The other robots watched, but didn't get in their way.

On the other side, it only took a few moments for their guide to find the right landmark and get them back on the safe path out again. They left the dead robot, and this time Parvi led with the guide and the shotgun.

Kugara hung back and let Nickolai help her limp along on her wounded foot. Once they were back on their way out, he asked her, "Was that a smart thing to do?"

"Can't let you take all the damn-fool risks now, can I?"

"I don't want to lose you."

"Then you had better keep up."

CHAPTER TEN

Atonement

"Heroism comes when all other options have been exhausted."

—*The Cynic's Book of Wisdom*

"A hero is no braver than an ordinary man, but he is braver five minutes longer."

—RALPH WALDO EMERSON
(1803–1882)

Date: 2526.8.5 (Standard)
Bakunin–BD+50°1725

Vijayanagara Parvi led her people through the back alleys of Wilson. She glanced back at Kugara, limping next to the tiger, and thought, *My people?*

She was appalled at herself, at her paralysis. In a sick way, it was why she was down here, and not with Mallory in what—if she was honest—had to be the most likely route to fight Adam. She had lost the ability to command. Having the responsibility over other people's lives had become an intolerable burden, and left her nearly unable to function.

Three times now, both Kugara and Nickolai had taken the initiative—and she didn't have the wherewithal to even raise an objection.

Above them, the sky was already gray with smoke, and the sounds of the battle seemed to be closing in on them.

If I continue as I have been, I will get us all killed.

Her knuckles whitened on the shotgun. After inadvertently killing an unarmed woman on the *Prophet's Voice*, she doubted she would ever be able to make that kind of split-second decision again. Not without second-guessing herself.

She led them to a mouth of an alley that opened up to a street, across from a block of office buildings that had burned down around the wreckage of a downed troop transport. Through the smoke of the smoldering wreckage, she could see the Wilson militia, only half of whom seemed to be wearing powered armor, making a retreat down the street, away from the main line.

She peeked around the edge of the building and could see flashes of energy weapons burning their way through the smoke. She ducked back around and felt her heart trying to slam its way through her rib cage. She tasted copper in her throat and heard a low growl from the tiger.

Of course, he can smell the fear . . .

It was worse than what she felt during the doomed resistance on Rubai, worse than what she felt on the *Prophet's Voice.*

"Okay," she whispered, reining in the panic. "This is what we have to do." She checked the shotgun and handed it off to Kugara. "You need to get everyone to the mountains."

"Me?" Kugara sounded incredulous.

Parvi nodded, solidifying her own decision. "We have two missions here," she told her. "Mallory wants to make contact with the PSDC."

"What?" It came from several people at once.

"Whatever you might find in the Dolbrian caverns, the PSDC is the last line of defense this planet has."

Everyone stared at her, and it was Flynn who spoke up. "Are you crazy, woman? The PSDC has to know what's going on in orbit; they ain't jamming their own communications. If they haven't contacted Mallory and his savior squad, it's 'cause they have more of a hard-on for running this effing planet."

"*Everything* we're doing is a long shot," Parvi said. "Besides, someone has to open a hole in the line so you can get through." She looked at Kugara and said, "It's your show now."

She glanced back around the corner, and made a dash for the wreckage across the street. As far as anyone saw, she was just an unarmed civilian, so no one targeted her. Behind her, she heard Flynn's voice say, "Jesus Tap-dancing Christ—" before the sound was washed away by something large and explosive taking out a trio of men in powered armor about fifteen meters away from her.

Even though she had no idea how she was going to open a hole, her heart had calmed, and her breathing had become steadier. She leaped over a crumbling wall and dropped into the ruins of the dead office complex. Twisted metal and broken ferrocrete towered over her, scorched black. She stood on a sliding pile of broken glass, gravel, and rubble that still steamed. The air choked her with black smoke and the smell of burned synthetics. Through watering eyes, she saw the armored side of the downed troop transport, more intact than it should be.

She scrambled toward it and found the side door open. The inside was hazed by white smoke from an invisible electrical fire and lit only by what little sunlight leaked in the open door. It took a moment for her watering eyes to adjust to the dim light and make out the details of the wreckage inside.

Two corpses sprawled across the interior of the wrecked transport. By the door were the remains of someone who'd had his upper body completely sheared away, probably by being half out the door when the transport hit. The other wore a helmet and comm gear that suggested he was the pilot. He was still strapped in a crash harness, and the impact had blown him to the back of the compartment, still attached to his chair.

She stepped over to the half-corpse, skidding on blood and the uneven floor, and relieved it of the sidearm holstered on its hip. The grip was sticky, but she was armed now.

She peered into the depths of the wreck. Underneath the corpse of the pilot, she saw a long box with yellow-and-black warning stripes stenciled down its length.

She had to push the pilot's chair off of it.

The wreck shook as something nearby exploded. She quickly checked the latches and opened the case. It was better than she had hoped, an AM grenade launcher with half a complement of grenades. It wasn't terribly common; few people wanted to take ammo into a war zone that would spontaneously detonate if the super-conducting casing lost a charge. It would be safer lugging around a tactical nuke.

But, apparently, the Wilson militia was pulling out all the stops, and she was just lucky that this thing hadn't detonated during the crash.

She shut the case, found the handle, and dragged it outside.

She could hear the firefight in earnest, closing on her position—and on Kugara and the others. She scrambled, one-handed, up the tallest pile of twisted metal next to the downed transport. She glanced across when she cleared street level, and saw the bloody edge of the retreating militia, a line of powered armor, facing up the street.

Across, in the alley, she saw Kugara at the corner of the building, holding the shotgun braced against the oncoming PSDC force.

That force included a pair of hovertanks flanked by heavily armored infantry. As she watched, one of the tanks belched a blinding pulse of plasma from its cannon, clearing the street of a dozen armored defenders.

Shit!

Parvi shoved the case onto a flat slab of ferrocrete about three stories above the battle, part of one building that hadn't completely pancaked together. She crawled after it. The space between the floors here was barely enough to open the case, and each time the tanks fired, she heard ominous creaking around her.

She barely had time to plan where she was going to aim as she pulled out the launcher and loaded a surprisingly heavy antimatter round. She didn't bother zeroing the sights; the tanks were so close that accuracy didn't much matter. She just raised it, thanked the gods that there was still enough distance that she could aim down and still have the shot clear the rubble below her, and fired.

* * *

Nickolai stood behind Kugara, his body an imperfect shield for the three other members of their party. Kugara glanced around the corner and said, "Tanks, they got fucking tanks!" She ducked back around and flattened against the wall as a shot of plasma took out a third of Wilson's defending line. "I don't know how she's going to make us a hole in that. We're going to have to back up and find another route."

Nickolai nodded, then froze when he saw something in the wreckage across from them; Parvi climbing up the wreckage, carrying a long case. He concentrated until the print stenciled on the case shot into focus.

"She's got an AM grenade launcher."

"She's got a *what?*" Kugara snapped.

Plasma washed the remaining defenders away as, above them all, Parvi readied the weapon. Nickolai yelled, "Everyone! Hit the ground now!"

No one argued, and Kugara dove behind him as he dropped. Quick as he was, he was still looking up when the grenade hit. If he had still worn the eyes he was born with, the flash would have blinded him. With the Protean eyes, though, he could see into the intense glare as half a twisted hovertank was blown down the street, gouging pavement as it tumbled like a child's toy tossed in a fit of rage. The noise was less a sound than an awful pressure on his skull and chest, a rumble felt though the ground that, for a moment, seemed to flow like water.

Then it was over, except for a muffled ringing in his ears and a burning feeling in the leather of his nose.

Behind him, through the ringing in his ears, he heard someone screaming, "My God! My God! What was that? *What was that?*" He thought it might have been Dr. Dörner.

Bits of gravel and debris still fell from the sky as he pushed himself up. He walked to the edge of the building and looked around the corner.

The street where the PSDC attackers had been was unrecognizable. A crater extended forty or fifty meters across, and the facades of the buildings on either side had sheared off and collapsed into the hole. Of the PSDC attacking force, the only sign was the turret of the other tank, twisted and wedged upside down on the second floor of one of the faceless buildings. Of the infantry, he saw a gauntlet and a single boot, both over twenty meters from the crater.

"We have our hole!" he called back.

Kugara called back to him, "Where's Parvi?"

He glanced across the street to look where Parvi had been stationed, but the wreckage had collapsed in on itself. There was no sign of where she had fired the AM grenade.

"She's gone," he said.

CHAPTER ELEVEN

Sins

"The more control one has, the more control one desires."

—*The Cynic's Book of Wisdom*

"Power is not happiness."

—WILLIAM GODWIN
(1756–1836)

Date: 2526.8.5 (Standard)
Earth Orbit–Sol

The Prophet's Voice orbited over a transformed Earth, an Earth populated by Adam's chosen. One of the few thousand incarnations of Adam stood on the bridge of the *Voice*, receiving the good news of His works. The impressions He received were not as direct as His knowledge of things on the *Voice*; this version of Himself had no direct connection to the surface. But His other selves, and the select ones among His chosen, broadcast their knowledge and their sensations to Him.

Even here He could see the cities rebuilt into more organic, rounded forms. Adam found the destruction and homogenization of chaotic human architecture almost as comforting as the transformation of humanity itself. Even though there was a long journey ahead of Him, now that man's cradle had accepted His salvation from the flesh, He knew that the final victory was His.

His creators would not have died in vain. They were the architects of life's final victory over entropy, over the Abyss. Adam's chosen would endure for eternity, transcending the Race, transcending Humanity, transcending even the ancient Dolbrians.

In the midst of the remade cities below, His chosen had built massive arrays of tach-receivers and transmitters, massive ears and eyes that saw deeply into the space around Him. Through them, He received news from other worlds that had accepted His word; Khamsin, Occisis, Cynos, Dakota, Haven, Acheron, Ecdemi, Paschal . . .

He also could hear from the planets that had yet to receive His glory. He could hear the unfortunate chaos and panic that gripped the ignorant in the face of any great change.

But there was something else. Something troubling.

He had not thought of Bakunin since He had defeated His Nemesis, Mosasa. The planet was irrelevant. Even the dim eyes of His resurrected AIs could have seen that the planet would collapse into chaos as soon as Mosasa's influence was removed. Bakunin couldn't maintain stability for more than a month without intervention. The planet's energy would be consumed by civil war and could be safely ignored in favor of planets with fleets and coherent states that might oppose Him.

Even the mass of refugees taching into Bakunin's system should only contribute to the chaos and confusion. By now, those ships should be cannibalizing themselves over too-limited resources . . .

But now Adam focused His awareness upon what He saw and heard from Bakunin. The refugee fleet, denied the surface of the planet, was not consuming itself as it should. The fragments of data His tach-receivers pulled from the ether told Him that they were, in fact, stratifying, forming organizational structures.

He now realized that the transmission from Khamsin had contaminated the social equation. A small variable that only slightly moved the stable planets of human space caused a major realignment in the shifting sands of Bakunin. It was an oversight He would have to deal with.

He ordered all His chosen who remained in orbit to
rally at the *Voice,* as the massive kilometer-long carrier
prepared to make the tach-jump to Bakunin.

Date: 2526.8.7 (Standard)
350,000 km from Bakunin–BD+50°1725

The more meetings he attended, the more disheartened
Mallory became. He sat at a long table with a dozen other
people in a conference room in one of the *Wisconsin's* endless series of luxury hotels. The table itself was lit by an
elaborate fixture dangling from the ceiling that doubled as
a holo projector, though no one seemed to have bothered
to put such a presentation together. The light from it bore
down on the people seated here, the glare making it appear
to Mallory that the participants at this table argued with
each other while surrounded by an abyss.

Mallory rubbed his eyes. Stress, lack of sleep, or his over-
driving implants made him sensitive to the light. Even so,
the metaphor was too apt.

"We need as many ships as possible under our banner."
The speaker was a thin man named Eric Tito. He was the
nominal leader of the Bakunin native fleet. He was an un-
repentant pirate and looked the part, down to a prominent
scar on his cheek and the habit of carrying three sidearms.

Leaning across the table to shout at Tito was a white-
haired retired general from Cynos who probably held the
highest military rank of anyone here—though it was a rank
in a military force that might not exist anymore. General
Lafayette said, "I maintain that our forces will not join with
a nation that attacked us without provocation."

"*We* were under attack!" protested the lone Caliphate
representative. "We defended ourselves from an unknown
enemy."

"By attacking us?" The general shook his head. "That is
unacceptable. We will not join with the Caliphate."

Mallory slammed his fist on the table and said, *"The Caliphate no longer exists!"*

Everyone turned to look at him. He kept his fist clenched
to keep his hand from shaking. He stood up and leaned forward. "You've seen the transmission from Khamsin?"

"Yes, but—"

"By now that scenario has played out on Cynos as well. Do you realize that?"

"You don't know—"

"And Occisis, and Earth," he slammed the table again, "and eventually *here*." He unwittingly found himself quoting Mosasa, "If anything trumps your narcissistic human political divisions, it's *this!*"

Everyone at the table stared at him, and after a few moments of silence, the woman from the larger of the Indi groups said, "Perhaps it is wise to take a break for a couple of hours?" The general started to object, but an ally of his, from one of the smaller Indi groups, placed his hand on his shoulder and said, "I second that idea."

After a few more perfunctory comments, everyone nodded and began filing out of the conference room. Mallory was the last to leave.

I need to hold myself together . . .

He eased back into his seat and looked at the too-bright light. "God grant me the strength and wisdom to do your will," he prayed, "however imperfect an instrument I might be."

He told himself that maybe, during the break, he could get some rest. He rubbed his eyes and swore that tonight he would force himself to get a good night's sleep.

He was the last to leave the room, and Toni met him. She opened her mouth, probably to tell him how bad he looked, but seemed to think better of it. Instead, she sighed and forced a smile.

"Please tell me it's good news." He prayed that someone had rounded up Karl's son. The young man had two missing people to his credit, and the fact that Mallory had brought the man to the *Wisconsin* had done a lot to poison what credibility he had outside his own group of Centauri ships. Mallory might have starred in a broadcast by the pope, but that had little sway with the Buddhists and Hindus making up the larger part of the Indi fleets that, just by dint of sheer numbers, were going to determine the course of Bakunin's defense whether or not folks from Sirius, Centauri, or the Caliphate wanted to admit it.

"I think it is," Toni said. "Alexander Shane's regained consciousness."

Mallory had a brief episode of disorientation. The reference to Shane was so distant from his here-and-now that he had to think for a moment even to remember who he was. Eventually his fatigued brain managed to pull the threads of Shane's existence from the disorganized mess of his other thoughts. "He's talking?"

"I just had a contact from the hospital. He wants to talk to you."

He had allowed Parvi to take an expedition to the surface because of things Shane had said in a half-delirium. If Shane was awake, Mallory could question the man directly, and gain at least some idea of what he had been trying to tell everyone.

"We have another two hours before this starts up again." He shook his head. "And I'm not sure what I'm contributing at this point. Let's go see him."

Going to the hospital required traveling to the Beta habitat, which meant taking one of the elevators up to the core and then taking another elevator back down. They passed by a number of armed security in *Wisconsin* blue, and in Mallory's still-tense state he thought that the guards were more for reassurance than anything else. The majority didn't appear to be looking around with any purpose, and they only paid attention to him and Toni so far as to check the IDs they'd been issued.

It sank in that the normal operation of this place probably only ever required a nominal security force, probably smaller than the number of guards just assigned within the hotel where they were meeting. The majority of these blue-suited guards must be operations employees with little or no training.

At each ID check, Mallory got the bad feeling that they were relying on security through bureaucracy.

The Beta habitat was denser with buildings, and had much less landscaping than the habitat they had left. Not a place for tourists.

The hospital was a stark blocky structure placed in the

center of a cluster of administration buildings. If he ignored
the multiple reflections of Kropotkin above him, it could
have been on any planet in human space, there was so little
to distinguish it.

Alexander Shane was in a semi-private room with the
still-unconscious Abbas. The blue-jumpsuited guard outside the room was an uncomfortable reminder that Stefan
was still loose somewhere with a cache of weapons.

Inside, lying on a bed with tubes and wires running into
him, Shane looked more than ever like a frail old man. The
stark lighting in the room shone off his naked scalp, making
his skin paler and the tattoos much more pronounced.

"Father Mallory," he greeted them, his voice less frail
than his body. "Who is your friend?"

"L—Captain Toni Valentine," she answered him.

He smiled slightly. "That's a Stygian accent, isn't it?"

"Yes." She glanced at Mallory and said, "I thought your
planet had no contact with anyone."

"It didn't," Shane said. "It just happens that Dr. Pak
made a hobby of collecting accents."

Mallory didn't want to be reminded of the mental rape
Shane had been a party to. "You wanted to speak to me?"

Shane nodded. "According to the staff here, you seem
to be in charge."

"That's overly generous." Mallory rubbed his temple.

"I know how disturbing this is for you," Shane said.

"No, you—" Mallory sighed. "Of course you do."

"What is it you wanted to talk about?" Toni asked him.

"The Dolbrians," Shane said.

"The Dolbrians," Valentine repeated.

"You know that Bakunin has the most extensive set of
Dolbrian ruins ever discovered, because of the unique ge-
ology of the planet, being tectonically stable for millions
of years. The quiescent nature of Bakunin's crust makes it
all the more likely that there is still some physical access to
other things the Dolbrians left behind."

"What other things?"

"What is the key mystery the Dolbrians left behind?"

Mallory sighed. "Why they disappeared."

Shane shook his head. "That's the common answer, the

one you gave your students. But that's the wrong question. All existence is impermanence. The question is not 'why they are gone?' The question is 'why did they leave these planets behind?'"

"What do you mean?" Mallory thought back to his xenoarchaeology courses in graduate school, and thought of the theories he had read; the terraformed planets were part of a colonization effort; or they were some sort of art form; or that the planets were naturally inhabitable and the ancient Dolbrians were there by coincidence.

"You've seen Adam, and the Protean, two sides of the same coin. That technology was the result of less than fifty thousand years of our evolution as a species. Just by dating the few artifacts and seeing the spread in time between them, the Dolbrians were active for at least fifty times as long."

"So?"

"They had no need for 'habitable' planets. They had lived long past the point where they must have been able to adapt themselves to any environment. Not only that, but the artifacts they left almost universally draw attention to themselves and the fact that these planets exist. Dr. Pak wrote a paper analyzing the content of all known Dolbrian writing. *All* of it relates to these planets or their locations. And, regardless of the relative dates of these artifacts, the script left behind shows no variation. His conclusion was that what we have left of the Dolbrians' language is one of two things. It's either a synthetic language or—"

"Or it's a sacred language."

Shane smiled. "I forgot you were familiar with the theory. Sometimes it's hard to keep track of who knew what." He raised a bony arm to press against his forehead. "Like the Latin of the Bible, the Arabic of the Koran, the Hebrew of the Torah . . . it's a common enough explanation. The Dolbrians created habitable planets as a form of worship. That idea is the core of the Dolbrian cult that has nominal caretaking duties for the ruins on Bakunin. It almost makes sense that the majority of the cult comes from the Fifteen Worlds—" Shane broke off for some unhealthy semi-liquid coughing.

"You were going to explain," Mallory said.

"Sorry, thoughts going around in circles. Things are still merging. But think; if these planets are an act of faith, would they be all there is to it?"

"What do you mean?"

"If the act of creation is a sacrament to the Dolbrians, what are they trying to create?"

Mallory narrowed his brows. "You haven't become a Dolbrian cultist, have you? They didn't create us. The latest signs of them not only predate hominids, but most mammals."

"No, but by seeding hundreds of planets, they knew that something like us was inevitable. They certainly were around long enough, and ranged widely enough, to have a good grasp on the probability of intelligent species developing. What if these planets were left specifically for us to find? What if the star maps with their common language were messages for us?"

"Great," Valentine said, her voice carrying a bitter edge of frustration. "If there are any universities left after Adam rapes the universe, maybe you can write a paper on it."

Mallory placed a hand on her arm. "Let him talk."

"Why? He's just telling us what we already know. This is a pointless exercise in academic masturbation."

"Captain Valentine?" Shane interrupted.

"What?" she snapped.

"I ramble because my thoughts ramble, but there is a point. A strong one."

"Get to it, then."

"The Protean, the entity that allowed Mallory and me to escape Adam's attack on Salmagundi, came from here, from Bakunin, hundreds of years ago. It survived some contact with Adam before crashing on my planet. It knew what Adam was, because the Protean was in some sense a mirror of Adam."

"And?"

"The Protean told us to find them, the Dolbrians. It knew what we faced. It also, most probably, knew what the Dolbrians left here."

"What the hell could they have left here that survived millions of years? A bunch of pretty rocks?"

"Knowledge," Shane said. "They left entire planets for a race they knew would eventually come. That wouldn't be all they left. If they were so forward-looking, they would have left more of themselves, their faith, for their successors. The Protean was telling us that it was our chance to defeat this Adam—"

Toni snorted. "I guess you'll be happy to know that we sent a bunch of people groundside with the *Khalid*, on your wild goose chase."

Shane sat up, dangling tubes and wires. "You did? What did they find?"

"They ditched in the ocean," Mallory said. "We've been out of communication ever since."

Shane leaned back down. "There *is* something there, I am certain of it . . ."

They were running late for the resumption of the conference, stuck waiting for the elevator to the core along with a bunch of *Wisconsin* security personnel in the midst of a shift change.

"That was pointless," Valentine said.

"It confirms Parvi's interpretation of what Shane was trying to say."

"You mean those two 'scientists.'" She managed to articulate the quotes around the word.

"Why are you so hostile to the idea?"

"I don't like baseless hopes masquerading as strategy. It cost us the *Khalid*."

"That was one ship among thousands."

"One ship with a radically improved tach-drive. Would you sacrifice your one suit of powered armor just because you have an army covered with chain-mail and good intentions?"

"We just have to—"

The elevator arriving interrupted him. They filed in with a group of a dozen of the blue-suited security personnel. None of them paid him, Valentine, or their conversation any mind as they chatted among themselves.

Again, he was apprehensive about the lack of professionalism he saw. *No wonder they haven't found Stefan yet . . .*

"We just have to what?" she asked him.

Mallory shook his head. "Go forward with what we have now. At this point it doesn't matter if Parvi's expedition was a mistake or not."

"I know. I was just telling you why the subject pisses me off."

Mallory nodded. His attention had shifted from their conversation to the group of guards here with them.

They rolled upward, the apparent gravity decreasing, and the floor seeming to tilt with the Coriolis effect, as they neared the axis of rotation. The view of the *Wisconsin* slid by the large windows, capturing Valentine's attention. She stared out at the stars while Mallory stared at the guards.

"Even if the Dolbrians left something, why didn't the Proteans do anything with it? How do we know it would even be comprehensible?" She snorted, slightly fogging the window next to him. "Even to someone with an advanced degree in cultural anthropology—"

Mallory placed a hand on her arm and said, "Shh."

"What?" She turned around.

One of the guards, across the elevator from them, was staring at a small comm unit and shaking his head. "Hey?" he called out after a moment, "any of you guys having trouble calling upstairs?"

"I was talking to Harris a few minutes ago," someone responded, pulling his own comm unit. After a moment he had the same puzzled expression. "That's funny, no answer."

The elevator began sliding home, and then the lights flickered.

Someone said, "What?" just before the elevator stopped moving with a horrid mechanical crunch and the lights failed completely. The elevator was nestled in the body of the central core, so the walls of the elevator shaft blocked the windows, and the only lights were from the telltales on the two comm units.

"Shit!" one of the guards said, "power failure."

"Get back," Mallory whispered harshly to Toni, pressing her against the window behind them. He caught her by surprise and they slid to the ground.

They hit the ground, and light flooded the elevator as the doors creaked open.

Someone said, "Good, now we—"

He never finished the sentence. The air filled with the sound of gunfire as three shotguns fired through the doorway and into the mass of guards. In a matter of seconds, the elevator was choked with the smell of gunsmoke and blood. He whispered into Toni's ear, "Don't move."

One of the guards fell down next to them with a breathless groan, trying to hold his blood-soaked stomach together with his hands. The gunfire stopped, and the only sound was ragged uneven breathing and someone softly cursing over and over.

From outside, a harsh voice called out, "Move your ass, get their weapons."

A skeletally thin woman in a dirty shirt and ragged khaki pants stepped inside, and stared at the massacre.

Outside, the voice called out, "Hurry up."

The woman lowered her own weapon and started picking up guns from the fallen guards and tossing them out the open door. When one of the guards, probably unconsciously, hung on to the butt of one of the weapons, the woman put her boot on his wrist, raised her shotgun to the man's face, and pulled the trigger.

Mallory saw that, closed his eyes, and tried not to breathe.

"Is that it?"

"Guns? Yes."

"Then move it. We can't waste time here."

He heard some sounds of movement, then only the groans of the wounded. After nearly a full minute, Toni whispered, "I think they're gone."

Mallory nodded and pushed himself just upright enough so he could survey the damage. He needed to help these people, but one glance told him that was hopeless. All of them had been hit in the upper body or the gut, most multiple times. The man with the stomach wound next to them had already stopped breathing, and groans of the living had faded to be nearly inaudible.

He rose, and Toni stood up next to him. "What the hell?"

"A refugee revolt, judging from the woman who came in," Mallory answered.

Toni bent down to look at the victims, but the elevator was now almost silent. "This is . . ." She shook her head, failing to find a word. "You think Stefan had a hand in this?"

"I wouldn't be surprised."

She reached down and retrieved one of the comm units. "They left these?"

Mallory edged toward the door and said, "They're disorganized and under-armed. They may not even be thinking in terms of cutting off communication." He crouched, so when he peeked around the edge of the doorway his head wasn't at eye level. The loading area by the elevator was largely empty, except for one blue-suited corpse lying on the ground halfway between them and the nearest exit. He ducked back around and faced her. "They had the sense to cut power to the elevator."

"Isolating the core from reinforcements."

Mallory nodded. "During a shift change, so this probably wasn't an isolated attack."

She looked at the comm. "There's probably no one left up here to call."

"We have to assume that these guys decapitated security's command and control. The guards were having trouble calling back to base already. Trying to alert *Wisconsin* security will probably only let the bad guys know we're here." Mallory let out a long breath. "And if the bad guys have control of the security systems, they'll know we're here as soon as we pass a security camera."

"Good lord. We're fucked."

"Maybe not. Can you raise other channels on that?"

CHAPTER TWELVE

Reformation

"The intent of all insurrections is to bring chaos out of order."

—*The Cynic's Book of Wisdom*

"The revolutionist ... knows only one science, the science of destruction."

—MIKHAIL A. BAKUNIN
(1814–1876)

Date: 2526.8.7 (Standard)
350,000 km from Bakunin–BD+50°1725

Toni II had spent the last forty-five minutes in the make-shift gym her younger twin had set up in an empty cargo compartment in the *Daedalus*. The gym consisted of a powered hardsuit tethered to the floor and ceiling, with the joint resistance jacked up to about three hundred per-cent normal. It had been necessary during their long stint in zero-gee, and it still was, now that they were docked. The ersatz microgravity here in the *Wisconsin's* core was just enough to give her inner ear a cue to up and down.

She ran in place, the tethers keeping the suit from flying into a bulkhead.

Her daily routine bore an eerie resemblance to her long stint on the observation platform in orbit around Worm-hole Sigma Draconis III. Wake up, spend a shift checking the ship's status, then go work out.

The world has been turned upside down, the Stygian Executive Command probably no longer exists, I'm a ghost, a pirate, and second-in-command to myself—and nothing seems to have changed.

She was perilously close to wishing something would happen, when the comm on her suit buzzed for her attention. "Yes," she responded, using the chin switch to open the channel without breaking her stride.

The voice was from of one of the Salmagundi crew working the bridge. *"We have an incoming transmission from Captain Valentine."*

She slowed herself as she said, "Okay, I'm coming up." She wondered what her twin wanted, and why she'd waited until this late to call in.

"No," came the word from the bridge, *"I'm routing it to you now."*

"What?" She realized that the Salmagundi tech sounded seriously spooked.

"Toni?" Her sister's voice was a whisper, distorted by the guy on the bridge upping the gain to make her audible.

"What is it?" Toni II asked, slowing her pumping legs to a standstill.

"We have a serious problem."

Ten minutes later, she was down in the *Daedalus'* air lock, shouting orders. She had seven of the remaining crew down here, three of the Salmagundi militia and four of the Caliphate techs. That left enough people manning the bridge to radio to the other ships docked here, and to pilot the *Daedalus* away if need be.

The rest of them donned the eight hardsuits they had, the two heavy-duty utilitarian models that the Tonis had brought on board, plus the custom-painted ones that had served Karl's crew before the Tonis had hijacked his ship. The powered suits were designed for heavy-duty EVA work, and weren't the best armor, but it was what they had.

Her impromptu squad was a garish sight. Karl's crew had been creative in painting their suits to be identifiable at a distance; one had a blue-on-orange tribal pattern, another had clusters of large purple eyes on a crimson field, another had a lemon-yellow and lime-green jigsaw puzzle pattern, one suit had a cherry-red flame job, another seemed wrapped by the tentacles of some alien creature, and the last one had been painted to resemble a bat-winged, goat-footed demon whose mouth gaped open to accommodate the suit's visor.

"Is everyone on the same channel?" she asked, once her people were suited up. She got seven assents.

She looked at the insane suit patterns, and the near-random assortment of weapons, and hoped that she knew what she was doing.

At least I probably have more military-trained people behind me than in front of me.

"Bridge, once we're through, evacuate the air lock and keep it depressurized."

"Got that."

It was a minor obstacle, but it would prevent anyone forcing entry short of overriding the mechanical systems. And if anyone tried that, the *Daedalus* could just decouple from the docking ring. With the air lock depressurized, they could do it cleanly even if the outer door was open.

"Bridge? Anything on the external monitors?"

"Nothing in our field of view."

Which didn't mean much. While docked, the cameras on the air lock could only really see into the *Wisconsin's* air lock, not beyond.

"Said," she called to the man in the other gray Stygian hardsuit, "You lead out the air lock and give the all clear."

Said grunted an assent and stepped though the air lock. She had him lead because he had the plasma cannon—and no one wanted to be between it and the enemy.

He made it through the interlock, and out the *Wisconsin's* air lock, and after a quick look back and forth, waved them all forward.

"Quiet," Mallory said, pressing himself against the wall. He and Toni were across from the elevator now, a few meters from the main entrance to the loading area in what seemed the only obvious blind spot from the security cameras. They had held position here for only fifteen seconds, and Mallory already heard motion in the hallway, coming closer.

He pulled out the comm he had liberated from one of the dead guards and whispered, "Give me yours."

Toni handed over its twin. Mallory opened a quiet channel on full, set the device on the floor, and kicked it so the small communicator slid across the floor all the way back to the elevator entrance.

The loping low-gravity footsteps came closer. It was hard to tell numbers, but it was more than one person. He held up a hand in front of Toni, spreading his fingers; he pointed at himself, then at the finger closest to the elevator. *I get the first one.* He pointed at her, and then at the finger closest to the entrance. *You get the one bringing up the rear.*

She nodded, her face set in a grim expression.

The flanking maneuver would be a lot more effective if Mallory or Toni were armed. But if they were lucky, there'd only be two people coming.

There were three; a trio of men with long greasy hair and scraggly beards. The lead one was thin and wore a bandanna wrapping his hair around a pale bald spot, the second wore a studded leather jacket and pants, and the third one was a head taller than either of them and easily topped a hundred fifty kilos. They all had shotguns at the ready, and stepped into the loading area with the situational awareness of a potted plant. They were already through the doorway before the first one even started to turn in their direction.

Thank God for small favors.

Mallory hit the alert button on his own comm, and the one by the elevator began whooping, drawing the attention of the shotgun-wielding trio.

He jumped at the bandannaed one. In the low gravity, his feet did not touch the ground between where he'd stood, and where he straight-armed the guy across the trachea. Mallory's victim was caught completely by surprise. He tried to bring the butt of the shotgun up to ward Mallory off, but he slammed into the floor before he got his movements coordinated. Behind him, Mallory heard a shotgun blast. He winced inside, but the shot came nowhere near him.

The man beneath him choked and sputtered and swung the butt of his gun ineffectively into Mallory's side. Mallory brought his comm down, smashing it into the man's temple. That was enough to stun him so he could wrest the shotgun away from him.

Another shotgun blast, and Mallory spun to bring his commandeered shotgun up to face the enemy. The guy in studded leather was still in the midst of falling backward, away from the doorway, his chest a shredded mess.

Toni stood in the doorway, smoke slowly curling up from the barrel of the gun she held. The huge man who had taken the rear was sprawled on the floor behind her, staring up at the ceiling with his head angled oddly.

The guy on the floor behind Mallory recovered enough to reach for the shotgun, and Mallory brought the butt of the gun down on the man's face, knocking him out.

After a couple of breaths, he turned back toward Toni.

"Now?" Toni asked.

Mallory pushed himself up from the floor and said, "The main control room."

Stefan stood on a catwalk overlooking the *Wisconsin*'s main control center. His takeover had been frighteningly easy. The *Wisconsin*'s security forces had collapsed in the face of an organized threat, and the communications had been simple to disrupt. It had taken less than twenty minutes to get from the habitat to where he stood now.

Below him, the control room spread out in three directions. To his left was security, to the right, traffic control, and in front, operations. The operations section was dominated by a schematic holo of the *Wisconsin*. In the wireframe representation, all the elevators between the core and the three habitats were flashing red. He had completely isolated physical access from the habitats to the core control section.

The communications channels were just now lighting up as the occupants of the space station began to realize something was wrong. The people who thought they were in charge were beginning to realize they weren't.

Down at one of the consoles in operations, one of Stefan's men called up to him, "I have the Regal, on-line." The Regal was the hotel where the faux leaders of Mallory's faux navy were meeting.

Stefan stepped over to a console mounted on the catwalk, and the holo obligingly lit up from hibernation when he approached. "Can you route the call up here?"

"Yeah, sure, give me a minute." It took the guy a bit longer than a minute. Stefan shook his head while he waited. Beggars couldn't be choosers, and he had had to settle for a rather lower tier of revolutionary when he massed his small army. Most were criminally inclined Bakunin natives, but the type of criminals that weren't particularly successful even in an environment where "criminal" activity was perfectly legal. Their main advantage was sharing Stefan's desire for self-preservation, combined with a rather low reluctance to use violence to achieve that goal.

After five minutes, Stefan's man downstairs figured out how to forward the call to Stefan's console. The spinning "W" logo in the holo dissolved in favor of a view of a meeting room somewhere in the Regal.

He looked at the faces present in the room and said, "Where the fuck is Mallory?"

One of the men spoke up, "Mr. Stavros, we—"

"*Shut up!*" he snapped. "I'm driving this thing now! That whole habitat can be vented to space if I want. Understand?"

Everyone in the holo slowly nodded.

"Now where's that damn priest?"

The same man spoke up again. "We don't know where he is."

"You. Don't. Know?"

"We were taking a recess in negotiations when—"

Stefan held up a hand and said, "Just stop talking." Mallory wasn't the reason he was doing this. It shouldn't matter if the damned priest was there or not. "Let me tell you what it is I want." He licked his lips. "I need three fully charged tach-ships and supplies, and I want them in the next hour." Enough for him and seventy-five people to evacuate themselves from this insanity.

The folks around the conference table all started talking at once.

He heard some commotion below him and said, "I'll give you ten minutes to discuss it," and muted the call.

He turned and bent over the catwalk to call down to the guys working the security consoles. "What the hell's going on down there?"

The woman working the main security console shouted back without looking up from her station. "We have a major problem off of dock thirty-six."

That was the berth for the *Daedalus*. He swallowed and called down, "What kind of problem?"

"Look."

The main holo over the security station switched to a camera pointing down one of the *Wisconsin's* corridors by the docking facilities. The corridor was long and four times as wide as it was tall. Air lock numbers were stenciled along the walls every fifteen meters or so. Just in front of the camera, a group of Stefan's people, about ten or so, ran down the corridor. Men and women bearing shotguns liberated from *Wisconsin* security.

Something flashed from down the corridor, and one of the leaders of the charge found a leg disappearing from underneath him. The charge broke apart as people hit the floor, or flattened against the walls, taking cover in the too shallow recess of an air lock door.

Silently, shotguns began firing down the corridor, and other weapons fired back. In the holo, Stefan saw ten of his people torn apart as shadows emerged from the gunsmoke haze.

"Holy shit," someone said from below him, "they got a whole squad of powered armor."

Stefan watched the screen and shook his head. Not powered armor, these were EVA hardsuits. He knew because he recognized the paint jobs.

"Hard core bastards," someone else said, as the suit with the demon paint job passed by in front of the camera. That one had been Stefan's EVA suit.

"Shit." If he had been thinking ahead, he would have sabotaged the damn suits. He just never thought of anyone wearing one into combat. One of the shotguns that *Wisconsin's* security favored *might* be able to damage one if it got close enough.

Stefan reached into his waistband and pulled out the gamma laser that had come from his own stores. Unlike military-powered armor, the EVA hardsuits from the *Daedalus* wouldn't protect much against energy weapons. He leaned over the catwalk and called down, "Davis, you got the plasma rifle—you and—" he pointed out three more people downstairs who had gamma laser sidearms—"you and you and you. Intercept that group."

"What the hell, Boss?" Davis stared up at him. "They got powered armor."

"They're wearing fucking EVA suits. They have zero mobility, and they're sitting ducks for any sort of energy weapon."

They stared up at him.

"Do you want to get out of this place or not?"

Davis grunted and waved the others toward him. Between the plasma rifle and the three gamma lasers, they should be able to hold off those bastards from the *Daedalus*, at least long enough for them to seize one ship. He ran over and shouted down at traffic control.

A shirtless bald man was bent over one of the consoles. He was one of the few good hackers Stefan had gathered for his crew. "Reggie! How are we on getting access to a tach-ship?"

"I'm throwing the stats up on the screen," he said. "Problem is anything big enough for us already has some crew on-board."

"Highlight the ships that don't have a crew present."

"Like I said, they're too small—"

"Just do it!"

A half-dozen berth numbers flashed across the screen. He noted the craft types; all two- or three-person ships. Two were on the opposite side of the *Wisconsin* from the control room.

"Unlock berths 87 and 102."

"Okay, but it isn't going to do us any good—"

Reggie was interrupted by cursing that seemed to come

from just below the catwalk. "*Quick!*" Stefan shouted down at him.

Reggie did something at his console and the green "docked" light started flashing amber. "There, but—"

Below, Stefan heard Davis' voice call out, "*Get the fuck out of my shot!*" Followed by two or three shotgun blasts.

What the hell? Between here and the *Daedalus*, there had to be at least twenty of his people. Even if they completely collapsed, that squad of EVA suits couldn't move quickly enough to get here.

"What's happening outside?" he called down to security. No one answered him. He looked at the other stations, as he heard another shotgun blast, but the consoles were deserted.

They could have gone to reinforce Davis, but somehow Stefan doubted it.

Well, if these bastards fold at the first sign of resistance, it just means I'm not obliged to worry about them.

He pulled out a grenade and his gamma laser.

Mallory and Toni turned up the corridor toward the main control center for the *Wisconsin*. They passed three dead and disarmed members of *Wisconsin* security and open doors marked "authorized personnel only." The one at the end of the corridor was still closed, but Mallory saw the dome of a security camera set above it. He leveled his shotgun at the camera and said, "When they come out—"

He never finished the sentence, because the main door opened and four of Stefan's thugs started walking right toward them. The one in the rear had a plasma rifle.

Mallory immediately lowered his shotgun as the guy with the plasma rifle screamed, "*Get the fuck out of my shot!*"

The three men in front of him scattered to flatten against the walls, but before he fired the plasma rifle, Mallory and Toni fired, hitting him in the chest and stomach and sending him in a microgravity tumble back through the doorway.

One of the three others pointed a gamma laser in Mallory's direction, and Toni pumped a shell into him. Another one fired, but had no idea how to aim from a prone position and merely melted the polymer sheathing on the ceiling behind Mallory.

With two more shots, Toni and Mallory cleared the hallway.

He and Toni held their position, flat against opposite walls, staring into the small slice of the control room visible through the open door. Beyond, Mallory could see ranks of unmanned consoles, and part of what looked to be a pile of blue-jumpsuited corpses piled against the far wall. His military training kept him from reflexively crossing himself, but he did offer a whispered prayer for the victims.

He saw some movement going away from their position.

Toni glanced at him, and he pointed at the open door, and made a gesture with his hand, *slowly*.

She nodded, and they eased up on the doorway along opposite walls, aiming the shotguns to give them a decent crossfire on the entrance. They were within a meter when a hand darted out from around the doorway, tossing a small round object into the hall between them.

He barely had the first syllable of the word "grenade" out his mouth when the world was filled by a blinding white flash and a roaring as if the *Wisconsin* tore itself apart around him.

Toni II stopped her squad when they reached the main corridor leading to the *Wisconsin*'s control room. She could see signs of a firefight, and she told the main body to hang back while she went forward.

No peep of resistance met her advance, and as she walked through dissipating white smoke, she saw a quartet of hostiles decorating the entry of the control room. The corpses weren't armed with the *Wisconsin*-issue security shotguns. She saw three high-power gamma lasers and a plasma rifle. Good thing they were dead.

Then she saw Toni.

"Shit!"

She bent down, fearing the worst. But, while Toni was unconscious, she was breathing. As she sighed with relief, she heard someone coughing behind her. She spun around and saw Mallory on his hands and knees, coughing and spitting up blood.

Toni switched on the external speakers on her suit and asked, "Are you okay?"

Mallory pushed himself up and looked up at her. "Someone hit us with a stun grenade!" he practically shouted at her. "Speak up!"

"Are you okay?" she repeated.

"Alive! They must have evacuated the control room!"

Toni groaned behind her, and Toni II bent over to help her up. Mallory stumbled past them, commandeering a gamma laser to go check out the control room.

Toni II called out, "Wait!"

"They're gone," Mallory called back. "All they left was a pile of bodies."

Next to her, Toni said, "I'm all right."

I'm sure you are, Toni II thought.

She walked Toni into the control room after Mallory. He had already taken over a console and was speaking to a holo that showed a conference room filled with very surprised-looking people.

Toni II set her sister down on a chair and asked her, "Are you sure you're all right?"

Toni blinked up at her. "Yes. Fine."

Behind her, Mallory said, "I think we're now commanding the *Wisconsin*." She turned to face him, and he was shaking his head at a blank holo, as if he wasn't sure what to do with the information. He looked at her and said, "You think your squad can secure the core?"

CHAPTER THIRTEEN

Father of Lies

"Never underestimate the ability to rationalize one's own self-interest."
—*The Cynic's Book of Wisdom*

"Life is the art of being well deceived."
—WILLIAM HAZLITT
(1778–1830)

Date: 2526.8.9 (Standard)
Bakunin–BD+50°1725

On the top floor of the tallest skyscraper in Godwin, General Alexi Lubikov faced the setting sun. The office he stood in used to belong to the CEO of Lucifer Contracts Inc., one of the largest private legal enforcement entities that had ever existed on the anarchic planet Bakunin.

It, along with nearly every other private security firm on the planet, had been absorbed into the Proudhon Defense Corporation, a fully owned and operated subsidiary of the Proudhon Spaceport Development Corporation. It was the inevitable end result of a long unstable existence.

General Lubikov leaned against the desk and pondered his own long, unstable existence. The body he wore was closing on eighty years, most of those in the employ of the Bakunin Mercenaries' Union. The BMU had treated him well, and he lived today mostly due to the large amount of hardware the BMU had implanted in his body; both arms and legs, both eyes, lungs, liver, heart . . .

Even so, he knew he was nearing the end of things.

Which was why he had accepted Mr. Antonio's offer nearly a year ago. And why, as he led the western command of the Proudhon Defense Corporation to take over Godwin and drive toward the sea, he had felt as if he was a near-invulnerable force of destiny. The entire course of the civil war here on Bakunin had played out exactly as Mr. Antonio had described.

Almost . . .

The last ten days had seen a divergence from the script.

He had seen the intelligence reports on what was happening off-planet, reports that did not pass below his own rarified security clearance. The PSDC had control of every known tach-receiver on the planet, and had securely clamped down on more conventional communication. So, as far as Lubikov knew, the knowledge of Earth's final transmission had not passed beyond Proudhon's leadership.

Even so, that transmission was more than enough to disturb the course of Mr. Antonio's prophecies. In it, the Vatican made a direct appeal to fight Adam, which in itself was probably enough to move a good part of the Christian population away from provincial concerns like a Bakunin civil war. But in the transmission was a graphic record of the fall of Khamsin, the Caliphate capital, showing Adam offering his transcendence of the flesh, and showing the ugly consequences of not accepting his gift.

Lubikov found the *existence* of the transmission disturbing. It was a flaw in Mr. Antonio's prophecy. Word of Mr. Antonio's master should not come before the master himself.

And, in the face of that communication, the flotilla of refugee ships above his head, which were supposed to be disorganized to the point of irrelevance, had begun aggregating into something like a fleet.

And the fire washing the sky . . .

No, the force I have joined with is not infallible.

But, then, nothing in this world ever was.

A sourceless voice announced, "The prisoner is here, General Lubikov."

He cleared his throat and said, "By all means, show her in."

Lubikov turned around as the door opened. A woman walked in, alone. She was short. Lubikov was not particularly tall, but this woman's head only came up to his sternum. Her hair was white where it hadn't been shaved by the medics, her skin a dark brown which made the high visibility of her yellow-green jumpsuit all the more intense. Her right arm was in a cast, and she walked with a pronounced limp.

Lubikov waved over to one of the chairs in front of the desk. "Have a seat."

Her eyes narrowed suspiciously.

"You should save the paranoia. I wouldn't have spent the effort to dig you out of that building and bring you here if I was going to do something untoward."

She sighed and shuffled over to the chair and sat down. She looked up at him and asked, "So who are you?"

Lubikov walked over to the bar service and poured himself a vodka. He didn't really metabolize alcohol anymore, but he had grown used to the warmth it gave him. "Care for a drink?" he asked her.

"No, thank you."

He poured a glass of water anyway, and set it on a table next to her chair. "In case you change your mind."

"What do you want?"

He chuckled and drained half his glass. "What do any of us want?" He set down his glass on the desk. "Another day. To see the sun rise one more time. That's all it really boils down to." He sat down on the edge of the desk and flipped a few switches embedded in its surface. The windows obligingly turned pitch-black, and the air filled with a near subliminal hum that faded to nothing more than a slight itch behind his inner ear.

"What I want from you, though, is a little conversation."

She glanced at the windows. "What did you do?"

"The prior owner of this office had reason to be even

more security conscious than most people in Godwin. We're quite private now."

"Who are you?" she asked again.

"I'm rather boring. Let's talk about you." He folded his arms and stared at her. "Vijayanagara Parvi, veteran of the Indi Protectorate Expeditionary Command. Assigned to the revolution on Rubai. When they pulled out, you remained with the Federal forces eight months after the central government fell to the Revolutionary Council. You came here and became a BMU member in good standing. Your last employer was Mr. Tjaele Mosasa of Mosasa Salvage, who has been notably missing since an attack on his place of business by a squad in the employ of the Eridani Caliphate—" He paused and gauged her reaction. "Have I got that right?"

"Yes. If you have access to the BMU biometric database, you know you do."

He picked up his glass and toasted her. "I approve of an admirable lack of bullshit on your part." He drank the contents and set the glass down next to him. "To answer your question, I am General Lubikov, commander of the Eastern Division of the Proudhon Defense Corporation. Which, as the successor to the BMU, you happen to be still an official member of."

"I see."

"I'm sure you do. And I suspect you knew the implications when you opened fire on our forces in Wilson."

She nodded. "You're going to treat me as a traitor."

"That remains to be seen. Given your history, I suspect you know that alliances are mutable things. Now, shall we talk about Mosasa?"

Parvi sat in the corporate office, talking to General Lubikov for over an hour. She had few secrets at this point, and she also had a mission to open a communication channel between the PSDC and Mallory. So she concentrated on answering most of the general's questions, trying to make an impression on him.

She told him what Mosasa was, and what his role had been in maintaining stability on Bakunin. She told him what she knew of Adam, about the destruction of Xi Virginis, and what had happened on Salmagundi. She told him of Mallory's plan to resist Adam, and what he had done toward that end.

Almost everything.

General Lubikov, thankfully, did not treat her like a raging madwoman. He listened, nodded, and prompted her with questions about what was happening beyond the surface of Bakunin.

"And the reason you're here?" he asked.

"Mallory wants to open a line of communication—"

"By committing a near-suicidal attack on a pair of my tanks and their infantry support?" He shook his head. "I believe you're omitting something."

"I was defending the civilians we brought down. We didn't realize what was going on down here on the surface. There's been no contact."

"And I toasted your lack of bullshit. You realize that you were in medical stasis for three days? More than enough time for my forces to engage your friends five separate times? The fact that one of them is a giant tiger makes them stand out. A bit."

Parvi stared at him, and he added, "Are you sure you don't want that drink?"

"No, thank you."

"I might also point out that since I do have access to the BMU database, I know who Nickolai Rajasthan and Julia Kugara are as well as I know who you are. What are they doing?"

Parvi debated whether to tell him. If the rest of her people had already engaged with Lubikov's forces, she wasn't going to tell him anything that he didn't already know. Except why they were going where they were going.

She also knew that, if she didn't give him a show of good faith, the gloves would come off, and they would make her give up the information. "Are you willing to help defend this planet?"

"That is an interesting question."

"Will you stand against Adam?"

He drummed his fingers against the desk. "Despite the

pretty lights in the sky, you have yet to convince me that such resistance is possible."

"Do you understand what this thing is? What it has killed, what it has destroyed?"

"I wonder if you do, or if you are like the king who had his archers shoot arrows into the sky to battle the drought that was killing his people."

"Adam can be fought."

"I am certain of that. Can he be defeated?"

Parvi opened her mouth and realized that she couldn't answer the question honestly. She was not certain that defeating Adam was even possible, much less with the resources they had at hand. She was not the best advocate for this fight. "Just open a communication channel with Mallory, and the fleet. Talk to them. It costs you nothing."

"Perhaps it depends how you define costs. But you haven't answered my question." He stood up and took his glass back to the bar. "That glass I gave you, it's only water."

Parvi resisted reaching for it, even though she was parched.

"Shall I make it easier for you?" Lubikov said. "We liberated a POW camp that was half full of 'passengers' from that little blockade run you pulled. They've all been debriefed. I have some idea what your team is doing, but I'd be more kindly disposed to your point of view if I heard it from you."

"They're our backup plan," Parvi said.

"A couple of mercenaries and some social scientists?" Lubikov shook his head. "Backup for a fleet of how many thousand ships?"

"It's a long shot."

"What do you expect them to do?"

"Make some contact with the Dolbrians."

Parvi heard glass rattle, but Lubikov said nothing. He didn't even turn around. The silence extended a long time before he repeated, "Make some contact with the Dolbrians?"

"Yes."

"They've been extinct for hundreds of millions of years."

"The Protean, on Salmagundi, strongly suggested we seek them out."

"I see."

"Like I said, it is a long shot."

Lubikov turned around. "Thank you for being so candid."

"You will talk to Mallory."

"I promise you, I am considering all my options. You, however, should get some rest." He walked over to the desk, tapped some controls, and the windows regained their transparency and a weight in the air receded, clearing Parvi's sinuses.

"Please," Parvi said, "I don't know how much time we have."

Lubikov nodded as a pair of guards came in the room to take her away.

Lubikov watched the guards take Parvi away.

How much time do *we all have?*

From Parvi's intel, Mr. Antonio's master, Adam, was limited to the speed of these new Caliphate tach-ships. More or less as fast as a normal tach-comm signal.

Unlike Parvi, Lubikov knew exactly why Adam had not yet made an appearance. Mr. Antonio—the old man who recruited him to Adam's cause, who Lubikov suspected was no old man—had provided Lubikov with a lot of information. Mr. Antonio gave him Adam's script of how Bakunin's future would play out for him, a script that Bakunin had followed up until the transmission from Earth.

According to Adam's prophet, Mr. Antonio, Bakunin and the space around it was supposed to devolve into a seething cesspit of self-destructive violence. As a military man, Lubikov could easily infer the reason. It made more sense for Adam to concentrate on the capital planets, the command and control centers with an interstellar reach. Bakunin was a mess that could be dealt with at leisure.

He wondered if Mr. Antonio knew that such mundane strategic considerations tarnished his master's claims of divinity. Not that Lubikov had cast his lot with the AI because he ever believed those claims. Lubikov, as always, simply played the odds in his own favor.

And as the activity around Bakunin began diverging

from Adam's script, Lubikov was sensing a slight shift in
those odds.

If he assumed the self-proclaimed deity would inter-
vene as soon as he was aware that things were not going as
prophesied, the earliest Adam could show up would be five
days after receiving that information. That was the shortest
travel time from a neighboring planet . . .

Five days.

When did he begin to notice things changing from the
script old man Antonio gave him? Ten days ago? Just
enough time for a tach-signal to go out, and for Adam to
come back.

Just enough time.

Lubikov eased himself into his chair, wondering what
his options truly were.

"Dolbrians?" he muttered to himself. Then he started
calling up commanders, ordering coverage to the main
eastern approaches to the Diderot Range.

CHAPTER FOURTEEN

Guardian Angel

"It is human nature to ignore the fate of nations when one's family is at stake."
—*The Cynic's Book of Wisdom*

"The destruction of civilization will always begin with the destruction of the family."
—SYLVIA HARPER
(2008–2081)

Date: 2526.8.9 (Standard)
Bakunin–BD+50°1725

Flynn Jorgenson drove a stolen groundcar cross-country along the plains about two hundred klicks northwest of Godwin. Tetsami had helped him disable every electronic component that wasn't needed to keep the wheels going. Even the running lights had been removed, and he drove through the night using a heads-up display set on passive infrared, giving the night a surreal monochrome appearance.

In the cabin behind him, everyone slept. He found it amazing that anyone could rest while that tiger snored.

"You there, Gram?"

"Yeah." Her voice was passive, almost resigned. Completely unlike the woman he'd shared his head with all his adult life. He glanced next to him, and saw her sitting in the passenger seat, looking as she always did, black hair diagonally cut, leather jacket, almond eyes . . .

Tears?

"Gram?" He wanted to reach out to her, even though the person he saw existed behind his eyes, not in front of them.

"I think it just hit me. It's all gone. Everything."

"I know," Flynn said, turning back to face the rolling gray landscape. After a few moments he asked, "If the Protean hadn't shown up, what would you have wanted us to do?"

"What are you talking about?"

"I'm saying, if the first we heard of all this was Adam plopping out of the sky and saying 'join me,' what would we have done?"

"Not a fair question."

"Isn't it? Somewhere there's a recording in the Hall of Minds that made that choice."

"No."

"You don't think Adam went to the Hall—"

"No, I mean what I was, what's there in the Hall … don't you remember how bad it was when you—you know if I was given a choice, then I would have said *hell, no.*"

Flynn paused a long time before he said, "I see."

"Christ on a unicycle, you know I didn't mean it like that."

"Sure."

"Damn it, however we feel about it now, we both weren't willing participants."

Flynn sighed, "I know you didn't mean it that way, Gram."

"You're the most family I've ever had."

"Same here."

"And for what it's worth, now I'm glad we weren't given the choice."

"So," he asked, "if Adam shows up now, and gives you that choice—his way or nothing—what would you do now?"

"That's not my say."

"Of course it is."

"This is your body, your life. I'm just a hitchhiker."

"Gram, after how long we've been together, this is as much your body as mine."

She didn't answer him immediately, and when he glanced next to him, she had vanished from the passenger seat. He looked at the empty seat and felt prickings of worry even though he knew she had never really sat there. *Gram?* he thought more than said.

He felt his eyes burn, and he reached up and wiped the tears off his own cheek.

"Thank you," he heard his own voice say.

But she never answered his question.

Date: 2526.8.10 (Standard)
Bakunin–BD+50°1725

Flynn, check your three o'clock.

He had driven in silence past midnight. The rolling plains and the rocking of the groundcar's suspension had lulled him into a near trance, and Tetsami's voice in his head cut through and he let the massive vehicle roll to a stop as he looked to the far right. Some light or other was out there, past the range of the passive thermal imaging.

Flynn pulled the vehicle to a full stop.

Immediately, he heard Kugara's voice from the cabin behind him. "What's the problem?"

I thought she was asleep, he thought. Then he realized that Nickolai had stopped snoring as well.

"Something up ahead," Flynn said as he powered down the heads-up display. Bakunin's moons had set, leaving the night lit only by a massive spread of stars above them. The mountains, their destination, were only visible as a high, ragged, horizon.

"Can you check it out?" Kugara said, and it took a second before Flynn realized she wasn't talking to him. Of course, why would she? He was a fifth wheel on this expedition, more useless than the still-sleeping scientists.

Don't get down on yourself.

Gram, I'm only here because you know the area.

The tiger opened the side doors, letting in the cold night air in a sudden breeze that made Flynn's arms break out in gooseflesh. Nickolai stepped out and became nothing more than a feline silhouette framed by the open door of the groundcar.

"What do you see out there?" Kugara asked him.

Flynn wondered if the tiger could see anything in the darkness, but then he remembered what the Protean had done to his eyes. He shuddered, and told himself it was the cold.

"PSDC," Nickolai said. "Airborne early warning and surveillance platforms. One to our southeast, another to our north-northeast. No question that they know we're here."

"Shit," Flynn said, "we got to get away from this thing before they show up."

"Don't worry," Kugara said. "They would have picked us up before we cleared the horizon. The fact they haven't sent anyone to intercept us means that they haven't classed us as a threat yet. One of those aircraft has to be tracking hundreds of thousands of civilian vehicles."

"The problem is they're between us and the mountains," Nickolai said. "The closer we get, the more likely they'll identify us." He stepped back into the groundcar. "If we spark their interest, we're already close enough for them to get a visual ID on us."

"Damn," Kugara said. "Just seeing you would be enough to set their alarms ringing."

Let me take over.

Gram?

I have a way past this . . .

Flynn let his mind drift back as he felt Tetsami turn his head to look at Kugara. He could feel himself smiling at her.

"I think I got good news for you."

A long time ago, back when Tetsami was living on Bakunin, she had worked for a man calling himself Dominic Magnus. He had been an arms dealer, and ended up being one of the final lines of defense against the last attempt by the PSDC to take over the planet. In the short period that Tetsami worked for him, she got to know his retreat in the Diderot Mountains—and the mountains themselves. The whole range was riddled with ancient lava tubes and natural caverns to the extent that someone could walk from pole to pole without breaking the surface.

It was the perfect place for someone to go to ground against an army. The number of options for retreat was endless, and thanks to Dominic Magnus' paranoia, some of those options were still firmly planted in Tetsami's mind.

"I know half a dozen coordinates by heart," she told the others. "These are the closest."

"It's also damn close to Godwin," Kugara said. "We were trying to avoid that."

"If they already see us, we'll be less remarkable going toward a population center than a mountain range," Tetsami said.

"And it's still twenty kilometers north of Godwin," Nickolai said.

"Okay," Kugara said. "Our goal is to reach the underground anyway. If there's a way in short of the mountains themselves, I'm all for it."

Tetsami turned the groundcar, and started going due south.

About ten kilometers north of their destination, the woods grew too dense for the car. Tetsami brought them to a stop and said, "We either cross over to a main road, or we hoof it."

"How much night do we have left?" Kugara asked.

"About ninety minutes," Tetsami said. After so long on Salmagundi, the sixteen-hour nights on Bakunin seemed endless. "Do you think you can make it on your injured foot?"

Kugara snorted, as if the question didn't merit an answer. She turned to the two scientists still asleep in the back. "Okay, everyone out!"

Well, Tetsami had the answer to her question. They were hoofing it. It was probably just as well; any maintained roadways would more than likely have some sort of PSDC checkpoint.

She turned on the console lighting, and bent down into the footwell by the driver's seat.

"What are you doing?" Kugara asked.

"Just a minute," Tetsami said, pulling a panel from underneath one of the driver's displays. She released a couple of spring-loaded latches, and the small display popped off in her hand. "Good—"

"What—"

Tetsami held up the display. "The on-board navigation system. Even when they're inset like that, they're generally the same add-on hardware as the after-market stuff." She yanked a couple of cables from under the dash. "Can I have your carbine?"

"For what?"

"This thing won't power itself on our good intentions," Tetsami said. "Don't worry, it just needs a trickle from the battery. It'd take a good ten years to drain the power cell."

Kugara unslung the rifle. "This is our only weapon. Are you sure you need to do this?"

"Unless someone here can tell longitude and latitude by looking."

She handed over the rifle. "Don't break it."

They walked through the woods, the sky slowly lightening above them. They followed Kugara's limping lead, while Kugara followed the jury-rigged navigation display Tetsami had attached to her rifle. Dawn came slowly, and Tetsami's breath fogged in front of her.

Flynn's breath.

"You awake?" she thought at him.

"Yeah, Gram," came back Flynn's voice inside her head. *"You want me to take over?"*

The matter-of-fact way he asked made Tetsami want to cry again. Whatever he might say, this wasn't her body. She was an interloper. Their relationship was freakish, even by Salmagundi standards. The whole process was supposed to merge identities, not leave multiple personalities inside the same skull.

"Only if you want to," she thought back.

"Then keep at it. I drove all night. I need a break."

"Great, so I get to feel our legs ache."

"You asked."

"Fly— Tetsami? Get over here." Tetsami looked up

ahead at the sound of Kugara's voice. Kugara stood at the top of a rise ahead of everyone. The mound was treeless, and seemed to be in front of a clearing. Beyond it was unobstructed rose-colored sky.

As Tetsami climbed the rise next to Kugara, she realized that the mound was too even and regular to be a natural formation.

When she reached the top, Kugara swept a hand toward the view in front of them. "Is *that* supposed to be there?"

"That" was an industrial complex of about thirty buildings surrounded by a twenty-meter–wide defensive perimeter consisting of two tall fences surrounding a no-man's-land. Perimeter towers rose every twenty meters, bristling with cameras and defensive weaponry.

Tetsami looked over at the navigation display attached to Kugara's rifle, and had her sinking feeling confirmed when she saw that the coordinates of Dom's old escape tunnel fell in the center of the mass of buildings.

"Jesus Mother-humping Tap-dancing Christ."

Kugara sighed. "That's what I was afraid of."

"Some bastard built this—"

"Within the past hundred-seventy-five years. I know."

Tetsami suddenly felt the weight of uselessness that Flynn must have been feeling. Worse. She had actually sabotaged the mission with her outdated information. They were now vulnerable, on foot, and way too close to Godwin, and the occupying PSDC, than was safe.

She put her head in her hands and cursed.

"Gram?"

"Please, I'm busy fucking everything up right now."

"Look at the nav computer again."

"What?"

She looked up and turned to Kugara who was already limping down the rise and saying something about turning back east to take on the mountains on foot. "Can I see that again?"

Kugara stopped, and Tetsami scrambled down and looked at the small map displayed on the navigation computer.

"What are you looking for?" Kugara asked.

"What am *I looking for?"*

"What's the odds that a random construction project would be perfectly centered on your coordinates?"

"It's not . . ."

It was.

She brought Kugara back up the rise so she could compare the map to the ground; judging by the topographical features she could identify, the complex wasn't just plopped down in the middle of nowhere. The perimeter was almost perfectly centered around Dom's old escape hatch, directly beneath the largest building.

It wasn't random. The complex was in a natural bowl, surrounded by woods, but in order to be where it was, it had been placed off-center in the natural feature and the construction had done a fair bit of excavating on the north side of the natural depression, where they stood.

The excavation, and the rise they stood on, wouldn't be necessary unless the builders wanted the complex exactly where they had put it. It wasn't as if there was any other infrastructure here, the complex was alone in the woods, with only a single road leading south, opposite where they stood.

"Nickolai?" she called down. "Can you come up here and look at this?"

The tiger mounted the rise next to them. Kugara asked, "What are you doing?"

"Can you read any of those signs down there?" Tetsami asked the tiger.

Nickolai started reading off a long litany of safety warnings, and other random bits of signage anyone could expect to find at an industrial site. After thirty seconds of his narration, Tetsami stopped him. "That's it. Our way into the mountain is down there."

"You lost me," Kugara said, "how do you know that?"

"Did you hear him read the company name?"

"Bleek Munitions? So what?"

"That's the company Dom took over, the one he ran from his headquarters in the mountains. It didn't cease to exist because we cashed out our shares. They built an expansion centered on one of the main access routes back to the mountain."

Kugara said, "That's a bit high on speculation."

"More than trying to hunt down Dolbrians?"

Nickolai turned to look at Kugara. "I think Tetsami's right."

"Why?"

"I can see signs directing employees to a subway system."

Kugara stared at him a moment, then looked at Tetsami with a grim expression. "I don't suppose either of you have a good idea how to get in there?"

CHAPTER FIFTEEN

Heaven's Gate

"When in doubt, move."
— *The Cynic's Book of Wisdom*

"Rapidity is the essence of war."
— SUN TZU
(ca. 500 BCE)

Date: 2526.8.10 (Standard)
Bakunin–BD+50°1725

For nearly four hours, Nickolai sat in the crown of a tree and watched the road that led to the industrial complex. Traffic was sparse, small vehicles and vans that were unsuited to Nickolai's purpose. Most traffic on Bakunin, even after a Pax Proudhon, was aggressively defensive. Anything of value, including and especially personnel, was hidden behind layers of armor. Direct attack, as lightly armed as they were, would do nothing except draw attention to them.

It wasn't until midmorning that he saw a vehicle coming that suited their purpose. It was a heavy wheeled transport, carrying a large piece of tarp-covered equipment on a flatbed. It was about five kilometers away.

He gestured to the others, and started climbing down the tree. They had about two minutes.

They had set themselves up on the inside of a blind curve that ran alongside a wooded ravine. The inside edge of the road had seen a fair share of erosion, and as he reached the ground, Kugara was shoving the laser carbine into a hand-dug excavation in the earth about two meters down from the road's surface.

"This better work," she muttered as she flipped the switch on the trigger guard.

Nickolai ducked behind a tree with the others, and Kugara dove in after him.

Tetsami's rewiring of the power cell worked as advertised, and the carbine whined and then released all its energy in a solid whoomp that shook the ravine floor beneath him. He looked around the base of the tree as dirt cascaded through the treetops like sleet. The road had been undermined, leaving a nasty crater that took a bite out of a third of the roadway.

"Okay," Kugara said, "That was our gun. We don't get a second chance at this."

Nickolai edged up to the road, pressing his body to the ravine wall and peering through the undergrowth. "They're still coming." He could hear the engines now, only a couple of kilometers away. "Get into position, we'll only have a few seconds."

The others joined him at the edge of the road as he heard the massive machine's gears shift and the brakes engage for the upcoming turn. Just as the first wheel passed their position, he heard the brakes lock and the wheels scream as the truck and its thirty meters of cargo tried to stop and avoid the sudden obstacle.

The last tire passed their position, and the cab was already around the turn. Nickolai jumped out onto the road, followed by the others. At this point, with the whole truck in danger of fishtailing off the road, the driver was not going to be paying attention to any rear-facing cameras.

Nickolai ran after the trailer, which was still screeching to a stop, the tires burning a reeking trail of scorched synthetics. He vaulted onto the back, grabbing and tearing free a corner of the tarp. The others were behind him, running, and he reached down and scooped up Brody by the good arm and tossed him under the tarp. Dörner jumped up on her own, and Kugara practically threw Tetsami/Flynn after

Brody. He reached down for Kugara, and she climbed his arm as if it was a ladder.

Everything shuddered to a stop.

Everyone froze in position on the back of the bed. Nickolai held his breath and flexed his claws, anticipating discovery.

Instead, the engine revved, and the truck started backing up. After backing ten meters or so, it began to move forward again, very slowly. As it rounded the curve, Nickolai saw the marks it had left in the pavement, leaving the road to avoid their sinkhole and chewing up five meters of ruts on the opposite side.

Once around the turn, the driver accelerated back to speed, and Nickolai dropped the tarp over himself and the others.

Kugara whispered in the darkness, "Okay, that worked, but we still lost our gun."

After a few more minutes, they rolled to a stop again. Nickolai crouched at the end of the truck bed, under the tarp, holding taut a heavy length of chain that had been one of four that had been securing one of the rear anchor points of the truck's cargo.

The machine was massive enough that the others had been able to move back and hide within a large recess between a pair of massive tanks. Nickolai stood guard at the rear, the chain their only real weapon. He crouched in the darkness and waited, as the truck sat idling.

For what it was worth, he prayed.

Light leaked into the world under the tarp, but not from his end. He turned his head, keeping the rest of his body still, silent, and ready to pounce.

Someone had lifted the tarp up near the cab. He heard someone talking to the driver. "Glad those Proudhon assholes finally let you out of Godwin."

"Yeah, how it works, ain't it? First comes an army, then the goddamn forms."

"Taxes will be next."

"Don't I know it, but whatcha going to do?"

This was Bakunin . . . wasn't it? Nickolai had no love for the lawless order that he had lived in during the years of his exile. The anarchy seemed fitting, the epitome of the Fallen themselves. But these men were talking in terms that would have been inconceivable to any Bakunin native a year ago. Not just the existence of a de facto State, but the fatalistic acceptance of it.

Could Mosasa's absence be so critical?

A man leaned his head in under the tarp, shining a light against the side of the machine. Nickolai froze, crouched in deep shadow. The man read off a long serial number aloud. Then he said, "Good. Our fabrication building has been running at two-thirds capacity ever since the old primary power plant decided to melt its core all over the place."

"You lucked out, this was the last terawatt reactor left in Godwin."

The tarp dropped. "And to hear management bitch, it was priced like the last one on the planet."

"Where's it go?"

"Follow the signs for the auxiliary fabrication building. There's a lot marked out for you. We'll get you unloaded within the hour."

The truck started up and slowly rolled forward. Nickolai whispered to the others, "I'll take the lead, get ready to follow."

He wrapped the chain tightly around his forearm, so he could carry it quietly, and crouched down so he could peer out from under the tarp while disturbing it as little as possible.

The truck weaved between buildings and drew to a stop near the center of the complex. When it stopped, Nickolai whispered, "This way."

They had pulled up next to one of the buildings, with little more than a meter to spare. It gave as good cover for them as he could hope for. The five of them slipped off of the truck, Nickolai in the lead, Kugara taking up the rear and landing with a sharp intake of breath. His muzzle wrinkled when he caught the scent of her wound. It needed attention.

Later, he promised himself.

He looked along the wall, and neither direction seemed promising. There was no access into the building along the length of the truck, and past the ends of the truck, no sign of cover.

"Down here," Flynn/Tetsami whispered. He looked down and saw him crouching to look under the bed of the truck. Nicolai looked underneath. A large grate was set in the pavement underneath the truck, part of a storm drain.

"You think we can slip out that?" he asked Nickolai.

The grate itself was big enough to accommodate a human, though Nickolai would find it a squeeze. He shifted through spectra until he could see a large volume of air passing through. "It's big enough—for most of us."

"Okay," Kugara said, "I'll get it open, you guard our rear."

He approved. *So if I get stuck, I don't block our escape.*

Kugara slid down on her belly and crawled under the trailer. After about a minute of quiet grunting, she had managed to slide the grate off the drain with only a slight scraping noise. She dropped down and waved the others after. Flynn went, then Dörner, and at last Brody who needed assistance with his arm in a cast.

Nickolai had just lowered Brody down the hole when the truck's engine started up. Below, he heard Kugara call up, "Move it!"

He was in trouble. He could hear gears shifting already, and there was no way he'd be able to squeeze down there in time. In the moment he had left, he pulled the grate back over the hole with no pretense of stealth. The clang of the heavy grate dropping home was mostly covered by the truck's engine. So was the sound of Kugara cursing him and asking what the hell he was doing.

The trailer was already rolling.

Nickolai reached up and grabbed an axle housing as it passed over him. He felt fur torn from his backside as he was dragged over the grate. He was dragged another ten meters before he kicked his legs up and pulled himself into the trailer's underside.

"What the hell is he doing?"

Dörner's sudden panic caught Kugara off guard, and she had to step forward, wincing on her wounded foot, and pull her off of the ladder to the surface. As she did, the truck's shadow moved away from the grate and blue sky shone down on them.

"What is he—" Kugara clamped a hand across the blonde scientist's mouth and gave her a stern glare. *Save us all from civilians in a combat situation.*

It should have been just her and Nickolai. They were trained for this sort of thing. She was more worried about Dörner and Brody than she was about Nickolai. The tiger could take care of himself.

And judging from the lack of any commotion above, he hadn't been spotted.

Kugara slowly released Dörner. The woman was shaking. Very quietly, Kugara whispered, "Get a grip on yourself. *Now.*"

Dörner shook her head. "We're trapped. What do we do now?"

Kugara hadn't reached that point yet. They needed to get to the subway, with or without Nickolai.

Preferably with.

Next to her, Flynn whispered, "Can you get me to a comm console?"

"I don't know where this goes," she whispered back. In both directions the storm drain led into inky darkness.

"Left goes deeper into the complex," Brody said. There was a stressed edge to his whisper, but he seemed more together than Dörner.

"Okay. Flynn leads, I'll take up the rear."

Dörner still shook, and Kugara squeezed her shoulder, "You can do this." *And I'll be behind you pushing your butt down the tunnel.*

It seemed an eternity without light, crawling on hands and knees through the slime, listening to Dörner's ragged breathing in front of her.

The air was cold, and stank so bad of mildew and stagnant water that she could swear she felt algae growing in her sinuses. At least crawling kept the weight off her foot; she did her best to keep the wound out of the accumulated muck running along the base of the drainpipe.

Right before they stopped, the tunnel had lightened enough that she could see the silhouette of Dörner's bony ass in front of her. Flynn whispered back, "Another grate ahead. I think it's in a building."

One by one, they all crawled into another catch basin beneath a meter-diameter grate.

Flynn was right, at least insofar as she didn't see sky above them, but the underside of a metal roof about twenty meters above them.

"Okay," she whispered, "all of you back into the drain-pipe, just in case."

She braced for some objection from Dörner, but it seemed as if her momentary panic had passed. When Kugara was alone in the catch basin, she climbed the ladder up to just beneath the grate. She did her best to survey the area from her low angle, but the best she could manage was the determination that she was looking up into some sort of motor pool. She saw a couple of vehicles, and one wall of the building seemed open to the outside.

Tactically, it was a bad way to enter a situation. A hostile could be crouching just three meters away from her hole ready to attack anything coming out. But the hostiles here had no idea they were here.

Yet.

She braced her good foot on the ladder and hooked her hand into the grate and slowly pushed up until there was enough clearance for her to look around at ground level. It was a garage. She saw several wheeled and tracked vehicles, even a couple of contragravs. Near the rear, a half wall sectioned off a mechanic's workshop where two partly disassembled aircars were parked.

The area was clear of anyone at the moment, and Kugara slid the grate aside as quietly as she could manage. "Come up," she whispered down to the others, then she scrambled out of the hole and crouched between two parked vehicles.

As the others crawled up out of the drain, Kugara split her time looking out the main entrance, hanging open to the rest of the complex, and the workshop at the opposite side of the garage.

As Flynn came up next to her, she asked, "What can you do at a comm console?"

"If I can jack into their network I can map out where we're going, and probably disable their security."

"Can you do it without giving us away? Our only advantage is the fact they don't know we're here."

"I think—"

Flynn's answer was interrupted by an unfamiliar voice. "What the fuck do we have here? *Don't move!*"

Kugara was so hyped that the thought of actually surrendering peacefully didn't cross her mind until her wounded foot was connecting with the man's throat. The guy was in greasy overalls, and had been in the process of unholstering a weapon as he spoke. Her foot was slamming him into the side of a blocky contragrav van before he got it out.

Even as the man started his stunned slide to the ground, Kugara saw a trio of other guys turning to face the commotion. They had been playing cards at a table that, as luck would have it, was set just out of sight of the storm drain. Two guys were grabbing weapons, and the third ran for the open doorway.

"Shit!" she muttered as she dove back between vehicles.

A gunshot thudded a hole through the skin of the contragrav next to her.

The first guy coughed and groaned, holding his neck. Kugara grabbed the gun from his holster. Then she cursed. The damn thing was more for show than anything else, a high-caliber slugthrower almost as long as her forearm. Yes, a .50 caliber round could put down just about anyone, and punch a hole in anything short of mil-spec powered armor. But it was a revolver and she'd only be able to do it seven times.

Not to mention the kick on the thing would make grouping multiple shots a bear even with her strength.

"Well, they know we're here now!" Flynn or Tetsami yelled across at her as another shot echoed through the garage.

"If you can do something," Kugara yelled back, "Do it *now!*" More gunshots, and Kugara popped up around the side of a grounded aircar and fired one shot at the two guys firing. The sound of the hand cannon firing shook the ferrocrete floor and the muzzle flash almost reached the groundcar next to the shooters. In response the two guys dropped for cover.

The guy running reached the front of the garage and slammed a big red button mounted on the wall. A button Kugara really didn't want pressed.

Klaxons started cutting through the air.

She ducked behind her aircar as return fire took out its windshield. "Flynn? Tetsami?" She glanced around and only saw the two scientists cowering back by the storm drain. She waved at them. "Back down, take cover."

She could at least keep them from being shot.

More shots, and the contragrav van sprouted more holes. She popped back out for another cannon shot to keep the other two pinned.

Four shots left. This will not end well.

"Flynn? Tetsami?" She looked around and saw Brody evacuating back down the sewer after Dörner. Did Flynn have the sense to duck down there first?

Then she heard the whine of the contragrav starting up.

PART EIGHT

Apocalypse

"Liberty is the condition of duty, the guardian of con-
science . . . Liberty is safety from all hindrances, even
sin. So that Liberty ends by being Free Will."
—John, Lord Acton
(1834–1902)

CHAPTER SIXTEEN

Blasphemy

"Ideals may create a revolution, but base human motivation recruits its foot-soldiers."
—*The Cynic's Book of Wisdom*

"Take mankind in general; they are vicious, their passions may be operated upon."
—ALEXANDER HAMILTON
(1757–1804)

Date: 2526.8.10 (Standard)
7.2 AU from Bakunin–BD+50°1725

The *Prophet's Voice* tached into existence in Bakunin's outer solar system. It appeared just as Adam's incarnations had already done dozens of times in other systems. Even if this particular copy of Him had only seen the direct conversion of three planets, other Adams in other ships had transmitted their own victories to Him. Through the lag of tach-space, their experiences became His own, and His became theirs.

Despite being distributed across light-years, Adam was one.

There was no question left of His ultimate victory, and He appeared before the glowing red pinprick of Kropotkin as if it was only a formality. The planet that his hated brother Mosasa had called home now bore no special characteristics, nothing to distinguish it from anywhere else Adam had brought His salvation. Even its chaotic political system had coalesced into a somewhat pedestrian State without his brother's constant intervention.

But He still had been forced to come here earlier than anticipated.

Even before He looked out upon the latest realm to receive His Glory, that fact drew His attention more than it deserved, a small canker on an otherwise perfect body. It shouldn't have concerned Him. It was not a flaw in His vision, simply a side effect of His servant's failure. The transmission from Khamsin should never have been allowed.

And those responsible should be punished . . .

But that was for later. Now He prepared to bring another world to Paradise. He opened Himself to His presence here.

And He felt only the void.

His cloud should be here, waiting for him, a diffuse mass great enough to envelop a planet within His embrace. But of His works, He felt no sign. He probed along frequencies known only to His chosen, and with the interminable hours of lag from light-speed communication, His agents on the planet itself responded to Him. They told Him of the plasma fires that had wiped His essence from the sky.

For a few brief moments, Adam refused to believe what He was told. Those speaking to Him were fallible tools, infinitely more prone to error then He was. They were wrong. Their observations were flawed.

But He could sense the still expanding cloud of inert dust, moving at improbable velocities away from where the *Prophet's Voice* floated in dead space.

And as denial faded, rage consumed Him.

His was the mission to save all life from entropy, death, extinction. Such an act, such defiance, it was a blow to existence itself. It was the ultimate definition of evil.

And Adam would crush all such evil before Him.

Adam's actions over the past twelve hours had taken Rebecca by surprise. For her, it had been just over three days since she had seen the Earth collapse under Adam's hand, since she had decided that her continued existence was not worth allowing Adam to go unchallenged, since she had found Jonah Dacham. It was barely enough time to earn his trust.

The man she had taken from beneath the Vatican was not just a man. He was an agent of Proteus, of the colony that had made a last dramatic stand against Adam's invasion of Earth. He was, in some sense, the father of the Protean colony that had hidden under the Martian surface. Nearly two centuries ago, he had shepherded the last Protean egg from the destroyed colony on Bakunin, and had taken it to Mars, where it grew into a new crystalline city duplicating the old.

So, when Adam threatened, before Proteus sent its ships to fight his fleet, it had sent Dacham to Earth on a diplomatic mission to the Vatican. He had been successful in getting the pope himself to transmit absolution for the Protean race, should they but face the evil that was Adam. But the real mission was not gaining that absolution.

It was the pope's transmission itself.

Not just the rebroadcast of the recording of Khamsin's fall to Adam, or Mallory's last tach-comm from Salmagundi—even though both were important warnings to a humanity unaware of Adam's approach. To the Protean strategy, the transmission was an important distraction.

It had drawn attention to the Proteans' military attack. Dacham's true mission was an exercise in massive misdirection. The whole operation was meant to distract from the Protean's *real* opposition to Adam, one much more subtle.

When he had explained himself and the Proteans to her and Mosasa, the Proteans' plans were obvious in retrospect.

Adam's major flaw was his own arrogance. He had inherited the long view of society and social systems that the Race had bequeathed to their AIs, but that was not omniscience. The AI Mosasa had been well aware of that, and Adam had used his brother's psychological need to fill in data holes to lure him out to Xi Virginis and to his own destruction.

But Adam, in his drive toward godhead, had ignored or forgotten his brother's own fatal lesson. Adam could no longer perceive the edges of his own knowledge; he no longer accepted the existence of unknowns in his view of the universe. It was why the Protean attack could be a surprise, and why Adam had shown no impulse to think any deeper about the Proteans after their destruction.

There were no secrets from God.

And just as she was getting her mind around Dacham and the Proteans, and had started formulating a plan, Adam surprised them all by a blatant display of his fatal flaw.

The *Voice*'s sudden departure to Bakunin was completely unexpected, as was the state of the system when they arrived. She had been as shocked as Adam was to find out that the people here had not only formed a vast fleet of refugee ships, but had somehow managed to neutralize the cloud of matter that was supposed to spearhead Adam's invasion.

For once, it was only the *Voice*. And Adam. And several billion souls that had sold themselves to him.

The *Voice* hung in the outer system seven AU from Bakunin and the mass of the opposition fleet. The majority of its "crew" existed only as minds within the thinking matter that now made up the whole of the carrier and the ships that rode with it. Almost none of Adam's chosen here were physically embodied. Being one of the first to accept Adam's offer of godhead, Rebecca was an exception, she still had a body that may have still had some slight continuity of existence with her prior human form.

Also, her experience during Earth's invasion had shown her that retaining a separate physical form was required in order to continue differentiating herself from Adam. The minds that swarmed the matter of the *Voice* might have retained some nominal individuality, but the border between their egos and Adam's seemed to degrade over time. Adam might not read minds, but his existence in and of itself was an attack on his subject's individuality.

Rebecca enforced the barrier between her ego and Adam's by keeping a physical body as much as possible.

Remaining separate was the only way that a fight against Adam was even conceivable to her. Now she saw, in the absence of Adam's cloud, a possibility that not only the fight, but Adam's *defeat* became conceivable.

Even as Adam rallied his attention to Bakunin, and the impossible resistance he found there, Rebecca turned her attention inside herself, into a realm that Adam couldn't perceive.

Dacham stood on a high platform in the mountains, overlooking the city of Godwin. He stared into the distance, the side of his face almost invisibly twitching.

"You have to move now," she told him, "while he is distracted."

Dacham turned to look at her, and his expression was grave. "No. He's still too distributed. Once we move, once he knows we're here, that is the end of our infiltration."

"Damn it! We have him isolated, one ship, alone. You want to wait until he burrows into *another* planet?"

He turned back to face the vision of Godwin. "Of course not!" He clenched his hands into fists. "But this is bigger than what I want, bigger than Bakunin . . . The plan is to build our strength."

"Adam is never going to be weaker than he is right now."

"You can't ask us to undo all that—" Something resonated through the virtual scene, a feeling of disruption, partly barely audible sound, partly a sense of dread. Dacham looked at her and asked, "What was that?"

"Adam is launching all the tach-capable ships on the *Voice*," Mosasa's voice came from behind them.

They both turned to face the tattooed pirate. Mosasa looked them over and said, "He's placed himself on each one of those ships, and every one of them is going to tach into the system in a moment. No ultimatum. He is going to take that refugee fleet and turn it into himself."

"He's breaking his pattern?" Rebecca said.

"You cannot know the depths of his rage," Mosasa told them. He turned to Dacham and said, "If now is not the time, it never will be."

"He is still distributed across the whole *Voice*. We still need to isolate him from ourselves."

Mosasa smiled. "There's something I need to tell you about myself."

Fifty ships spread out from the *Prophet's Voice* in response to Adam's orders. On board each were the embodiments of Adam's chosen. Most still resembled human beings; others had made a fuller break with their humanity. All the ships carried a fragment of the embodied Adam with them, their omnipresent God directing their actions.

Adam had decided that there was too much at stake to allow any individual's decision to interfere with His plans. The defiance here could not be allowed to stand, and all His people would have to see and appreciate the fruits of such defiance.

Though Adam saw only the shell around the minds of his chosen, He saw that they all understood what it meant when He did not grant His offer to these people of Bakunin. They all understood that these people had passed beyond saving.

The ships spread out, facing a fleet of thousands massed insystem, refugees from all the nearby corners of human space.

Aboard each of the fifty ships around the *Voice*, tach-drives began powering themselves up, as Adam integrated Himself into the sophisticated Caliphate navigation systems. The systems in control of the tach-drives were, in many respects, the descendants of the hardware that had given Adam His birth—and allowed Him to become the brain of fifty ships.

Adam faced His opposition without fear and without any reservation. Before Him was the rump end of an extinct humanity, an evil reflex moving a body already dead. Nothing these still-breathing corpses could array against Him could blunt the tide of destiny or turn it aside.

He had faced much more with much less.

At His command, all fifty ships leaped into tach-space, and for a little less than three and a half seconds, they ceased to exist.

Date: 2526.8.10 (Standard)
350,000 km from Bakunin–BD+50°1725

Mallory's people had cleaned up the control center of the *Wisconsin*. The only signs of the attempted takeover were a few scars in the walls and bloodstains where the bodies had fallen. Crew from the Daedalus manned the room now, the *Wisconsin's* own crew having been decimated by Stefan's attempted coup.

Mallory led the other commanders of the fleet into the room, and they all filed in to stand behind the traffic control console. On the main holo, an image of a large spaceship floated. The coordinates scrolling by on the bottom of the image showed that the ship was seven AU away, roughly where the cloud had been.

The other Valentine sister was sitting at the main traffic control console below the holo. "It tached insystem about eighty minutes ago," she told them. "The tach-pulse from the arrival was huge—thought I was seeing another wormhole for a moment."

Mallory had never seen the Ibrahim-class carrier that the Caliphate had developed, but he knew that was what he was looking at.

Tito, leader of the Bakunin fleet, squinted at the holo and said, "Doesn't look like much."

The general from the SEC shook his head and said, "My God."

"What?" Tito didn't seem to get it.

The general explained. "That dot, floating off the starboard side? That's a Medina-class troop transport."

"No, you got to be—" Tito leaned forward. "Damnation and Taxes, that thing is huge."

"About half the size of the *Wisconsin*," said the Valentine by the console.

More dots were flying off the carrier, almost as if the kilometer-long craft was disintegrating.

It's launching everything.

"Any transmissions?" Mallory asked. "Has he broadcast an ultimatum yet?"

"Not a peep."

The change in tactics felt ominous to Mallory. Still, right

now they had the advantage in numbers. "We need to attack, now."

"Are you sure?" one of the Indi leaders asked. "Maybe—"

"Now," Mallory said, "while he's physically isolated. While his forces are confined to his ships—"

Red lights and angry beeps erupted from the consoles all across the traffic control consoles.

"What the hell is happening?" yelled the SEC general.

Valentine shook her head, "Tachyon bow shock from forty or fifty ships incoming. I got dozens of ships calling for attention."

"What?" The general looked up at the holo where the *Voice* was slowly disgorging its fleet.

"That image is an hour old," Mallory said. "He tached his fleet insystem."

The general shook his head. "You can't use a tach-drive tactically—"

Mallory snapped, "We did, with less accurate drives."

"No, the accuracy isn't—"

"I'm picking up detonations," Valentine said. She looked up at them. "We just lost contact with fifteen Indi ships."

Mallory slid to a comm console and pulled up his own channel and started transmitting orders to his fleet. The other members of the leadership only hesitated a moment before taking their seats and opening channels to their own fleets. In that brief hesitation, Valentine kept calling out casualties: Five Centauri ships, three from the SEC, another from the Bakunin fleet.

"These are the most advanced ships out there," Mallory said, "but we have numbers. Tell them not to engage one to one. Group four or five of ours to concentrate fire on one of theirs."

Another three Indi ships, a loss for the Union of Independent Worlds, a Centauri ship wounded but still with life support. And, finally, a confirmed kill of one of the hostile forces.

Above them, Valentine called up a holo that gave a strategic view of the space around Bakunin. Mallory glanced up and saw a great swath of blue dots, and in their midst, only a tiny sprinkling of red.

The numerical advantage was overwhelming.

"Concentrate your fire," Mallory told his fleet. "Concentrate as much energy in as small a space as possible."

Another red dot went gray—along with twenty blue dots. The horrifying thing was, with the lopsided numbers, that kill ratio was acceptable.

God forgive us, Mallory prayed.

CHAPTER SEVENTEEN

False Prophet

"Power will always fall to weaknesses it has denied possessing."
—*The Cynic's Book of Wisdom*

"Power always thinks it has a great soul and vast views beyond the comprehension of the weak."
—JOHN ADAMS
(1735–1826)

Date: 2526.8.10 (Standard)
1,500,000 km from Bakunin–BD+50°1725

Stefan Stavros slept uncomfortably in the cabin of a stolen three-passenger tach-ship. The old *Xanadu* had been designed in the most decadent days of the SEC, before the Caliphate existed. Even if this ship was a reproduction, it had been the toy of some mega-rich corporate mogul. Inside, it was all gratuitous leather, brass, and hardwoods. The control console was all inlaid with ivory and mother-of-pearl.

Also, it stank. The air was rank with the smell of piss and feces. As well as the sweat and blood crusted on Stefan's clothes.

His escape had gone perfectly, up until he was ten minutes away from the *Wisconsin* and tried to engage the fully charged tach-drive.

The bastard computer had asked for a password.

Somehow, the idea that some paranoid corp type had owned his escape route had never entered into his plans. His repeated attempts to engage the tach-drive all failed. And when he gave up and tried to pilot the craft conventionally, to remove himself from the doomed fleet, he had found out that the prior owner was a vindictive sadist.

"You don't think I'd let you do that now, do you?"

The words still glowed on the holo above the unresponsive controls. Life support still seemed to work, but the waste recycling had stopped. And the *Xanadu* piloted its own course, going somewhere without Stefan's intervention. Some preprogrammed rendezvous for the owner to track? Or was it just randomly launching itself out of the system to teach the would-be thief a lesson?

For three days, Stefan had been learning that lesson. He had torn free the nails on his hands trying to pry access panels from the cabin walls, and he had smeared filth on his blue jumpsuit by trying to force the waste recycler to work. His hair was matted, and he wore three days of beard. His mouth was dry. He was dizzy from hunger and dehydration, and every passing hour made drinking his own urine seem like a more attractive option.

He slept in fits and starts, startling himself awake with the vain hope that Mallory's dupes had found him and were going to take him into custody. Each time, nothing was there but empty space, and each time the air was a little staler.

The irony was he was trapped here because he didn't want to die.

Now he held a barely charged gamma laser, and fantasized about emptying the charge into his skull.

In the pit of his despair, he saw a light flash. He blinked several times; half-convinced he had begun to hallucinate. The barriers between his dreams and his waking moments had been slowly crumbling . . .

Another flash; multiple ones crossing the starscape unrolling before him. His brain slowly began to register something out there. He saw stars occluded by tiny motes of spacecraft flying—in astronomical terms, right next to him.

He reached for the display controls—one thing the

sadistic prior owner of the *Xanadu* did not deny him. He zoomed in on the flashes, thousands of kilometers away.

He gasped.

Tumbling under Kropotkin's bloody glare, he saw an endless cloud of floating wreckage. He had no idea how many ships had been consumed. He saw engine fragments from six—no, eight—different varieties of spaceship, sections of hull, corpses and pieces of corpses, chairs, electronic components, pieces of contragrav reactors, air lock doors floating surprisingly untouched, all tumbling outward in a cloud of shimmering ice crystals.

The *Xanadu* was headed directly at the expanding field of debris.

He spun the ship's sensors around, and saw himself surrounded. The *Xanadu* had drifted into the midst of Mallory's grand fleet, and now on every side of him, he could see the fruits of Mallory's futile war.

He could point his view in any direction now and see the remains of ships that had been torn apart. His heart raced as he saw a sleek Caliphate vessel pivot into the midst of a group of cargo haulers not that different from the *Daedalus* and tear them apart like a rabid wolf dropped into a nursery.

He stared into the heart of battle after battle as he drifted uncontrolled through a war zone, waiting for the strike that would peel the hull apart like an onion. But the *Xanadu* drifted through the chaos unscathed.

He watched with impotent rage at the priest and his minions. What right did he have, to sacrifice these people in some vain impossible fight?

The proximity alarms began wailing at him.

He reset the display to the default view forward, and found himself gripped by a fatalistic chuckle. He wasn't going to die in Mallory's battle. It would be a collision with a random piece of space junk.

The *Xanadu*, improbably, was aimed right for a large debris field from the battle. It was already passing through the gossamer glitter of an expanding cloud of frozen gases, and part of a control cabin larger than the entire *Xanadu* tumbled by him within a hundred meters. The original vector of the destroyed craft was close enough to the *Xanadu*'s that the wreckage passed by him with an almost majestic grace, showing first a curving metallic hull that slowly rotated to reveal the charred and melted interior.

Ahead of him the stars started winking out.

"What?"

At first it seemed a flaw in the display. Perhaps something had collided with the sensors causing the bind spot. But the hole within the darkness wasn't static. It grew. The *Xanadu*'s velocity relative to the wreckage was only a few meters per second, but the blackness was approaching faster than that. As he watched, a section of a winged lifting body belonging to a Centauri dropship drifted in front of the darkness, briefly shining in Kropotkin's light, hanging in front of complete nothingness. Then it vanished.

As the *Xanadu* drifted toward the darkness, Stefan stared into the gaping maw of the Abyss.

He could feel it staring back.

The blackness expanded in front of him, hiding the stars and consuming wreckage until the view out the display was completely blank. He braced himself for an impact that never came, even as all the telemetry data of the frozen controls stopped reading any velocity or direction at all. According to the ship's sensors, the *Xanadu* had stopped moving.

It was as if, outside the hull, the universe had ceased to exist.

The interior lights went red, and a small insistent beep started warning him of the exterior air lock door opening. He pulled his gamma laser out and turned the pilot's chair around so he could face the air lock. The door was directly to the rear of the crew cabin, between the two access ways that led aft and down to the two small cabins that were all the living space on the *Xanadu*.

The air lock door was an oval of polished brass etched with delicately ornate scrollwork, the only view inside through a porthole modeled after an ancient sea vessel. Because of the tiny size of the window relative to the door, and the slight tilt downward, Stefan could only see vague shadowy movement inside the air lock itself.

The red light in the cabin began flashing, and the electronic warning beep became a screaming alarm as the elaborate latches holding the air lock door shut began to unscrew themselves.

Stefan's eyes widened and he glanced at the console. According to the display, the outer door was still open. The interlock had failed or had been overridden. When the air lock door opened, it would expose the cabin to vacuum.

Stefan started hyperventilating, trying to suck in enough oxygen to survive until he got the door shut again. He pushed himself up out of the chair to float toward the air lock, just as the door opened.

He grabbed a tooled leather strap to anchor himself against an expected outrush of air. But the air remained impossibly still as the brass entrance of the air lock folded up into the ceiling on well-oiled hinges.

His visitor stood flat on the antique carpet of the air lock as if the *Xanadu* had its own gravity. Surreally, the man was naked, wearing not so much as a belt. Stefan stared, disbelieving his own eyes showing the open outer door of the air lock. Beyond the naked man, the darkness writhed, throwing whips and eddies of itself into the air lock, but not past his visitor.

The man's nakedness did not project vulnerability. Instead, the man's pupilless eyes bored into Stefan projecting arrogance and an unspeakable power.

When the apparition spoke, Stefan's bowels turned to water.

"You have sinned against Me." The voice came from a too-human throat, but the words resonated through the hull of the *Xanadu* as if the darkness itself spoke.

"No, no, I haven't," Stefan said, shaking his head and crying. He lost his grip on the laser, and it floated between them, ignored.

"I have offered My hand, and you have raised your hand against Me."

The words were like blows, and Stefan curled himself into a ball, shaking his head and saying, "No, no. It was them, not me. I wanted no part of this fight."

"Yet here you stand in the midst of this evil."

The man was not a man. Stefan knew he faced Adam, Mallory's Antichrist. And, joined with the terror that racked him, Stefan felt an explosive kernel of impotent hate for the priest that cast him here, alone.

Adam walked from the air lock, ignoring the absence of gravity as he strode to where Stefan floated. Adam reached out and touched Stefan's face. It felt nothing like the hand of God or the Devil. It felt human as Adam raised Stefan's chin so he faced him.

"So here you are. Do you have any reason why I should not send you the way of all flesh?"

Stefan looked into Adam's face and blurted, "I'll kill the priest for you."

Adam stopped moving, and Stefan caught something like surprise in his expression, in the hesitation.

"I know where he is," he said. "I can take this ship, find him. He's caused all this. You must want him to suffer—"

Adam's grip tightened just enough so Stefan stopped talking. "Do you presume to know the mind of God? You are an insect, less than nothing. Obscurity headed for oblivion. What can you give Me that I will not take for Myself?"

"He *expects* you to kill him," Stefan said.

"So I will."

"But if *I* do it, it will hurt him more."

Adam stared at him, the surprise now deeply etched in the otherwise perfectly sculpted face. His grip loosened on Stefan.

"Let me," Stefan said. "Let me rob that man of his destiny. Let him die not in the glory he seeks, but at the hands of someone he chose to discard. Let my obscurity be his final punishment."

Around them, tendrils of darkness floated, curling, probing the walls, slipping into the control systems of the *Xanadu*. Adam let him go, and Stefan floated, and caught himself against the swirling darkness. The black curled around his legs and arms, sliding inside his jumpsuit. Its touch was cold and light, like the last breath of a corpse.

"Will you serve Me as your God?" Adam asked.

"Y-yes!"

"Then, as you ask, you will become My instrument of vengeance."

The darkness poured over Stefan, filling his eyes, nose, and mouth. His fear died in a single explosive burst, and when the smoke cleared, Stefan Stavros was left with only a single glowing coal of hate.

Date: 2526.8.10 (Standard)
7.2 AU from Bakunin–BD+50°1725

Barely six minutes passed between the time that Mosasa's revelations convinced Dacham to go ahead with the Proteans' plan against Adam, and the time Adam lashed out in his rage, taching half of the *Voice*'s fleet insystem.

It felt an eternity to her.

Adam's attack consisted of the fifty most advanced tachships human technology had been able to produce. Each of the fifty ships carried an army, a virtual world, of Adam's chosen on board, and each one carried an embodiment of Adam himself.

It was also the starkest demonstration of Adam's central flaw that Rebecca had yet seen. Adam's self-image as a God meant that omniscience was an integral part of his identity now. The thing that was Adam literally could not accept an unknown into his universe; it threw the would-be God off-balance, caused more mistakes, and rendered Adam's own reactions unpredictable.

The situation on Bakunin caused him to completely break his pattern. Here, he was no longer interested in ultimatums, or conversion. Here, he was only interested in punishing defiance, turning his attention to the world that so defied him.

And when he launched those ships, he had no idea that defiance was much closer to hand. At the instant the attack ships vanished into tach-space, the only embodiment of Adam for light-years was the eidolon on the bridge of the *Voice*. The only presence of Adam's mind was within the thinking matter infecting the *Voice*. For three and a half seconds, fifty other Adams would be lost in the tach-space between the *Voice* and their opposition.

For a people freed from the constraints of the flesh, three and a half seconds could be a long time.

Mosasa moved first.

His revelation to Dacham and Rebecca had been what made this possible. She had suspected, on Earth, that Mosasa was not quite as limited to her mind as he had implied. He had confirmed that. His individuality was as distributed as Adam, every convert to Adam's reign beyond the flesh carried some small fraction of him, less a whole version of Mosasa, than a single cluster of neurons in a vast network, more rarified than even Adam's chosen. The chosen may live only as thoughts within the pattern of thinking matter that made up Adam's body; Mosasa's mind was made of patterns implanted within those thoughts.

Rebecca's mind just happened to house the part of Mosasa that had achieved self-awareness again.

It also meant that, in the confines of the *Voice*, when Adam was at his weakest, most alone, and most psychologically unstable, he was suddenly confronted with a billion images of his Nemesis, Mosasa. Mosasa had no effect on the physical world, but he could manifest himself across the breadth of Adam's chosen, appearing before all of the senses Adam possessed.

It was enough to completely break Adam's tenuous grip on sanity. The God attacked his own, striking down millions of his chosen to burn out the image of Mosasa. Mosasa seemed unmoved in the face of the onslaught and pushed himself into the God's own mind.

The battle of wills was opaque to Rebecca; she suffered the same limitation as Adam, unable to see within another's mind. It was a limitation Mosasa did not seem to share. The only thing Rebecca could see of the battle was the spasms of Adam's identity though the physical matrix that infected the *Voice*.

For a moment, it seemed that Mosasa might single-handedly defeat Adam . . . But less than a second after the attack began, she heard an unearthly scream echo through her own head. A scream in Mosasa's voice.

Following the scream, she heard Dacham's voice.

"Our turn."

The Proteans' plan to attack Adam had been much more insidious than a straightforward military attack, as powerful as the dead Protean colony was.

Dacham had not been the only agent they had sent to Earth.

They had sent thousands. All to await Adam's call. All to accept it.

All of them had been perfectly human in form, as Dacham had been. And thanks to the Protean attack, and the pope's broadcast, the possibility that such wolves were in the midst of the human sheep had never occurred to the god Adam.

So Adam had brought all of them into his bosom. Ten thousand human beings carried the minds of the ancient Protean cult. Ten thousand humans who already had the knowledge of living centuries without a fixed fleshy form.

Unlike untold billions who found Adam's transformation paralyzing in its novelty, the Proteans were at home in Adam's environment. Some had lived within such a state longer than Adam had existed.

In his rage, first at the defiant Bakunin seven AU away from him, then at the monstrous appearance of Mosasa within his own mind, he paid no attention as the distribution of the minds within the *Voice* shifted around him. The first few microseconds, the chosen in proximity to him—the ones damaged or erased at his lashing out at Mosasa—were replaced by certain members of the chosen from Earth. In his battle with the phantom Mosasa, Adam did not pay attention as his consciousness flowed like water back toward his embodied self on the bridge of the *Voice*.

Adam showed no reaction to the Protean presence, until the body within the *Voice* began a physical separation. The continuous swarm of nanomachines that filled every space on the *Voice*—the structure, the wiring, the air itself—had been forcefully split into two groups. Adam's tenuous, almost autonomous, connection to the body of the ship had been forcefully cut.

"What is this?" Adam screamed. His voice resonated in the walls of the bridge, but no further. While his fully conscious incarnation realized that he was encapsulated on the bridge of the *Voice*, hundreds of Protean agents roamed the remaining environment of the *Voice* finding the semiconscious remnants of Adam's psyche that had been severed from their conscious direction.

On the bridge, Adam lashed out at his confinement. The bulkheads twisted, shedding electronic equipment as the metal superstructure began to flow and remake itself. Around Adam, the walls themselves formed into dozens of long segmented arms that tore into the bulkheads, ripping at the invisible barrier, trying to tear free into contact with the greater cloud infecting the *Voice*.

Somewhere, seven AUs away, Adam's tach-ship fleet winked into existence, completely unaware that Adam's incarnation on the *Voice* had been trapped.

The physical structure of the bridge tore itself apart, as if the room was having a psychotic tantrum. Matter threw itself against the walls, piercing the envelope Adam found himself in, but the cloud within the mass of the *Voice*, now a Protean cloud, withdrew from any physical contact with the matter piercing the bulkheads of the bridge.

A third cloud formed, a buffer between the bridge and the rest of the ship, a spherical presence invisibly englobing the bridge and Adam's incarnation. The invisible sphere was made with the minds of a thousand Proteans, a cabal of the first ones. The thousand had lived the longest; they had tread upon the surface of Titan before a terraforming accident consumed all life upon that moon and spawned the ban upon self-replicating nanomachines.

Each one of the thousand had been human long before a pirate named Mosasa found his derelict spacecraft and participated in Adam's birth. Each one of the thousand, if not for the Protean creed they had founded, could have become Adam themselves.

Adam screamed again. "What is this defiance? Who raises their hand against the living God?"

The bridge was no longer recognizable as a human construct. The mass that had formed the walls, the chairs, the holo displays, the air itself, had all coalesced into glowing streams of coherent matter whipping around, striking at the sphere englobing it. The only thing still recognizable was Adam himself. His body, naked and perfect, floated in the center of a perfect sphere of boiling chaos.

As Adam railed, the *Voice* itself fired a series of maneuvering jets, giving it a very slight vector down, away from the bridge. Above the bridge, bulkheads dissolved, leaving a hole large enough for the globe containing Adam to drift out into space.

The *Voice* increased its thrust, separating itself from the flickering irregular sphere containing Adam's wrath. Within, Adam's fury had begun to consume matter itself, the temperature increasing as the swirling mass became a barely controlled plasma. When Adam cursed them now, it was no longer in a human voice; there was no air for speech, and his human embodiment had begun to burn.

I shall destroy anyone who defies Me.

As one, the thousand responded, *We know.*

And then there was light.

CHAPTER EIGHTEEN

Holy Ghost

"If you shoot, shoot to kill."
      —*The Cynic's Book of Wisdom*

"We should regard all force with aversion."
      —WILLIAM GODWIN
       (1756–1836)

Date: 2526.8.10 (Standard)
Bakunin–BD+50°1725

"If you can do something," Kugara yelled. "Do it *now!*"

Kugara was barely three meters from them, popping around cover and snapping shots from the biggest handgun Flynn had ever seen.

"*Let me drive,*" Flynn called out inside his own head, grabbing Tetsami's attention as forcefully as possible.

"Sonny, you remember what happened the last time you did that in a firefight?" Tetsami didn't even try to subvocalize as they cowered behind an aircar. Alarms began sounding all around them. Tetsami muttered, "Fuck."

"*Damn it, Gram, do you want to get to a terminal or not?*"

"What are you—" A gunshot blew out a windshield, peppering them with clear polymer fragments.

"We don't have the time!" Flynn shouted, reaching the end of the sentence before he realized she had relinquished control back to him.

He sprang up from his crouch and dove for the contragrav van, putting it between him and the shooters. He heard shots slam into the side of the van, but he made it. He pulled open the cabin door and crawled inside. It took a moment to orient himself from ground level, but before the door swung shut behind him, he started charging the contragrav.

The whine of the generators was enough to draw more fire. Slugs blew holes in the thin skin of the craft, and the windshield shattered.

"Where the hell are you going in this thing?"

"Only thirty meters, Gram." He maxed out the generators so the bricklike vehicle achieved a negative buoyancy and started rising. Once they had risen ten meters or so, Flynn risked a look up. He figured his head was out of sight from shooters on the ground now.

Even so, he only popped up long enough to confirm his impression of the motor pool layout. At the rear, opposite the doors to the outside, was a workshop separated from the parking area only by a two-meter partition wall. He looked down inside the shop and saw it was unoccupied except for a pair of two-seater aircars. It looked as if someone had been cannibalizing the parts from one to maintain the other.

What drew Flynn's eye, past the diagnostic equipment and cabinets of tools, was a rolling cart with a comm unit on it, covered in a protective plastic tarp.

Good enough.

He ducked down, goosed the jets to give some forward momentum, and cut the contragrav power by 58%.

Cut to about a third of its mass below neutral buoyancy, their brick obligingly plunged in a slow-motion parabola to nose into the far wall of the motor pool a bit less than three meters above the ground.

The impact slammed him into the footwell, but he recovered to jump out the door.

Inside his head, he heard Gram's voice shouting the words *"Jesus. Fuck."* Over and over again.

As he rolled across the oil-stained ferrocrete floor, he thought at her, *"Get ready to do your thing!"*

He came to a stop under the more gutted of the two aircars.

Behind him, holes peppered the partition wall, and some energy weapon blew a burning chunk out of it close to where the contragrav van continued its slow descent, crushing tables, rolling carts of tools, and grinding a massive hole in the wall with a screeching of abused metal that threatened to upstage the alarm system.

He crawled along behind the aircar back into the corner with the comm unit. He reached up and yanked the plastic sheeting from it and said, "Now, Gram!"

He mentally withdrew, and felt her pick up the slack as she pulled the main comm off the cart. Bullets slammed into the aircar bodies behind them. She muttered something about interface cables, pulling a mess of cable out of their pocket. The object was like a multicolored octopus with too many legs, cables of various colors and thicknesses led into a hard ball of emergency repair tape. The kludgy object had followed them from the *Daedalus*, custom-made by Tetsami. One black optical cable, about a meter long, led back to a small magnetic socket that fit into the dimple in the base of their neck. That had come from a security camera back on Salmagundi. The rest of the device was made from salvaged cables that Tetsami had picked up from the *Khalid* and the *Daedalus*. The homemade adapter was necessary for her to use her skills with a neural interface whose specs were two hundred years out of date.

Tetsami found the right port on the comm and plugged in a short lime-green cable. Two little lights embedded in the knot of tape shone green up at her. Flynn felt her smile as she took the black cable and attached it to the port on their neck. Flynn felt the click of the connection in the bones of their jaw.

Flynn braced himself mentally as his view of the world dropped away.

The two of them shared the same sensory input, so when Tetsami dropped into a software interface, he dropped along with her.

The world went black and silent, and he knew from experience that it meant that whatever Tetsami had jacked into had no actual interface for someone using it like this. The void only lasted a moment. Tetsami walked across the face of the deep and pulled existence out of nothingness. A blue field, an infinite plain, emerged from the dark, covered by geometric forms in every color that Flynn could imagine. Glowing trails sprouted between the shapes, arcing and looping in a three-dimensional tangle.

Flynn knew that she was designing a user interface on the fly, and he was somehow seeing the network this comm was connected to.

Then, he felt Tetsami using their hands, or some analog of their hands, to start picking up the shapes, twisting them, manipulating them, pulling conduits from one and plugging into another. Soon, her individual actions were indistinguishable as shapes and lines sped by too fast for him to absorb. He was left with a staccato sequence of machine-gun impressions.

Embedded in the abstract movement of shape and line, he caught flashes of the outside world: Kugara firing her massive cannon at the closing gunmen; twenty armed men charging the entrance of the motor pool; people in some sort of control room yelling commands; a warehouse with workers abandoning crates of weapons to run toward the exits; Nickolai standing, fur matted with blood from a shallow wound in his side, holding a gory length of chain, five men face-down on the pavement in front of him.

Over all of this, his ears remained in the real world, hearing gunshots and sirens.

Tetsami's voice came to him, almost too fast to understand, "*holyshitgetouttotherealworldnowdamnitnow*"

He felt a mental push and the virtual world tumbled away, and he found himself blinking and looking at the underside of the motor pool's ceiling. "*keepmepluggedingodhelpuskeepmepluggedin*"

He blinked and reached behind his neck, feeling the cable still firmly plugged in. Above him, something blew through the partition wall, sending burning debris raining down on him. He raised his arms to protect his face.

"*damnitsonnymoveyourasshescomingaroundtheaircargrabaweaponnowmoveitnow*"

Flynn sat up and grabbed a large wrench, just as a man with a gun rounded the corner of the aircar. He was lucky because the guy was focused on eye level. He swung the wrench overhand to land in the guy's crotch. The man doubled over. Before he recovered, Flynn cocked back and brought it down on the guy's unprotected head.

Holy . . . did I just kill someone?

"grabthegungrabthegun"

Flynn reached and felt a tug on the back of his neck, and he clamped his left hand there to keep the cable in place. He stretched again, and heard the comm unit scraping on the ground.

"dontunpuguspleasedontunplugus"

The siren cut out, and somewhere near the front of the motor pool, something mechanical started grinding.

His fingers brushed the handle of the fallen gun just as someone else stepped through the hole blown in the partition wall. He grabbed the butt and scrambled back around the side of the aircar as a bullet whizzed by, striking sparks and shrapnel off the ferrocrete floor, close enough to draw blood from his cheek.

Flynn raised the gun as the figure came around the corner.

They fired almost simultaneously.

"FLYNN!"

The gunshots echoed through the suddenly quiet garage, and Flynn's attacker fell to the ground with a large-caliber hole disfiguring most of his face. Flynn's wrists ached from the recoil.

"I'm fine, Gram."

He wasn't. He knew that as soon as he took a breath to speak. Something hard and painful squeezed his gut. He looked down and shook his head. "We'll be fine, Gram," he lied. "Keep up what you're doing."

His abdomen was scarlet, deepening to black where a crater formed above his left hip. He balled his left hand into a fist and shoved it against the wound.

"fuckfuckfuckfuck"

"Get a grip and finish the job," Flynn whispered. *We knew this was a one-way trip anyway.*

Flynn raised his knee so he could brace the gun one-handed, and waited for the next attacker.

We are so fucked.

Kugara risked a look out from the cover of a bullet-riddled aircar and saw a group of guards charging the entrance of the motor pool. The brief glimpse she got told her that the new guys were actual security personnel, with body armor and guns with more than seven shots in them.

At least one of them had a powerful energy weapon, because as soon as she moved back behind the aircar, its paint bubbled and the interior burst into flame.

She dodged and ran down an aisle of vehicles, away from the burning aircar. Three cars away from the fire, she saw one of the guards ducking around the end of a six-wheeled earthmover. He led with his gun, but the angle wasn't directly on her, and before he brought it in line, she swung her massive fifty-cal hand cannon down, pistol-whipping the guy's wrists where there was a gap in his armor. The laser carbine fell from his hands, but the strap was still wrapped around his upper arm.

She didn't know what backup he had behind him, so she grabbed the strap with her left hand, pulling him forward to bring his exposed face down on her knee. She leveled her gun across the guy's back with her right hand as the next guy came around the back of the earthmover.

She fired the last bullet she had into that guy's face.

She backed up, tossing aside the empty weapon as she untangled the laser carbine from guard number one. She had to knee him again, in the side of the temple, to get him to stop fighting her. When the carbine came free, she took it and jumped into the cab of the earthmover. Just as she dove inside, a trio of guards came around to back up their two fallen comrades.

At least the sirens had stopped.

She dove out the other side of the earthmover as the guards started peppering the cab with laser and gunfire. She hit the ground on the other side and brought the carbine up while she was still prone. She faced the main door, which was rolling shut with a grinding noise.

At first she thought they were sealing them in here, but she saw five or six of the guards outside, trying to hold the thing up with their hands. As she watched, two of the men lost their grip and the door slammed to the ground.

No one was in front of her, so she rolled on her back as she thumbed the controls to max the power and the aperture of her commandeered carbine. She swept the carbine around to cover the aisle behind her just as one of the guards looked around the other end of the earthmover. The man ducked behind the cover before she could draw a bead on him, so instead she focused on a nearby passenger aircar, aiming through the windshield and into the cabin. She held the pulse on for a full second, long enough for the window to turn rainbow colors and warp before the plastic padded interior flashed over, blowing out the half-melted window in a belch of black smoke that would have to do for cover.

She rolled over, under the next aisle of parked vehicles. She no longer had any idea how many guards she was dealing with, or where they were. She rolled out from under the vehicle and found herself up against the wall of the motor pool.

She flattened her back against the wall and cast glances up and down the line of vehicles, and the only sign of the home team was the upturned card table by the front door.

She crouched and ran in the other direction, heading toward the rear where the mechanics shop was, and where Flynn had crashed the contragrav.

I hope one of him knew what he was doing.

She heard more gunshots as she ran, none anywhere near her. Above her, the ceiling had nearly disappeared behind toxic black smoke. Whatever fire-control measures the building had were unresponsive, even with two vehicle fires going.

Was he able to disable that? Along with the door and the alarm?

She reached the partition wall and looked down along it. The half on the other side of the garage had been severely damaged, first by the contragrav van blowing through part of it, then by several hits by energy weapons more potent than the carbine she held.

A gunshot came from that end of the garage, from behind the van and a couple of disabled aircars. She could barely see past the wreckage of the wall.

In response, she saw a white flash from a focused plasma weapon. Unlike most lasers, this was very visible and left an afterimage on her retinas. The burst tore through another chunk of the partition wall and washed against the van and the nearer of the two aircars. Both burst into flame.

If Flynn was still back there, another shot like that would probably take out whatever cover he was using. She needed to neutralize the guy with the plasma weapon. She needed the high ground.

She leaped up on the back of a small flatbed truck, then, from there, climbed up on the cab. A quick survey showed her nothing, so she jumped the two meters from the top of the cab to the undamaged part of the partition wall. Her wounded foot objected, and she almost fell off, but she steadied herself. In a balanced crouch on top of the wall, she swung the carbine around. The plasma guy obligingly revealed himself by firing at the truck she had just vacated.

She blinked the afterimage from her eyes, and fired a swath down on his position, pulsing the beam until, almost by luck, it clipped his weapons containment cell in the midst of charging. The plasma sniper disappeared in a flash of blinding white fire that consumed the five vehicles nearest him.

She looked around the motor pool, and it seemed now that half the building was on fire. Columns of black smoke billowed to the ceiling, and the shroud covering the ceiling had descended to just above her head.

She didn't see any hostile movement.

She jumped down from the wall and limped around to the other side of the garage, past the burning van and aircar. She stepped over four guards to get to Flynn. "Are you all right?"

He groaned, and his leg slid down, revealing the wound in his gut.

Oh, shit.

"Found our subway," he muttered.

"Got to get you out of here," she said, setting down the carbine.

Flynn waved his hand and said, weakly, "No."

"What? You're shot."

"Gram's working," he slurred.

Kugara only then noticed the cable leading from a small comm unit to the back of Flynn's skull. "Jack out, then. There're still who knows how many armed assholes crawling around here. It's not—"

"Four."

"What?"

"Four left, and they're headed out the fire exits."

"And the place is burning dow—" Kugara was interrupted by the sprinklers coming on full blast everywhere but their little corner of the garage.

"Get the others," Flynn said. "Gram's getting you out of here."

CHAPTER NINETEEN

Underworld

"Live each day as your last, remembering that it might not be."

—The Cynic's Book of Wisdom

"None meet life honestly, and few heroically."

—CLARENCE S. DARROW
(1857–1938)

Date: 2526.8.10 (Standard)
Bakunin–BD+50°1725

Nickolai operated on the assumption that the rest of his party was in the direction of the most chaos. Ever since the sirens began sounding, he'd headed toward the sound of gunfire. While he tried to keep to cover, twenty people had attempted to get between him and his objective. Only one had managed to do more than slow down his progress. The man had stabbed him in the side while he'd been concentrating on two others armed with guns.

The sirens had since ended, and he barely thought about the shallow wound across the left side of his rib cage. His chain, now tacky with blood and hair, was wrapped diagonally across his chest, providing impromptu storage for five pistols he had liberated. A sixth and a seventh, a gamma laser and a slugthrower, he carried in his hands.

The last three people he had come across had taken one look at him, seen his snarl, and had run the other way.

He should be making his own way to the subway. Their mission was to get to the Dolbrian sites in the mountains. But he didn't know what use he would be alone. It was the scientists who might be able to figure out what the Protean had been directing them toward. He was to get them there, not to go there himself.

More importantly, he was not going to leave Kugara here with a trio of humans who were useless in a fight.

He stopped across a large courtyard from the obvious site of the gunshots. A massive garage sat off to one side of the compound. A group of twenty or thirty armed men surrounded it, backed up by three armored security vehicles.

Smoke billowed up from the building's roof and out a few open windows. Nickolai squeezed the butts of his two undersized weapons until his knuckles cracked.

If he charged, he could probably kill or disable six of them before he was in hand-to-hand range. Then three more, before someone put a shot through his skull. He might risk charging eight or ten, in a desperate situation. Not thirty.

Not without a few grenades anyway.

He was still pondering his options when a four-story-tall rolling crane gantry moved into view. It rolled slowly on two sets of three wide tracks, each one as big as a good-sized van. The crane itself, suspended above everything on its skeletal legs, was lowering a massive claw as it moved.

The first tracked foot passed Nickolai, giving him cover from the guards surrounding the burning building. He ran forward, shoving the slugthrower into his chain bandolier, and grabbed one of the massive metal treads as it moved up the back of the leading foot, pulling him up on top of the massive track.

As the tread made its slow progress up and over the rolling track, Nickolai hooked the claws of his feet into a lower tread and sprang up into the superstructure supporting the gantry.

When he was secure, he swept the gamma laser to cover any guards who might have seen him climb aboard. No one was paying attention to him. They were running away.

With good reason. The gantry was headed right toward

them, and the building they surrounded. The foot below Nickolai pitched up as it rolled over one of the security vehicles, crushing it. The gantry kept moving forward, turning very slowly until another security vehicle was straddled between its two sets of legs. Nickolai watched as the vehicle's occupants piled out the doors in a panic, just before the massive claw under the gantry went into free fall, slamming the vehicle into the ground.

Nickolai prepared to jump from his perch before the machine started rolling through the building, but the gantry stopped short of the structure. Whatever was happening, the machine was not out of control. He looked up, but there didn't seem to be any obvious control cabin—it was probably automated . . .

"Nickolai!"

He looked down and saw Kugara. He didn't realize how tense he had been until he saw her, and some deep part of his psyche relaxed its grip. As this point, death didn't concern him so much as did facing it without her.

Nickolai jumped to the ground between the gantry's legs as Kugara emerged from the smoke-filled building. As she approached him, he saw that the scientists followed her. Between them, they carried a pale, wounded Flynn.

"What happened?" he asked.

"Bastard was shot," Kugara said. "What's your better hand?"

"Right—"

"Grab his right leg, then."

She had been leading, carrying both Flynn's ankles. Nickolai reached down and took Flynn's leg in his left hand, keeping the gamma laser in his right. "I can carry both," he said.

Kugara looked at him, and then at Flynn's foot dwarfed by Nickolai's grip. "Forgot how big your hands are. Here, don't drop him, he's driving."

Nickolai took a grip around both Flynn's ankles, tucking them against his hip. He glanced back and saw the two scientists holding Flynn's shoulders. Flynn looked unconscious. His torso was stripped naked, and the contents of some first-aid kit had been sprayed on his abdomen, and the spray bandage was already turning rust-colored at the edges.

He's driving?

A black comm unit sat on his chest, one end of a rat's nest of cables plugged into it. Another cable snaked from the tangle to go around Flynn's neck.

She couldn't mean—

The gantry started moving.

"Come on," Kugara told him, running ahead to the forward moving part of the gantry and unslinging a laser carbine.

Progress was nerve-rackingly slow, the gantry never moved faster than a walking pace—a walking pace for someone with a stride considerably shorter than Nickolai's. He felt as if he strode through molasses.

At least the guards had decided that they had enough. No one came after them while they walked underneath the lumbering gantry.

After what seemed to be an eternity, the gantry came to a stop and Kugara looked back at him and said, "We're here."

They walked up next to her and saw that the gantry had crunched to a stop about fifteen meters shy of crushing a small outbuilding. The single door on the structure had a sign reading, *"Maintenance Access. Authorized Personnel Only."*

"That's our way down."

"How do you—"

As if in response to Nickolai's half-spoken question, the door popped open with a pneumatic hiss.

"Move it," Kugara said, running across the open space to the cover of the door. Nickolai followed, slowly, so that the scientists could keep up. The back of his neck practically burned with how exposed he was. He watched Kugara swing her carbine from inside the doorway providing covering fire that was only visible as infrared trails of superheated air. They didn't take any return fire.

Nickolai crouched through the doorway, and a second later he heard the door hiss shut behind them. They were in a large storeroom, filled with tools and spare parts piled on shelves lining the walls. A cylindrical elevator shaft dominated the far end of the room. As he watched, the elevator dinged, and the doors slid open.

Nickolai leveled the gamma laser at it, but the elevator was empty. He glanced back around at Flynn, who was still semiconscious and groaning.

Next to him, Kugara said, "His Tetsami alter ego is still wired into the network here." She reached out and touched Nickolai's chest. He looked down at her as she said, "Carbine's drained. I need to raid your arsenal." She pulled one of the other gamma lasers from his improvised bandolier. "Let's get moving." She gestured to the elevator.

The elevator took them down four sublevels and let them out into another storeroom. They put down Flynn, and Nickolai handed Dörner and Brody the last two lasers he carried.

Dörner looked up at him and said, "Why are you giving me this?"

"Because you probably can't handle the recoil of this," he said, taking out one of the slugthrowers.

He joined Kugara by the door to the storeroom. It opened a crack, and Nickolai could see out on to a subway platform crowded with people, about half heavily armed. He counted at least fifty in his line of sight.

"So what's the plan now?" he asked.

Before Kugara could answer, an electronic voice echoed across the platform. "*I'm in control here, so nobody fucking move!*"

There was a metallic screech from out of their line of sight from the storeroom. He could hear someone out there groaning in pain. The echoing PA system said, "*That was so not a good idea. Get the hell away from those controls.*"

"What the hell?" Kugara whispered.

Inside the room, a speaker above them said, "*Okay, chicky. You and the tiger better clear them out.*"

"Tetsami?" Kugara whispered.

"*Christ in a sidecar, who do you think? Move it, you think this is easy for me?*"

Nickolai cast a glance back at Flynn as Kugara pushed her way through the door. She yelled to the mass of people,

"Okay, everyone, toss weapons on the ground and move yourself out the nearest exit. Now!"

Nickolai followed and found himself on a long wide platform in a massive arched chamber. A maglev train sat on one of two sets of tracks, the front end smoking slightly with the smell of overheated ceramics. The driver was backing away from the controls as if they had just bit him.

Nickolai stood behind Kugara and growled.

Over the PA, Tetsami called out like the voice of God. *"You heard her. Drop the guns and move it. You do not want to piss off her friend."*

The mass of people moved toward the exits, away from him and Kugara. Only about half tossed weapons down, but Nickolai didn't much care about the others as long as they didn't choose to level their weapons in their direction.

In less than a minute the platform was empty, and he heard doors sliding shut, sealing them off.

Next to them, the train stood on the track, doors open.

Kugara turned to him and said, "Get Flynn."

The maglev smoothly accelerated and slid into a tunnel aimed deep at the heart of the Diderot Mountains. Flynn took up one of the passenger benches, the bandage on his gut now mostly dark with blood. Kugara and Dörner had found a first-aid kit by the driver's compartment and were trying to improve on the wound's dressing.

Nickolai wrinkled his nose because Flynn had already started smelling of death.

Kugara reached to peel away the old bandage, and Flynn grabbed her hand. "No time," Flynn groaned.

"Lay back," she said, "we're on the way to the mountain. We need to stop the bleeding."

He shook his head. "No time. Gram did what she could, but we're cut off from the network." With a shaking hand, he reached up and pulled the socket out of the base of his skull. "We're out of range of where this thing works."

"The train," Dörner said, "it's still moving?"

"Autonomous." He pulled himself into a near sitting position to lean against the window. "We only have five minutes."

"Five minutes for what?" Nickolai asked.

Flynn looked up at him and smiled, his teeth glistening red from his own blood. "Your stop."

Flynn had them carry him to the controls at the front of the train. Nickolai listened as Flynn told them, haltingly, that Tetsami had managed to penetrate far enough to see that Bleek Munitions' HQ in the mountains was very aware of the attack on their facility, and they had been ramping up their security since it started. And unlike the facility they had just left, the security in the mountain consisted of a unit of PSDC military.

There was no way through at the end of the line.

However, the train flew through caverns only slightly modified from the lava tubes that Tetsami remembered. While in Bleek's network, she had been able to pull a full map of the known tunnels, and there were several places where the tunnels intersected with the subway.

Flynn sat at the controls, doing something to override the computers piloting the train. Then he leaned against the wall and whispered to himself. Nickolai barely heard the words, "Ten. Nine. Eight . . ."

At three, Flynn pulled the emergency stop and the train screeched to a halt. "We're here," he said.

"Okay," Kugara said, "Nickolai, get his feet."

"No," Flynn said, shrugging away from Kugara's reach.

"What do you mean, 'no'?" she said.

"I'm too injured," he said. "I'll slow you down, and bouncing me around isn't going to help what life I got left. Without me, you'll have half a chance."

Kugara shook her head as Nickolai gently pulled her away from Flynn.

Flynn said, "Look, wherever you're going, I'm not making it there like this. At least, driving this thing, I can make you harder to follow."

Whatever Nickolai's faith might believe of Flynn, or the transgressions his people had made, Flynn had been a worthy ally. He had the soul of a warrior. Nickolai placed his right hand gently against Flynn's bandaged wound and breathed in the scent of blood. He whispered, "May the spirit of Saint Rajasthan join you in your final battle."

The blessing felt blasphemous spoken in the tongue of the Fallen, but Flynn deserved to hear it. Flynn looked up at them and said, "Go on, move it!"

When Flynn was alone on the train, he shut the doors and started it moving again.

"Just you and me, Gram."

He heard a sniff and looked next to him and saw Tetsami's effigy standing there right where the tiger had been. Her cheeks were wet, and she was semitranslucent, as if she was leaving the land of the living before him.

"Don't cry."

"I'm not crying," she said, his own burning eyes making her a liar.

"We had a hell of a ride."

"Yeah," she said.

"Ever wanted to see how fast something like this can go?"

He reached up and started turning off parts of the train's navigation system. Turning off collision avoidance sensors, and the computer that held the train under a safely controllable speed.

The velocity sensor started cranking upward, and the tunnel lights began shooting by impossibly fast, becoming a blurred streak in the windscreen.

The frictionless maglev only gave a slight pressure of acceleration as it climbed toward double the velocity it was rated for. The only sound it made was air ripping by outside, muffled through the train's skin.

"I always thought I'd die on this hellhole," she said.

"If I could, Gram, I would have sent you off with the others."

The velocity peaked, hovering around eight hundred klicks an hour. At this rate, in thirty seconds the train should slam into the station like a bullet. Fast enough that he probably wouldn't even be aware of the collision.

"If Adam came now," Tetsami said, "I think I'd say yes."

"Gram?"

"My last resurrection went pretty well," she said, "and I don't want you to di—"

A violent rhythmic thudding interrupted her, as the train suddenly started trying to shake itself apart.

"What the hell?" Flynn shouted at the console. It was vibrating too hard to make out clearly, but the velocity meter was racing backward. The accelerator was on full, but the train was still slowing down.

"Damn it, they figured out some way to slow us down."

It took a second for him to realize what had happened. The HQ always had, as a last resort, the ability to shut down the track. If they nuked the magnets holding this beast up, the train would stop—but at the speed it was going, it would stop catastrophically, probably taking out a good part of the tunnel with it.

Instead, someone had the bright idea of shutting off every *other* magnet in the track. Not enough to have the train fatally kiss the ground, but enough to slow it down violently.

"Shit!" Flynn called out, the train forcing his voice into a vibrato and trying to shake his intestines out the wound in his belly. The velocity dropped under a hundred klicks an hour, and the shaking got worse, and now it sounded as if a massive hammer was trying to pound the underside of the train apart.

Now only every third magnet is powered, Flynn thought, holding on to the bench with a death grip. His heart pounded, as the fear gripped him. They had dropped far below the speed of instant death. At seventy-five klicks an hour, there was a good chance that he'd live through a collision at least long enough to feel it.

But whoever was playing the track knew what they were doing. The train slowed to little over twenty klicks per, and it finally ground itself to a halt, sliding into the station with a hideous screech and a shower of sparks.

Through the windows he saw a welcoming committee of about twenty guys in powered armor.

He sucked in a painful breath, amazed that he was still alive, and said, "It may disappoint the tiger, but I'm leaning toward surrender."

CHAPTER TWENTY

Anathema

"Hell grows out of a desire for Utopia."
> —*The Cynic's Book of Wisdom*

"Fear is pain arising from the anticipation of evil."
> —Aristotle
> (384 bce–322 bce)

Date: 2526.8.10 (Standard)
350,000 km from Bakunin–BD+50°1725

Mallory and the other commanders watched the main holo on board the *Wisconsin*. Across the holo, a galaxy of blue showed the largest fleet ever formed by man. The adversary only had fifty ships.

Only fifty.

But as Mallory watched blue lights blink out, he began to wonder if the numerical advantage mattered. The battles were akin to watching a squad of Occisis Marines go up against an army of UN peacekeepers from the 21st century. The red dots showed some attrition, but not nearly enough.

A flash obliterated a red dot, and the Indi commanders said something to each other in Mandarin. Tito said quietly, "We got one."

Mallory nodded gravely. Adam was down to thirty-eight ships, but at a cost of over two hundred of theirs. Those losses were barely sustainable, and of a magnitude to make him pray that he hadn't chosen the wrong path.

At the control console, the other Valentine said, "Oh, no."

Her sister said, "What is it?" before Mallory got the question out himself.

"The *Othello* just wiped out three merchantmen attached to the *Adam Smith*."

"What the hell?" Tito snapped at the mention of the *Adam Smith*. It was the largest and most heavily armed of the Bakunin native fleet. The *Othello* was part of the SEC forces, a dreadnought that was one of the more sophisticated military vessels in the fleet. He turned toward General Lafayette and said, "Do you train your people?"

"It must be some mistake—"

"Damn right it is! Three ships to friendly fire. *Three?*"

"Eight," Valentine said. "The *Othello* has claimed eight ships now, including the *Adam Smith*."

Both Tito and General Lafayette were stunned into silence.

"The *Othello* is compromised!" Mallory shouted. "It's part of Adam's fleet now! Concentrate fire on it!"

Valentine passed on the orders, but color drained from her face as she did. She shook her head and started reading off the names of ships, "*Sun Tzu, Liverpool, Ulysses, Mjöllnir, Lincoln, Shiva*—damn it, we've got dozens of ships suddenly turning on our own fleet."

It's like fighting a virus. "Same rules of engagement as Adam's fleet. One of ours starts attacking, give it a wide berth and concentrate fire."

Valentine typed at the console, and suddenly the lonely red dots in the midst of their fleet were joined by another twenty yellow ones.

Now there were over fifty enemy ships to contend with, and the losses were no longer sustainable. He heard muttering from the command next to him and realized that they had come to the same conclusion.

"We need to stage a retreat to regroup." Tito said.

"We'll be slaughtered like this," General Lafayette said. "We need to disperse our forces."

One of the Indi commanders asked, "Can we reprise the attack you made on the cloud?"

"No," Mallory said, "That was a static target, and we had time to synchronize hundreds of tach computers. We don't have a known fixed target, or time. But we do need to retreat to buy time." He addressed Lieutenant Valentine. "Every ship that has a charged tach-drive, jump at their own discretion off the ecliptic and away from Bakunin."

"It's too dangerous to use tach-drives tactically like that," General Lafayette said.

"It's all we have," Mallory shook his head.

After a few minutes of tense silence, Lieutenant Valentine said, "We have tach-pulses from our ships." On the holo, blue dots began winking out. "Several ships have their drives disabled. We've lost the *Independence.*"

"We need a strategy to segregate Adam's ships," Mallory said. "They're vulnerable in isolation."

"We're getting stronger tach-pulses . . ." On the holo, the remaining red dots began winking out, leaving the yellow, infected ships behind.

"They're retreating?" Tito asked.

Mallory realized that the Caliphate ships had drives an order of magnitude faster than any his fleet had. They were following the retreating ships' trajectories—and they would be there waiting, crucial seconds before the slower ships fell out of tach-space; thirty-eight red dots, facing the refugee fleet one-on-one.

He had just signed the death warrants for thirty-eight more ships.

But their fleet was spreading out, less of a target. It was the right order for the vast majority of their forces . . .

God help them all.

"I have a ship headed for the *Wisconsin.*"

"Ours or theirs?" Mallory asked.

"A single unarmed luxury passenger ship. Transponder IDs it as *Xanadu.*"

General Lafayette said, "It's the ship that bastard stole after his attempted coup—"

"Warn him off," Mallory said.

"Warn?" General Lafayette sputtered. "Shoot him down."

Mallory glared at the general. "Warn him off, and if he doesn't change course, *then* shoot him down."

A smaller holo popped up, showing the approaching craft. Telemetry data sped by below, enough for Captain Valentine to say, "That's not a docking vector, and he's still accelerating."

Lieutenant Valentine said, "He's not responsive."

Mallory shook his head, "Shoot him."

The being that had been Stefan Stavros watched as the *Wisconsin*'s defenses locked onto the *Xanadu*. Even a nominally peaceful entity like the *Wisconsin,* in the lawless sphere of Bakunin, had an impressive array of defensive measures. Any attacker that came toward one of the habitats would face arrays of missiles, and energy weapons ranging from chaotic frequency lasers that would tax any ship's Emerson field to pulses of coherent plasma that contained enough energy to render many such fields irrelevant.

The *Xanadu* was rocketing down the *Wisconsin*'s axis of rotation, and facing one of the more intimidating defenses. The *Wisconsin*'s linac accelerated its mundane iron-nickel projectiles along its two-kilometer length before directing them out a cannon along its axis.

Stefan grinned as the linac discharged a tight grouping of shots, balls of metal smaller than the tip of his finger, but tearing through space at a speed near a third of light-speed. A dozen iron marbles spread out in a circle about thirty meters across, intersecting the *Xanadu's* path.

Only one of them hit.

That was enough. The kinetic energy of that small projectile was enough to vaporize it and about fifty cubic meters of the *Xanadu* instantaneously. The stress of the impact caused a massive failure of the structure, the ship fragmenting along its length, its hull buckling, and the engines—losing the containment for their reaction chamber—erupted into a fiery ball.

In less than a microsecond, the *Xanadu* had been transformed into a cloud of wreckage made of boiling gases and fragments not much bigger than the linac bullet that had hit it.

Stefan no longer had a face to smile with.

If he had, he would have grinned harder.

He no longer inhabited a body. His flesh had only been a vessel, much like the *Xanadu* had been. His identity now lived in a complex matrix of microscopic machines that had permeated the matter of the *Xanadu*. Adam's machines were as hardy as bacteria, and the linac attack had only sterilized a fraction of those machines where Stefan's identity lived.

As the cloud moved, only slightly deviated from the *Xanadu*'s original vector, the small chunks of solid matter within it dissolved. Stefan consumed them, transforming the wreckage into more of the cloud containing him. Less than two seconds from the destruction of the *Xanadu*, all that was left was an undifferentiated cloud of matter.

Matter that was almost entirely Stefan.

On the holo, the approaching ship disintegrated after a single salvo; vaporizing into a cloud of wreckage that glowed briefly before turning completely dark. Mallory stared at it with unease, sensing an ugly familiarity in what he was seeing.

"Is anything going to hit the *Wisconsin?*" he asked Lieutenant Valentine.

"We're not picking up any solid mass left, the ship entirely vaporized. It's going to blow right by us."

"Damn," Tito said, "Lucky shot—"

"No," Mallory said, "That cloud, what's left, is that going to hit the *Wisconsin?*"

"It's on the same trajectory, more or less. It will brush the Gamma hab—"

"Evacuate the Gamma habitat now!" Mallory shouted. "And fire everything you can into that cloud!"

With the alien sense of the cloud, Stefan saw the *Wisconsin* resume its attack upon him. It was too little, too late. Projectiles and lasers penetrated through his unsolid mass, and while the plasma weapons burned away some of himself, his cloud was moving so fast that, by the time they were in range to do damage, he was already touching the *Wisconsin*.

The tiny machines that made up the whole of Stefan

Stavros struck the surface of the rotating Gamma habitat, remaking themselves into something more cohesive; a liquid condensate forming on a hundred-meter stretch of the great windows facing the core. Below the condensate, thread-fine holes burrowed through meters of insulated and armored plastic, glass, and polymer. Millions of holes drilled down from vacuum to air, none much wider than the individual nanomachines.

Beneath, on the underside of the great blue-tinted windows, the view darkened, the surface clouding as Kropotkin's reflected light was further refracted by Stefan's entrance. The white clouds embedded in the window's surface darkened as if they were actual storm clouds.

And like a storm cloud, there was, eventually, rain.

This rain, however, was solid black, and where it fell, matter melted and pooled, becoming more of itself. Beneath the storm, people ran toward the elevators to the core, but some were unlucky enough to find themselves beneath Stefan's rain. People screamed as the black drops scalded their skin and burrowed inside their flesh, mechanically disassembling them on a molecular level, until their bodies lost cohesion and they fell on the already black ground, skin bursting apart to spill more black liquid onto the pulsing ground.

At the center of the chaos, a pillar formed, the matter reassembling itself into a copy of Stefan Stavros. In a human body again, Stefan looked around with human eyes, amazed at what he was wreaking.

For a hundred meters in every direction, the living, moving shadow that was him, had claimed the surface of the habitat. The edge of his influence pushed itself outward, to the base of one of the gaudy tourist hotels. Stefan's darkness climbed up the edges, to embrace the building, pull its matter into itself. Stefan poured himself through the doors and windows, consuming the structure until its own mass pulled it down, crushing itself and the people still trapped within.

Stefan's blackness crashed over the mound of debris in a wave, covering it, flattening it, digesting it.

So this is what a God feels like, Stefan thought.

His fury was immeasurable. Not only had the priest played with all their lives, risking everyone in a futile war against Adam, but Mallory had also conspired to deny him *this*.

The priest, and all who followed him, deserved the unmerciful hand of judgment. His minions would die, and the priest himself would be torn apart.

As Stefan's anger grew, the mass around him became more agitated, growing tentacles and feelers that whipped by, cracking like whips, smashing into themselves and their surroundings. He walked forward, to the edge of his circle of influence, and past it, leading ten thousand square meters of boiling chaos like a cape behind him.

He spread his arms and looked up toward the artificial heaven, and the core beyond the false tint of the sky. "I'm coming for you, Mallory!"

On the command holo, they watched Stefan raise his arms, as behind him the Gamma habitat dissolved into a barely coherent mass of undifferentiated movement.

Toni II watched the chaos at her console and muttered, "That evil little bastard."

"How do we fight something like that?" said one of the fleet commanders behind her.

"First, we get people out of the way," Mallory said. "Evacuate the *Wisconsin*."

"You're going to abandon—"

"Yes, because, by the grace of God we have that chance." Mallory leaned over her and pointed at the holo. "This isn't Adam, and he doesn't know what he is doing. Adam takes things over, subverts them. Even when he was destroying Khamsin and Salmagundi, he was building as much as he was tearing down."

"This is an attack," the general said. "There wasn't even the pretense of offering conversion."

"I know, and if this was Adam himself, he would be in control of all the systems on this platform before manifesting like that." Mallory asked Toni, "How long before we can evacuate everybody?"

She swallowed and found her mouth painfully dry as she

spoke. "I don't know if we can. The Alpha habitat is packed with refugees. The elevators can only handle so much traffic to the core." *The poor bastards in Gamma are already piled twenty deep around them,* she thought.

Mallory turned to Toni the younger. Toni II took one look at her own face looking back at her and realized that her sister felt the same drag of guilt that she did. It was their fault, however inadvertently, for bringing Stefan Stavros here. Their act of piracy on the *Daedalus* had, in large part, created this monster they faced.

"Captain," Mallory said, "can you go to the docks and make sure that there's an orderly evacuation, and make sure none of those ships leaves half empty?"

"Yes."

"And get the command off on the first ship out." He waved at the others, the nominal leaders of their massive disintegrating fleet. "They'll need to establish command and control somewhere else."

"What about—"

"I'm staying. I'm praying my presence will keep Stefan focused here and give everyone a chance to escape."

Her sister nodded and snapped at the others, "Come on, let's move it."

They left Toni II and Mallory alone in the control center. On the holo, it looked as if Stefan had taken over a full quarter of the Gamma habitat. He was approaching the first axis elevator.

"Where's his father?" Mallory asked her.

"I don't know. But I think he's down there, somewhere."

CHAPTER TWENTY-ONE

Heavenly Host

"Do not underestimate anyone's capacity for irrational hatred."

—*The Cynic's Book of* Wisdom

"God is a sadist."

—ROBERT CELINE
(1923–1996)

Date: 2526.8.10 (Standard)
350,000 km from Bakunin–BD+50°1725

Karl Stavros walked away from the hotel that had served as the diplomatic center of Mallory's war against Adam. The structure was abandoned now, emptied by people fleeing to one of the main elevators up to the core. Karl knew the math, and suffered no illusions that he might make it to the core and an outbound ship.

From where he was, he could see what they were all running from. Looking down Gamma's axis, he could see a stain, as if someone had spilled ink across the whole of that end of the habitat; ink that moved, pouring toward him.

Refugees and guards alike ran away from it, past him.

He watched as the threads of darkness wrapped themselves around the vast glassy pillar that was the aftmost elevator. He could see thorough the windows enclosing it, into the elevator cabin and the tiny figures of way too many people inside. The darkness formed a chaotic helix around the shaft, and as he watched, the material shattered, an implosion of vaporized plastic disintegrating into boiling white clouds. Only a second later he heard the sound of it, the sound of a mechanical giant screaming in agony. Then, he saw the elevator cabin tumbling downward to disappear into a writhing mass of black threads and smoke. Even over the cacophony of the shaft falling apart, he thought he could hear the people scream.

He walked toward the destruction because he had heard the monster's voice.

How can he do this?

He was through the crowd now. Everyone who had managed to run from the spectacle before him was now behind him. The air had become cloudy from the collapse of the elevator shaft, the toxic smoke made his eyes water, his skin itch, and held the visibility down to ten or fifteen meters. It smelled of burning rubber, acetone, and overheated transformers combined with an oily stench as dark as the chaotic stain Stefan had brought on board with him.

Around him, out of his sight now, he heard tearing metal and the crumbling of buildings.

"Stefan!" he called out. "*Stefan!*" He broke off, coughing in the acrid air.

Around him, the air suddenly filled with whipping black tendrils, tearing around him in a wide circle, blocking his path forward or back. They reached in toward him, not quite touching him. He froze where he was, and in front of him he heard his son's voice.

"Father."

The writhing mass of black parted to reveal Stefan. He stared at Karl, the same as he had always been, except for his face. The Stefan that looked at Karl now had erased almost all emotion from his expression. Karl looked into his son's eyes, and could have been looking into the soul of a machine.

"What have you done, Stefan?"

"What have I done? *What have I done?*" he stepped toward Karl, out of the whirling chaos. "I have become something more than you ever expected of me. I come here as the vengeance of a God."

"You've sold your soul."

"You sold my birthright for much less, old man."

"Is this what you are? A mass murderer?"

He grinned at Karl. "I'm much more than that."

Karl shook his head and said. "No. You aren't." He looked into the eyes of the thing that was once his son and said. "It is *all* you are. You are only defined now by the blood you shed."

"Father?"

"I have no son."

Stefan screamed and the swirling darkness collapsed and consumed them both.

"We've lost contact with the Gamma habitat," Toni II said to Mallory. She flipped through sensor after sensor, but the assault on the *Wisconsin* had finally taken its toll on the larger structure. The stress had caused system failures across the board, and the change in mass distribution showed warnings all across the structural indicators.

The rotating *Wisconsin* had already picked up a dangerous shimmy, the oscillation period was over five minutes, not fast enough for the occupants to feel it, but each time she called the schematic up, she saw three or four more major structural elements pushed past their design specs.

"How's the evacuation?" Mallory asked.

Well, we're still here . . . "Two thirds of the craft have undocked and are underway. People are still coming up from Alpha and Beta. There aren't going to be enough ships."

"I know."

"The computer is recommending that I stop the habitat's rotation."

"What?"

"Damage to the Gamma habitat is throwing the whole platform off-balance. If the center of gravity shifts too far off axis, the whole place could fly apart."

Mallory rubbed his face, and she wondered how this guy found himself in this position. To look at him, he was asking himself the same question, and it aged him. "We have to do it, then, don't we? We have to maintain the integrity of this place as long as possible."

"Yes, sir," she said, sending the commands to the computers of the *Wisconsin's* control systems. Alarms sounded in the control section as the computers began to prepare the emergency jets to bring the rotation of the *Wisconsin* to a halt.

Something about the act made Toni II aware of her own mortality. This was a desperate act, firing massive jets of matter tangent to the platform's rotation. It was such a desperate move that there was no immediate way to resume the rotation once it stopped.

All the habitats were going to suffer a lateral acceleration of nearly a quarter gee for close to a minute. The havoc that would cause didn't bear thinking about . . .

In the core, the sense of movement wasn't nearly as bad, but she experienced a feeling that her chair was tilting as amber warnings all across the operation's systems flashed over to angry red.

She glanced up and saw the destruction evident in the holo of the Beta habitat. Her eyes focused on one of the ornamental rivers that snaked through the landscaping around the administration buildings. It had sloshed to the side, spilling over the left bank, until the rotation ceased. Then water left its bed completely, to disperse into the air.

She shut down the display and turned to Mallory. "We should go."

Mallory shook his head. "Stefan is focused on me."

"And how will he know you're on one of those ships? Magic? There's nothing left to do here, and you're at least the symbolic head of this fight."

"If you want to go—" Something buzzed from the control consoles, interrupting him. "What's that?"

"The tachyon—" She turned around and stared at the display. "Oh, my God."

"What is it?"

She changed the main holo back to the schematic of the battle, and the chaos of blue-and-yellow dots. A new red dot appeared in their midst. One of Adam's tach-ships had returned insystem.

"*The Prophet's Voice,*" she said.

The small red dot suddenly spawned fifty children as the *Voice* launched the remaining ships in its fleet.

"God help us," Mallory whispered.

Date: 2526.8.10 (Standard)
1,780,000 km from Bakunin–BD+50°1725

The damaged *Voice* appeared in the midst of battle, ahead of the explosive light from its Adam's demise. Its arrival caused engines to overload on thirteen nearby ships which had otherwise undamaged tach-drives. Half of those were ships claimed by Adam and his followers.

With the *Voice*'s arrival, several hundred Adams queried and sent information, each intending to commune with another part of Himself and expand His omniscience. The lie of that omniscience was proved by the Adams' confusion at the unresponsiveness of the *Voice*. Such was Adam's arrogance that not one of Him considered the implication of the massive hole in the *Voice*'s hull, clearly excising the bridge.

As the *Voice* plunged through the thickest heart of the fighting, it launched the remaining half of its complement of ships. Adam's first salvo had been made with fifty tach-capable ships, heavy craft, heavily armed. What remained were another fifty highly maneuverable fighter craft, not tach-capable, but even more heavily armed.

Adams queried these ships, sending orders, directing them to troublesome spots in the battle. It wasn't until those ships ignored Him that He began to realize, collectively, something was wrong.

The realization was confirmed by the obliteration of a score of his captured ships in a hail of antimatter missiles. The Protean fighters tore through the mass of the fleet, taking on Adam's chosen and vaporizing those who still clung to their master.

Unlike Adam's last encounter with Proteus, he now faced an opponent as numerous, and more maneuverable. Worse, his chosen were immediately faced with his fallibility as his own vessel, *The Prophet's Voice*, began unloading its own considerable arsenal, eliminating would-be attackers in miniature imitation of the furious immolation of the first Adam to die.

And at the expanding edge of the new Protean advance, a small fighter threaded its way past an exodus of refugee craft, toward Bakunin's moon, Schwitzguebel.

Date: 2526.8.10 (Standard)
350,000 km from Bakunin–BD+50°1725

Stefan was vast. He was now the entire Gamma habitat, and his body had begun probing into the core of the *Wisconsin* for his Nemesis. The elevators between the core and the Gamma habitat were gone, but pillars of blackness extended up from the habitat as Stefan reached for the heart of the *Wisconsin* with clumsy new fingers.

It took care, though, to feel his way inside. His sense of scale was upended by this new existence, and his first attempts to connect with the computers that ran the *Wisconsin* had the effect of a human trying to pick gnats out of spider's web. His control over the blackness that was himself was not fine enough, and he ended up tearing pieces of the habitat apart in frustration.

He had to calm himself. Flailing blindly, he could inadvertently kill the object of his hate, and he wished to face Mallory and see him suffer.

As he had watched his father.

He felt a twinge of something when he thought of that. He did his best to ignore it. He had a purpose here, and as unfamiliar as his new existence was, he knew enough to be able to complete that purpose. If he couldn't control his new body as finely as he needed, he always had his old one.

And he had as many of those as he wanted.

The shadowy conduits that connected his mass to the *Wisconsin*'s core began pulsing with mass moving inward from the Gamma habitat. Inside the core, the massive interlocking doors that sealed the now nonexistent shaft began crumbling as the darkness consumed them from the inside out. When there was no longer enough strength to bear their weight, the doors folded themselves into Stefan's darkness, pulled in by swirling black tentacles.

Stefan pulled himself out of the chaos, floating weightless into the loading area. He watched the boiling darkness as he crawled out of it again. Then another Stefan, and another, and another.

From out of every connection to the Gamma habitat, duplicate Stefans floated out of the darkness. Each one exactly the same, each one wearing the same apocalyptic grin.

He was a legion unto himself, and he would have his vengeance.

Stefan invaded the corridors of the core. Some of him went to computer consoles to begin shutting down what was left of the *Wisconsin's* brain. Others hunted the people who tried to flee his wrath. They'd shoot, but his bodies were more than what they had been, and the machines that lived within him, that created his body, repaired the damage as soon as it happened. Slugthrowers, shotguns, lasers, it didn't matter.

And all he needed was for one of him to reach out and touch his victim, and he could tear though his attacker's body the way he had torn through the Gamma habitat. They would scream sometimes, as their organs were disassembled within their bodies, then their skin would split open and spill out a pool of Stefan's black essence as they completely dissolved. And given the raw material, and because it amused him, the black pool would reassemble itself into another copy of Stefan.

See, Mallory, I have my own army.

Captain Valentine burst into the control center and screamed, "What the hell are you two still doing here?"

Mallory looked up from the console next to Lieutenant Valentine and said, "There's an incoming fighter from the *Voice*. It will be here in—"

"*Fuck that!*" Captain Valentine said, "We need to move!"

Mallory realized that she wasn't holding a shotgun anymore. From somewhere, she had picked up a wide-aperture plasma cannon, complete with backpack generator. It would be hard to pick a less safe weapon to use onboard any space-borne environment.

Her sister said, "She's right. I can't get the defenses on-line—"

Captain Valentine pushed off the wall with her foot, grabbing Mallory's arm to stop her forward motion enough to plant her feet on one of the consoles that had died during the course of Stefan's attack. Her grip was like steel, and her eyes shone with a hard desperation. "We go *now*, before one of them gets here."

He wanted to tell her to take her sister and leave him, but they were both right. There was nothing left to be done here. More than half the consoles were dead; they had no outbound communications left, and only spotty data coming from sensors that hadn't gone off-line. The status of the *Wisconsin,* from life support to structural integrity, was all now a matter of guesswork.

He allowed her to push off with him in tow, and her sister pulled herself along after them.

In the corridor beyond, the absence of even the small measure of "gravity" from the *Wisconsin's* rotation caused the air to be filled with all manner of floating objects: trash, pens, clumps of dirt, a shoe . . .

There was no one immediately evident, but Mallory could hear a distant scream, and something like a laugh followed by a surreal echo.

She pointed to an upward curving corridor. "We haven't launched the *Daedalus* yet, and I think we can make it around on the Beta side of the core."

They had pulled themselves along the wall and the ceiling, toward the intersection, when Mallory heard a familiar voice shout his name. The sound was almost a chorus . . .

He turned to look behind him.

The corridor behind them had filled with copies of Stefan, dozens of them, crawling on the walls, the floor, the ceiling. Worse, the copies themselves were imperfect. Some had missing or extra limbs; some were missing mouths or noses, or had them in the wrong place. Some had extra joints in their limbs, or had them freakishly elongated.

All the Stefans filled the corridor and pushed themselves forward, crawling over one another, reaching toward him as if he faced a Hieronymus Bosch vision of Hell come to life.

A hand grabbed his collar and pulled. "Get behind me, damn it!"

Captain Toni passed by him, pulling herself forward as she pushed him back. She was already aiming the plasma cannon down the corridor.

As soon as he cleared her, she fired. The corridor in front of her flashed a brilliant, painful light, washing away the distorted Stefans. The afterimage in Mallory's eyes lasted much longer than the burst from her cannon. When he blinked the corridor back into visibility, it was a feature-less charred black, the air filled with a uniform gray ash.

"Come on," she said. "That's only going to hold him back a moment."

CHAPTER TWENTY-TWO

Black Mass

"The most lethal combination is evil and stupidity."
—*The Cynic's Book of Wisdom*

"Evil is easy, and has infinite forms."
—BLAISE PASCAL
(1623–1662)

Date: 2526.8.10 (Standard)
350,000 km from Bakunin–BD+50°1725

Alexander Shane hobbled through the streets of the Beta habitat. The mass of people, most much quicker than he was, had disappeared, gone in their panicked evacuation. He moved slowly and deliberately, partly because of the barely closed wound in his chest, mostly because he had a semiconscious Sergeant Abbas leaning across his shoulders.

He probably should have left her as the staff fled the hospital, but something in him, perhaps the overlay of the priest's personality on top of his own, prevented him. He hadn't actually considered leaving her behind, even though he had seen her kill Dr. Pak, owner of one of the minds that formed his own remade personality.

Perhaps knowing what had happened on Salmagundi had just made him too aware of the value of human life. Anyone's life. And only partly because he suspected that those who died out here would not have their minds given unto posterity.

Then again, maybe between the onslaught of four fresh minds on him, along with a gunshot wound and the destruction of his home planet, he wasn't thinking particularly clearly.

He wasn't aware of what the new alarms meant, and barely noticed as the ground beneath him seemed to tip out from under him. Not until everything seemed to fold out from beneath him and both his feet left the ground. The sensation was so unexpected that by the time he realized what was happening, he was out of range of anything he could grab to stop his drift.

Abbas groaned against him, and he gripped on to her as the ground drifted slowly away from them.

The reality of the situation began to sink in. The rotation had stopped. That meant they were probably far beyond evacuation. If he meant to evacuate from this place, the way the alarms and the announcements told him to, he needed to make it to one of the elevators that rose up into the too-blue canopy above him. Now, that goal, only a hundred meters or so from him, might as well have been on Salmagundi.

Hanging on to the unconscious Abbas, he realized that he could push against her mass, casting her doomed body away to direct his motion back at the ground, where he would be able to pull himself along.

Which would gain him what? If he reached that elevator, could he make his way through the people crowding there? It wouldn't be an easy task, even if he were young and healthy. So he could cast her away for a chance to scrabble through a panicked crowd, and have the act be a shadow over his final few minutes.

Or he could stay with her, floating, with his self-respect intact.

There was something peaceful about floating here, removed from the chaos. Abbas had even stopped groaning.

He lightly brushed the hair from her face. He looked at her and wondered if it was better to be aware of what was happening as the world ended, or better to sleep through it and never see the end coming.

He looked up and saw a shadow on the windows above,

where mirrors shone down a hundred reflections of Kropotkin. It moved slowly, almost gently, above the sky, despite showing the deadly outline that Mallory's memories told him were of an advanced Caliphate fighter design.

Shane did not know the exact details of where he was, but in the dozens of minds' worth of knowledge that made him himself, he knew that that fighter was not flying anywhere near where spacecraft were supposed to go.

His instinct was confirmed with a hideous crunch as the fighter above them touched the window holding in the sky.

He held his breath as he watched the shadow stop moving. The sky below it clouded with a strange icy, almost pearlescent sheen. He heard distant sounds of cracking and snapping, as if the giant window was breaking apart.

The strange cloud grew more opaque, more solid, hiding the shadow from view. In seconds, the cloud grew to have a mass and a texture, as if some giant was pushing his finger through the surface of the window, and instead of breaking apart, the window stretched downward—

Shane watched, fascinated.

His trajectory was taking them underneath the bulging formation. He could see clearly that the cloud was no longer a cloud, but a massive crystalline stalactite, growing downward as he watched. The object was strangely familiar, a helical pillar twisting downward, and within semitransparent walls were more helixes, mirroring the form of the pillar. Structures within structures.

The thing the Protean built . . .

Shane remembered the Protean's landing site, and how, when it awoke, it had transformed half the camp around it into a strange set of crystal structures that resembled the helical pillar he floated toward.

He heard Abbas gasp. He looked down at her, and saw she had awakened, and was staring wide-eyed at the formation hanging in the air before them. It had already grown all the way down to the ground of the habitat. At the base, structures were folding into themselves, twisting and turning into something else.

"God save us," Abbas whispered. "What is that?"

Dr. Pak had bequeathed him enough Arabic to answer

her. "A Protean artifact," he said, "and it is where we're going."

She looked down around them, then at him. "You—you surrendered Salmagundi to the Caliphate."

"Neither exists anymore."

"Where are we?"

"A space station in orbit around a moon of Bakunin."

She shook her head and looked down. At first he thought she reacted to their height above the nominal floor of the habitat, but she raised a hand covered in blood. "I—I'm bleeding."

He reached down and put pressure on her wound, which had pulled open at some point during their evacuation. It was nearly impossible to do, suspended in zero-gee, he ended up having to hug her, and with his upper body strength it wasn't near enough. She started coughing.

"I remember," she said quietly. "I was shot . . ."

They floated, a trail of ruby red spheres marking their slow drift toward the helix. As they closed, an opening seemed to appear within the ridges of the pillar. Shane couldn't tell if the walls twisted apart in front of them, or if it was simply some trick of perspective hiding the opening until they were right in front of it.

"I was trying to save them all," Abbas said. "God knows, that is all I tried to do."

"Save your strength," Shane told her, as they drifted into the pillar through the sudden opening. In moments, he lost sight of the outside, and the world became an endless series of crystalline facets without a definitive up or down.

They gently bumped up against a wall, or floor, or ceiling, that had a slight curve. The surface was disconcertingly warm, and vibrated a bit, almost as if something moved within it.

"Save it for what? We have fallen into the Adversary's clutches." She coughed and a cloud of red drops englobed their heads. "Adam will have his way with us soon enough."

"This is not Adam's domain," came a voice from the crystal chamber around them. The voice spoke English and was eerily familiar to Shane, though he had never met the speaker. He looked up and saw a shadow moving in the translucent walls, it drew closer, folding inside itself and back until it was no longer a shadow, but a person emerging though some hidden pathway.

Rebecca Tsoravitch?

A rather unremarkable red-haired woman floated in the chamber with them now. She looked at Abbas and said softly, "You are dying."

Abbas stared at Tsoravitch. "Who are you?"

"My name is Rebecca, and I represent Proteus."

"Proteus?"

"And we can save you, if you wish it."

Abbas shook her head, "I will not deny my faith."

"We are not Adam, and we do not ask for worship."

"What do you ask for?" Shane said.

"Nothing," Tsoravitch said. "But should we heal you, you become one of us, with all that implies. If you ask for our aid, you are asking to join us."

Abbas shook her head. "No." She closed her eyes and Shane stared accusingly at Tsoravitch.

"How can you allow this woman to die?"

"Because that is her wish."

Abbas' breathing became shallow and Shane pressed against the wound, but he couldn't do anything. She was already in shock, and he felt her heart shudder and stop. He tried to revive her, but there was nothing he could do.

He looked at Rebecca, unaccountably angry for a woman he barely knew. She quietly said, "If we are to oppose Adam, we must be different from him."

He took his hands off of Abbas' wound and stared at them. They were slick with blood.

"She refused us," Rebecca said, her voice defensive.

"She didn't know what she was saying," Shane said, staring at the bloody mess in his hands. "She wasn't aware—"

"She was lucid," Rebecca's voice sounded sad, and Shane found himself reliving memories of her from four different perspectives: Pak seeing her as brilliant but scatterbrained, Dörner's quiet disdain for someone nominally her peer but without a doctorate, Brody's vicarious appreciation of her youth and enthusiasm, Mallory's unease over her innocence and her closeness to Mosasa.

He knew that this was not the same woman his other selves knew aboard the *Eclipse*, and yet, she was.

"If she hadn't woken up?" he asked.

"If she had not been able to express her refusal, we could have saved her. Reluctantly."

"Reluctantly?"

"We must allow consent to the Change. Denying someone consent is a grave transgression."

"Graver than letting someone die?"

"What Proteus does, what Adam does, is more transformative than death. When you're touched by the Change, willingly or unwillingly, you cease being unique. To become us—"

"The pilgrim must provide consent, devotion, and information," Shane said.

"You know of us?"

Shane chuckled. "In my head right now are several years' worth of study on the Protean cult, from three different people. The point, the preservation of your culture, is the archival of all the souls who give themselves to you." He smiled grimly. "Did you ever make it down to Salmagundi?"

She hesitated a moment before she said, "Yes."

"Then you know that I have as good an idea of the implications of that as anyone." He rubbed his temples and thought about the four people he had taken into the Hall of Minds. Mostly he thought about Dr. Leon Pak, who had been so damaged by his involuntary ascension into the Hall, and who now lived only as a piece of Alexander Shane. "And I know what you mean by consent."

"I am sorry about your friend."

Shane shook his head. "She was not my friend. Far from it. She killed Dr. Pak."

"What? How do you—"

"She was a Caliphate sergeant who found herself in command. She tried to hold the chaos together, but she was out of her depth. I was. We all were."

"Who are you?"

"The name Alexander Shane would mean nothing to you. Without Salmagundi, it probably means nothing, period. But I have received the minds of those you do know, Pak, Brody, Dörner, Mallory."

Rebecca stared at him.

"I see I've surprised you."

"Yes, you have."

"Would it surprise you that being a pilgrim of Proteus would be the closest I can come to fulfilling my duty to my posterity without the Hall of Minds?"

"You wish to accept the Change, and all it implies?"

"If you answer me one question."

"What is it?"

"What exactly have the Dolbrians left behind on Bakunin?"

Stefan threw himselves against his enemy.

He created copies of copies, building the flesh of himself from whatever matter drifted into the path of his anger. He paid little attention to the finer aspects of these bodies. They were simply mechanical tools to bring his mass in contact with the hated one. They crawled through the corridors of the core, filling them to the point that their limbs tangled, and the weaker of his bodies found themselves crushed against bulkheads even in zero-gee.

It didn't matter. Each of his bodies was a personification of his white-hot rage, and nothing would halt its advance, not even other instances of himself.

He multiplied them, hundreds, thousands. The bitch with the plasma cannon could only hold him off for so long. Her resources were finite, his weren't. As she vaporized one wave of his anger, he created twice as many of himself behind it. Each time, he sank his anger deeper into his creations, growing their teeth into fangs, fingers into talons, giving spikes to the bone that penetrated through the flesh.

His legion backed them to an air lock to a dock that had been long since evacuated. The narrow corridor they were trapped inside met the main corridor in a T, and the host that was himself fed the main corridor from both directions, pushing itself toward them. He scrambled over himself, the stronger of his avenging personas crawling over and through the weaker. They moved through a haze of their own skin and blood.

One pulse of light, and his advance was erased in a haze of gray ash, but there were more than enough bodies to spill in and fill the gap. Stefan, as distributed as his mind had become, focused all his instances of himself on his enemy's narrow corridor, a corridor filled with choking gray ash and covered by a thin black tarlike char. For several minutes he pushed wave after wave of himself against them, reveling in the uselessness of the bitch's plasma cannon. But unease came from another source.

He felt something, a growing sensation akin to having a leg go numb. At first he focused himself only on his mission, but the sensation persisted and spread until he could no longer ignore it. Furious at being diverted from his game, he turned his attention to the strange numbness within himself.

And what he saw terrified him.

We're dead, we are so fucking dead. The words kept tumbling through Toni's head, almost disconnected from her body. She braced on one knee, forward foot hooked in a support strap on what had once been a wall, rear foot pressing hard against a floor-to-ceiling light fixture. Her position on the wall was about five meters in front of Mallory and her sister. She held the plasma cannon facing down toward the main corridor, her aim rock solid on the center of their corridor. The aperture was focused just tightly enough for the cone to wash the walls just three meters ahead of the intersection.

That intersection had become a pretty good approximation of hell. In the moment before the next wave, every surface by the intersection steamed. The only light came from the undamaged corridor behind her, and the exposed parts of the bulkhead that glowed red. The air was a noxious combination of burning chemicals and burning flesh. It made her gag and made her eyes water.

Then the attack came again. The demonic things erupted out of the corridor, pulling themselves into Toni's line of fire. Each round, the things seemed less human. They scuttled crablike along the walls and each other, unconcerned when their skin burned from contact with the superheated bulkheads, or their talons gouged out the flesh of their slower companions. They moved fast, filling the corridor with grasping claws and teeth—

And Toni closed her eyes and fired a pulse from the cannon. She opened her eyes, her vision still intact, and glanced at the readout on the cannon's instrumentation.

The energy level had fallen deep into the red. One more shot, maybe two.

So fucking dead.

She heard the scramble of claws, and the sizzle of flesh touching red-hot metal, and prepared for her last shot—

And the entire corridor wrenched itself to the left. She barely held on to the cannon, but she lost her anchor and had to scramble with her feet to keep from losing her position on the wall. She awkwardly brought the barrel to bear against the still unseen horde and screamed to Mallory, her sister, and any God that was listening, *"What the hell was that?"*

Stefan looked outward with his new, uncertain senses. He tried to see what was happening to the Gamma habitat and the larger portion of himself, but he was blind to that part of him. The best he could do was to peer outward, down the elevator shaft his essence had used to enter the core.

As he watched, the *Wisconsin* suffered a wrenching vibration. The shock was not only felt in the structure of the space platform, Stefan felt it in himself, as if someone was twisting a knife in a still too-human gut. Another shock followed, and another, and Stefan's numbness flared into the fiery pain of an amputated limb.

For a moment he looked out and saw nothing, just a blackness where the Gamma habitat was. Then, as a thousand invisible hammers tried to smash apart the *Wisconsin,* the shadows fell away from his view. He saw into space—a black sky dominated by Schwitzguebel's horizon and the blue crescent of Bakunin hanging in the sky. At first he didn't understand what had happened. A whole third of the *Wisconsin* was missing. He should see into the Gamma habitat—

Then the mirror blocking his view tumbled away, taking its view of Schwitzguebel and Bakunin with it.

A thousand other mirrors tumbled free between the core and the Gamma habitat. The two-kilometer-long cylinder hung before him, behind a mass of floating wreckage, torn mirrors glittering like stars in the midst of twisted girders and fragments of pipe. The habitat itself was black, the great windows into the habitat opaque with Stefan's presence within.

But something else clung to the surface. Along every support that held the habitat to the core, Stefan could see a crystalline deposit, almost like frost, coating the scaffolding that held the *Wisconsin* together. And the crystals were venting gases, each one the root of a growing, sterile cloud.

He tried to reach out to himself within the habitat, but it was like trying to touch the moon below him. And, unlike Adam, he had not been given a century to become confident in his own omnipotence.

More shocks tore at the *Wisconsin,* and the last pieces of scaffolding holding the Gamma habitat in place fell away. Stefan watched it drift, driven by the gas venting from the alien crystal frost growing on its surface.

He watched it tumble with agonizing slowness, down toward the moon's surface, trailing a cloud of ice crystals.

When he felt the numbness extend into what was left of himself in the core of the *Wisconsin,* he did not ignore it.

Around them, the *Wisconsin* tried to shake itself apart. Toni had to let go of the wall, because floating in the center of the corridor now was a more stable firing platform.

Whatever was happening, it was violent enough to threaten the structural integrity of the *Wisconsin* itself. She found herself hoping for a hull breach. Dying in a vacuum seemed preferable to being torn apart by a horde of mutant Stefans.

Whatever was shaking the *Wisconsin* apart, it was enough to give their attackers pause. The demon horde held back.

The bad thing about it was that she had more time to think, beyond the mechanical process of firing again and again. She licked her lips and called back, "Is there still power to the air lock?"

"Yes," Mallory said. "What are you—"

She heard the air lock door to the empty docking bay open as the whole station groaned. He sister called out, "You think we can make it?"

Toni pressed her lips into a hard grin. "Your guess is as good as mine." *You know what I'm thinking.*

She heard them back into the air lock as another, weaker shock wrenched the corridor around her. She stretched with her foot and kicked back toward the air lock. "Aim for the air lock across the axis. It's the most straightforward for you to get to. Kick out as hard as you can. At most, you have half a minute before you black out." She stopped next to the controls and looked back at Mallory and her sister. She saw her own face drain of color as her other self realized what she was doing.

"Wait—"

The scrambling noises resumed, and Toni saw the Stefan things reaching around again to pull themselves into her corridor. Toni hit the controls to shut the air lock. "Sorry, I got to keep this asshole away from this door."

CHAPTER TWENTY-THREE

Lake of Fire

"Nothing is inconceivable to a doomed man."
                    —*The Cynic's Book of Wisdom*

"He who has a why to live can bear almost any how."
                    —FRIEDRICH NIETZSCHE
                    (1844–1900)

Date: 2526.8.10 (Standard)
350,000 km from Bakunin–BD+50°1725

Lieutenant Valentine pushed him into the air lock, and before he could react, the door was closing on them. The other Valentine faced the door and said, "No."

Mallory pulled her shoulder. "She's giving us this chance. Breathe."

She nodded and started sucking in deep breaths along with him, oxygenating the blood as much as possible. Holding their breath would end up doing severe damage to their lungs, and the pressure differential between their body and the vacuum outside would kill them a lot sooner than the lack of oxygen.

Survival tips drilled into everyone who left a gravity well, though Mallory didn't know anyone for whom the knowledge made a difference.

She reached down and grabbed a strut on the floor that allowed her to crouch down and squat against the floor even in the zero-gee. Their legs would be the only propulsion they had. He mirrored her squat, then let go of the wall so he could break the cover on the emergency air lock release, and looked across at Valentine and held out his hand. She took his and nodded, not wasting the air to say she was ready.

He pulled the release and, above them, the outside door thrust itself open in a rush of air that went suddenly silent, a silence that became agonizing as each throb of his pulse plunged daggers into his ears. They crouched, and together pushed off.

The core was a massive cylinder with the docking space on the inner surface. The *Wisconsin*'s docks were mostly empty now, the inside covered with air locks and docking gantries. Directly across the center of the core, a twin of their air lock hung before them. Less than seventy-five meters, but it could have been another planet.

His eyes burned, and began to ache. His skin began to itch and burn as all the moisture sublimated from his skin. His tongue went dry and numb in his mouth, and it felt as if someone painfully twisted his testicles.

So slow. They were drifting toward the air lock so slowly. Nearly ten seconds and they hadn't reached it yet.

He looked across at Valentine, and the only sign she still lived was the fact she blinked, once.

His gut was cramping now, his bowels trying to equalize the pressure. His chest was on fire as the vacuum tried to freeze-dry the tissues in his lungs. Every part of his body ached, and he felt his consciousness slipping.

Not now. Please, God, not now.

They were almost at the new air lock. His vision was horribly blurred, and he squinted to see the emergency entry lever.

Then they struck the surface. His reaction was sluggish, and he hit face first, smashing his nose and mouth into the air lock window. He felt the bones of his nose give way and a tooth come free, almost as if he was a bystander. He barely felt it, even as the blood burned frozen patches on his skin and mouth.

It was all he could do to keep his grip on Valentine, though his muscles were so cramped now that he doubted he could have let her go.

He pulled his brain together. His implants burned, dumping whatever they had left into his ragged metabolism. They were probably the only reason he was still conscious. He belatedly realized that they had reached the opposite air lock, and now they were drifting away.

He reached for the emergency lever and fumbled for it with a hand that felt as if it was wrapped in a mitten, a mitten that was on fire. For nearly half a second he pulled without any effect. The disorientation was great enough that he just kept pulling, without realizing he needed to anchor himself to have the leverage.

But he kept pulling and the effort dragged him and the unconscious Valentine back in contact with the door. Once he could no longer move forward, the lever moved backward, and the door slid open in front of him. They floated into the air lock.

Thank God. Thank God. Thank God . . .

But he was still losing consciousness. His vacuum-numbed mind took way to long to start looking for the control to close and pressurize the air lock. He was almost blind now; his vision blurred, blood red, and focused on a tiny window in front of his face. When he found the control, he couldn't even be sure that it was the right one.

With a last prayer, he hit the controls and blacked out.

The air lock door shut behind her and she leveled the plasma cannon at the onrushing horde. Her aim was not quite steady because of a lack of anchorage, so she opened the aperture on full, and waited for the monstrous rush to come a full second closer to her.

Hey, whatever happens, there's still another me running around.

For a while at least.

She closed her eyes and fired the last burst from the plasma cannon. The point of contact of the plasma and the wall was too close to her. She felt superheated air sear her body, pressing her against the air lock door. Somehow, despite the agony of having her clothes melt into her flesh, she managed to hold her breath and not scream. Her body curled into a fetal position, the pain shattering her consciousness, destroying most of her coherent thoughts.

She maintained enough will and muscular control to pull the trigger again.

Nothing happened.

She opened her eyes, and her vision was blurred from pain. Her breath came in short gasps, the air still so hot it burned her mouth and lungs, but nothing like the agony that gripped what was left of her skin.

The corridor was dark now except for the red glow from the metal bulkheads. She floated, turning slightly so the corridor spun around her. The sounds of Stefan's demons were muffled through her damaged ears. She tried to yell at them to come, finish her off, but all that came out was a horrible groan that tasted of blood.

She saw them, shadows emerging from the edges into the barely-lit corridor, the red light carving inhuman high-lights on the otherwise shadowed forms. They slowed as they approached, no longer scrambling at her, as if they knew the delay was more painful than anything they could do once they reached her.

Do it, you goddamned bastard, DO IT!

Her attempts to scream left a haze of saliva and blood droplets in front of her.

But they left her floating as the light in the corridor slowly increased. A point in the floor, or the wall, or the ceiling, appeared to open, allowing in a soft yellow light. The spot grew, the light seeming to push back Stefan's creatures. A faceted, translucent form unfolded from the light. The object grew as if it emerged from another dimension where the normal rules of geometry didn't apply. Even through her blurred vision, the repeating facets twisted around themselves to the point where it seemed that there was much more inside the crystal than its volume could contain.

The demons seemed afraid of it, and tried to retreat back where they had come. But they stopped because a similar light was emerging from behind them.

The light seemed to reach out from the crystal, to touch the things that used to be Stefan Stavros, and the demons dissolved into the light. The monsters screamed as their bodies vanished around them, as if in a slow-motion replay of their deaths before the plasma cannon.

Toni closed her eyes. Stefan wasn't going to end her suffering. She tried to shut herself down, remove herself from her body, from her life, by will alone. She found a dark place inside herself, as far away from the pain as she could manage, and huddled there, whimpering.

"Captain Valentine? Can you hear me?"

She was delirious; she couldn't be hearing the voice she was hearing.

"Please, can you still hear me?"

She forced herself to open her eyes. Around her the world had changed, the walls were faceted crystal slabs that glowed softly. And floating in front of her was Alexander Shane, with a deep expression of concern furrowing his tattooed brow.

Of all people? You? How . . . random . . .

"If you understand, can you nod?"

She did so, weakly, wondering if she was conversing with a pain-induced hallucination.

"I want to help you, but you have to consent."

She nodded.

"I'm with Proteus now. They have the capability to save your consciousness, but only if you join them."

"P-roteus?" her lips cracked and bled as she forced the word out.

Shane nodded. "You would become one of them, and there's no going back."

She uncurled her burned hands from the trigger of the plasma cannon and reached out to him. She touched the white topcoat he wore, smearing red-tinted fluid across the front. She felt him there, through the pain, and the touch convinced her she wasn't hallucinating.

"I don't want to die," she whispered through bleeding lips.

Stefan watched the Gamma habitat implode in a flash of light upon the lunar horizon, and then all his eyes that saw outside went blind. He vainly tried to finish his one purpose here, the destruction of Mallory, the root of all the ill that had befallen him, but his attack dissolved into this alien light, a light that came like a cruel abrasive wind, tearing apart the pieces of his extended self.

He screamed for Adam's help, but his new God didn't answer. He didn't hear, or He had better things to do.

The alien presence pushed aside his attempts to force his mass past it. The coherent mass of nanomachines that he controlled, that could force itself through steel and flesh in equal measure, broke upon their walls like a feeble breath against the side of a mountain.

He tried to escape, to vent himself out some breach in the *Wisconsin's* skin, and flee into space to regroup and re-build himself. But every avenue he tried, every bulkhead, every door, every tiny route to the outside was blocked to his passage. The others had wrapped themselves completely around the vessel, trapping him inside.

His identity coalesced as they sliced away more and more of him. His body reduced itself until he was nothing more than a single malformed fleshy golem, pulling itself along one of the many corridors paralleling the dock in the inner core. The thing that was what remained of Stefan Stavros couldn't think properly anymore, too many pieces of his own consciousness had been lost with the parts of himself they had killed. He had not been quick enough to pull all of his mind back into himself.

He had also been sloppy in the creation of this one re-maining body. Its legs were twisted and floated useless behind it, one arm was far longer than the other, and it stared at the corridor before it with a single off-center eye. What remained of its broken mind was just enough to know what it had lost.

And to know fear.

It came across a woman in the corridor, and it attacked. Its world now only consisted of itself and the enemy, and the woman was a resource. It could cloak itself in her flesh and gain a more useful body. It attacked, even though it had mostly lost the knowledge of how to do such a thing.

It struck out with its claws, swinging its oversized arm, digging its hand deep into her back, so deep it felt its fingers brush a beating heart. It forced its last reserve into the wound, pushing itself into her body.

But the heart kept beating, and it could not push itself into her.

It tried to remove its hand, but it was trapped inside her body, and it began to scream as the sensation in its claws and fingers were gradually lost.

She spoke to it, without turning around. "You are evil," she said quietly, almost inaudibly beneath the thing's keening pain and terror.

The thing that had been Stefan Stavros fell away from Rebecca's back. She turned to face it. It held a truncated arm accusingly toward her, its twisted muscles throbbing and writhing unnaturally beneath its skin. It stared at her with a single cloudy eye embedded in a noseless face. Its twisted face was dominated by slavering fanged jaws that probably couldn't form words even if this thing still understood language.

She stared at the abomination and said quietly, "You are evil, and you must be destroyed."

The stump of the arm that had attacked her began glowing. The cloudy cyclopean eye widened, and it shook its limb as if trying to extinguish a fire. The glow grew, sliding into its body, outlining the veins beneath the skin.

Before the glow consumed it, it proved her wrong by possessing enough language to croak, "Adam! Help me!"

Its words remained longer in the air than it did.

The first sensation Toni II was aware of was a burning in her lungs. She sucked in breath after breath, gasping, as she slowly became aware that she breathed air. Her lungs burned, her joints ached, her mouth was numb, and it felt as if someone had kicked her repeatedly in the stomach, but she was alive, and breathing air.

It was a few moments before her memory came back fully, and she remembered what they had been running from. She opened her eyes. They burned and watered in the light. Her arms flailed for a handhold to orient herself as the full horror of what had happened sank in.

No, not her. The reality of it struck her harder than the

aftereffects of being exposed to vacuum. Her sister, her other self, had given herself over to the demons to give them the chance to escape. It wasn't right. Toni was the real one; she was Toni II, a ghost. She was the interloper in this universe. She should have been the one to sacrifice herself.

And if they blew it now, the guilt would be even worse.

Her hand found the edge of a supply cabinet, and she grabbed it as if it was a lifeline. Holding onto it, she looked around for Mallory.

He floated only a meter away from her in the air lock, his face a mass of blood and bruises.

Fuck.

She grabbed his shoulder with her free hand and pulled him over. His nose and mouth were clogged with blood that had nowhere to go in zero-gee. She opened his mouth and shoved her fingers in to dislodge a gory mass of half-frozen blood. He was still unresponsive, and she released her anchor so her other hand could support the back of his head as she bent over him to provide rudimentary rescue breathing as she racked her brain for the medic training on zero-gee chest compressions.

To her relief, that wasn't necessary. She only gave him five breaths and he started coughing into her mouth. She let him go and spit out a mouthful of Mallory's blood.

He gasped and wheezed and said, "Made it?"

"Yes, and we need to get out of here and to the *Daedalus*. If it's still here."

He nodded and said something about getting spacesuits next time. He fumbled for the air lock door with bruised and swollen fingers. Toni II stared at the door, realizing how mundane it looked. Utterly ordinary—while on the opposite side of the *Wisconsin* things had become Hell itself.

How close is Stefan to us now?

The air lock slid open, and someone waited for them on the other side. A woman blocked their path, upside down in relation to them, unbound red hair fanning out around her head. The woman was smaller than Toni II, pale, freckled; a complete stranger to her.

Not, apparently, to Mallory.

"Tsoravitch?" Something in Mallory's voice made this woman's appearance seem suddenly ominous.

"Sergeant Fitzpatrick," she said. "Or should I call you Father Mallory?"

Sergeant Fitzpatrick? Who the hell is Sergeant Fitzpatrick?

The woman turned and looked at Toni II, "You must be one of the Toni Valentines." She smiled and said, "Don't worry about your sister, we got to her in time."

The statement brought relief and apprehension in equal measure.

Mallory's voice sounded shaky. "The *Voice* picked you up with everyone else who stayed on the *Eclipse.* How did you escape Adam?"

"I didn't," Tsoravitch responded.

Toni II stared at her. "You didn't?"

Tsoravitch kicked lightly against a wall to cleanly rotate herself so that her vertical orientation matched theirs. "I was one of Adam's chosen. When he gave me his choice, I took it."

Mallory shook his head. "It's over now, then. You know I won't join him."

"I said *was.*" Her voice lowered and her expression became grim. "You wounded him worse than any physical attack. You hit him in his most vulnerable point, his self-image as a God. Were he here now, there'd be no talk of conversions. He has condemned this entire system and everyone in it."

"I know," Mallory said. "I knew it when he attacked without giving his ultimatum."

"Not *everyone*," Toni II said, "he did something to Stefan, if the thing wrecking the station is Stefan."

"It probably amused him to send one of your former allies to destroy you." Tsoravitch shook her head. "I have seen Adam up close for far too long, and his personality is far from divine. He is angry, vain, arrogant, vindictive, petty, narcissistic . . . and he is not quite sane."

"If you aren't one of Adam's chosen," Mallory asked, "what are you?"

"Proteus."

CHAPTER TWENTY-FOUR

Infidels

"Never assume another's beliefs are irrelevant to your own."
—*The Cynic's Book of Wisdom*

"The religion of one seems madness unto another."
—THOMAS BROWNE
(1605–1682)

Date: 2526.8.10 (Standard)
Bakunin–BD+50°1725

The tunnels under the Diderot Mountains were interminable. With every branch, Kugara was reminded that she had wanted Flynn with them because Tetsami was the only one they had with direct experience with these passages. The four of them moved slowly through the underground, their only light coming from a cheap flashlight from the same emergency kit she had used in her doomed attempt to patch up Flynn.

They followed Nickolai, because he had the best vision, even if the black Protean eyes gave his face an empty skull-like appearance. He saw much deeper into the caverns than the flashlight reached, and warned them away from drops and dead ends.

And, occasionally, he would direct Dörner and Brody's attention to some part of a cave wall. Kugara would see nothing, but more often than not the two chatted about

Dolbrian carvings and wished aloud for Dr. Pak, the linguist.

Either they were going in the right direction, or the remains of the Dolbrians were particularly thick on the ground down here. She bet on the latter.

She had been pushing them forward ever since Wilson, focused on the reason they came here, but now that they had escaped all the intermediate obstacles, it sank into her exactly how hopeless their job here was. They didn't even have a clear idea of what it was that they were looking for, or where.

She didn't like the ugly thought that she hadn't considered the end of their little mission before now because she had expected them to die long before they had reached this point. It was as if the universe was using their own survival to mock them.

Dr. Brody seemed oblivious to the fact that they were on a Snark hunt, when he called over, "Can you bring the light closer over here?"

Kugara obliged, walking closer to the edge of the passage by Brody and Dörner. The two scientists stared at the wall, and as Kugara brought the light closer, she could see the odd script that she was already sick of—complex interpenetrating lines looping around and through themselves to form repeating triangular patterns.

Dolbrian graffiti, as far as Kugara was concerned. It was unlikely that any random chicken scratches would make a bit of difference.

"No," Dörner said, "This is wrong."

"What's wrong?" Kugara asked.

"This writing is supposed to be a hundred million years old," Dörner said. "But I can see tool marks and scratches that should have worn away a long time ago. This is much more recent."

From the darkness, Nickolai said, "Perhaps there are still Dolbrians down here."

"I seriously doubt it," Dörner said, "A hundred million years is too long for—"

"Listen," Nickolai hissed.

The chamber fell silent.

At first, all Kugara heard was their own breathing. Then, slowly, she became aware of something else. A soft, rhythmic, clicking noise that was vaguely familiar.

It was the same sound Nickolai made when he walked barefoot through the caverns with them. The sound of claws on stone, and it was coming from a lot more than two feet, from more than one direction.

"Where?" Kugara whispered, stepping in front of Brody and Dörner.

"Everywhere," Nickolai whispered in return. His muscular back emerged from the shadows, coming toward her. He moved like a spirit, his black stripes almost a part of the darkness beyond. He had removed two more guns from the chain wrapped across his torso.

Kugara's stomach tightened as she heard growling animal sounds emerge from the caverns around them. What kind of monstrosity could evolve down here after a hundred million years? The noise seemed to come from everywhere at once, filling the darkness around them.

"What's out there?" she whispered.

Then, all at once, a blinding light emerged from the darkness, from at least three sources, pinning their shadows against the wall behind them. She squinted against the light, briefly unable to reconcile the animal grumbling and the scrape of claws with the floodlights washing over them.

Then she realized Nickolai growled back.

Brody muttered something behind her that sounded like, "Of course."

A figure emerged from the shadows, a human figure. He wore a long robe of undyed linen, and had long blond hair and an untrimmed beard that came halfway down his chest. In contrast to his hermitlike appearance, he carried a sleek EM rifle that was the grown-up cousin of the little needle-gun she had left on Salmagundi. His rifle probably had a similar rate of fire, and could pump out flechettes at twenty thousand rounds a second. The main difference was that it could do so a lot longer, with ammo that massed four times as much—almost as destructive as a plasma cannon.

Kugara stared at the new arrival as she whispered to Brody, "'Of course,' what?"

The robed man looked them all over and said, in a somewhat hoarse voice, "I am Brother Simon, and I welcome you to the caverns of the Ancients." He hefted his rifle. "But I must ask you to surrender your weapons, out of respect."

Nickolai growled something, and to Kugara's surprise, Simon growled back.

Behind her, Brody whispered, "The Dolbrian cult, that's what."

Nickolai walked up to Simon and started handing the man his guns. Kugara watched, nonplussed, as the weapons passed from Nickolai to Simon, and Simon passed them to someone out of sight behind the spotlights' glare. When he stepped back, he turned and looked down at Kugara. When she hesitated about disarming herself, he told her, "Beyond the lights are twenty heavily-armed monks. Let them have the gun."

Kugara nodded, noting that Nickolai still kept the chain wrapped around his torso.

She walked up and handed her gun to Simon. He smiled. "Thank you." He handed it off, and Kugara saw the hand that received it: furry, brown, and half again as large as Nickolai's.

Simon slung the rifle across his shoulder and said, "Welcome, friends. It has been a long time since we've properly received any pilgrims. Come with us and receive our hospitality."

As cheerful as Simon sounded, it was obviously not a request.

Once they were Simon's "guests" and the lights no longer shone in her eyes, Kugara could see the monks that Nickolai had mentioned. Only Simon was human. The rest of them were all nonhuman denizens of the Fifteen Worlds, descendants of the same period of history that gave rise to Nickolai's ancestors, and hers.

None were quite Nickolai's kin. There were at least three felines, with fur ranging from spotted to jet black, but all were smaller than Nickolai, with narrower faces and finer bone structure. There were shaggy gray-and-brown canines, and a couple of small sleek forms that weren't close enough for her to put a name to, and, most intimidating, an ursine that stood half a head taller than Nickolai, massed probably thirty percent more, and had to spend most of his time hunched over so badly she thought he might be more comfortable on all fours.

She had been trained by Dakota Planetary Security how to handle most of the races of the Fifteen Worlds in hand-to-hand combat. She was good enough that she knew that she could beat Nickolai in a fight, maybe not a *fair* fight, but if you ended up grappling with a four-hundred-kilo tiger, "fair" shouldn't be a top concern.

The ursine—even in the confined tunnel—*that* she'd run from.

Looking at their nonhuman escorts, she began to wonder if Simon might have the same Dakota ancestry as she did. She wondered what she felt about that. More, she wondered how Nickolai felt. He had been living with the "Fallen" for so long, she wondered what it meant to him to be among God's chosen people again. He didn't give her any signs of what he was thinking. He followed their hosts, watching them with his expressionless black eyes.

She did notice that the group herding them cast occasional uncomfortable glances at Nickolai. She didn't know if that was due to caution on their host's part, or something else.

She walked to the rear, placing the two scientists safely between her and Nickolai, not that they had any real chance to protect them if things should turn ugly. There were just too many well-armed opponents too close.

As they walked down natural corridors, deeper into the mountains, she whispered to Brody, "What do you know about these people?"

"Dolbrian worship has been around for centuries, ever since the first artifacts were discovered. But it wasn't organized until the fall of the Confederacy. The Fifteen Worlds—the Seven Worlds then—brokered a defense pact with Bakunin; the protection of their sovereignty against the other arms of the Confederacy, in return for the largest

Dolbrian site ever discovered. The belief system found a center here, and among the populace of the Fifteen Worlds, it found ready converts—and the nature of the Fifteen Worlds meant that any citizen coming to Bakunin for the sake of a permanent presence here was probably one of those converts. Few others would willingly dwell on a human world."

Brody went on, at length. Many of the details were lost on Kugara, but she understood that they were, in some sense, treading on the soil of the Fifteen Worlds, and for a century or so, this nonhuman monastery had been the only official State presence on Bakunin, and could probably be considered a theocratic city-state, like a smaller cousin to Vatican City.

Bakunin's founders were most likely spinning in their graves so fast that they reached relativistic speeds, shrank inside their own event horizon, and disappeared into another universe.

Kugara could see the attraction to this faith, though, especially after seeing firsthand the kind of mental violence Nickolai had done to himself because his belief that mankind—in some sense his creator—was, in fact, damned for hubris. Wouldn't it be more comforting to place everyone on the same plane, having mankind be just another creature engineered by some ancient race? These guys also had an advantage over St. Rajasthan's followers, and most other religions Kugara could think of; they had evidence of the existence of their god lying all over the place.

More of the Dolbrian carvings covered the walls, but it was clearly of more recent vintage. Brody commented that he suspected it was either a sign of the monks' devotion, or a decoy to lead any unwanted treasure hunters astray.

Like us, you mean?

She wasn't expecting it when they reached the monastery itself. They walked through a cavern mouth, and suddenly, there it was: a massive cavern, large enough to park the *Daedalus* three times over within it. Across the vast space, a tiered wall faced them, covered with bas-relief carvings, arches, and fluted columns. It was almost a cathedral carved out of the stone itself. Below the wall, an amphitheater had been carved into the cave floor, with arcs of stone seats stepping down to a central podium.

They were taken past all that, through one of the many archways in the cathedral wall, down a few dark passages, to end up in a large room with a heavy door. Simon told them to wait inside, then he shut the door behind them.

Kugara turned to try the door, but on this side there wasn't a handle, or any other obvious way to open it. She pushed against the brushed metal surface, but it didn't budge. She shook her head and muttered, "Now what?"

Brody walked over and sat down in one of several overstuffed chairs that filled the room. He groaned and rubbed his cast with his good arm. "I think we should be thankful no one is shooting at us for the moment."

Kugara spun around, about to say something sharp, but she saw the exhaustion in his face and held her tongue. He and Dörner weren't soldiers, they were academics, and between the two of them he seemed to be doing better than she was. Dörner had folded herself into another chair, one built for someone Nickolai's size, and almost seemed to disappear within it. On the *Eclipse*, Kugara remembered her as being cold, assertive, confident and—most of all—in control of herself.

This Dörner stared into the middle distance through threads of stringy blonde hair, and her steely blue eyes now seemed to speak not so much of cold reserve, but of a thin sheet of ice that could fracture at any moment, releasing the dangerous rapids contained beneath.

Nickolai didn't sit. He kept pacing, and Kugara wondered what he was thinking.

Kugara walked to her own chair and sat down, nodding. "Get your rest when you can." She looked around the room. It certainly wasn't a prison cell. There were the chairs and tables and tapestries hanging on the walls and thick carpets trying to hide the fact that they sat in a hole carved in a rock.

The tapestries, in particular, were a reminder of who held them right now. Even without an explicit explanation, she saw the religious nature of the scenes they showed. One on the far wall depicted a featureless glowing white form, reaching down to shine light on the curving horizon of a lush planet. And, receiving the light, a naked human form imitated the gesture of the light-shrouded form above, and seemed to direct that light down on a congregation of all manner of creatures, some of whom had begun picking up tools. Kugara noticed Nickolai looking at that one as well.

The other tapestries had the similar figure, made of undifferentiated white light, presiding over other scenes; a desert sprouting to life, a cascade of planets falling across a starry background, a mixed congregation of humans and nonhumans kneeling within a vast room whose walls were covered in Dolbrian writing.

"Do you have any idea what they're going to do with us?" she asked Brody.

"Normal times, I suspect they have a standard procedure for unexpected visitors. This is Bakunin, after all—"

"That includes heavily armed squads of monks?"

"Times aren't normal. The threat from Adam aside, the PSDC is pushing their authority everywhere else."

Kugara nodded. The nominal sovereignty of the Fifteen Worlds down here was a rather thin shield to hide behind. "So?"

"I suspect we'll be brought before some sort of adjudicating authority."

"A judge?"

"A judge. They'll want to determine if we're a threat—a secular one, or a theological one."

Kugara couldn't help but look at Nickolai, who still stared at the first tapestry.

Great.

In her opinion, the last thing they needed was to have Nickolai get into a theological debate with these guys.

"I think they know," Dörner said quietly.

"What?"

"I think they know what the Protean wanted us to find." She turned to look at Kugara, her expression calm, but fragile as a porcelain doll. "We're close to intact Dolbrian construction here."

"How do you know?"

"I saw the signs on the way down here," she said. "You can see the architecture through the mineral deposits. The tunnels become more regular, the angles less random."

Kugara sighed and said, "That's good, if we can convince them to lead us where we want to go. But from what I see here, what we're looking for is probably their holy of holies. How do we convince them to allow a bunch of infidels there?"

Brody rubbed his chin and said, "You could convert."

"I doubt it will be that straightforward," Kugara said. "And I doubt I could convince them of my sincerity."

"No," Nickolai grumbled, turning to face them.

Brody looked over at the tiger and said, "Don't get angry. I was being facetious."

Nickolai shook his head. "I understand. But there is only one way to convince them to take us where we want to go."

"Which is?" Kugara asked.

"We convince them that Adam is truly bringing the end times to us all."

CHAPTER TWENTY-FIVE

Reliquary

"No organized religion can survive direct confirmation of its beliefs."

— *The Cynic's Book of Wisdom*

"For those who proclaim to love God so much, they seem reluctant to meet Him."

— BORIS KALECSKY
(2103–2200)

Date: 2526.8.11 (Standard)
Bakunin–BD+50°1725

They waited hours for their keepers to come for them. The others slept, but Nickolai found he could not. He had never felt so alone in his faith. Here he was, among others of his kind for the first time since his exile, and they were all pledged to something that the priests of Rajasthan would consider an abomination.

Not that he would fare any better in their eyes.

In my own eyes . . .

What did he believe anymore? He had blessed Flynn sincerely, despite the fact that the nature of Salmagundi's veritable worship of AI—even if it was in the form of their own ancestors—would make the whole society damned on a level beyond even the Fallen.

And whatever stain Flynn had in the eyes of St. Rajasthan, the stain on Nickolai's soul would be worse. He lived now only due to the touch of Proteus, and the thing had permanently marked him with its alien eyes.

And yet, he stared at the tapestry showing God reaching down to man, and man reaching down to his creation. It was not an image of a fall.

He could not condemn the Protean's act to save his life. He could not condemn what he felt for Kugara. He couldn't call damned the people who fought this evil, Adam, despite the guilt of their species.

The tenets of his faith crumbled around him, and he was finding it harder and harder to find anything to replace them. He prayed to God for the wisdom to truly know His will, and the only answer was the sound of his own breathing.

As degraded as his moral compass had become, he did have one fact to hang on to. Adam was evil. That he knew down to his soul. For all that he questioned the faith he was born to, he still knew that much. Adam was evil, and if he failed to do what he could against that evil, he would share in it, more than he already had.

He stared at the tapestry, his alien eyes making out each individual thread, the fibers within each thread . . .

I'm no longer who I was.
I'm no longer what I was.
Who am I?
What do I believe?

When they came, they came for Nickolai. It made sense—he was one of their kind—but he could tell that the others, especially Kugara, seemed uncomfortable with him being separated from the group.

They took him to another large room, this one with no furniture or tapestries in evidence. The walls had been polished until they were nearly mirrorlike, and the light came from pits recessed into the upper walls near the ceiling.

Dominating everything, recessed in a ten-meter-square wall opposite the entryway, was a massive slab of carved rock. The edges around the carving were rough and unfinished, as if the surface of the surrounding rock had fallen away to reveal it. Its irregular outlines reached within a meter of the ceiling, and a couple of meters from each wall.

Even without any study of the matter, to Nickolai the carving was clearly of Dolbrian manufacture. He could stare into the marks on the rock and see how precise they were, and he could see a molecule-thin coating covering them. It was something that could survive a hundred million years, or longer.

Standing in the room, a tawny-furred canine had his head bowed toward the carving. After a moment, he said, "Your name is Nickolai Rajasthan?"

"I am," Nickolai answered. "You know me?"

"I know of you." The canine turned around to face him, looking Nickolai up and down with severe blue eyes. "We are the official presence of the Fifteen Worlds here, and when a member government decides to dispose of a problem on Bakunin, we do know of it—even when they try to be secretive."

"I see."

"Despite the best efforts of the Rajasthan priests." The canine's smile showed no teeth, but still felt like a challenge. And it left Nickolai uncertain . . .

"So who is it I am talking to who knows my history so well?"

"My name is Brother Lazarus, which will mean less to you than your name means to me."

Nickolai did not like being on the defensive. If he were in a fight, he would be pressing an attack right now. Instead, he forced another question, "So what are you here?" He thought of Brody's comment. "A judge?"

Brother Lazarus shook his head and Nickolai noticed that the left half of his face bore scars across his muzzle and cheek, and he was missing a small piece out of his ear. When he laughed, that side of his mouth didn't move quite as far as the other. "Perhaps more a bailiff. Judging will be left for the Ancients upon their return." He stopped chuckling, "If you believe that."

"I follow the faith of St. Rajasthan."

"Do you now?"

Nickolai's hand was in the air before he even realized he was reacting to the insult. His claws were extended and might have added to the monk's scars, if Brother Lazarus still stood where he had been. But the monk had moved while Nickolai's body was still deciding what to do.

Brother Lazarus was on the other side of his arm, his elbow folded over Nickolai's wrist and the palm of his other hand pressing against the point of Nickolai's elbow. "You should remember two things, scion of Rajasthan. We are not a pacifistic order. And my ancestors in Rhodesia were bred to hunt the likes of you long before any man knew what a gene was, much less how to engineer them."

Nickolai turned to look at the monk, who was still smiling, though now Lazarus allowed just a hint of his teeth to show. Nickolai shook his head and said, "I don't wish to fight you."

"You have an interesting way of expressing that sentiment." Lazarus let go of Nickolai's arm. "And I think that is not the arm that you left here with."

"How—"

"As I said, we are the official presence of the Fifteen Worlds here. When Proudhon decided to rationalize the political structure of this planet, they had a decision to make. Were they or were they not going to continue the *de jure* relationship between Bakunin and the Fifteen Worlds? They made a wise decision."

"You are working with them?"

"We are in contact with them. Diplomatic relations are more preferable to both sides than an ongoing insurgency through these mountains."

"Diplomatic relations?"

"Please don't feign naïveté; it does not wear well on a scion of House Rajasthan. You, of anyone, should know the futility of divorcing spiritual concerns from the political. You still live because of a political compromise the priests of Grimalkin made on behalf of your family."

Nickolai spat a one-syllable curse on the bodies of those priests.

Lazarus still smiled. "Perhaps it is a good thing I am

not one of those priests, even if you follow the faith of St. Rajasthan."

"Perhaps."

"But again, I think, we face another compromise concerning your welfare."

"What do you mean?"

"As I said, we have diplomatic relations with the PSDC. Our relationship has gone hot and cold throughout their conquest. Right now, things are particularly chilly. Until an hour ago, I was in a conference with General Alexi Lubikov, the gentleman now in charge of the western half of the continent. He was quite interested in you, and your friends from the *Eclipse*."

The statement left Nickolai without any words.

Lazarus shook his head. "General Lubikov characterized your departure as 'not particularly subtle.' I suspect the same could be said of your return. He has quite a dossier on you. Now I am left with the question of what to do with you."

"What do you intend to do?"

"Prudence would dictate that I maintain a working relationship with the new masters of this planet. What would it gain me to antagonize the PSDC?"

"So you intend to turn us over?"

"My last question wasn't rhetorical, Nickolai. And I suggest you take your hand away from that chain."

Nickolai lowered his hand. He hadn't been quite aware that he had been reaching for the chain that still wrapped his torso. His thoughts were raging. They couldn't be stopped this close to their goal.

"Why are you here, Nickolai?" Lazarus asked. "Why would a group of mercenaries that left over nine months ago voluntarily return to the middle of a civil war just to force their way down here? What is it you are attempting to accomplish?"

The monk watched him intently, head slightly cocked. His body language, even his scent, spoke more of inquisitiveness than of assertiveness. Nickolai wondered just exactly how much he knew.

"Do you know what's out there?" he asked the monk.

"Having diplomatic relations with the new government does not free us from their signal jamming. We're as isolated as anyone else on this planet. Perhaps you can tell me?"

"What is out there, Brother Lazarus, is the end of the world."

Nickolai told the monk of the *Eclipse*'s ill-fated journey to Xi Virginis, the missing star. He told him of their trip to Salmagundi, the lost colony. He told him of the creature Adam, which had named itself God. He told him of the Protean, and of the flood of refugees filling Bakunin's solar system. He told him of the fall of Khamsin, and he told him of Mallory's resistance fleet.

"The plasma fire that shone in the sky a week ago. That was Mallory's attack on Adam's invasion. It may be the only reason why we are alive to stand here and discuss this."

"I see."

"Did your friend General Lubikov tell you any of this?"

"He is not my friend." Lazarus turned away from him and walked up toward the wall with the giant Dolbrian carving. "And you haven't told me why you are here. You seem to support this resistance, and it is unlike a member of your house to travel away from a battle."

"The battle will follow me here," Nickolai said. "And I will face it with both feet on the ground."

"Why *this* ground, Nickolai?"

Would you understand if I said I don't quite know?

"I believe that the Protean was directing us here."

"You believe?"

"It is why we took a ship and landed here. The Protean came from here, and said to find those that came before it."

"The Ancients."

"The Dolbrians."

Brother Lazarus shook his head and looked up at the massive carving before him. "I don't suspect a scion of the line of St. Rajasthan has been schooled in the tenets of my faith. But what you speak of is the cornerstone of our belief, the knowledge that one day, when we are ready, we will once again find the Ancients." He reached up and lightly touched the carvings in the wall. "They left us this. They did not abandon their creation. They're only waiting."

Lazarus' hand dropped and he turned to face Nickolai, a look of sadness, almost melancholy across his face. "But, I'm afraid that there is nothing here for you. We have studied these tunnels for more than a century, and the Ancients left nothing here but the gift of this planet, and a few carvings to mark their achievement."

CHAPTER TWENTY-SIX

Congregation

"There are never only two sides to a conflict."
—*The Cynic's Book of Wisdom*

"From the true antagonist illimitable courage is transmitted to you."

—FRANZ KAFKA
(1883–1924)

Date: 2526.8.12 (Standard)
Bakunin–BD+50°1725

General Alexi Lubikov stood in the corner of an executive suite in the residential part of Bleek Munitions' mountain headquarters. Both his injured guests had recovered enough to give him withering stares. Parvi repeated herself for what seemed to be the tenth time, "If you've opened a channel to Mallory, let us speak to him. He may have information that will help."

Lubikov shook his head and said, "I can't allow that. You two are prisoners of the Proudhon Defense Corporation for good reason. There's more than a fair share of casualties counting against both of you, and the only thing standing between you and a summary tribunal are my good graces."

"You haven't contacted him, have you?" Flynn asked, looking at him in a way that made Lubikov suspect it was the other personality, Tetsami, peering out at him from beneath the arcane tattoo on his head. If he hadn't known firsthand about Adam's talent for possession, he would have found the presence of another person in Flynn's body hard to credit.

"Are you purposely trying to antagonize me?" Lubikov asked.

Flynn's face broke into a sarcastic smile as Tetsami said, "I've known a lot of liars, and you're not a particularly good one."

Lubikov smiled and said, "And I've known a lot of prisoners, and it would take more than that kind of weak rhetorical prodding to prompt me into doing anything . . . self-defeating."

Flynn's smile shifted in a remarkably steady attempt not to reveal that Lubikov had precisely identified exactly what Tetsami had been doing. It was why you never let amateurs interrogate prisoners. A bad one can take things personally and reveal more information than they got from the prisoner.

"So, since we can't seem to more clearly identify what your friends are looking for in this mountain, and where they may be going, I'm afraid I have more productive tasks to attend to." He walked over to the door, which opened as he approached.

"How's it going," Parvi asked, "the fight with Adam?"

Lubikov turned and looked at Parvi, and found the thread of hope in her eyes a bit disturbing. "Better than I would have expected. They've cut off the invasion into separate pockets, and are fighting to sterilize them."

He let the door shut on her.

We're all doomed.

Not that Lubikov had lied about how Mallory's forces were doing. The only real falsehood he had provided them was the fact he had communicated anything with Mallory. Such a gambit, while possibly useful, was outweighed by the certainty that Adam would perceive it as a slight against his power, and Adam had agents on Bakunin waiting for his call.

He was perhaps the only one who found the absence of such a call disturbing.

There was a full-fledged war occurring though the system. He was one of the few within the PDC power structure high enough to see the intel reports from off-planet. Parvi's resistance was remarkably holding its own against the onslaught of Adam's forces.

But he knew, at best, Mallory's "fleet" would have a pyrrhic victory.

He walked down a hallway toward Bleek Munitions' communication center. The several Marines guarding the area snapped to attention for him. He told them to stand down and asked, "Is the meeting room ready?"

"Yes, sir."

Lubikov nodded and walked past, into a plain-looking conference room. Seated around a table were twelve men and women from all parts of the Proudhon hierarchy: military, civilian, executive. He allowed the door to slide shut behind him with a hiss, sealing out most of the EM spectrum that wasn't explicitly cabled into the room.

"I apologize for my tardiness. I had another meeting that ran a bit late."

The room broke out into simultaneous chatter, though it was mostly the civilians. The military folks in attendance, even the two who outranked him, showed a little more deference. He let the questions hang in the air as he took a seat at the conference table.

Everyone's here . . .

He continued, as if everyone wasn't trying to talk over each other. "I also want to thank you all for coming. I suspect this is the first time most of you have met each other, in any context."

"What exactly is this?" asked the loudest questioner. Geoff Talbot was an engineer and chief of PSDC's air traffic control operations. He was well placed to control not only physical access to the planet, but off-planet communications as well. If Bakunin was locked in a box, he held the keys. "ATC Operations are not under military jurisdiction."

"This is highly irregular," said a dark woman named Kim Hyung. She was deputy CFO, and in charge of the day-to-day financing of the PSDC and its military machine.

Lubikov smiled and looked at the faces of the people

staring at him. "You are all here because the situation we face is highly irregular."

All of the people he faced were holo projections. They had all called in from various points around the planet, and none of them had been told who else would be attending. One of the military attendees, General Yolanda Davis, Eastern Division Command—roughly Lubikov's peer, though she functionally outranked him by being in charge of the forces around the PSDC's capital, the city of Proudhon—looked at him and said, "You said that this was an intelligence briefing, General Lubikov. What are civilians doing here?"

"The same thing you are, General Davis. Asking what could possibly bring this group of people together. This *particular* group."

Lubikov wasn't particularly surprised when he saw Talbot's eyes widen slightly. The people in this room wouldn't be here if they were stupid. And Lubikov suspected a few of them would actually understand as soon as they recognized who they were in the meeting with.

For the ones who hadn't yet put the pieces together, Lubikov said, "If you look across this table, you'll see representatives from every segment of the PSDC. The people here, in large part, run this planet now." He folded his hands in front of him and leaned forward. "That is not all we have in common."

The talking ceased. Everyone here had reached a point of actual power, where his or her decisions made a definitive impact on the PSDC and, by extension, the whole planet. They were perhaps the twelve most strategic people on Bakunin at the moment, and he had spent months quietly finding out who they were, ever since he realized that he could not have been the only person recruited by Mr. Antonio.

General Davis broke the silence by asking, "What, exactly, are you saying, General Lubikov?"

"That each of us here has given allegiance to someone other than the executives in Proudhon." Objections began cascading across the table, and Lubikov added, "to someone calling himself Adam."

The brief pause the name caused in the objections was all the confirmation he needed, had he needed any. The pause was followed predictably by loud denials. Of course, none of these people were willing to admit such a thing.

He leaned back and said, "I have proof, of course."

That led to a slowly growing silence.

"What possible proof can you have?" someone muttered.

"Choosing to be an agent of this being, Adam, impacts far more than your loyalties. He grants rather particular gifts to his agents in positions of power, a foretaste of what he has promised you. But this gift does mark you, in subtle and very specific ways."

Kim Hyung shook her head and announced, "I am not going to indulge you any further. I am going to report—"

"Please sit down, Ms. Hyung." He squeezed all his considerable command experience into the order, and she responded like a green recruit being verbally smacked by a drill sergeant. Lubikov stood himself, looming over the holo representatives around the table. "Each one of you, were you not servants of Adam, would be dead right now."

General Davis dropped all of her military pretense. "What the hell are you talking about, Alexi?"

"I've researched all of you for months, and all of you were specially targeted over that time frame. An agent of mine, at some point in the recent past, hit each of you with a C-rad weapon."

"What is—" Hyung started.

"Coherent Radiation," Davis answered. "A nasty black ops weapon, like a gamma laser, low enough energy that the target doesn't even feel it—until their teeth fall out and they start puking up their stomach lining."

"Oh, my God . . ."

"Every one of you should have died of radiation poisoning over the last three weeks," Lubikov said.

"You're lying," Talbot said. "You're insane."

"More important," Lubikov said, "if the PSDC Board of Directors receives this information, I have little doubt that Adam would be displeased by the quality of your service."

Someone started to say, "You can't . . ."

Davis shook her head, "Of course he can. You've always been a ruthless, self-serving bastard, Alexi."

Talbot looked across the table at her, "You can't seriously be suggesting that he—"

"Shut up, Geoff, I've known about you for at least a year."

Talbot just stared at her and gaped.

Davis looked around the table then back at Lubikov. "I think you have everyone's attention. And I do not think this little gathering has Adam's approval."

"No." Lubikov steepled his fingers. "But if you were given the same information I was, I suspect you all know that Adam's stated plans have seriously diverged from what we were told to expect."

Several people nodded slightly.

"You did not gather us all here to tell us that the refugees cluttering up the system are more organized than expected," Davis said.

"No. Not even to tell you how they've managed to beat back Adam's advance for now." Lubikov noticed surprise on several faces. Not everyone here was high enough in the hierarchy to have fresh intel from off-planet. "Adam has reinforcements. His opposition does not. Nothing extraplanetary need concern us."

"What, then?" Davis asked.

"Currently, there is an attempt on the part of this opposition to recover some as-yet-unknown Dolbrian artifact."

If his audience was not still in the throes of shock and denial, he expected his statement would have been met with derisive laughter. As it was, he was met with a sea of blank, disbelieving virtual stares.

"You're right, Geoff," someone said, "he is insane."

Lubikov touched the surface of the table, calling up a holo in the middle of the table. In it, Nickolai Rajasthan was in the process of neutralizing five armed men, armed with nothing more than a length of chain. The scene flipped between that and Julia Kugara shooting up the motor pool. "This group secured entry into the Dolbrian tunnels under the Diderot Range."

One of the junior officers present looked at Lubikov

and spoke for the first time, "With due respect, sir, how can a group of three or four insurgents be of any importance, wherever they are?"

"Those insurgents are the only people to have successfully run our blockade of the planet. They come directly from the organized opposition to Adam. They came here with the specific intent to access these Dolbrian artifacts, whatever they might be."

General Davis shook her head. "What makes you assume they understand any more about Adam's strengths, or his hypothetical weaknesses, than we do?"

"Because they are facing his advance now and winning, for the moment. Because they've faced him before, and survived." He changed the display, and started giving them a short history of what he had reconstructed of the late Tjaele Mosasa's expedition. He gave them a history of the *Eclipse* and the people who had been on it. When he was done with his summary, he leaned back and said, "These actors know and understand what we've pledged allegiance to, perhaps more so than we do. Which leads me to suspect that the battles we're watching above us are a distraction, a feint—and the real threat lies under our feet."

General Davis shook her head. "A group of four people? This is in your jurisdiction. You should be quite able to task a squad, a dozen squads, to deal with them."

"Oh, they will be dealt with." Lubikov smiled.

Talbot's face was actually changing color, and he seemed so angry he was having difficulty speaking. "Good lord! Then why the hell have you pulled us all together? You're risking exposing all of us."

"I am hoping one of two things. First of all, I need to know if any of you know from your contact with Adam or his agents, what it is this 'group of four people' are looking for. What the threat actually is."

No one spoke up.

"No one?" Lubikov spoke.

"I think you know more about this than any of us," General Davis said.

"And the other thing you're risking all of us on?" Talbot snapped.

"Do any of you have the capability of warning Adam of this threat?"

Again, silence.

"None of you?" Lubikov asked incredulously. "None of you have a means to contact Adam?"

Talbot shook his head. "And if I did, the first thing I'd do would be to tell him what a reckless servant he has in you."

"I know," Lubikov said. He scanned the faces across the table, looking each one of the holo images in the eyes. He figured he owed them all that much respect. As he did, he typed out an order over an encrypted channel.

General Davis sighed. "Now what, Alexi? You've crawled out on a limb here. Any more grand plans?"

He nodded, "Always."

Across the table Hyung's image vanished in a flash of white light and static.

Davis, and several others barely said, "What?" and four more attendees followed Hyung, vanishing. Talbot stood and screamed at him, "You traitorous motherf—" his words consumed by a white light.

General Davis' eyes were wide as she stared at him and said, "Alexi?"

Three more attendees vanished around them. The remaining ones were scrambling out of their seats trying to run.

"You said I was a ruthless, self-serving bastard," he told her as her own holo disappeared in a flash of light.

Lubikov leaned back in his seat, alone in the conference room now. On a display inset into the table, text scrolled by as a dozen Special Forces squads messaged back the code words for a successful mission.

Adam's agents all met their fates in varying ways, but all involved extreme overkill that vaporized not only them, but the buildings they had been transmitting from. He disliked the collateral damage, but the gift that Adam gave them would mean that there was a possibility of surviving anything short of complete destruction.

And since he had the means . . .

He tapped a few more commands out on the console, and even the encrypted history of this meeting, and his orders out to his men, began to erase itself. No one person knew the scope of what he had just done, and he had placed enough layers of deniability between the act and himself that no one should connect it to him, especially since there were twenty-five other attacks, killing strategic personnel within the PSDC who had no particular connection to Adam, including key leadership positions within the Board.

He waited a few minutes, and then the door started buzzing insistently. He touched the controls to release the seals on the door, and said, "Come in, my conference is over."

The door slid open and a breathless Marine ran in and came to attention.

"At ease, son. What is it?"

"Sir, we've just received words of a coup."

Lubikov straightened in his chair and said, "A coup, you say? An insurgency?"

"We don't know, sir. We've just heard of a series of co-ordinated attacks all across the planet. At least fifteen, including a bomb that took out the top floor of Proudhon corporate headquarters."

He stood up and asked, "The Board?"

The Marine shook his head, "We don't know if there were any survivors."

Of course, there were survivors. Lubikov had carefully planned the survivors as well as the victims, and while the Board that was left would, of course, know nothing of the attack that placed them in power, none of them would have any reluctance in seizing the opportunity. They might even, in fact, exploit the general perception that they had been behind the "coup." Fear was a useful emotion in wartime.

And all would help camouflage Lubikov's own actions.

"Do we know the source of the attack? Was it Proudhon Defense Corporation personnel?"

"Sir?"

"If it was a coup, the attack was probably staged by our own forces."

"No word yet."

Lubikov nodded. "I want everyone under my command to shift communication protocols. All comm traffic to any unit is to come though here on an encrypted channel. Complete blackout otherwise, and I want reports on anyone breaking that order."

"Yes, sir."

For the time being, Lubikov would be the de facto ruler of everything west of this mountain range. He also guessed that it would take several days for the PSDC to recover from the event. But they didn't have several days.

That meant that he had to take advantage of what he did know now, before Adam regrouped and took this planet. He intended to be on the winning side of this—

Whoever won.

CHAPTER TWENTY-SEVEN

Doubt

"They never help you for *your* sake."
> —*The Cynic's Book of Wisdom*

"It is folly in one nation to look for disinterested favors from another."
> —GEORGE WASHINGTON
> (1732–1799)

Date: 2526.8.12 (Standard)
350,000 km from Bakunin–BD+50°1725

The *Wisconsin* had changed. The Proteans had rebuilt the structure after the damage of Stefan's attack. In less than a day, a new *Wisconsin* hung in orbit around Schwitzguebel, glittering like an alien jewel. Pieces of the original remained, melding into the new Protean artifact. Toni II suspected that those areas only remained to appease the sensibilities of the few living occupants who remained human.

The very few.

She, Mallory, and a handful of crew from the *Daedalus* were the greater part of those remaining. Everyone else had evacuated, died during Stefan's attack . . . or didn't count as human anymore.

Toni II stayed in the *Daedalus*, in the cabin she had shared with her "sister." It was one of the few places she had access to that was free from the influence of Stefan, or the Proteans.

Her injuries weren't that severe for someone who had gone EVA without a suit—some bad bruises, a horrible earache, and lungs that insisted on coughing up blood every twenty minutes or so. She had suffered worse in basic training on Styx. Even so, they gave her an excuse to stay there, nursing her injuries, trying not to think of what was happening outside the *Daedalus.*

What had happened to her sister. Her other self.

She slept in fits and starts, interrupted by her own coughing, and nightmares of a thousand Stefans crawling over each other to reach her. And when she woke, she felt waves of self-loathing for retreating into this cabin while the battle raged around them.

The Proteans are in charge of that now, aren't they?

The Proteans actually seemed to have some chance against Adam's forces.

She was pretty much irrelevant. She didn't even belong to this universe. A cosmic mistake, an irrelevancy . . .

She was coughing up more of her lungs into a bloody rag when the buzzer sounded on her door. She lowered the rag, careful to keep the fabric wrapped around the contents so that the mess wouldn't fly free in the tiny microgravity aboard the docked *Daedalus.*

"What?" she called out, her voice hoarse and weak.

"Can I come in?" her own voice answered.

"I—" Her voice choked on the taste of her own blood. She hadn't seen or heard her sister since Toni shoved her and Mallory into the air lock. She had learned since how Toni, her younger self, had survived, and Toni II didn't know if she wanted to face that.

She didn't know if she could.

Outside, herself said, "Please?"

Toni II finally answered, "Come in."

The door slid open, and Toni pulled herself into the cabin. They looked at each other, and Toni II stared into her other self's face, looking for some sign of a change, some mark showing that she had joined the Proteans. She didn't see any, other than the fact that her sister was still alive.

Toni stared back into her eyes, as if she was looking for something as well.

Toni II shook her head and said, "You look good."

"You look like hell."

"Apparently it's not particularly healthy to breathe vacuum."

Herself nodded and said, "Neither is breathing plasma."

Toni reached out to her, and almost involuntarily, Toni II flinched away from the touch. Toni's hand withdrew, and a painful sadness crossed her face. "I'm still me," she told her. "Whatever happened, I'm still me."

"I'm sorry. I don't think I can." The words were hard to say. She could feel her throat bleed as she spoke.

"No. I'm sorry for abandoning you."

"You didn't abandon me. You saved us—"

"No, I've been abandoning you ever since we left Styx."

"What?"

"I just took the lead in everything."

"I let you—"

"Because you have the same stupid idea I do, that somehow the fact you came out of that wormhole, that you're a ghost, makes you less of me. Makes you less of you."

"That isn't—" She had to cough a few times into her rag before she could continue. She was more aware than ever of her ears throbbing, and she didn't know if it was her coughing or Toni's words.

"Are you saying I don't know how we think?" Toni asked her.

"I'm an alien here, this is your universe—"

Toni knelt down next to her, slowly in the microgravity. Her sister reached out and touched her face, and this time she didn't flinch. "How does that matter now? How does that even make sense? We are far beyond the point where anyone except us cares . . . Neither of us has a past now— not one that matters to anyone but us."

"I don't want to lose you."

Her sister, her other self, gazed into her eyes and said, "You haven't lost me."

"But you've become one of . . . one of them."

"Yes."

"You didn't have a choice?"

"Yes, I did. I chose what I did, freely."

"Why?"

"I didn't want to lose you."

Toni II suffered a strange wash of feelings for her twin, and wondered if she was at heart, a narcissist.

"You should come back with me," Toni said. "You are a part of what is happening here, as much as I."

"What *is* happening here?" she asked her sister.

Toni took her to a conference room in the core of the re-made *Wisconsin*. Mallory was seated at a table, and she wondered if she looked as bad as he did. He had deep bruises under bloodshot eyes, and his cheeks were threaded by spidery hemorrhages under the skin. His fingernails had all turned dark purple or black.

In the room with him were Alexander Shane, whom she had only ever seen conscious on a surveillance video from the *Khalid*, and Rebecca Tsoravitch, the woman who had greeted her and Mallory when they had emerged from the air lock.

She looked around the room, and only saw grave expressions.

"What's the matter?" she asked. "I thought we were winning."

"We are," Mallory said. "For the moment, we have."

"But?"

"We may have driven Adam from this system," Tsoravitch said, "But it was only once. Our forces are weak, and it is only a matter of time, hours or days, before more of his army appears. His ships are probably in tach-space now."

"Then how do you intend to stop him?"

"They don't," Mallory said.

"What?" Toni II said. "What the hell are you talking about?"

Tsoravitch sighed. "We can't fight him like this continually. Our only hope is injecting our agents into his body. It worked here, but it came too early." She shook her head. "At least that is the consensus of the body of Proteus."

Toni II stared at all of them in turn, dumbfounded. They had *won*; they had beaten this thing back. It made no sense. When she looked at her sister, Toni told her, "Now you see why you needed to be here."

"This is insane!"

Tsoravitch shook her head. "Not from the Proteans' point of view."

"You're talking as if you're not one of them."

"Oh, I am, by the rules of their particular game. But that doesn't mean I think like them yet."

"What the hell does that even mean?" Toni II cried at them. "Why would they give up?"

"They aren't giving up," Shane said. "But Rebecca is right. They don't think the same way you do. Not even the same way I do, and my culture had more than a passing similarity to theirs. This battle here, to you, to Mallory, even to me—it was the endgame. The last stand. To Proteus, it was an opportunity to advance their plans a decade or two."

"A decade—what?"

"Within Proteus, the concepts of individuality and mortality have eroded to the point that they are truly alien. They sacrificed an entire world of themselves as a feint to inject themselves into Adam's collective. They fought this battle less to save this world, but to grant them the capability to disperse themselves and their pilgrims throughout human space ahead of Adam. There are dozens of worlds where he has yet to reach. Now, on each one, there will be Proteus, dormant, waiting." Shane leaned back. "A few decades from now, just a moment to the Proteans, they will be in a position to do to Adam everywhere what they did here."

She opened her mouth, but she couldn't bring herself to say anything.

Shane continued, "Proteus took this chance only because Mallory's efforts earlier made it possible to overpower his presence before he could communicate with other selves."

"Proteus has already started taching out of the system,"

Mallory said, "They and their converts are going every-where throughout human space, using what is left of our fleet."

"But that means that—"

"He will win," Mallory finished. "He will win, and maybe, sometime in the future the Proteans will overthrow his rule. But mankind, as such, will be long dead."

Toni II looked at her sister and said, "So you are leaving me again."

"No," Toni said. "I'm staying here."

"I don't understand," she said, trying to wrap her mind around the end of everything. "You're saying Proteus is abandoning us."

Tsoravitch shook her head. "No, they aren't, we aren't."

"They're leaving just enough of their force behind to make a credible fight when Adam returns," Mallory shook his head. He looked very weary. At the moment he looked older than Shane. "I can't even posit a viable counterar-gument. They're right. With their resources, it makes no sense to focus everything on one point where Adam can concentrate all his forces. Not when they can disperse and slip inside all his defenses." He shook his head and chuck-led. "They even have the sanction of the Bishop of Rome."

She looked at Tsoravitch, "How can you slip inside his defenses if he knows what happened here? If he's expect-ing what you're doing?"

"The one thing he can't do is see into someone's heart, and when he comes to the new worlds where Proteus is waiting, all he will find are people otherwise indistinguish-able from anyone else. That, and his arrogance will con-vince him that when he finally defeats us here, he will have defeated Proteus completely."

"Damn it," she snapped, "Why can't we defeat *him*? You've done it once already."

"Even if all of Proteus stayed here," Tsoravitch said, "we do not have the resources to repeat that battle."

"Then don't repeat it. Find some other way. This bastard isn't God. *Stop treating him like it!*"

Everyone stared at her, and she realized that she had allowed a note of hysteria to creep into her voice. Even her sister looked at her as if she had suddenly turned into someone else. She kept going, "You rebuilt the *Wisconsin* in what? A day? What else can you build? How quickly?"

"There aren't enough of us to build and crew a fleet like—"

She shook her head, her thoughts tumbling over each other. "Not a fleet, or a crew, for that matter. What about a tach-drive? How big does one have to be to make an interplanetary jump—can you make one as sophisticated as the one on the *Khalid?*"

"Yes, but—"

"What Mallory did to his cloud, do it to *him*. Have small drives sitting out there, waiting, and when he pops out of tach-space, tach the SOBs *into his ship*."

There was a long pause and, slowly, Mallory said, "They'd have to power up from a cold start . . ." The weight didn't leave his shoulders, but from the way his head lifted, it seemed he found more strength to bear up under it. "But could you reproduce the Caliphate's new control systems?"

Tsoravitch nodded, "We could do that, but it would still require a huge effort, and we couldn't cover all the potential arrival points . . ."

"Just the likely ones, then."

"And what about our people on the planet?" she asked. The room went silent.

"What? What happened?" She looked at Shane. "You sent them down there. What happened?"

Shane's face looked pained. "I know. And I now know what's down there. I'm sorry, but I didn't understand before joining Proteus—"

"What? What's down there?"

Shane looked up at her with a hollow expression. "Death."

"I don't understand."

Shane didn't look her in the eye. "There is something, in the deepest part of the caverns. It is a barrier; something is enclosed within it. The Proteans have known about it for centuries, but in their time on Bakunin, no one has lived to pass through it, and they know nothing of what is beyond it."

"Send some machine through, then."

Tsoravitch said, quietly, "Nothing that passes though the barrier ever comes back out."

She stared at Shane. He said, "They don't know why the damaged Protean on Salmagundi would direct you there. They know no way in it, past it, or through it. If your friends test it, they will be lost."

PART NINE

Deus ex Machina

"The universe is but one vast Symbol of God."
—Thomas Carlyle
(1795–1881)

CHAPTER TWENTY-EIGHT

Meditation

"Security is only 100% effective when protecting
something no one wants."
                    —*The Cynic's Book of Wisdom*

"When you're guarding the front door, they come in
the window."

                              —MARBURY SHANE
                              (2044–*2074)

Date: 2526.8.12 (Standard)
Bakunin–BD+50°1725

Their captors kept the four of them in a comfortable suite,
and neither Simon nor Lazarus came to see them again.
Nickolai told his fellow prisoners of the conversation he
had had with Lazarus, such as it was. And he had told them
how convinced he was that Brother Lazarus was lying
through his canine teeth.

Despite what he had told the dog, it was not enough.
Nickolai had had his fill of mysteries, and of holy men who
were the gatekeepers. He had been brought here by the
grace of God, and by that grace there should be no more
secrets. It didn't matter how profane or tainted Lazarus
thought his guests might be; the fact that they were here at
all argued for them.

Kugara and the scientists saw things differently. While
they didn't argue with the premise that Lazarus lied, their

thoughts went toward escape and a resumption of their search through the tunnels.

Nickolai knew that approach would be doomed.

What they sought, Lazarus knew of and could lead them to it. He just needed to be convinced. And, instead of sleeping, Nickolai spun theological and moral arguments in his head, trying to discover the key to Lazarus' thinking, what the dog needed to hear to deem them worthy.

That was almost a mental equivalent of wandering guideless through the dark tunnels under the Diderot Mountains. He was not a monk or a philosopher. He had been as mediocre in his religious training as he had been exceptional in the skills of a warrior. And his spiraling thoughts led him to a core of self-doubt that pondered if those deficits in his upbringing were responsible for his new understanding of God.

I know what is right.

If the Ancients had the foresight that Lazarus believed, if they were truly the hand of God in the universe, Nickolai was convinced that whatever remnants they left behind would be with this in mind, something like Adam. If the Ancients' creation was divine, free from the hubris of Mankind's creation of their ancestors, wouldn't they have left them some means to know their mind?

Perhaps some way to call upon them?

That was it. It had to be. Like Nickolai's faith, like Mallory's, Lazarus' had a defining moment for the end times. For the monks here, the end point of the current world was the return of the Ancients.

What if, buried in these caverns, was something that Lazarus believed would call them back? If so, Nickolai could now understand the lie, the reluctance. What kind of burden would it be to hold the secret of the end of the world, to have the responsibility of deciding when and how it would start?

Even if he didn't share Lazarus' faith, he understood the burden. If Nickolai had the means, how easy for him would it be to open the door of Heaven and allow the vengeful spirit of St. Rajasthan to descend upon the Fallen and the Saved alike?

He knew his job would have to be to convince Brother Lazarus that it was time to open that door.

Brother Lazarus had fasted and meditated since the exiled scion of Rajasthan had left his sight. He sat on the floor of his meditation chamber, facing the embedded slab of rock bearing the Ancients' hand. He sought to empty his mind of all distraction, all the clutter the external world tried to pour into his flawed vessel of a being.

He needed to see the chaos around him, around the universe, with the perspective of the Ancients, where the distance of a million years rendered them all so much dust drifting though the tabernacle of the Ancients' creation.

From that distance, did what Adam bring upon them truly matter?

The decision weighed heavily upon him.

He did not only protect the small bit of the Fifteen Worlds' sovereignty on this planet. He also protected the secrets they had found here. It was disturbing, a sign in and of itself, that Nickolai suspected that there was anything here to find. However limited his knowledge, the fact that the Barrier was here, under this mountain range, was only known to six people. All of them resided in the monastery. No one who knew about it was ever permitted to leave.

Now it seemed, according to Nickolai, that the Proteans knew of the Barrier.

Did Adam?

Was either of them so much closer to the Ancients than he was?

He looked up at the rock covered with the script of the Ancients; the stone was passive, as it had been all the millions of years since the Ancients' departure. If he had been of another faith, he might have prayed for wisdom.

He had three choices.

First was to do nothing. If Adam came to the Ancients' world here, take that as enough sign that this Adam was to be their successor in the Ancients' plan.

Second was to accept Nickolai's sincerity, and take him and his companions to the Barrier.

His last choice was uncomfortable to contemplate. The

first of his faith to come here and discover the Barrier had decided what it must have meant. It was a doorway to the Ancients themselves, a doorway that had to be protected from those not ready to pass through. They kept its existence a secret, and to prevent its premature revelation, they buried explosives throughout the complex network of caverns leading to it. Every monk to hold Lazarus' position had a detonator implanted in his skull. With a thought, he could seal the Barrier beneath a hundred million tons of the Diderot Mountains.

Perhaps it would be safe then . . .

But perhaps not.

And perhaps the Barrier itself would be destroyed in the process.

Was now the time for their return, and if it was, or wasn't, did his decision matter? Was the decision his, or was he deluding himself? His faith called upon him to see in terms of millions of years; the thought that it all fell upon *his* head was the height of arrogance. He was nothing.

What was his duty?

His reflection was interrupted by a high-pitched whine. His nose immediately picked up the scent of vaporized metal and superheated rock.

He sprang to his feet. Someone was shooting.

He heard a cry, and the scent of blood mixed with hot metal and smoke. He ran for the door, his thoughts perilously close to firing the explosives that would bring the mountain down around them.

Through the doorway, he heard more EM rifles, one cry had become a chorus, and the blood he smelled now merged a half-dozen species. His hermitlike existence meant he had never succumbed to the local tradition of bearing arms at all times. He now regretted resisting that impulse.

In the hallway, he took one step toward the armory as Brother Simon ran around the corner toward him. He had been a native convert, and would have carried a weapon, if his right arm still extended past his elbow. He clutched the bleeding stump as he ran, eyes glassy and skin pale, obviously heading toward Lazarus even though he seemed unaware that his leader was in the hallway until he was almost upon him.

When Simon saw him, he stopped short, stumbled, and fell into Lazarus' arms.

"Proudhon betrayed us," he groaned.

Heavy footsteps preceded a large shadowy figure into the hallway after Simon. The figure filled the corridor, almost as wide as it was tall. It moved deliberately, with a mass that shook the stone floor beneath it. In form it was a headless armored torso as wide as Lazarus was tall, with legs thicker than Lazarus' torso, clawed hands large and powerful enough to tear even Gregor the ursine in half with a twist of the wrist. One of those claws pointed at Lazarus and Simon, aiming a cluster of weapons at them, any one of which would probably leave them a thin smear on the ground.

"Brother Lazarus," it called to him.

The voice was familiar.

"Brother Lazarus," it repeated in General Lubikov's voice, and something whined as a red light came on above one of the barrels emerging from its forearm.

"Yes," he responded.

"You will order your people to stand down."

When Lazarus hesitated, it repeated, "You will order your people to stand down, or they will all be killed."

They didn't have the resources to repel this kind of military attack. He looked at the thing and said, "How?"

"Give the order. It will be broadcast."

Simon looked up at him and whispered, "You aren't going to—"

He gave the order, and he heard his voice echoed through the corridors. After speaking twice, the sounds of battle, if not the smell, began to recede.

Simon muttered, "Why?"

"Suicide is not a virtue," Lazarus told him.

CHAPTER TWENTY-NINE

Desecration

"The most dangerous threats are the ones you assume you understand."

—*The Cynic's Book of Wisdom*

"Their team has the bad habit of changing the lineup when you aren't looking."

—Sylvia Harper
(2008–2081)

Date: 2526.8.12 (Standard)
Bakunin–BD+50°1725

Nickolai and Kugara were immediately awake at the first sound of gunfire. Nickolai stood in the center of the room, holding the chain that was his only weapon, as Kugara roused Brody and Dörner.

"What the hell—" Brody started to complain, but he stopped talking as soon as he saw the expression on Kugara's face.

Nickolai listened to the sounds coming through the sealed doorway. The grinding of machinery, the whine of EM rifles, the cries of the wounded.

"Adam?" whispered Dörner.

Nickolai shook his head, "Not unless he's now using heavy powered infantry." He could hear the footsteps of the armor, five times the mass of the powered suits he'd confronted in the woods outside Wilson, the kind of weight that ground errant gravel into powder.

There had been some dim night-cycle lighting in their suite/cell, but now the orange lights along the base of the walls winked out, leaving them in darkness. His new eyes adjusted instantly to see by infrared, in time to see Dörner fumbling to switch on the dead lighting.

"Power's cut," he said.

"Proudhon?" Kugara looked past him.

"Probably."

"Are they after us, or the monastery?"

Nickolai wrapped the chain around his arm. "Perhaps both." He slammed his body into the sealed doorway, leading with his metal-wrapped arm.

"Shit!" Dörner called out, "What's happening?"

Her voice dripped with fear, and Nikolai could smell the panic from where he stood. He'd forgotten they were blind in the darkness. "I'm trying to open the door," he said. He backed up and struck it again. The resonating impact tried to shake the teeth loose from his head, but the door was unmoved.

"They may be trying to preempt us," Brody said. "The local generalissimo has a file on all of us—he may have figured out why we're here."

Nickolai struck the door again, tuning out the conversation as he continued trying to break it down. To his chagrin, the door was constructed with people like him in mind. Repeated attacks only hurt his shoulder. When it was clearly futile, he backed away, panting, trying to think of another escape.

Kugara must have read his thoughts. "It's the only way out. I checked earlier, and all the walls are solid rock except for a few tiny ventilation holes."

Nickolai shook his head and let the chain spiral off his bruised arm to clatter on the floor.

Wait. That was all they could do.

Beyond the door, he heard Lazarus' canine voice order his people to lower their weapons, the words repeated several times from several directions, and the sounds of battle slowly ceased.

"Is it a bad thing if they find what the Protean sent us to find?" Dörner whispered, her voice small and shaky. "It's to fight Adam, as long as they aren't him—"

She was interrupted by the door rattling and slowly opening before them, letting in a flood of new light.

Backlit in the open doorway, Brother Lazarus stood facing them. As Nickolai's alien eyes shifted their spectrum and sensitivity, he could make out the source of the light flooding the room from behind the monk.

It came from floodlights mounted in the shoulders of a wall of ambulatory metal. Nickolai took an unconscious step backward once he saw the thing. The suit was remarkable enough that Nickolai still remembered the name of it from his abbreviated training at the BMU; Bleek Munitions Goliath Series V. It was the heaviest class of powered infantry armor ever created. So heavy, in fact, that the mobility tradeoff made it of limited tactical use. A hovertank was faster, cheaper, and had more firepower.

Under the Diderot Mountains would be one of the few environments where that kind of bipedal tank would make sense. The thing could shrug off most any small arms, it was EMP hardened, had integral Emerson fields powerful enough to soak up the energy from a small AM grenade, and could engage a small armored cav unit in hand-to-hand combat. It bore pretty much the same relation to the armor he'd faced by Wilson as Nickolai did to *felis domesticus.*

With the machine looming over him, Lazarus said, "Come with me."

They were marched out of the monastery, and into the huge cavern that had greeted them on arriving. It no longer seemed quite as huge with a squad of Goliath armor standing guard over thirty disarmed and injured monks. The tiered wall of the monastery itself had suffered damage to its facade, many of the carvings cracked, pitted, or scorched. Above them, a gray haze hid the ceiling from the artificial lighting, which now only came from the floodlights mounted on the armor, making the shadows long and surreal, wrapping around the rock like flaws in a broken holo projection.

The prisoners had been massed in the dishlike amphitheater, as if they were about to receive a sermon. The armor surrounded the outer edge, like demons guarding a tiny circle of Hades. Their personal Goliath ushered them into the front row, right before the podium.

Brody looked up at the Goliaths and whispered, "This can't be good."

A few minutes passed, and then the cavern filled with the sound of hydraulics and mechanical whirring. Nickolai realized that the Goliaths were all standing at attention.

A man walked out from the darkness beyond the reach of the Goliaths' floodlights. He was not particularly tall for a human, but his body language compensated for it. Every motion was economical and confident, no step careless or accidental.

He wore a uniform; gray fatigues that were recognizable as BMU issue despite the redesign of the patches to read "Proudhon Defense Corporation." On the collar were embroidered the stars of a general.

The man walked up to the podium. From him, Nickolai didn't even smell the casual subliminal fear that most humans emitted in his presence. He stood facing the forced congregation and said, "I am General Alexi Lubikov, and I am in charge here."

The prisoners started speaking, but Lubikov raised his hand slightly, and suddenly the area was filled with the sound of moving machinery as Goliaths pointed their arms toward the crowd.

"I would prefer not to be interrupted," Lubikov said.

The objections died down.

"Thank you. As I said, I am in charge here. I am backed by the full force of the Western Division of the Proudhon Defense Corporation, and due to some recent instability in the PSDC, at the moment I answer only to God. Do we all have an understanding?" He stared out at everyone, and Nickolai had the thought, *How do you define God, General?*

"I come ahead of an invasion. An entity called Adam will soon come to this planet. The first few battles have already raged above the atmosphere. He's been momentarily defeated, but that resistance has a consequence. When he does come, and he *will* come, it will not be as a conqueror. It will be as a destroyer."

Nickolai wondered how much truth the man spoke. He suspected that it was more than he would like.

Lubikov turned so he was addressing Brother Lazarus directly. "Since you had the remaining crew of the *Khalid* in your custody, I am quite certain you were aware of this. I am also sure you know why they came to you."

Nickolai looked at the general, disconcerted by how much the man knew.

"They are going to cooperate with me, not only because we have the shared goal of preventing Adam from destroying this planet, but because I am sure they would like to be reunited with their comrades."

Nickolai heard that and knew that Flynn had been captured. Despite his warrior ethos, he couldn't find it disappointing that Flynn had survived his final battle.

Then the last word struck him. *Comrades.*

"Parvi," Kugara whispered next to him.

"You will cooperate with me as well, Brother Lazarus."

"Why?" the canine half growled. "You desecrate a place of worship. You attack my people. You violate a sovereign territory that has pledged its stewardship of a treasure whose value you don't even understand. Why would I cooperate with you?"

"Because martyrdom would be pointless if I still find what I am looking for."

Nickolai smelled the canine's anger in the air as Lazarus glared at the general. For a moment, Nickolai thought the monk might leap and attack Lubikov, despite the armored sentries surrounding them. But the monk remained still, staring as if his look alone could kill.

Then, without any explanation, Lazarus' expression changed. His mouth twitched downward, and the hard glare in the eyes gave way to uncertainty. His posture sagged slightly, drawing inward, and the smell of anger drifted away, toward fear.

Lubikov shook his head as if negating an inaudible conversation between himself and the monk. "I never take a battle to a territory I haven't studied beforehand. Those bombs may be buried deep, but not so deep as to avoid notice."

Lazarus grumbled something. To human ears it would have been an inarticulate growl. Nickolai heard the words within the growl. *"You're jamming ..."*

"And, thanks to your transmission, we now have the activation codes as well as the frequencies." He leaned forward slightly. "Would I be wrong in assuming that by following the trail of those explosives, I would find myself in the heart of your Dolbrian mysteries?"

Lazarus looked defeated.

Lubikov smiled, "It shouldn't be a hard decision. All you're doing by cooperating is saving my time, along with the lives of yourself and your fellow monks."

CHAPTER THIRTY

Forbidden Fruit

"Beware of your allies' secrets."
—*The Cynic's Book of Wisdom*

"Lying to ourselves is more deeply ingrained than lying to others."

—FYODOR DOSTOEVSKI
(1821–1881)

Date: 2526.8.13 (Standard)
350,000 km from Bakunin–BD+50°1725

Rebecca stood on a dusty red plain, under a sky that wasn't quite the right shade of blue. The ground under her feet was not quite barren. Spidery tendrils of grass had a tenuous hold on the near sterile soil, enough that the air was close to breathable. The sun above was bright and hard and cold.

Centuries of effort had been expended to make this place habitable, and Adam had erased it all in less than an hour. This Mars now only existed in the memories of Proteus, and even though she had never set foot there, in her own.

Jonah Dacham stood on the plain, facing away from her. He looked up at the sky and shook his head.

"I'm trapped, aren't I?"

"I'm sorry." She didn't know what else to tell him. "If I hadn't—"

"I know. I had that conversation with Mosasa. If Adam had seen me, it would have tipped Proteus' hand. None of us realized where Adam had come from, or that he had been here before." He turned around and smiled weakly. "I should be glad I retain some sort of identity, shouldn't I?"

Rebecca stared at the horizon. Some of the hills in the distance resembled a human face. "If I could, I would set you free." *And Mosasa, if he still existed here.* "But minds don't work like that."

Dacham shook his head.

"I've been trying to solve this problem since Adam took me and I found Mosasa waiting for me." She had been spending a good part of the new awareness that Adam had granted her in examining her own mind, with the dispassion of a software engineer trying to decompile code. She thought she now knew more about the low-order workings of her own consciousness than Adam did his own. "I didn't find him an exit, and you are just as much a part of me now. It's like pouring three vintages of wine into the same bottle, then trying to only pour one back out."

"Mosasa must have managed a way," he said.

"I don't think so. I just think he existed across too many minds. When he attacked Adam—" She found it difficult to speak. For some reason she had a hard time thinking the phantom pirate had actually sacrificed himself. Even though Mosasa probably existed replicated across Adam's whole existence, the loss of him *here* affected her more deeply than she would have credited. "I think whatever part of him is left in my mind isn't enough to remain sentient. I've found no objective means to segregate one thought from the next, despite who's thinking it."

"My existence is an illusion, as much as the Face over there."

"No, I don't think—"

"But you do," Dacham said, "you think me." He crouched down and looked at the Face on the horizon. "In fact, I am probably more you than me. I feel your thoughts the way I used to feel the air I breathed, when I breathed. It's why I know you're bringing questions for me, not sympathy."

Rebecca didn't respond, because Dacham was right.

That, and he was privy to the same things she saw and heard, he would know of her talks with Shane, and his obsessions with the remnants of the Dolbrians.

"Why don't you ask?"

"Don't you know my questions already?"

He nodded. "I also know what you will do with the information. You will go to Shane, and he will go to the humans he is still so attached to."

"Would I be wrong?"

"I really don't know."

"Shane believes that the Proteans—you—are lying."

There was a long silence before Dacham said, "It's unfortunate that I don't even have a rationalization for the deception. After all this, I only have the faith that, for good or ill, there was a reason."

"A reason for what?"

"Promise me something."

"What?"

"A trade, for my knowledge."

She stood there mute. She didn't know what offended her worse, the fact that Shane had been right and the Proteans were lying about the Dolbrian remnants on Bakunin, or the fact that Dacham was making some sort of game of all of this. After all that they had lost. All that *she* had lost. She felt rage building, and Dacham looked as if he sensed it as well—

"Please," he said quietly, "think of it as a belated last request from a man who has died at least two more times than he should have."

"What do you want?"

"When there's an expedition to the surface, go with Shane."

"No one's suggested there would be—"

"When you hear what I have to tell you, there will be. And, like Shane, there are humans I have more connection to than a disciple of Proteus should."

"Fine," Rebecca said, "now tell me the truth."

"It's not that we've lied," Dacham said, "so much as omitted some details . . ."

*   *   *

When Mallory finally slept, he slept for a long time, his body collapsing into a dreamless coma that lasted far too long. When he finally awoke, even in the microgravity in the core of the *Wisconsin*, he felt old. It was as if the past couple of days had burned out all of his training, and left him an arthritic old man.

Some of it, he expected, was aftereffects from being exposed to a vacuum. His lungs still felt raw, and the inflammation of the soft tissues couldn't have been good for his joints.

He kept going, partly due to the grace of God, partly because he didn't know how to stop. It took him longer than it should have to make his way down to the control center.

The room was empty when he arrived. He hadn't expected anyone. The nexus of control had shifted elsewhere, somewhere into the collective brain of the Proteans who had deigned to stay behind. He slid into a seat at one of the control consoles, and started pulling up displays of the state of Bakunin's solar system.

Again, on the schematic view, the dots were all blue. They had, for the moment, retained control. On another display, showing the surface of the moon below, he could see a long curving spine rising up from a flat plain. The crystalline object was several hundred kilometers long and gradually curved skyward to point up out of Schwitzguebel's gravity well.

The Proteans had barely started building the thing when Mallory finally had gone to his cabin to sleep. Now, in less than a day, it looked fully functional.

He zoomed the image until he was only looking at the end of the massive structure. From far away, the thing looked delicate and fairylike, a crystal web-work of gossamer threads. Close up, the scale of it became clear. Those gossamer threads were pillars the diameter of one of the *Wisconsin*'s habitats, and they wove together into a braid that formed the ridge on top of the kilometers-long spine.

Buried in that ridge, barely visible at this distance, was a tiny hole that was probably a hundred meters across at least. It drilled into the end of the spire as if it was the barrel of a massive gun.

And that would be a pretty accurate description of what the object was.

As he watched, a tiny speck emerged from the hole. Fired down the length of the spine, it had a speed ten times the moon's escape velocity, and a trajectory that would take it out of Bakunin's orbit as well. On the schematic holo of the system, he could see a new blue dot emerge from the vicinity of Schwitzguebel's orbit.

It traveled out, safely beyond most of the other blue dots, and winked out—taching to somewhere in the outer system.

Lieutenant Valentine's suggestion had given birth to an entirely new class of weapon. Copying the drives, and more importantly the navigational systems, of the new Caliphate tach-ships, the Proteans had shrunk the disparate elements as much as possible until they had a dense silver sphere about fifteen meters in diameter—nothing but sensors, computers, and an unshielded tach-drive. It didn't even have the reaction mass to maneuver itself; it relied only on the precision of its tach-drives and its navigational computers. And the sensors on board would be able to detect another ship like the *Voice* taching in and aim for it based solely on the tachyon radiation released by its reappearance in the real universe, and in theory it would be able to anonymously jump to the site of the target long before the light of its appearance reached it.

That last capability meant that the whole system could be effectively covered by a number of ships several orders of magnitude smaller than could be done with conventional mines. In fact, it took several hundred hunter-killer satellites for the PSDC to deny low orbit over the one strip of a continent on Bakunin.

They were looking to create a denial area out to 15 AU.

Another small speck shot out of the spine on the moon below. They were shooting out one every thirty seconds. Nearly three thousand in a day.

Maybe they could do this.

But for how long?

He folded his hands in front of him, and prayed for wisdom. He understood the Protean strategy. Adam had the whole rest of the universe to plan, regroup, attack as many times as he deemed necessary. However impressive their defenses became, Adam could afford to test them until he found a weakness.

Mallory couldn't see a way out.

"Mallory?"

He turned around and saw the ghostly figure of Alexander Shane standing there. Now that the man, if he was still truly a man, wore clean clothes and didn't have the stooped posture of the wounded and infirm, he more resembled someone who might have once been at the helm of a whole planet's political system.

Mallory nodded an acknowledgment as he silently concluded his prayer.

"Yes, Mr. Shane?"

"I came to apologize."

"For what?"

"For abusing you and your people on Salmagundi." He walked over and sat on a chair next to Mallory, looking up at the holo of the spine, shooting out another shiny tachyon mine. "I disregarded my own society's norms to do what I did. And by taking your own living minds into my own, I ironically gained an exhaustive understanding of what a violation that was for the rest of you."

Mallory's hand unconsciously went to the back of his neck. The implant at the base of his skull, where Shane had connected him to the Hall of Minds, was no longer raw. But the scabbed scar tissue was painfully inflamed after his space walk. He winced and said, "You are welcome to what forgiveness I have left."

Shane shook his head and said, "Joining the Proteans, accepting their change, it is no small thing."

"I expect not."

"I don't believe I was aware of how mercifully clouded my thinking was before they remade me. All of me. Dozens of selves, all now equally present, equally clear. And many are unhappy with the choices I have made. The part of me that is you has convinced me, us, to act in some measure to redeem ourselves in our own eyes."

Mallory looked at Shane and tried to imagine what it must be like to have so many individuals trapped in one brain, one of them himself. Could it be anything but hellish? Was there really anyone that could be called Alexander Shane, anyone inside himself that he could identify as himself, or was all of him only pieces of others?

"I was as dissatisfied with the Protean answers about Parvi's mission as you were. By definition. Perhaps more so, since I bear some responsibility for setting those people on that path."

"It was the Protean's own words," Mallory said.

"And mine."

"And Dörner and Brody."

"Mine as well. The Protean answer was not satisfactory—"

Mallory nodded. "Only death remained in the Dolbrian caverns."

"It seems that that was only half of the truth."

Mallory leaned forward. "There's more to it?"

"Not as much as I would wish. The parts of me that mirror those who left, Brody and Dörner, weren't satisfied with the answers I gave you. Why would the Protean on Salmagundi send people to certain death?"

"Why?"

"Logically, because that poor doomed creature came from here at a time when the barrier did not exist."

"What, you told us the Dolbrians left the barrier here . . ." He trailed off because Shane was shaking his head.

"They never actually said that, did they? I figured out that much on my own, but your comrade Miss Tsoravitch was able to dig out the actual story for me."

Mallory stared at him and said quietly, "The barrier you spoke of, the Dolbrians did not leave it behind. The Proteans did."

"Yes."

"What's it protecting, then? What were we being sent to?"

"They don't know—"

"How can you not? If the Proteans built this wall, they must know what's behind it."

Shane shook his head. "At one time they did, but not now."

"What do you mean?"

"When they placed the barrier, every soul in Proteus purged their own memories of what lay beyond it." He shook his head. "They also purged all knowledge of how to penetrate or disable the barrier."

"Why?"

"Fear. Those who existed when the decision was made are still barely able to speak of it, despite their incomplete memories. They did not even trust themselves to own the knowledge of what it was."

Mallory shook his head. *Fear? What does Proteus fear that much?*

"Do they know you're telling me this?"

"Probably."

"Probably?"

"I made no secret of my interest, or why. I am just . . . uncertain how my new peers think. After centuries like this, they have changed."

More so than you from Salmagundi?

"Proteus sees itself as a guardian of its knowledge. They have restrained themselves, prevented their existence from bleeding beyond their own self-imposed boundaries. They know what damage can be wrought were they to defer to the base instinct they inherited from their human progenitors."

"What instinct is that?"

"The instinct to power." Shane turned toward the schematic holo where the tiny tachyon mines floated away from their lunar orbit to vanish into tach-space. "The most basic and necessary feature of intelligence is the desire to control the environment, to make it more favorable to oneself, one's family, one's tribe. Without that, no species would pull itself out of the mud that spawned it, much less reach the stars. But that will to control does not cease when it reaches another person. That will is why we have language, mathematics, science, and can be sitting on a space platform orbiting a moon sixteen light-years from the planet that birthed us."

He turned to look back at Mallory. "It is also why we have slavery and murder and war, and a creature named

Adam that will not stop short until every voice in the universe praises his name as a god."

"Not *a* god," Mallory said.

"Proteus saw the seeds of Adam within itself, and built itself to prevent that from ever happening. And what I see when I look at the Proteans, is to some extent they have crippled themselves. And for all they see Adam as an abomination, they have self-limited to the point where I wonder how effective they will be in stopping him. But I think they know this, and I think they may accept that their new converts may have differing ideas."

"What kind of ideas?"

"I think some of us should return to Bakunin."

CHAPTER THIRTY-ONE

Ascension

"Unless you love yourself, you cannot love another."
—*The Cynic's Book of Wisdom*

"Take away love and our earth is a tomb."
—ROBERT BROWNING
(1812–1889)

Date: 2526.8.13 (Standard)
350,000 km from Bakunin–BD+50°1725

Toni II's sister found her near the air lock where they had made their last stand before Stefan. There was no sign left of the battle, the corridor had been rebuilt by the Proteans, changed so that her only indication that this was the place where she and Mallory launched themselves into the vacuum was the schematic of the *Wisconsin*'s core.

She was sitting, leaning against a curving semicrystalline wall, when Toni approached her. She looked up into her sister's face, *her* face, looking for some recognition of where they were.

She was comforted when she saw some echo of her own emotions. She was still in there. Whatever heretical powers had claimed her other self, she was still in there. A version of her, anyway.

"How are you doing?" her sister asked.

Toni II almost responded, "You know how I'm doing." But did she? They had started from exactly the same place, at one point had been the same person. Their experiences since she had come back from the wormhole had been mostly shared. Before Stefan, they had still occasionally finished each other's sentences; each had known what the other was thinking.

Now, they were no longer the same . . .

She told her sister, "I was just wondering how many Rubicons one person can cross."

Her sister knelt down and placed a hand on her shoulder. This time she didn't flinch at the touch.

"Only as many as we need to," Toni said.

"It frightens me," she said. "*You* frighten me."

"I know."

"You're no longer me."

"No, I'm not. But I never was, not since we became separate people."

Toni II reached up and placed her hand on Toni's. It was warm, and felt human. "What is it like?"

"It *is* scary. You have to concentrate to keep your identity enclosed within itself, and part of the deal is they have the right to copy you, take everything you are and reproduce you somewhere else."

"God knows, we wouldn't want that to happen."

When her sister laughed, Toni II felt a small weight lift off of her heart.

"And there are rules," Toni said, "what can and cannot be done."

"The whole consent thing."

"More than that. The only reason Proteus can move as it has been doing is because Adam has poisoned the well—"

"Poisoned the well?"

"He brought the 'Change' here, however unwillingly. Beyond simple self-defense, moving as they have done in the world of men is taboo. Their highest commandment is to never grant mankind the means to destroy itself."

She looked up at her sister and tried to understand herself. "But they're leaving us to him. There isn't going to be a mankind left—"

"They aren't omnipotent, and they are much fewer than

Adam's host. They are working to stop him the best way
they know."

She realized something in what her sister was saying.
"You keep saying what 'they' are doing. Aren't you a part
of them?"

"Come with me, I want to show you something."

"Oh, my God," Toni II's voice caught, barely a whisper.

Her sister's hands were on her shoulders and she whispered into her ear, "I wanted you to see this."

They had walked out an air lock, an extreme measure
of trust for Toni II, and into a small craft that seemed little
more than a featureless white sphere with one slightly flattened wall. When the entry seamlessly sealed itself behind
them, the sphere accelerated until the flattened wall became the floor.

Then, after a few more seconds, the color, the walls
themselves, drained away, leaving nothing but the space
beyond.

She stared out at the universe, gaping. There seemed to
be nothing between them and the stars. To their right, the
surface of Schwitzguebel was dark but still faintly visible
in the reflected light from Bakunin, a ghostly landscape in
blue-black. To their left, the planet Bakunin glowed blue-
white, showing a hemisphere of ocean to reflect Kropotkin's light toward them.

Around everything was a near painful spread of stars.

"It's beautiful."

"I wanted to remind us why we left Styx in the first
place."

Toni II bit her lip and stared out at the blackness. There
were too many stars to make out Sigma Draconis, or even
to tell if she was looking in the right direction. "It really is
all gone," she whispered, "Not just the wormhole, but Styx
as well. Everyone, everything . . ."

The starscape blurred, and Toni squeezed her shoulders
and whispered, "Not everything."

Toni II realized that she was blushing as well as crying.
"We always enjoyed the view from space, didn't we?"

"Yes."

"I'd forgotten it. Nearly a year orbiting that damned wormhole."

"The damned loneliness." Toni's arms lowered, to embrace her from behind. Her chin rested on her shoulder, looking out at the stars with her. "We're not alone."

"But—"

"You asked why I keep saying 'them' when I mention Proteus."

The question on Toni II's lips had been, *but you're no longer human.* Of course, Toni would know that.

"Yes."

"Proteus can no longer contain its own. It governed by consensus for centuries. Consensus by a small elite, self-selected group that infinitely propagated itself—but this past battle they not only took me, but thousands of others, all recently human. Proteus is changing in spite of itself."

"What does that mean?"

"I don't know." The way she held her, chin on her shoulder, Toni II felt Toni's cheek against her own, felt the warmth of her breath against the side of her face. Whatever she had done, whatever bargains she had made, Toni still felt human. "I don't know what any of this means. I think anyone who does is lying to themselves."

"Why . . ." Toni II trailed off, unable to finish the question.

Toni's response was to turn and lightly kiss the side of her neck, below her ear. Even though she had expected the response to her barely spoken question, the light touch of her other self's lips on her skin send a ripple of fire down the whole length of her body.

She swallowed a painful doubt and whispered, "I don't know if I can join you."

"I'm not asking you to."

"But what you've become?"

Toni turned her around to face her. She reached up and gently wiped a tear off of Toni II's cheek. "I won't leave you. Leave us."

She stared into Toni's face for several long moments. Her skin was bluish silver in the light reflected from Bakunin's ocean. She had never been particularly vain, but somehow, seeing her face on another person—on Toni—made it beautiful.

Toni's expression seemed to collapse into a vulnerable sadness that made Toni II's heart ache for her. She began to say, "I never wanted to—"

She grabbed Toni's shoulders and pulled her into a sudden, impulsive kiss. Toni stiffened a bit in surprise, and then fell into the embrace as if it had been her idea. Which it had been.

They kissed each other, holding on as if they could become one person again; every touch incredibly alien, and incredibly familiar; the motion of each tongue mirroring the other. With their tongues' mutual caress, Toni II felt aches awaken in her body that she hadn't known existed.

They pulled away from each other at the same moment, and Toni II saw her own bemused expression staring back at her.

They both said, simultaneously, "I know this is weird, but . . ."

The words trailed off as they both realized that, for all that had happened since Toni II had popped out of Wormhole Sigma Draconis III, they were still enough the same that their thoughts still echoed each other. Echoed each other enough that they moved in silence as the sphereship's motion caused Bakunin's orb to set behind Toni's left shoulder.

They removed each other's clothes, allowing the brief touches of hand to skin to send warm shudders through the other. They both slowed as the excitement built, until their motion had a near ritualistic gravity. When they stood to face each other's nakedness, they both quietly said, "I love . . ."

Again the simultaneous statement trailed off, this time more in a mutual embarrassment for the narcissism of the words. They both reached for the other's face, thumbs tracing lower lips, and they both responded by kissing the other's hand, taking the thumb into their mouth. Both closed their eyes and shuddered at the contact of tongue on skin.

Then they embraced, pressing the whole length of their naked bodies together, kissing each other again. When the kiss broke, Toni II allowed herself to realize that she held a naked woman in her arms. Some part of herself that still lived on Styx prompted her to quietly say, "When did we become gay?"

"You know," Toni said, "since Proteus touched me, I don't have to be—"

Toni II placed a finger on Toni's lips, quieting her. She shook her head, smiling and wondering at the fact that, for the moment, she was taking the lead. "I know you could be anyone now." *Anything.* "You could be a man if that's what we wanted." She caressed Toni's face. "But this is still *you*, isn't it?"

Toni nodded slightly, and Toni II felt her breath hot on the skin between her thumb and forefinger.

"*That's* what we want," she told her.

Tentatively, awkwardly, surrounded by stars, they made love to each other as if it was the first time for both of them.

Much later, Toni II lay on her back staring up at the universe with Toni curled up on top of her. *I need to stop thinking of her as my sister . . . things are weird enough already.*

"What now?" she asked herself.

Herself lifted her head up from between her breasts and looked down on her, "Whatever it is, it's together."

"You make it sound easy."

Her other self placed her head back down on her chest and said, "If it was easy, this would have happened *before* we both nearly died."

"I guess so." Toni II bit her lip. "What about Proteus?"

"What about them?"

"Will I have to . . ."

"Only if you ask for it."

"What if I can't?"

"I won't let that come between us. I won't let anything do that."

Toni II stared up at the stars. "Just us against the universe?"

"Just us," Toni said.

*   *   *

The return to the *Wisconsin* was an unwelcome return to reality, or what was masquerading as reality nowadays. If she could have, she would have prolonged their orbit around Schwitzguebel, if not forever, at least a bit longer than they did. But she couldn't abandon everyone, especially since she bore some responsibility for Stefan and what he had done. She knew, without discussing it, that her Protean self felt the same. They felt a duty here almost as strong as they felt toward each other. And, as inconvenient as that was, without that part of themselves, they probably wouldn't feel nearly as deeply for each other.

Whatever happens now, though, we have that.

They walked out of the air lock, and Mallory was waiting for them. Toni II felt Toni's hand brush hers and wondered what the priest would make of their relationship.

"Captain," Mallory said to Toni. He turned to her and said, "Lieutenant." His eyes were still shadowed from the bruising vacuum, and Toni II figured that was how he was telling them apart. There was a distant, almost fatalistic look in his eyes, and just as she recognized it, Toni squeezed her hand.

"What is it?" Captain Toni asked him.

"You were concerned for our mission to the surface."

Toni II thought of the people that were probably lost now, Parvi, Kugara, Flynn, Nickolai, Dörner, Brody—people she barely knew ... but, even so, she asked, "You have news about them?"

"About what they face."

"What?" both Tonis asked in unison.

"The obstacles in their path are more recent than the Dolbrians. Whatever the Protean on Salmagundi wanted us to find, it is sealed behind a barrier erected by the Proteans themselves."

Toni II turned to Toni and said, "That means that they can remove it, right?"

She felt Toni's grip tighten on her hand, and her voice was cold when she spoke, "Why didn't Proteus tell me this?"

Toni II opened her mouth, but then it sank in. Her other self had accepted Proteus' bargain, and she hadn't stopped to think of what it would take to make her agree to it, to allow an alien machine to burrow into her, take her apart and reassemble her, to know her more intimately than she could possibly know herself. To embrace something that, for all her life, she'd been taught was an evil. Maybe *the* evil.

To face that, accept that, and discover that what had embraced her had betrayed her.

Toni II felt the anger, and read it across her own face.

She squeezed her hand back, a silent acknowledgment that Toni still had her.

Mallory had been explaining the logic of why they hadn't heard this from the Proteans, but it didn't really matter. What mattered was what he said next:

"I need a pilot."

CHAPTER THIRTY-TWO

Cathedral

"Before you search for something, make sure you understand what is before your eyes."

—The Cynic's Book of Wisdom

"I think it better that in times like these a poet's mouth be silent, for in truth we have no gift to set a statesman right."

—WILLIAM BUTLER YEATS
(1865–1939)

Date: 2526.8.13 (Standard)
Bakunin–BD+50°1725

It took General Lubikov several hours to secure his position in control of the monastery. Kugara thought the delay had more to do with a pathological thoroughness on Lubikov's part than it did with any effective resistance. All the prisoners remained in the amphitheater, with oversized suits of powered armor playing baby-sitter over them.

It at least gave them some time to rest.

An hour or so into the waiting, Dörner whispered to her, "What are we going to do?"

She sighed and said, "Get some sleep. We have no idea when will be the next time we're going to get some rest."

"But aren't you planning an escape?"

Kugara shook her head.

"But—"

"Rest," Kugara said, and the blonde xenoarchaeologist shut up.

She didn't blame Dörner, much. The woman was an academic and probably didn't see any difference between their situation now and all the other crazy risks they'd taken so far. But it *was* different. They were held by trained military, rested, undistracted, and vastly overequipped for the job. They were in a confined space with a finite number of escape routes, also covered by their opposition. Lubikov's men were aware of their captives' history, and were expecting something.

Most importantly, Lubikov showed every intention of taking them where they were planning on going anyway.

Still, it didn't make it easy, doing nothing.

Nickolai sat on the ground and leaned up against one of the stone benches. His eyes were closed and occasionally he'd grumble a feline snore. She slid down to sit next to him, leaning her head against his massive chest. He grumbled again, and his arm shifted to reach around her, pulling her to him. Even half-conscious, his hug was bruisingly strong, and would have been a struggle to escape, had she wanted to.

She ran her fingers along the fur on his chest, tracing where his stripes faded to white. It reminded her that there was a reason she was doing this. In the personal and moral vacuum she had been in since Mosasa hired her, she could have seen herself giving in to Adam's bargain. Her independence aside, what would she have been giving up, really?

With Nickolai, she knew what she'd lose. For all that she seethed at his self-flagellation, his angst, his superior attitude—she knew that deep down she found him admirable. For all the physical prowess engineered into him, his real strength was a commitment to what he thought was right. She had lived a long time in a world where expediency and power ruled the day; she had accepted that ethics and morals were simply obstacles to overcome. What was right began and ended with what worked.

She met him as a fellow traveler in Mosasa's band and grew to see him as just another pious idiot. Initially she saw

it as a pose, the same sort of hypocrisy that she saw in all
ostentatiously religious people, the sort who advertise their
faith out of some need for social or psychological advantage, or who needed an excuse to do what they would do
anyway.

But he wasn't like that, especially since the brunt of his
theological excoriation was borne solely by himself. The
self-pity was infuriating, but a mark of a sincerity that she'd
never seen before, in anyone. And he wasn't a static dog-
matist either; she could see him trying to understand, trying to reconcile himself to the upended world they found
themselves in. She could see him trying to figure out what
was right, even when his religion failed him.

He gave her an anchor in the midst of the chaos, one she
could not let go. She knew why she wanted to fight Adam;
because she knew that Nickolai would never submit, and
she would not continue in a universe without him.

Very quietly, she whispered into his chest, "Thank you."

When Lubikov returned, he took the four of them and the
canine monk Lazarus. Three of the Goliaths followed along
with five more conventionally armored soldiers, making
Lubikov's warning against any attempted escape somewhat redundant.

They walked down a complicated set of tunnels, Lazarus leading the way. The deeper they went, the less natural
the stone walls became. In places, Kugara began to discern
sharp angles and surfaces too flat, tunnels too straight.

After the first hour or so of walking deeper under the
mountain, Dörner called out that she saw something. Under the glare from the Goliath's spotlight, she ran to one of
the sections of wall too flat for nature.

The patch of wall was covered with carvings almost too
faint to see, the spotlight's glare deepened the shadows to
the point where the worn scratches in the rock were visible. The cuneiform knotwork of the Dolbrian script was
unmistakable—triangles within triangles. She touched the
surface and said, "This is the real thing."

"Can you read it?" Kugara asked.

"Give me a moment."

Lubikov turned around and said, "Move it. We aren't sightseeing here."

"This could be important," Dörner called back toward him.

"Do I need to remind you that is not your decision?"

Dörner started to say something, but Brody patted her on the shoulder and said, "Let's keep going."

They sighed and resumed marching down the tunnel. After a few minutes, Lazarus said, "That was a position marker. The numbers there refer to a complex coordinate system, angular measures of where we were in relation to the center of the planet, where the planet was in relation to Kropotkin, where Kropotkin was in relation to the center of the galaxy at the time they carved it."

It marked more than that.

It marked the point where a hundred million years began to fade away. After they passed that patch of naked Dolbrian writing, the character of the tunnel began to change. The artificial flatness and angular nature of it was no longer hinted at beneath layers of rock, and even the floor evened out until the irregularities in the surface became a ribbed stairway. The walls flattened around them until the tunnel became a pentagonal prism. The carvings deepened, covering every surface now.

Kugara had no idea that anything of the Dolbrians had survived so intact. Where they walked now seemed less than a hundred years old, much less a hundred million.

Something covered the walls down here, a transparent coating that gave off a subtle sheen when the Goliaths' spotlights traversed it. When Kugara touched it, it felt as smooth as glass, even over the carvings. Her fingers seemed to float a hair's breadth over the surface.

The deeper they walked, the more age seemed to fall from the walls, the carvings acquired color beneath their protective shell; reds and golds buried in the depths of each line cut into the rock, bleeding outward as they descended, joined by silvers and blues, until they were wrapped in a multicolored universe of looping triangular patterns.

Dörner and Brody stared wide-eyed at the display, but the soldiers wouldn't allow them time to gawk, pushing them forward every time they slowed. Lazarus offered no more explanations, and Lubikov kept picking up the pace.

Kugara held no more doubts that there was something down here. Where they walked held no resemblance to a natural cavern anymore. The edges of the bottom-heavy pentagon were knife-edge sharp now, the floor flat and sloping down now at a forty-five–degree angle, making the ribs every half meter necessary to avoid tumbling forward.

Necessary for those without armor, anyway. All the normal powered suits with them had gyroscopic stabilization aiding them, and the Goliaths, which barely fit and had to follow them down single file, had a center of gravity so low that they probably would have to make a conscious effort to trip.

They reached the end of the corridor where the walls disappeared and the floor flattened out beyond a darkened doorway. Kugara could sense a massive chamber beyond even before Lubikov and Lazarus disappeared into the darkness. They followed, and she could hear Nickolai's sharp intake of breath before the Goliaths walked in with their spotlights.

When the chamber was illuminated, she felt her breath catch as well.

Where they had entered, the ceiling was barely above the top of the Goliaths' armor, but it sloped up, and up, and up, until it met five other massive slabs of rock a hundred meters overhead. She looked up at the underside of a massive five-sided pyramid. Each face was crowded with Dolbrian writing, not only the triangular script, but concentric circles, ellipses, dots. Thousands of circular symbols spread across the ceiling in a gigantic star map.

Above them, the circled dots varied in size, and their color ranged from white-blue, through yellow, to orange-red. If she had to guess, the pride of place at the tip of the pyramid would go to Kropotkin, Bakunin's star.

The Dolbrians' place in human history was assured, not just by the planets they terraformed, but because of star maps like this one. Just fragmentary pieces of star maps like this one spurred the golden age of human colonization during the Confederacy—shards covering at most ten light-years had been hoarded as leads to more terraformed planets, more wealth, more political power.

The value of such things had declined with the demise of the Confederacy, as controlling actual planets meant more to internal stability than finding new ones. But still this artifact was priceless in most ways Kugara knew how to assign value to it.

"This is what the monastery was set up to protect," Nickolai whispered.

Dörner walked out onto the floor of the chamber and pointed up. "I think that is Xi Virginis." The circle she indicated was close in to the peak, and Kugara had to revise her sense of scale. The starscape above had to be several times the diameter of known human space. When she stared, she could even see some of the structure of the Milky Way in the stars distributed above her head.

The vastness of what the Dolbrians placed here only highlighted how vast everything else was. Here was a slice of space ten times greater than anywhere humans had ventured, and she could just make out the uneven distribution that marked the boundary of a small part of a spiral arm of the Galaxy.

She stared at the tip of the pyramid, and the small volume marked at the fringe by Xi Virginis; such a tiny area. It made Adam's claim of godhood laughable. And it made the fate of humanity, and its bastard children like her and Nickolai, irrelevant.

Nickolai whispered, "I now know why the monks feel close to God here."

"How do you do that?" she asked him.

"Do what?"

"I see this, and all I can think of is how insignificant everything is."

"We aren't insignificant," Nickolai said. "No one is."

"I just—" she found herself interrupted by the tail end of an argument between Lubikov and Lazarus.

"Are you trying to tell me that this is it?" Lubikov snapped.

"This is the heart of the Ancients' presence here." Lazarus said. "You said yourself you can trace what it is we're protecting."

Dörner and Brody were looking at each other, as if they were wondering, "Did the Protean actually send us here?"

Kugara looked up at the star map. Could it be pointing somewhere, to something they could use against Adam? If so, they were fucked. She didn't see any of them getting off of this rock again.

"No, Brother Lazarus," Lubikov said. "I don't believe these people were sent for a star map. This is why you're here, but it's not what you're protecting."

"I assure you—"

Lubikov raised his hand slightly, and the Goliaths moved, pointing their weapons at the monk. The other soldiers in powered armor made a point of stepping away from him. Lubikov stared at the tawny canine and said, quietly, "You are a terrible liar."

"I can't—"

"What is that?" Nickolai said, loudly enough to draw attention away from the standoff.

Lubikov turned to face him, "What is what, Mr. Rajasthan?"

"Brother Lazarus?" Nickolai asked. "Why is the floor where you stand different than the floor where I stand?"

Kugara could see nothing special about where Lazarus stood, but the way the canine turned and glared at Nickolai told her all she needed to know.

"How different?" Lubikov asked.

Nickolai walked up to the standoff, looking down. His alien matte-black eyes gave his face a skull-like appearance in the spotlight's glare. "It's very well hidden, almost a mirror of the remaining stone floor. But the temperature is a fraction of a degree warmer."

One of the solders said, "I don't see anything in IR."

Nickolai bent at Lazarus' feet. "Your equipment is probably not sensitive enough." He reached out with a finger, extending a hooked black claw, and drew the tip across the floor at the monk's feet. He traced a razor-straight line in the dust. He continued, walking around, marking the floor, until Lazarus was contained within a perfect pentagon, ten meters on a side, one flat side parallel to and nearly touching the nearest wall.

Nickolai faced that wall. It rose straight up five meters to meet the sloping pyramidal roof. Unlike the rock above them, the wall was unadorned, stretching from the doorway they had entered, to another similar pentagonal opening underneath another vertex of the giant pyramid. Kugara couldn't see the whole pyramid, but she assumed that it was symmetrical and had a doorway in each corner.

I guess the Dolbrians had a thing for fives.

Nickolai took a few steps, still facing the wall, his back to everyone else. She could tell he was studying the surface, even though there didn't seem to be any significant variation or irregularity in the blank wall.

She glanced at Brother Lazarus, and it appeared the canine monk was holding his breath. Nickolai was onto something.

The Goliaths swept their spotlights to cover him, causing his orange-and-black fur to stand out brilliantly against his shadow on the wall. Every muscle in his back seemed to be carved in higher relief by the stark light.

She glanced over to Brody and Dörner and tilted her head slightly, making a point to step forward, across the line Nickolai had drawn in the floor and into the pentagon. The two scientists glanced at her, and followed suit.

When he was centered, just inside the wall-facing side of the pentagon, Nickolai grunted slightly. The sound had a satisfied ring to it.

Lazarus said, "Don't—" while simultaneously Lubikov said, "Wait—"

Then Nickolai touched the wall and the ground fell away beneath her feet.

CHAPTER THIRTY-THREE

Benediction

"People will more readily give up their lives than give up their beliefs."

—*The Cynic's Book of Wisdom*

"Wherever an altar is found, there civilization exists."

—JOSEPH DE MAISTRE
(1753–1821)

Date: 2526.8.13 (Standard)
350,000 km from Bakunin–BD+50°1725

Father Francis Xavier Mallory stood in a large auditorium in one of the still-intact habitats on the *Wisconsin*. He stood at a podium and faced an audience made largely of holo projections. It reminded him of the classes he'd taught on Occisis.

There were a few flesh-and-blood people here, refugees and staff who hadn't managed to evacuate, and for whatever reason had yet to leave. The remaining space was crowded by projections from every part of the fleet that remained. Even after the dire losses they had suffered, and after so many had joined the Proteans and left the system, there were enough people in the audience that, had they been real, there would have been no room to breathe.

He faced them from his improvised altar and said, "In the name of the Father, and of the Son, and of the Holy Spirit."

About half mirrored his sign of the cross and responded, "Amen."

"The grace of our Lord Jesus Christ and the love of God and the fellowship of the Holy Spirit be with you all."

Again, about half responded, "And also with you."

He looked at them and thought, *This could be all that remains of the Church.* Of the ones here ignorant of the responses, he wondered how many of them were lapsed and how many had never received before. How many weren't even Christian?

He didn't think it mattered.

"As we prepare to celebrate the mystery of Christ's love, let us acknowledge our failures and ask the Lord for pardon and strength."

After a moment of reflection, he led the mostly unreal congregation in the Penitential Rite, giving pauses in the responses so those unfamiliar with the Mass could catch up, following their brethren. He led through the Gloria without benefit of even a recorded choir, and the presence of so many time-lagged voices gave the hymn a quality that was both dissonant and ethereal.

He ignored the liturgical calendar for the readings, not because he didn't have a Lectionary, but because the time they faced was unique. This Mass, here, transcended any particular date, saint, or feast. He read from Ezekiel and Matthew, and for the homily he spoke of Christ's temptation in the wilderness.

"We face the same trials as our Lord faced in the desert. Satan has taken us to that same high mountain, and has shown us all the kingdoms of the world, and their glory. And Satan has said to us, 'All these things will I give you if you fall down and worship me.' "

He spoke of the fallacy of many interpretations of Christ's temptation in the wilderness, ones that held that because of His divinity, Christ *couldn't* be tempted. Those interpretations missed the point. If Christ couldn't feel the same temptation that men did, there would be little point in relating the story in the Gospel. In fact, it was a diminishment of Christ's love for mankind to assert that He was somehow untouched by Satan's offer.

God gave His only son, but Christ gave *Himself*. It was clear from the Gospels that there were many opportunities for Him to turn aside, to escape the fate that awaited Him. But for the sake of mankind, He accepted that fate. He was allowed that choice.

"Our choices are what define us," he told his congregation. "You cannot have good or evil without choice, without free will. Our Lord wishes us to be good, but the only way we can *be* good is if we are *allowed* to do evil. Should we ever abdicate that responsibility, we lose our free will, what makes us human, and we commit spiritual suicide."

After the Mass, he walked out into the habitat proper. A fragmented Kropotkin still shone down through the false blue sky, but the habitat itself was wrecked. Buildings had been damaged, landscaping uprooted, vehicles had been tossed about at random. It looked as if he stood in the aftermath of some great natural disaster—the temporary loss of gravity had torn apart the *Wisconsin*. Even if they managed to hold Adam's advance, and the world here returned to some semblance of normalcy, Mallory doubted that the station would be revived.

The comm on his hip beeped for his attention.

He sighed as he answered it. For a couple of hours he had been only a priest. He didn't want to return to his role as a revolutionary leader. Or was that counterrevolutionary?

"Mallory," he said. "What is it?"

One of the Valentine women was on the other end. "I've been trying to reach you for an hour. Did you switch off your comm?"

"I was conducting a service," Mallory said.

"You were what?"

"What is it?"

"We have a communication from the surface."

The holo was distorted by digital artifacts, the speaker's face periodically erased by solid blocks of color scrolling across the image. The man's voice had lost most of its human character as the computers reconstructed his speech from the bits of data escaping through the jamming on the surface.

"Have you been able to respond?" Mallory asked.

"No," Lieutenant Valentine told him. "This guy was able to exploit some weakness in the broad-spectrum jamming going on down on the surface—the broadcast is coming from the jamming satellites themselves. I doubt he even has a mechanism to receive a transmission. It's a looped recording anyway."

On the holo sat a man in a uniform that looked like a slightly modified version of the fatigues sold by the Bakunin Mercenaries' Union. He was somewhere around thirty years standard in age, and showed a few days' beard growth. There was a shift as the transmission looped back to the beginning.

"I am Colonel—bzt—arl Bartholomew, acting commander of the Eas—bzt—vision of the Proudhon Secur—bzt—peration. I am sending this m—bzt—to forces remaining in—bzt—wer not made aware of the situation—bzt—ot until the leadersh—bzt—in an attempted coup. The situation on the—bzt—is deteriorating. We are facing an imm—bzt—oss of control, which will damage any defen—bzt—abilities we have. But if we align wit—bzt—mmand of the forces defending the outer—bzt—we may be able to negotiate—bzt—a reunified force."

Mallory stared at the transmission and shook his head. This is what he'd been hoping for since arriving back in this system. The forces on the ground on Bakunin were the last line of defense.

But, looking into the haggard face of Colonel Bartholomew, he couldn't help but think, *Too little, too late.*

"I have assumed the author—bzt—attempt contact and negotiate an all—bzt—behalf of the Proudhon Defense Corporation. The Wes—bzt—Division has ceased communication with us. We have been trying to—bzt—control of jamming and ATC facilities. We have—bzt—evy resistance. But we do have opera—bzt—control of Proudhon and the spacep—bzt—ssfully avoid orbital defenses we guarant—bzt—passage for any representative in—bzt—airspace."

"Do you think you can repeat Parvi's gimmick?" Mallory asked.

"Toni—the other Toni—she can. We're trained pilots, but since she—when they—she'll react a lot faster than Parvi could have."

"Good," Mallory said, "I want to meet with this colonel."

Valentine turned around and looked at him. "I thought you were sending us to the mountains, to back up Parvi's team?"

"Only some of us," Mallory said.

CHAPTER THIRTY-FOUR

Tabernacle

"It is larger than you can imagine."
—*The Cynic's Book of Wisdom*

"So many worlds, so much to do, so little done, such things to be."

—ALFRED, LORD TENNYSON
(1809–1892)

Date: 2526.8.13 (Standard)
Bakunin–BD+50°1725

When they brought them into the presence of the Dolbrian artifact, Nickolai knew that they were close to Brother Lazarus' holy of holies. Even as the general began to argue, Nickolai could sense the tension in the monk's posture; the defensiveness and the smell of fear. It was not the aspect of someone who had led them to a dead end.

Lazarus still acted as if he hid something, and Nickolai looked around the Dolbrians' work with his alien eyes, searching for something that the monk would be trying to conceal. As he looked deep into spectra beyond the visible, he saw the Ancients' work in impossible detail, the map above their heads a frighteningly dense snapshot of the universe a hundred million years ago, highlighting the planets the Ancients had terraformed.

So many.

He wondered if it was possible that no one had set foot on a planet they hadn't touched beforehand.

The detail of the map was there and vivid in all the wavelengths he could see, which is why he turned his attention to the floor. It was a surface devoid of any interest, made of featureless stone, polished smooth.

Whatever he looked for, it had to be accessible to the monks.

It was under Lazarus' feet, a large pentagon in the floor radiating at a different temperature than the surrounding stone. The temperature gradient was so slight that it could have been just natural variation—if the edges weren't so obviously artificial.

Even with his Protean eyes, he had to concentrate to see the seam between the pentagon and the rest of the floor. He talked to the others, but his attention was riveted by the ground at Lazarus' feet.

A door.

He traced the edges in the dust, looking for the mechanism to open it. There was nothing obvious on the floor. The next place to put some sort of actuator was the wall facing the bottom of the pentagon. He stood, facing the wall, staring at it. Behind him, he heard Kugara and the scientists follow him into the pentagon.

His shadow spread over the wall in front of him as spotlights focused on him. He blinked a few times and his eyes compensated for the variance in light reflected from the stone in front of him. Like the floor, the wall here was featureless, absent the dense detail carved in the ceiling, or even in the corridors leading to this place. Any markings should have been obvious on the plain wall, but passing aeons made it hard to detect.

He did find it. The placing seemed logical, and explained why the monks would have been able to find it without equipment with the tolerances of his eyes; a small spot on the wall, midway between floor and ceiling, and centered along the base of the pentagon on the floor. Unlike the floor, there were no seams, no temperature gradient, making it much harder to find. All that showed it was a slight pattern of wear that almost invisibly distinguished it from the rest of the wall. A rough circle about fifty centimeters in diameter showed some smoothing from repeated touching.

Nickolai reached out and touched the spot on the wall.

The floor dropped out from beneath his feet. He fell backward, painfully twisting his tail underneath himself. General Lubikov still stood at floor level, but had quick enough reflexes to jump down onto the descending platform next to Brother Lazarus before they had fallen more than three meters. Two of the soldiers in the light powered armor followed, falling nearly ten meters to crash down next to Kugara and the scientists.

Lubikov called up, "Hold your position!" at the receding pentagonal hole above them. Two of the Goliaths bent over to shine their spotlights down on them.

Thirty meters and Lubikov turned to Brother Lazarus, who had braced himself and was the only one standing upright, "Where is this going?"

"Where you want to go, General," Lazarus whispered. He turned to look at Nickolai and said, "Do you know what you've done?"

Nickolai pushed himself upright and said, "Only what you didn't have the heart to do."

"The Ancients are not to be trifled with! Only when the time is right will the Barrier fall."

Nickolai shook his head. "I smell your fear, Lazarus. For you, the time will never be right."

The others got slowly to their feet, and Lubikov's solders made a point of backing to flank their general and cover both Lazarus and Nickolai. The platform accelerated its descent, the chamber now more than three or five hundred meters above them. The air was noticeably warmer, and carried a charged potential, as if he stood next to a massive transformer. He caught a whiff of ozone that became steadily stronger.

The light from the Goliaths became diffuse, little more than a pair of stars above them now. He realized that the shaft they descended angled slightly, and after another hundred meters the Goliaths above weren't able to shine their spotlights on them.

The potential in the air began to charge his fur until every slight movement seemed to crackle. After they fell out from under the lights of the Goliaths, they were left illuminated only by the weaker flashlights from Lubikov's men.

And still they descended.

Kilometers passed by before the platform slowed. Then the walls of the shaft vanished above them, and they were washed by an electric blue light.

Kugara whispered, "Good Lord."

The space was vast, an order of magnitude larger than the pyramidal void far above them. The pentagonal platform slid through the ceiling, the pentagonal shaft ending in a single facet of a vast geodesic dome. Above them, Dolbrian markings covered the whole domed ceiling, close to a kilometer in diameter. And the markings themselves illuminated the huge space below, masses of tiny glowing points swarming above them in an arc of artificial sky.

As they continued to descend, and they could see the shape of the mural across the ceiling, the form became obvious. When the platform stopped, and they were on the ground of the chamber, the dome above held a glowing image of the entire galaxy. The Milky Way hovered above them, its arms reaching across the underside of the dome, the markings so far away from them that it looked real, as if they stood on the surface of a planet hovering thousands of light-years away.

"How can that still be glowing?" General Lubikov whispered.

"S-some sort of bioluminescence," Dörner said. "They engineered something that can feed off the environment, the air, the rock . . ."

"For a hundred million years?" Lubikov said.

Kugara walked up to Nickolai and placed a hand on his arm. "Remember what I said about feeling insignificant?"

"Yes?"

"I didn't know what the fuck I was talking about."

Brother Lazarus walked off the platform and knelt down, bowing his head. The two soldiers followed him, flanking the monk. General Lubikov lowered his gaze from the galaxy above and said, "So, were you trying to hide another star map?"

Nickolai walked off the platform, and took a few more steps into the chamber saying, "No, I don't think so."

Unlike the chamber above them, this one was not empty. Beneath the glowing artificial stars, a black hemisphere sat in the center of the floor. Even with his Protean eyes, the smaller dome was hard to see at first. It did not appear to reflect or emit any radiation at all, and despite being three-dimensional, Nickolai's brain kept trying to interpret the thing as a shadow.

"What is that?" Nickolai asked.

"That is the Barrier."

The Barrier ... the words echoed uncomfortably in Nickolai's skull, the voice alien and halfway familiar. The echo was gone before he could focus on it.

The Barrier seemed deceptively small in the gigantic space. It was only possible to overlook it at first because it was nearly half a kilometer away from them, centered under the arc of the glowing Milky Way. Even with his Protean eyes, which were far better at estimating distance than even the artificial eyes they'd replaced, it took a moment for the enormity of the distance involved to sink in.

The hemisphere of the Barrier had to be close to two hundred meters in diameter. It could easily enclose the Dolbrian pyramid above them, and have volume to spare. It rested on a flat stone floor, which, unlike the floor of the pyramid, was generously carved with lines of Dolbrian script. Dörner and Brody called to one of the soldiers to shine the light on the floor in front of them. The nebulous blue of the faux starshine was washed away by the stark white of the soldier's flashlight. It cut shadows deep into the intricate carvings underneath a transparent protective coating. The two scientists stared at the carving with almost the same expression as Kugara wore, staring at the ceiling. Reading human expression was still a new experience for Nickolai, but he suspected that it was something like awe.

"Can you read it?" Lubikov asked. "What does it say?"

Dörner's voice cracked, "I—I—damn! I studied this, but this isn't mathematics, or stellar coordinates. There are words and symbols, I don't know . . ." She looked up, at the plain all the way to the Barrier. "It covers the whole floor?"

Brother Lazarus reached out and touched the surface of the floor. "It is our scripture," he whispered. "We have studied it for nearly two hundred years, and about ten percent, maybe fifteen, we have so far translated."

"How could you keep this secret?" Dörner stared at him, her voice cracking. "This is the most important archaeological discovery in the entire history of—"

Lazarus growled at her. "This place does not exist for the amusement of idle academicians!" He rose from the crouch, and his body language was so tense that both soldiers moved to train weapons on him. "Your concept of history, of time, of species—it is all nothing in the eyes of the Ancients. They left us words and artifacts millions of years beyond our understanding—"

"Brother Lazarus," General Lubikov interrupted. "I would like to remind you who is still in charge here."

"I brought you to the Barrier," Lazarus responded. "What else do you want from me?"

"Perhaps you might go on a bit about the part of that 'scripture' you've managed to translate. I'm guessing it might have something to do with what's on the inside of that barrier of yours."

The Barrier . . .

The voice was a whisper, an echo of an echo as Lazarus spoke. The words itched inside Nickolai's skull as if a memory just on the cusp of consciousness. Lazarus continued talking lowly, as Lubikov led them across the chamber toward the Barrier itself.

Lazarus was giving his interpretation of what he knew of the Dolbrians and what they left here. It was hard to tell if he was speaking the whole truth, though the attitude of resignation that hung on the canine seemed to argue that they'd hit the end of his secrets.

According to Lazarus, the Dolbrians—the Ancients— were a self-created God. The Ancients had seeded not only the few dozen planets popularly ascribed to them, they had seeded everything. All life that anyone was aware of was the product, directly or indirectly, of the Ancients' intervention. What artifacts they left behind were landmarks for whatever sapient life came after their creation—messages to be unraveled when their creations were ready for ascendance.

"Ascendance?" Lubikov asked.

"The Ancients were not some monolithic entity," Lazarus said. "They were thousands of races over millions of years, races that shared a single faith; a faith that moved them to give us all life, and a faith that calls those who are ready to join them."

"Your faith?" Nickolai asked.

Lazarus bowed his head. "I know far too little to claim such. There are depths beyond which I lack the understanding to see, and this is how I know we are not ready."

"Uh-huh," General Lubikov said as they reached the edge of the Barrier. He gestured at the black dome, so featureless it seemed a flat wall before them now. "So how does this fit into all this?"

"The Barrier is not mentioned in what we've translated. I do not know what is beyond it."

Lubikov shook his head slowly. "Brother Lazarus, have I mentioned what a rotten liar you are. I can hear in your voice when you hedge. What do you *suspect* is behind this thing?"

"It's a doorway," Lazarus said. "It is the way through which our kind will meet the Ancients."

"How do you get through this thing?"

"You don't."

Lubikov looked over at the scientists and Kugara. "This is what you were looking for, wasn't it?"

Yes . . .

Nickolai rubbed his temples. The alien voice in his head was becoming stronger. He was afraid that again he might start losing volition, might start seeing Adam or Mr. Antonio emerge from the shadows. He backed away from the side of the Barrier.

Dörner nodded and looked at Brody, who said, "Yes, I'm sure the Protean was directing us to use this, somehow. The Dolbri—the Ancients clearly would have the capability to defend against Adam."

Lazarus whipped around to them, warning, "This is not a weapon!"

"But," Dörner said, "if it's a doorway, a means of contact, can't we ask for help?"

"It doesn't work like that," Lazarus said.

"Yet you've never been inside," Lubikov said. He waved one of the soldiers forward. "Sergeant? Are you carrying a bomb kit?"

"Yes, sir."

"Okay. I want you to get a probe out and see some analysis on this dome."

"Don't test this," Lazarus said.

"Go ahead, Sergeant."

"Do not test this!" Lazarus ran toward the man, but the other soldier stepped forward, blocking his way.

"Don't worry, Brother Lazarus," Lubikov told him. "No one is touching this thing until we know what it's made of."

Lazarus moved fast and managed to slip by the soldier, but only received a gauntleted fist to the back of his head. The monk dropped to the ground.

Yes . . .

Nickolai kept backing away, and Lubikov started shouting orders to back up and give the sergeant some clearance. The one soldier dragged Lazarus' semiconscious body away from the Barrier, and the general led the civilians after him. They stopped about thirty meters away, fifteen meters past where Nickolai stood.

Kugara stopped by him and asked, "Nickolai? Are you all right?"

Yes . . .

"I don't know." The word still echoed in his head, and he couldn't take his gaze off of the Barrier. He sucked in a breath and corrected himself, "No, I'm not."

"Come on," she said, pulling him back to the others. He didn't turn around, his gaze locked on the sergeant kneeling at the base of the Barrier. He noticed something as the sergeant worked on constructing a small device.

The edge of the Barrier, where the black surface met the ground, cleanly intersected the innermost line of carvings nearly in half. *Why would the Dolbrians do that? Why cover their own carvings?*

They didn't ... came the response to his thought, the words painfully alien in his brain—dark, monotone, familiar.

"Who?" he whispered to himself, even though he was already beginning to understand the answer. He stood, unmoving, unsure if he was unable to move because of the alien presence in his skull, or because of the shock of understanding what it was.

Near his feet, Brother Lazarus grumbled and pushed himself up from the ground. General Lubikov called out, "When you're ready, Sergeant."

The sergeant nodded and took a few steps back with a control unit. He manipulated the controls, and a trio of small triangular drones rose from the site where he'd been kneeling.

"No!" Lazarus shouted, as the drones flew a small formation into the Barrier. The drones moved as if the blackness didn't exist, disappearing inside with no resistance at all. A half second passed, and the sergeant called back, "Sorry, sir. I lost contact as soon as they crossed—"

A grinding noise filled the chamber, resonating through the floor, screeching painfully in Nickolai's ears. Then the Barrier came alive, sprouting huge black tendrils, whipping through the static-charged atmosphere fast enough to crack the air. Someone shouted, "*Run!*"

Before the sergeant could move, a black mass slammed into him, crushing him to the floor hard enough that Nickolai heard the servos on his armor seize up and snap. Another black tendril slammed down, hammering across the man's upper torso, pieces of it splitting apart to drill into his body so when it lifted, it took the sergeant's corpse with it.

Nickolai stood frozen to the spot, staring at the suddenly animate Barrier, listening to the alien voice in his skull.

They didn't build this.

We did.

Nickolai started walking forward.

CHAPTER THIRTY-FIVE

Apparitions

Planning is always necessary, but never sufficient."
—*The Cynic's Book of Wisdom*

"Don't tell me what *can* go wrong, tell me what *will* go wrong."

—August Benito Galiani
(2019–*2105)

Date: 2526.8.13 (Standard)
7.2 AU from Bakunin–BD+50°1725

The *Prophet's Sword* emerged from tach-space four and a half days after departing from the converted planet Ec-demi. Adam had left the 61 Cygni system as soon as He was aware of the first tach-comm signals showing that things were not right in the system around BD+50°1725. Bakunin was a core planet, but not a capital, and His view of the social, cultural, and political webs binding Bakunin led Him to relegate it as a low priority. Without His brother's influence, and with the influx of refugees, the anarchy should have been busy consuming itself awaiting His salvation.

Instead, He heard the death rattle of the cloud awaiting His return. It was an echo in tach-space that resonated twenty light-years away. He had felt the resonance as hundreds of tach-drives exploded, wiping His presence from the system.

Adam responded to the insult, even though he knew

that the *Prophet's Voice* had tached away from Earth. The
timing meant that His Earth self had left before the impressions of the vaporized cloud could have reached Sol.
Earth's Adam had left not knowing the extent of the resistance, the *evil*, that had grown around Bakunin.

The Adam from Ecdemi knew what He might face.

And when the *Sword* tached into orbit around Kropotkin, at nearly the exact location His self from Earth had
arrived, Adam was unsurprised when the *Sword*'s control
systems saw hundreds of tach-drive signatures, all on vectors
toward His ship. He stood on the bridge, spreading His arms
as if to welcome the incoming horde of small tach-ships.

He smiled.

Date: 2526.8.13 (Standard)
350,000 km from Bakunin–BD+50°1725

"We have a tach-signature," Toni II said, staring at the unexpected reading on the dropship's navigational computer.
The dropship was a virtual twin of the *Khalid*, without the
damage. She sat next to Toni in the crew cabin, while their
three passengers—Mallory, Rebecca, and Shane—sat in
the back.

"Close enough to affect navigation?" Toni asked her.

"It will be when the mines—" She exhaled slowly as the
display lit up with dozens, if not hundreds, of overloaded
drives blowing apart and dumping energy into imaginary
space. "Holy—"

"Is it Adam?"

"You mean *was* it Adam?" Tach-bursts still sent waves
across her sensors. "There's going to be nothing there now
but highly charged plasma. We're in for a hell of a light
show in about an hour."

Toni flipped on the intercom and told the passengers,
"We just had sensors pick up an intrusion into the outer
system. The tach-mines seem to have destroyed it—but
we will have to sit tight for a bit before we fire ours." She
turned to Toni II and asked, "You think our mines will zero
in on our drive?"

"They're supposed to only target things originating
from outside the syst—what?"

"What?"

"Another tach-signature, smaller, same type of drive—" She watched dozens of mines go after the newcomer.

"I don't get it?" Toni II said, "The timing is just too . . ." She trailed off and looked at Toni as if she might be able to dissuade her from the thought that had just occurred to her. But from Toni's expression, the exact same thought had occurred to her.

"He launched his fleet before he tached insystem."

The second wave of explosions was still happening when a third tach-signature appeared. Mines swarmed it, but not as many.

"That's fifty ships," Toni II said, "At the rate these are consuming mines, he'll have a clear shot after another four or five ships tach in."

Toni turned on the intercom. "We're going now. It might be a little rougher than we expected."

"Do you think—" Toni II started.

"I'd rather deal with tach-radiation messing with our drive than with one of Adam's fleet. If we wait for it to clear, they'll be in."

Toni II nodded.

The sensors lit up with another of Adam's martyr ships. Almost every reading on the tach-drive was in the high yellow. All pushed into the red as Toni primed the ship for the jump.

"Here we go!"

Date: 2526.8.13 (Standard)
Bakunin–BD+50°1725

The cabin resonated with a massive smashing sound, and suddenly Toni II was thrown against the harness holding her in the chair. The acceleration kept up, trying to throw her out of her seat. Another crunch, as if something was slamming into the skin of the dropship, and the whole thing began vibrating and she had the sense of spinning violently.

The gee-forces were so intense that she could barely lift her head to look up at the main holo. Her eyes widened; all that appeared in the holo was a view of the ground, their ship pointed nose down at the spine of Bakunin's only continent, descending so close and so steep that she saw nothing of ocean or sky.

Every readout below the main screen, those that still worked, showed dangerous levels of everything, from airspeed to surface stresses. The temperature sensors had maxed out, and the gee-forces tach-drive itself showed a string of zeros, as if the drive had not followed them along for the jump.

We tached into the atmosphere? God help us.

She couldn't lift her arms, and her vision was going gray from the spinning acceleration.

"We're going to make it," came her voice, but not from her. She moved her eyes so she could see the pilot's chair, and Toni still sat at the controls. Even against the forces trying to shake the dropship apart, she sat upright and still, hands palm down on the console in front of her. Toni kept repeating the words, like a mantra, but to Toni II's graying vision, she didn't seem to be doing anything else. She wanted to scream at her to fire the maneuvering jets, fire the contragrav—but even with her dimming vision she saw that that side of the control console was dark. Like the tachdrive, the contragrav and the maneuvering systems had died so thoroughly that they might not even exist anymore.

They were a brick in free fall, and there wasn't anything they could do.

The shaking was so violent, the acceleration so bad, that Toni II began to hallucinate. The walls of the cabin around her seemed to stretch and ripple as if they had become semiliquid. In front of her, the view of Bakunin approaching them shrank as if the planet was retreating down a tunnel—right before the screen went blank.

The cabin descended into darkness as even the displays that still worked flickered and died. After a half-second, the emergency lights came on, giving the cabin an otherworldly red glow.

The shaking had eased, and Toni II realized that she no longer felt on the verge of passing out. She could move, too. She turned toward Toni and asked, "What happen . . ?"

She trailed off when she realized that Toni seemed completely unaware of her now. She sat upright in the pilot's

chair, eyes rolled up into her head, and didn't even appear
to be breathing. Toni II reached out to her, but stopped before she touched Toni's shoulder.

Toni still held out her arms to the control console, but
now her hands had sunk into the console, as if she was now
part of the dropship.

Toni II lowered her hand. Whatever Toni had done, or
was doing, it seemed to have gained control of their descent. The last thing they needed was to have her distracted.

She wanted to check on the passengers, but the views-
creens were all dead.

However, now that their flight felt stable, she could
undo the crash harness and push herself upright. On wobbly legs she moved back and opened the manual release on
the door to the passenger cabin.

She looked in on the red-tinted cabin and was gratified to see Mallory in his seat, conscious and apparently
uninjured.

But he was alone.

She looked at him and said, "Shane, Tsoravitch?"

Mallory pointed over at the air lock.

The dropship appeared in the upper atmosphere in a burst
of displaced air and radiation. The engine housings boiled
white hot, shedding heat shielding like curls of burning
paper as it tumbled down toward the ground below. The
dropship shuddered and yawed as it plummeted, the air
slamming against the asymmetry of the damage, spinning
it around its downturned nose.

Boiling, molten fragments of the engines trailed behind
it, granting a throbbing red underglow to the plume of
white smoke the dying craft dragged through the air. The
skin of the ship glowed now with the friction as it slammed
through layers of air in a near vertical descent.

Close to the tip of the nose, a black patch appeared, a
dead spot on the glowing skin of the dropship, perfectly circular. The spot grew, a growing circle of black that ignored
the friction of the atmosphere, and absorbed the energy
without comment. The blackness rolled back over the descending ship, hugging it like a second skin. It pulled itself

over the burning engines, collapsing against the remaining structure, enveloping the flames and cutting off the plume of smoke.

The dropship, now little more than a blackness cut out of the sky, stopped yawing, and without a visible means of propulsion, it began to level off its angle of descent. Five kilometers up, and it was no longer plummeting. It flew along the spine of the Diderot Mountains, going five times the speed of sound.

Its presence altered dozens of units of the Proudhon Defense Corporation, some of which had devolved into autonomous commands attempting to hold on to one city or another, others that believed they still owed allegiance to a larger mission. Some of the latter had never received any orders rescinding the blockade, and those scrambled fighters to intercept the alien craft.

The ones who radioed warnings, received a rebroadcast of Colonel Bartholomew's broadcast and a statement that the ship was on a diplomatic mission to Proudhon.

But some didn't radio warnings, and some ignored the responses.

Energy weapons cut across the blackness of its skin, absorbed into the alien ship. Missiles fired at it failed to lock on properly, exploding fore or aft, or tumbling down into the mountains.

The one-sided dogfight followed the ship along the spine of the mountains, until it passed by the mountain outpost of Bleek Munitions. As the ship passed over the camouflaged outpost, two shadows separated from the speeding ship, so small that none of the trailing fighters spared them any attention as they plummeted into the side of the mountain.

The black ship made an impossible right-angle turn and accelerated toward Proudhon. Below it, black shadows melted into the snow below Bleek's hidden outpost. The shadows rolled uphill, gathering mass from the snowpack and the rock beneath, coalescing into two humanoid figures.

When Rebecca had knees again, they felt a little weak. The hyperawareness she'd gained as Adam's disciple had not gone away, even if the scope was more limited now, and she had viscerally lived through Toni's chaotic descent into Bakunin's atmosphere. And even though their jump to the surface wasn't any different than multiple prior descents she had made as part of Adam's host, this had been the first time as an individual. Her brain, rewired and distributed it might be, still had a lifetime of training that what she had just done was supposed to be fatal.

But she and Shane had managed to reassemble themselves in front of Jonah Dacham's goal, the mountain facilities that had—long ago—housed his own company during the Confederacy's assault on Bakunin. Here they could find passage into the mountain's complex set of chambers, and find the Protean barrier, and possibly have a chance of disabling it.

The pair of them walked past the edge of the holographic projection that masked the site from outside observers. On the other side they were greeted by twenty soldiers from the PDC, braced, weapons leveled at them.

The hostile fighter escort broke off from the dropship as they entered Proudhon's immediate airspace. True to the colonel's word, they had safe passage once they got within range to communicate. The ship set down in the midst of a half-abandoned spaceport, and once it touched ground, the black second skin withdrew and faded, leaving the smoldering remains of an unflyable aircraft.

Mallory was first to disembark.

He walked out into blazing daylight, on to the surface of Bakunin, and into a surreal negative reflection of the first time he had come here, nine months ago. Then, it had been night, and he couldn't see the city for the landing lights. Today, Kropotkin shone down oppressively on a bleached-white skyline that looked like the bones of some giant creature sinking into the desert.

Before it was all lights, and movement, and noise ... now the silence was as stifling as the heat. The few aircars he did see moving didn't feel like the lifeblood of a bustling city, they felt more like flies buzzing around a corpse.

The cluster of white towers marking the center of

Proudhon were marred by soot and fire damage, and one ended slightly short of the others, the roofline ragged and black. He felt as if he was looking at a ruin.

There was another stark contrast to his prior arrival. The last time he arrived, which could have been to this same LZ, he hadn't been challenged. The anarchic flow of immigrants was allowed to mix into Proudhon without any obvious intervention by any authority. He had walked straight from the air lock into the city proper without so much as filling out a form.

This day, fifteen soldiers stood between him and the concourse, about fifty meters away, wearing uniforms that seemed slight modifications of the jumpsuit Parvi had worn when he had first met her.

He stood at a safe distance and made no sudden moves. Behind him, he heard the Valentines deboard the ship after him.

He called to the soldiers, "My name's Father Francis Xavier Mallory. Colonel Bartholomew invited me."

The soldiers split into two groups flanking an aisle to the concourse. One of them stepped forward and waved at Mallory. "Follow me," he said.

The three of them stepped forward to follow the soldier into the concourse. Mallory spared a glance back at the dropship.

It was never going anywhere again. The rear engine housings had collapsed in on themselves, and were still steaming. Half the skin of the ship looked as if it had peeled away.

Inside the concourse, he faced more wholesale changes. It was a different place than the one that greeted him last time, but it was obviously part of the same complex, the black granite floor with the accent of stainless steel was familiar. But it wasn't spotless. Trash had gathered in the corners, and the surface was dull, scuffed, and stained.

There was no surging crowd. The halls were mostly empty except for a few military personnel and the occasional guard. Above them, the crystal skylight that had once shown an enhanced view of the sky above was a flat dark gray. And the few terminal kiosks they passed all seemed to be dead.

The three of them were led through the concourse, to a near-abandoned subway, where a single train car took them into the center of Proudhon. As they rode on in silence, Mallory said a short prayer for the people who used to inhabit this city.

The train came to a stop in a vast station lined with marble and neoclassical columns. Advertising holos were inset into the walls, but all showed a graphic logo for the Proudhon Spaceport Development Corporation. He didn't read all of the flashing text, but what he did read was enough:

"Order will be restored, with your cooperation."

"Serve public safety, report suspicious activity."

"PSDC: Order, Security, Strength."

In nine months, Bakunin's anarchy had slid into fascism.

He expected to be led into one of the central towers above them. Instead, their military escort led them through two checkpoints down into a utilitarian sublevel. It gave Mallory another strong feeling of déjà vu. The corridors they walked down mirrored the subbasement at St. Marbury University, where he used to teach. He had only visited those maintenance levels once, when Cardinal Jacob Anderson had recruited him.

That was almost a year ago . . .

They walked into a large room that had been retrofitted to serve as a communications center. Disassembled shelves and other debris had been piled along one naked concrete wall, while the other had been lined with comm consoles manned by a host of young, earnest, and very tired-looking personnel. They were led past the impromptu command center, stepping over power cables, toward a smaller room in the back that was guarded by a pair of serious looking men holding rifles at parade rest.

The one on the right acknowledged them and typed something on a keypad, and the door slid open. From inside, he heard a voice, "Come in, Father Mallory."

Mallory walked into the room and Colonel Bartholomew stood and smiled. "Thank you. We need help."

"I have limited help to offer," Mallory said. "I'm hoping you can provide some last-ditch defense on the surface." *I'm hoping for a miracle.*

"But your presence is helpful by itself. We had an attempted coup here, and the result destroyed our chain of command. The PDC has degenerated into autonomous units. Worse, in the chaos, the details of what our leadership knew about you and the fighting in the outer system leaked out. It damaged Proudhon's credibility."

Mallory's eyes narrowed. "You didn't know?"

"The blockade was, is, on information as well as physical traffic."

"God help us all," Mallory whispered.

"But because of that leaked information, they know who you are. A message from you and we can unify our forces again under a single command."

"Colonel," one of the Valentines told him, "we already have a second wave of Adam's forces taching into the system. There are only limited forces left in the system to combat him. We may be seeing an invasion within an hour."

Colonel Bartholomew stared at Mallory with an uncomfortable intensity. "We better get moving."

CHAPTER THIRTY-SIX

Souls

"You cannot argue with high explosives."
>
> —*The Cynic's Book of Wisdom*

"In a war of religion, it is more important to crush the enemy's God than the enemy himself."
>
> —BORIS KALECSKY
> (2103–2200)

Date: 2526.8.13 (Standard)
7.2 AU from Bakunin–BD+50°1725

The eighteenth ship from the *Prophet's Sword* was the first to tach into the system and not be greeted by a swarm of self-directed mines. None were left to greet it. The Adam who dwelled aboard it perceived the still-boiling plasma that was all that remained of seventeen sister ships and the carrier that berthed them.

Even though He had foreseen the possibility of what had happened, it did not diminish His rage. This cursed place would be scoured of every scrap of life. He would walk the planet and personally tear the souls from the people who had so conspired against Him.

He pushed his awareness out, to see what forces were arrayed against Him, and He saw less than five hundred ships. As a force, they were barely relevant. He also perceived the mark of the Proteans on Bakunin's largest moon, and He deduced that they were responsible for the plasma cloud his ship drifted through.

As the twentieth ship tached into the system, Adam began planning how He would punish those who defied Him.

Date: 2526.8.13 (Standard)
Bakunin–BD+50°1725

"Where the hell is he?" Parvi said.

"Hm?" Flynn said, not taking his eyes off the chessboard. He finally moved his king's pawn and gave his hand over to Tetsami for her response.

"Lubikov? Where is he?"

Flynn watched his hand reach out and take his pawn. *"Your turn, sonny."* Instead of responding to the gambit, he leaned back and looked at Parvi, who sat on the edge of the couch staring at the door. "You were enjoying his little interrogations?"

Parvi turned and looked at him. "That bastard is the only conduit of information we have."

"Information he wants us to have," Flynn said. "We have no way to know if he's just making stuff up."

Parvi shook her head.

"Don't beat yourself up," Flynn said, "you're why we made it as far as we did."

"I just wish I—" She was interrupted by a large muffled bang that resonated through the walls of the suite. "What the hell?"

More muffled bangs and rattles. And Parvi slowly stood up, shaking her head. "Gunshots?"

"Maybe it's something else . . ."

Flynn realized that it wasn't something else once the alarms began blaring. *"Gram, I think our game's done."*

"No shit, sonny."

Parvi backed to the wall next to the door to the suite. Flynn grunted, clutching his still-healing gut as he stood and mirrored her position on the other side of the door. "Okay, you're the mercenary. We're unarmed and injured, what do you expect us to do?"

"If one person comes—" She hesitated a moment, and while the contrast of her white hair made her skin appear darker than it actually was, Flynn thought it went a bit ashen as she spoke. She stared at the floor a moment. "One person alone, I'll distract them and you overpower them, get their weapon."

"Okay." The sirens still blared, and the sounds of gunfire and people shouting were coming closer. Flynn looked around for something that could be a weapon. He grabbed a nearby endtable, flipped it upside down, and kicked one of the metal legs until it broke free. For a few long seconds he held his stomach, staring at the ground.

Kicking is a bad thing. Got to remember that.

"You want me to do this?"

"I got it, Gram."

He reached down, making a point to bend with his knees, and picked up the metal table leg. The improvised club was disappointingly light, and Flynn wondered if using it would be any more effective than tackling someone unarmed.

"More than one," Parvi said, "or someone in powered armor, we surrender."

They stood there, the air thick with tension and the sound of fighting. The siren blared constantly, setting Flynn's nerves on edge. Then the sounds of fighting retreated.

After about fifteen minutes, all that was left was the sound of the siren. He had the realization that they might not be a priority for either attackers or defenders. Flynn stared across at Parvi and said, "What if nobody comes?"

She didn't answer.

When the door opened, it was without any sound as preamble, and it startled him so badly that he almost dropped his makeshift club. He took a step back as a single elderly figure walked into the room. He took one look at the bald scalp dotted with tattoos, and his club slid from his fingers to clatter on the ground.

Alexander Shane looked at both of them in turn and said, "Flynn Jorgenson, Vijayanagara Parvi? I think you may want to come with me."

Flynn followed Shane into the hallway, followed by Parvi. In the back of his mind he heard Tetsami. *"Where the hell did he come from?"*

Outside, in the hallway, Flynn smelled, faintly, the odor

of overheated metal; a weapon discharge, but distant. Not from Shane; he was unarmed.

Nor from the soldier whose unconscious form lay crumpled on the floor of the corridor across the hall from their suite. Flynn knew the smell didn't originate with that man, because the unconscious man's weapon was in discreet disassembled pieces scattered on the floor around him.

"You recovered rather quickly," Parvi said as Flynn remembered the tach-comm on Salmagundi, the Protean disarming its opponents and repairing the damaged tiger.

"I had help," Shane told her. "Where's the rest of the team?"

"Why should I trust you?" Parvi asked.

"We're on the same side."

"I'm not even sure who you are."

Flynn looked up at Shane and said, "You're with Proteus now, aren't you?"

Parvi turned to look at Flynn, "What the hell are you talking about? The Proteans were wiped off this planet centuries ago."

"They came back," Shane said.

"Nickolai!"

Kugara screamed at the tiger as he walked toward the monk's barrier. She started to run toward him, to grab him, drag him away from the twisting chaos that barrier had become. Something hit her blind in the back, and her muscles went to jelly. She twisted on her wounded foot, and the dagger of pain through her leg made her topple.

As she fell, she saw writhing black tentacles whip by Nickolai, as if he approached the maw of a giant mutant anemone. For some reason, it made her think of the Protean on Salmagundi.

She slammed to the ground as one of the barrier's tentacles whipped by where she had stood. She heard the others scrambling away from her. They hadn't moved far enough away from the thing. She heard yells, and someone, probably Dörner, called her name.

A length of pure blackness the thickness of her torso slammed into the ground a meter in front of her face. The sound of the impact rang in her ears. She looked up at the thing as the tentacle in front of her withdrew; she watched it rise up and readied to dodge one way or another.

Out of the corner of her eye she still saw Nickolai.

The black tentacle started down, and she rolled away, focusing on where Nickolai was. Somehow he had made it to the original surface of Lazarus' barrier without being grabbed or crushed. In fact, the writhing tentacles seemed to spread apart for the advancing tiger, giving Nickolai a clear path inward.

The tentacle she had dodged slammed into the ground next to her.

Another came slamming down on her and she attempted to dodge again, rolling away too slowly. She saw the black silhouette eclipsing the artificial galaxy above her.

Before it hit her, it vanished.

She blinked, her body too tense to breathe and unwilling to relax. But it *was* gone. Not only the tentacle above her, but also the sound of the others whipping and cracking through the air. She pushed herself upright and saw that Nickolai was gone, too.

The barrier had resumed its original form, a blank, black hemisphere, completely inert.

She stared at it and whispered, "Nickolai?"

Kugara was certain that the attack had ceased as soon as Nickolai had crossed the threshold. But she didn't know if it meant he was alive or dead. But now that she stared at the black hemisphere, she couldn't help but picture Nickolai's eyes, and the Protean.

The Protean had sent them here.

What if the barrier hadn't been left by the Dolbrians?

What if the Protean had given Nickolai more than a new set of eyes?

"Damnation and Taxes!"

She turned around at the sound of Lubikov's voice. He stood about twenty meters away from her, underlit by a flashlight lying on the ground. Next to the flashlight was the other soldier who had accompanied them down here.

Half of him, anyway—the barrier's attack had bisected the man's torso, clean through the layers of armor. Kugara tensed immediately because there was no sign of the dead man's rifle.

She looked around for the others and saw Brody and Dörner, but no sign of Brother Lazarus.

Shane led Flynn and Parvi down through several levels of the Bleek Munitions outpost. By the time they had descended three levels, the alarms had silenced themselves. All the way down, Flynn saw evidence of the Protean attack; barriers dismantled, weapons disassembled, mercenary soldiers collapsed on the ground.

How did Alexander Shane, of all people, become part of this?

When they reached the lowest level, where the walls became polished stone and the conduits for power and data were exposed, one person was left conscious to greet them.

Parvi stopped, staring at the woman, and said, "*You?*"

The short redhead shrugged her shoulders and said, "Me."

"You know her?" Flynn asked.

"Tsoravitch was part of our expedition to Salmagundi. She was taken aboard the *Prophet's Sword* when I was." Parvi stared at the woman. "How did you escape that?"

"I didn't."

Parvi stared at the woman.

"Gram, does that mean what I think it does?"

Tetsami was unusually silent within his skull. But Tsoravitch answered for her.

"I was taken by Adam. At this point, the flesh I'm wearing is irrelevant."

"What the hell?" Parvi shouted at Shane. "What did you lead us into?"

"It's all right," Tsoravitch said. "I served Adam, but I changed my mind."

"What?" Parvi said.

"Later," Tsoravitch said, turning to Shane. "Where are the rest of them?"

"Already gone."

"Damn. We better move, then." Tsoravitch turned and started down a corridor where the polished stone gradually gave way to unworked tunnels of rock. Shane ushered Flynn and Parvi to follow. As they moved, Shane asked, "Do they know where they're going?"

Parvi shook her head. "Not until you tell us what she meant by, 'changing her mind.'"

Shane gave them the story of the Proteans, and how they had subverted Adam with Tsoravitch's help. As he told the story, they walked deeper into the tunnels under the mountain, and Tetsami finally spoke up in the back of Flynn's mind, *This is getting too familiar.*

What?

Everything...

Shane explained what had happened on Earth, how the Proteans who had been on Mars had infiltrated the population, to become parts of Adam's chosen. Flynn found himself asking questions, prompted by Tetsami, until they came so quickly that he ceded control over to her.

"Who was he?" Tetsami asked with his voice.

"Who?" Shane said.

Flynn watched himself step up to Tsoravitch and grab her shoulder. "Who was he?"

The woman looked into his face and shook her head, "Later, there's no time now."

Flynn stared into the woman's eyes, and he felt his heart begin to race. "Tell me. Who, of all the people in contact with Proteus, who would this Adam have known?"

"We need to—"

"*Who?*" Flynn felt an edge in his own voice as Tetsami spoke.

Tsoravitch stared into Flynn's eyes—Tetsami's eyes—and said quietly, "Jonah Dacham."

"Dom?" Flynn's voice whispered. He could feel tears burning the edge of his vision.

Tsoravitch placed a hand on Flynn's shoulder and said, "We need to move. The rest of your team is in danger if they try to—"

She was interrupted by the sound of an explosion.

Brother Lazarus ran. He had started running as soon as the enraged Barrier had bisected the soldier holding him.

His mind was in a panic, not just from the physical danger, but from the spiritual as well. He did not know what kind of threat angering the Ancients would mean, but he knew that it was beyond his understanding. What the soldiers had done ...

It wasn't only a threat to their existence; it was a threat to the very *meaning* of their existence. By prematurely approaching their creators, they might cancel that creation, destroy the path their descendants had toward their enlightenment.

This blasphemy had to be stopped, and he only had one tool to do it.

He ran while the Barrier went mad with bloodlust. He found the edge of the chamber and ran along the wall, away from General Lubikov, away from the signals jamming the implants in his skull.

He reached the opposite side of the chamber from the general, and he could feel the implants make contact with the network of explosives that filled all the caverns between here and the surface.

A rumble shook the ground beneath his feet, and above him, the Milky Way began breaking apart.

CHAPTER THIRTY-SEVEN

Angel

"The greatest mysteries we face are those we hide from ourselves."

—*The Cynic's Book of Wisdom*

"Why should we honour those that die upon the field of battle? A man may show as reckless a courage in entering into the abyss of himself."

—WILLIAM BUTLER YEATS
(1865–1939)

Date: Unknown
Unknown

Nickolai walked into darkness. The Barrier let him through as if it had less substance than a shadow.

What is this?

It is what came before . . .

His stomach tightened at the Protean's voice in his head, but with it came an odd sense of peace, as if he had found the path he was meant to take. Even in the darkness, he kept walking forward.

The air he breathed was dry, stale, and very still. He heard nothing except the scrape of his claws on stone as he walked forward. He stopped when he thought he should have walked beyond the other side of the Barrier.

He stood there wondering. This place couldn't be empty, since it made no sense that the Proteans would place such a barrier around an empty spot on the ground. He asked the voice in his head, *What is it? What were you protecting?*

No response.

"What is it that came before?"

The Protean voice was gone.

He felt an ache in his eyeballs and he rubbed them. They felt odd in a way, and in another way, they felt almost normal for the first time in two years.

Nickolai shook his head. "You led me here! Where did you go?"

An oddly lisped female voice said, "Sorry, Kit."

He raised his head and blinked his eyes. It was disorienting for a moment, because he couldn't adjust the spectra and magnification of his vision. He had to wait for his eyes to adjust to the light, and it sank in that his eyes were, suddenly, normal. He looked toward a brighter spot on the floor and realized that he saw with the same vision he had been born with.

He walked toward the spot of light, an island in the darkness, and saw a body laid out beneath the sourceless illumination. The body was onyx black, muscular, male, and polished smooth of not only every imperfection, but of most fine detail. No hair, no nipples or fingernails, no small wrinkles . . .

It was the Protean from Salmagundi.

"It's a shame, Kit. You bring him all this way and he just doesn't work out. 'Course, none of them did; guess that's why they bottled this up." The voice was heavily accented, and it was hard for Nickolai to make sense of it.

He looked up from the Protean's body and called into the darkness, "Who are you?"

"Sheesh, no need to shout." The darkness retreated from a figure standing about ten meters from him, a nonhuman figure. Like him and the other natives of the Fifteen Worlds, this stranger had descended from some human's design. In this case, her ancestors had been built from a lepus strain.

She was a large rabbit and her presence here was completely incongruous.

"Are you from Brother Lazarus' monastery?"

"You effing serious?" She laughed at him. He noticed

that a scar on her cheek pulled her mouth up in a sarcastic smile. "Do I look like a nun to you?"

"Who are you, then?"

"Call me Angel."

"What are you doing here?"

"Talking to you, Kit."

He looked down at the inert body of the Protean. "What did he do wrong?"

"He didn't ask the right questions."

"What are the right questions?"

"That's a good start."

The air filled suddenly with the squishy sounds of human language. It was a language that Nickolai did not understand. He blinked a few times, uncertain of where he was. The air was cold, blowing down on him from a vent in the ceiling, rustling his fur. The floor was no longer stone under his feet. Instead, he stood on a slick linoleum floor. The air smelled faintly of unfamiliar chemicals and warm electronics.

Flanking him were ranks of shelves that held bulky electronic components, blinking lights, snaking cable. Light came from outside the room, from an unseen window.

"Where is this?" he whispered quietly. The human voices continued their own argument, ignoring him.

No one answered, and Nickolai thought of Angel's warning.

He asked the wrong questions.

He sucked in a breath of air-conditioned air and decided not to ask anything else before he understood what he was asking and why. If there was a reason for him being here, it would become apparent.

He walked by the racks of equipment, toward the voices, the light, and the unseen window. Something about this place, this room, felt wrong. Nearly at the end of the aisle of equipment, he realized that the wrongness came from the ceiling. It was made like nothing he had seen before, large square tiles nested in a thin metal frame. He reached up and touched it, and the tile lifted off of the frame, and he saw the ends of crude wire suspension holding up the metal.

He let the tile fall.

He turned and took a closer look at the rack next to him, trying to identify the equipment. There were labels, some handwritten, marking the sockets where the cables entered. Again, the script was unfamiliar.

He concentrated on the people speaking. The voices seemed to come from the other side of this rack of equipment. He still couldn't make out the sense of it, but the accent began to feel familiar to him. The speakers, two men, had a tang to their voices that reminded him of Parvi.

He edged past the end of the racks and looked around to see the human speakers. They had their backs to him, one older and tall, the other shorter, rounder, and a few decades younger. A large clunky holo display stood between them. Semitranslucent, hovering over the archaic holo projector was an exploded view of someone descended from St. Rajasthan. He saw bones and teeth, muscles diagrammed on half the body, furless skin pulled taut across the other half.

He looked at the racks of equipment—old, ancient computers of the same vintage as the holo between the men.

No, that isn't a descendant *of St. Rajasthan.*

He stood in an ancient laboratory. Hundreds of years gone, where mankind first conceived of their Fall. He stared at the scene, fascinated and repelled.

Why would I be shown this?

The older man shook his head and spoke with a shaky voice. He turned away from the holo of Nickolai's unborn ancestor. Nickolai saw the man in profile and saw that his cheeks were wet. The younger man took his arm and spoke gently to his elder. Nickolai watched in confusion, wishing he could understand their tongue. The old man was upset, and what caused the distress, the tears, the why of it, was suddenly very important to Nickolai. Was there something about his origins, his ancestors, that he should know? Something that brought this long-dead man to tears . . .

Why was the old man upset?

He looked at the young man comforting his elder and realized that it wasn't the right question. The two men

were paying no attention to the holo with the anthropo-
morphic tiger that could have been the dissection of one of
Nickolai's cousins. Their incomprehensible speech could be
about anything.

Anything.

Nickolai saw the grief and pain in the old man and realized that it might have nothing to do with St. Rajasthan, or
the Fall of Man. This human, this *person*, had life beyond
the holo, beyond this room, beyond Nickolai. He saw an
old man in pain, and a young man attempting to provide
comfort. These men might be the midwives of his species,
but that did not define them.

Nickolai blinked, and the men were gone. He stared off
into the blackness wondering what it meant.

"You already know, Kit."

He looked to the side to see Angel standing, looking off
in the same direction he had been staring.

The words hung in the suddenly still air. "You know my
thoughts?"

"Sorta have to do that to do my job."

"What are you?"

"I'm what you can understand, Kit."

An explosion ripped through the cabin. Nickolai was
thrown against the wall, and he dug his claws into combat
webbing to keep his feet as the floor tilted down and the rotors above began to oscillate ominously. The cabin around
him vibrated with the rotors. Smoke filled the cabin, and
Nickolai smelled fire.

The rotor sound suddenly got much louder as a door
slid open. The smoke vanished in a great roar of sucking
air, revealing other figures. His eyes still watered from the
smoke, and at first he only made out the bodies. At least
three victims had been too close to the explosion when it
ripped through the wall of the cabin. Under a ragged slice
in the wall, Nickolai saw partly dismembered bodies dangling from crash harnesses. The bodies were almost fully
covered by inert armor, except where limbs and heads had

been torn free, and for a brief moment he thought they were humans.

But they were too large.

He heard shouting over the rotors and the roar of wind. Looking up from the three casualties, he realized that these *weren't* humans.

Holding on to the edge of a door opening into a swirling darkness, he saw a figure that could have been pulled from the legends of his ancestors. Nickolai knew he looked at an image out of the past, because of the white fur in the tiger's snarling profile. There had been no white tigers born to his kind since shortly after the time of St. Rajasthan.

The white tiger was half a head taller than Nickolai and had broader shoulders. He wore woven fabric armor colored a muddy camouflage brown, streaked with soot. He had been wearing a helmet at one point, but the only signs of that now were the bloody mats in his fur where the straps had pressed down on his skull. In one hand he held an ancient belt-fed machine gun.

The white tiger shouted the same unknown language the humans had been speaking, and a line of other tigers, fully armored and helmeted, dove past him, out the open door and into the darkness beyond.

The white tiger leaped out after his squad.

Nickolai jumped out after them, just before an RPG shot through the darkness and into the open door behind him. A burning hand spiked with shrapnel pushed him down into the muddy ground as the helicopter exploded behind him.

He raised his face from the mud and looked up.

An ambush, Nickolai thought, *the enemy saw the landing . . .*

It was night, raining, and because of the light from the burning helicopter behind him, he only saw a circle around the immediate clearing. The terrain was rocky, mountainous, and the only sign of the enemy were muzzle flashes from outcrops that were little more than shadows. The tigers, his warrior ancestors, were pinned down behind the poor shelter of a couple of boulders.

This is why we were created, why humans made us. He

was looking at a battlefield on Earth, a war where his kind served as man's proxy. His fingers dug into the muddy ground beneath him, as a part of him ached for armor or a weapon. He tried to push himself upright, but then he felt where the shrapnel had torn across his back. He fell back down with a groan inaudible for the gunfire.

He looked at his doomed ancestors and shouted at them. "This is man's war. You're sacrificing yourself for—"

Nothing?

Was that what he was being shown? Was that what he wanted to take from this scene?

The white tiger stood up and shouted something in that unfamiliar language, leveling his machine gun at the hidden enemy. The meter-and-a-half-long barrel hammered fifty caliber rounds into the night, the muzzle flashes lighting up the whole mountainside. The white tiger ran toward the enemy, screaming words inaudible under the roar of the weapon in his hands. The area around the enemy position exploded with dust and fragmenting rock, and they attempted to return fire.

Nickolai thought he saw the white tiger struck twice before he reached the outcrop that sheltered the ambush and disappeared behind it. After a crescendo of gunfire, everything went silent.

For several moments the only sound was the crackling of the burning helicopter, and the rushing of the storm around them. The white tiger's comrades started calling after him, but there wasn't an answer.

Nickolai knew there wouldn't be one. He could smell the blood.

He watched the others cautiously stand and take stock of the situation, one stepping into command. They all ignored Nickolai as they assessed the perimeter and started moving out.

He watched them go, to continue their original mission.

The white one's sacrifice wasn't for nothing.

"What, then?" Angel asked him when the darkness returned.

He pushed himself up from the stone floor. The wounds

from his vision were gone. He looked at the rabbit facing him and said, "He did it to save his comrades."

"And?"

"And for himself," Nickolai said. "As limited as his choices were, he still had a choice. For all that man might have made him, and placed him where he was, he was still himself."

"I think I like you, Kit."

"What I'm seeing, is it real?"

"As real as you are."

"What about you?"

Angel laughed.

Nickolai faced a wall. Painted on the surface was an old symbol, an eagle, wings spread, holding the schematic image of a planet in its claws. The icon was a symbol of the Terran Council, the totalitarian Earth government that preceded the development of tach-drives and the rise of the Confederacy.

The symbol was splattered with blood.

Nickolai turned his head and saw a long corridor, strewn with bodies. Dozens of unarmed humans lay where they had fallen, their blood staining the floor red. Looking down at the closest victim, he saw claw marks—more than would have been necessary to kill.

He walked along the corridor, passing the dead. Claw marks gouged the walls, and some of the bodies appeared partially eaten.

His journey ended by the doors to a large hemispherical room. The walls were transparent, revealing a shining blue planet hanging in a black sky, its reflected light washing away the stars behind it. Nickolai saw the tracery of the continents below the swirling white clouds and knew the planet he looked at.

Haven.

Haven and Dakota, the twin planets orbiting Tau Ceti, were the first home of Nickolai, Kugara, and Angel's nonhuman kin after their exile from Earth. Seeing the planet, after the ancient emblem of the Terran Council, made him uncomfortably certain who it was that sat in the center of the observation dome in front of him.

Even though the tiger staring up at Haven was smaller than Nickolai, and certainly less powerfully built than the ghostly white warrior of his last vision, Nickolai knew that he looked at St. Rajasthan himself.

St. Rajasthan turned to look at Nickolai and said, "Who is there?"

CHAPTER THIRTY-EIGHT

Last Supper

"The only things that do not change are those things that have ceased to exist."
— *The Cynic's Book of Wisdom*

"Loss is nothing else but change, and change is Nature's delight."
— MARCUS AURELIUS ANTONINUS
(121–180)

Date: 2526.8.13 (Standard)
Bakunin–BD+50°1725

Colonel Bartholomew sat Mallory at a massive array of communications gear that had been set up in an impromptu command center under the heart of Proudhon. Around him, dozens of other people were in contact with the parts of the PDC that still remained under centralized control. Those parts were re-coalescing as Mallory talked to colonels, captains, and lieutenants who had been cut off from their command structure by the failed coup.

It seemed that rumors of what was happening off-planet had propagated far enough that just seeing Mallory's face and a retransmission of the pope's last broadcast from Earth, gave Colonel Bartholomew enough gravitas to knit the chain of command back together.

One place he hadn't been able to communicate with had been the temporary HQ of the Western Division Command—the man there was a General Lubikov. If he

were there, he would be one of the highest-ranking opera-
tional commanders surviving.

The man had also taken his command at an outpost in
the Diderot Mountains, right where he had dropped off
Shane and Tsoravitch. That was why he kept trying the
connection periodically. The general was on top of the Dolbrian ruins that his people were trying to reach.

He was shocked when he finally got a response to his
transmission.

A young man's face filled the holo in front of him, shouting, "—request you send assistance. We have suffered an
attack by unidentified hostiles. Enemy has entered the
chambers under the—"

Colonel Bartholomew pushed in front of Mallory, "Can
you describe the enemy? How many? How were they
armed?"

"There were two of them."

"Two?"

"A man and a woman."

Shane and Tsoravitch.

The colonel sounded incredulous, "How could two—"

He was interrupted when the view in the holo shook,
and the man in the image turned around. Then the holo
went dark. There was an upsurge in chatter around Mallory, as other communications channels began lighting up.
"What happened?" he asked as he tried to get the channel
to Bleek Munitions reestablished.

One of the other men in the communication center
said, "We have reports of seismic activity centered on the
Diderot Range, east of Godwin."

*Seismic activity? Bakunin is supposed to be tectonically
dead.*

Several others began repeating the report; someone
mentioned "subsurface explosions."

Mallory prayed for everyone inside the mountain.

"Flynn?"

"Yeah, Gram?"

"I can't see anything."

"It's dark."

"Can you move?"

"No."

"What happened?"

"Cave in, I think."

"Christ on a crutch, these caverns hold up for umpteen million years, then fall down on us?"

"Bomb, I think."

"Shit. You think Parvi . . ."

"I don't know."

"What about Shane and the redhead?"

"I don't know."

"Fuck! What do you know?"

"It's dark, we can't move, and we're probably going to die."

"Hello?" Kugara yelled. "Is anyone out there?"

No one responded.

She lay on her back, staring at a fragment of the galaxy that had fallen from the ceiling. It was huge, about ten meters across, and probably weighed several hundred tons. Somehow, it hadn't completely sandwiched itself against the floor, and the space underneath was almost enough for Kugara to stand upright—if her left leg hadn't been pinned under another massive chunk of rock.

Of course, the rock falls on my uninjured leg.

She tried pushing the rock, but there was no way she could move it. Not only was it over two meters tall, it was holding up the fragment of the Galaxy that still glowed down on her. Surprisingly, it didn't hurt nearly as much as she expected, probably because there wasn't any more leg below where her thigh disappeared under the stone.

"Hello?" she called out again. "Brody? Dörner? *Nickolai?*"

She lay back down because she was out of breath. She felt chilled and clammy, and slightly faint. She was probably in shock. She should stop trying to pull her leg free. The pressure from the rock was the only thing keeping her from bleeding out.

Everybody dies, she thought.

"Where are you, Nickolai?" she whispered. "I wanted to face this with you."

Date: 2526.8.13 (Standard)
7.2 AU from Bakunin–BD+50°1725

Adam had learned well. As His chosen and His embodied host tached into the system around Bakunin, He could read the signs and understand what had happened. The awareness bequeathed by the Race bore upon Him with an unnatural clarity, the tactical defeat of His predecessor selves cut through His hubris. The presence of the Proteans on Bakunin's moon had enlightened Him.

His broadly-knit plans, as wide as all of human space, were incomplete. His model of human society was imperfect, it did not account for the Proteans, and when He fed the heretic culture into His model of the universe, when He took the uncharacteristically humble step of reassessing His view of the universe in light of their presence, He saw the foundation of His world change.

And He saw what they must do, how they must strategize.

The battle here was a feint, a way to draw His attention, to anger Him and distract Him from what He must do. And Adam's cold fury, duplicated thirty-three times across the surviving ships of the *Sword*, was all the worse for the fact that He had almost allowed their defiance to stand. He had never conceived that some of those He brought into His Glory would be, in fact, agents of the Protean heresy. He understood now that the agents of Proteus must be concealing themselves in the mass of humanity He had yet to confront, yet to offer salvation.

But, now that He understood this, He could combat it. Thirteen of his ships tached back out of the system, each traveling to part of Adam's far-flung host to warn Himself of the Protean menace.

He would purge such heresy from His body the way He would purge it from this system.

His remaining ships tached into the system, toward Bakunin.

Date: 2526.8.13 (Standard)
350,000 km from Bakunin–BD+50°1725

On the surface of the moon, Schwitzguebel, a trio of Adam's ships tached very near the surface, close to the spine where the Proteans launched their mines into the outer system. The arrival was sudden, and close, and in the fraction of a second it took for the Protean guards to raise a shield around their outpost, Adam was already within it.

Outside the defensive hemisphere around the spine, the universe faded, the light from outside red-shifted and slow. Within its confines, the trio of warships floated on their contragravs like deadly insects trapped in amber.

Weapons formed along the spine, firing bursts of plasma at the invaders, but before even the first shot connected, the ships disintegrated, blowing apart into a uniform cloud that consisted of little more than matter and Adam's will. The cloud settled to the lunar surface, and began incorporating mass into itself.

The Proteans tried to extend their reach as well, but they had spent too much of their energy and attention on the organization of the spine, the shield, the defensive weaponry. When they pushed outward, through the mass of the moon, they found Adam surrounding them.

The ground around the spine glowed, and began shooting gossamer threads, injecting itself into the mechanism. Many were severed or absorbed by black tentacles reaching out of the spine itself, but many got through. The threads wove themselves around the spine, sinking in, constricting the existence of the occupants.

The shield fell, and the spine began launching mines again.

This time, however, it fired on different targets.

Suddenly the Protean defenders, arrogant in their opposition to the one true God, found themselves and their vessels confronted by their own creation. Their ships would be consumed in tachyon plasma, and one of the first to vanish in Adam's purifying fire was the *Wisconsin*.

Now that this Adam had a villain to focus His anger upon, *this* Adam broadcast His ultimatum to Bakunin.

Date: 2526.8.13 (Standard)
Bakunin–BD+50°1725

It took a long time to convince the command of the planetary defenses to rejoin the centralized PSDC control.

The personnel in charge of the orbital shield enforcing the blockade of the planet had been purposely segregated from the normal chain of command of the Proudhon Defense Corporation; their organizational tree branched off at a much higher level than Colonel Bartholomew had started. They were intelligence and covert ops people who were naturally suspicious of the chaos in the military.

However, the fact that they had coalesced about ninety percent of the ground forces under Bartholomew's command, made their argument more convincing. More convincing than Mallory's presence. And the staff with those duties also understood the situation beyond Bakunin's immediate orbit.

And that situation was deteriorating.

The remaining defending ships were facing off with new forces from Adam, and they weren't doing well. The defending Protean ships were exploding in bursts of tach-radiation even before engaging with Adam's forces.

One of the Valentines said quietly, "He must have attacked Schwitzguebel . . ."

Mallory nodded. Adam had turned their defensive apparatus, such as it was, against them. He turned to Colonel Bartholomew and said, "We're going to have to defend ourselves here, on the ground."

The colonel shook his head. "How do you fight that?"

"Put as much energy in as small a space as possible," Mallory said. "Dump everything you have into the target from as far away as possible. He only has a few vehicles for the attack, we can orient the orbital linacs at them as they approach, and AM-bomb whatever lands."

Interference rippled across all the displays in the comm center, each one suddenly showing Adam's face.

"I am Adam. I am the Alpha, the God of the next epoch of your evolution. I will hand you my universe. Reject the Protean evil that denies me, or face their fate. Worship me and you will partake of my paradise forever."

Behind Mallory, one of the Valentines said, "Oh, fuck."

Next to her, Toni said, "Oh, fuck." Toni II watched Adam's transmission with her and wondered why she was surprised. They knew this was coming, and they knew what long odds they were facing. When he mentioned the Proteans by name, she reached out and grabbed Toni's hand.

"If I go back to our dropship," Toni said, "I can help organize defense of the city."

The colonel turned away from Mallory and looked at the two of them. "You?"

One of the soldiers in the comm center with them said, "Sir, while the ship appears to be a Caliphate design, heavily damaged, it was not showing a normal profile or maneuvering capability in flight."

The colonel nodded and looked at Toni. "It's a Protean artifact, isn't it?"

"It is now," Toni said.

The colonel turned to the soldier who had spoken. "Sergeant, make sure they get back to their dropship."

The sergeant said, "Yes, sir!" Then he pivoted to face her and Toni. "Follow me," he said, leading them back out of the comm center.

As they walked out into the maze of corridors under Proudhon, Toni II asked her other self, "You think you can defend against *that*?"

"We have a chance, don't we?" she whispered. "A little time and I think we can seed a shield that might keep him out. For a bit."

For a bit.

They walked on in silence for a long time. Toni II began to realize that their borrowed time was almost up. With Adam closing in on them, they probably wouldn't last the day. Even Toni, her Protean self, probably wouldn't escape Adam's wrath. Toni didn't even have the illusion of choice, having embraced Proteus; Adam had already marked her for destruction.

Toni's thoughts must have been traveling in the same direction. She said, "You know, if it ends up being death or joining him—"

"No, Toni."

"If you can survive by—"

She grabbed Toni's hand and said, "No."

Not without you.

They followed the sergeant back up through the nearly empty concourse, and to the landing zone. They pushed through a small knot of solders to go back outside to board their ship.

It wasn't there.

"What?" Toni II said, running up to the edge of where their dropship had landed. The ship was gone, as well as most of the landing surface itself. Instead, she stood at the edge of a ragged crater twice as wide as their ship's footprint.

Toni whipped around to their escort and said, "What happened to our ship?"

"An AM grenade," came the response. The voice came from farther behind them than she had expected. Toni II turned, just in time to see the flash from a plasma weapon.

Behind him, Colonel Bartholomew shouted orders, and soldiers ran from the comm center to carry out various tasks to shore up the defense of Proudhon. Mallory called back to the colonel, "We only have a limited time to get the orbital linacs on-line—"

"Just a moment, Father Mallory. We'll handle everything."

Mallory frowned. The colonel was ordering his men out of the comm center, but he hadn't started giving commands to the PDC forces they had just managed to knit back into a single force. Most of the planet was waiting for word back from this room.

Something wasn't right.

He started organizing open channels on the console before him, so they could give global commands to the entire planet. As he did so, he heard the colonel tell him, "Father Mallory, can you step over here a moment?"

Mallory pushed his chair around to face the colonel. There were only four people left in the communications center, and the other three were all looking at him.

"What is it, Colonel Bartholomew?"

"I want to thank you. After the disastrous assassinations that wiped out a good fraction of the PSDC command, you were able to help me knit the whole back together. Without that . . ." He gave Mallory an unnerving smile.

"Thank you, but I think that army is waiting for some direction from the command here."

"I know. But we need to come to an understanding first."

"What?"

The colonel nodded slightly and the two remaining solders got up and grabbed Mallory's arms, lifting him up from his seat.

"I want you with me," the colonel said.

For some reason, it didn't surprise Mallory. He shook his head. "You mean you want me with Adam."

"You know you're fighting a doomed battle. Even with the Proteans, it's hopeless. He is much too powerful."

"He is evil."

"Is worship so high a price for what He grants us?" The colonel smiled at him. "Besides, you know your opposition to Him ends here, one way or another."

CHAPTER THIRTY-NINE

Beatification

"God speaks to fewer ears than hear him."
—*The Cynic's Book of Wisdom*

"You cannot know God as He is if you cannot know the world as it is."

—St. Rajasthan
(2075–2118)

Date: Unknown
Unknown

Nickolai took a step back in surprise. No one in his prior visions had seen him. Of course, in both cases, the participants had been otherwise occupied.

St. Rajasthan narrowed his eyes, and Nickolai noticed that the left one was cloudy with a dilated pupil. The fur around the saint's muzzle was thinned with age, and he was missing his left canine tooth. The hand he gestured with was gnarled with the beginnings of arthritis. All those details were overlooked in the accounts of him Nickolai was familiar with.

"You smell odd, son. Do I know you?"

"No, you don't."

"Are you here to kill me?"

"No!" The words stung Nickolai, even though he knew that St. Rajasthan had stayed aboard the colony ship, like Moses, never stepping foot in the Promised Land. There were apocryphal scriptures that told of unbelievers who also remained behind to murder him.

That couldn't be his purpose here.

"Your denial is too sharp. Why else would you stay behind on a dead ship? But sit down, my friend. We will pretend you speak truth." He patted the bench next to him, and Nickolai walked around and eased himself down next to the founder of the only faith he had ever known.

"You are one of the Atavists, aren't you?" he asked Nickolai.

"I don't know what you mean."

"You wear no clothes, my friend." He turned to look at Nickolai with his unblind eye. "Then, again, you deign to use language."

Nickolai looked at St. Rajasthan and noticed that he did wear something like a human jumpsuit tailored for digitigrade legs and a tail. He wondered what the point of it was.

When did we stop emulating human dress?

"I am not from this place," Nickolai said. "Or this time."

St. Rajasthan turned to look up at Haven. "So am I to think you are lying, or insane?"

"I am not a liar."

"I shan't fault you for your madness, then. Do you care to say what place and time you do come from?"

"The year is 2526, I come from a planet named Bakunin."

"Four centuries in the future? Our kind still lives?"

"Only for the moment. We are facing an evil that may be the end of us, and them." Nickolai nodded back toward the corridor where the human corpses were.

"What evil do you face?"

Nickolai explained Adam, and what Adam was. When he was done, St. Rajasthan chuckled. "You seem to be a much more interesting prophet than I."

"I am no prophet."

"That's right, we agreed you were insane." The Saint folded his arthritic hands before him and bowed his head. "I have been praying and meditating here for days. Asking for some sign from God. Do you think you are that sign?"

Nickolai stared at the old tiger, and saw the weight of age as well as a much heavier weight. It was unsettling to him. St. Rajasthan had always been an abstraction, a label for a set of writings, of ideals, of immutable rules. Part of Nickolai wanted to dismiss the image before him as some deception, a challenge to shake what little faith he had left.

But something in him knew that what he saw was truth.

Our prophets come from the same clay we all do.

He searched his mind for the right question, and responded, "Why did you stay behind, instead of going with your people to their new home?"

"To take responsibility for my sins."

"What sins?"

"Are you blind, as well as mad?" He snapped at Nickolai, raising his head to stare at him. "Do you not see the slaughter?"

"But they were . . ." Nickolai was about to say, *only the Fallen,* but the words tasted like ashes in his mouth. It was a hard, lifelong habit he forced himself to abandon at that point. He looked back at the corridor and no longer saw "Man" as defined in the scriptures. Instead, he saw only men, a series of individuals with their own lives and their own burden of history to bear; but only their own—not their brothers' not their fathers'.

"They died for others' evil," Nickolai whispered.

"And what do you know of evil?" St. Rajasthan snapped at him.

What do I know of evil?
What is evil?

Nickolai whipped around and faced Angel. "Why did you bring me back here?"

"Easy, Kit. You saw everything you needed to see."

"I had so many questions."

"Only one that mattered."

Nickolai wanted to grab the rabbit, force her to send him back to St. Rajasthan so he could discover what scriptures were true, and what were embellished by four centuries of priesthood. But he stopped as he understood how pointless it would be.

What is evil?

Angel looked at him and asked, "Do you have an answer?"

"Is this the Dolbrians asking?

"No, this is *me* asking. I just got the job to decide if you go any further." She folded her arms and cocked her head so her ears tilted to the side. "So, an answer?"

"The men who made people like me, to fight their wars by proxy. That was evil. Adam, demanding his people worship him as a God, or face destruction. That is evil. Executing a man only because he is the same species as those who did evil. That is evil."

"Why?"

Nickolai looked at her, and found himself fumbling to articulate an answer. He wasn't a philosopher or a theologian. He was an exiled prince, a warrior, and a mercenary. He only thought about these subjects because his life kept spiraling into places where his old pat understandings did not make sense. His faith was a continually eroding structure that required constant maintenance to keep upright. He wondered if all the effort was worth it, if it mattered.

He looked at her and answered as best he could. "If we have free will, we can act, we can make moral choices . . . Acting to deny that of anyone else, removing their ability to make moral choice, negating their morality, their will, their life, their individuality to serve your own. That is evil."

"Then what is good?"

He wanted to say, *opposition to evil*, but that was too simple. He paused to gather his thoughts before he said, "Preserving our ability to make those moral choices—preserving our own will, individuality, and life—in the face of that which would take them away. Defending that for ourselves and others."

"Yeah, Kit. Do you believe it?"

He stood in the darkened corner of the temple, and he saw St. Rajasthan again, four centuries removed from the ancient self-exiled tiger in orbit around Haven. In the apocalyptic mural, bearing the flaming sword to cut down the unrighteous, he was young and fierce and tall as a mountain. This mural had been the last thing he had seen with the eyes he had been born with. He stood in the rear, with a crowd of acolytes, his gut tightening as he expected to watch his own mortification.

But the priests did not drag a younger Nickolai through the doors of the temple. That would be too easy.

Instead they dragged in a lowborn panther servant, her expression blank with shock after witnessing the death of her children. Nickolai's children.

He did not want to watch this. He didn't want to hear the priest's invocation of God and St. Rajasthan. He didn't want to hear her screams. He did not want to see the blades pierce her skin during the slow execution.

They strapped her to the altar, and the priest raised the ritual knife, and Nickolai could no longer bear it. He pressed through the crowd of acolytes shouting, "No!"

He was on his hands and knees, hyperventilating, the darkness so thick now that it constricted his chest. "Why didn't you let me stop them?"

"This isn't time travel, Kit. They were just part of my boss' memory, just like I am."

Nickolai closed his eyes and shuddered. "How could they invoke God and do that? It was *wrong*."

"Why?"

He turned his head and looked up at Angel. He had the impulse to reach out and snap her lepine neck for asking that question. If it was part of their memory, they knew exactly why . . .

Angel waited patiently for the answer.

"You're testing me, aren't you?"

"Getting to know you, Kit. You gave a nice speech on good and evil. Tell me about it in real life. These priests honor the same God you do. They follow the word of that tiger you left in orbit around Haven. She shagged you of her own free will, knowing the potential consequences. But the priests are wrong? Why?"

How could he articulate the pain in his gut?

"It just *is*. You know it is."

"So what they did to you was wrong, too?"

Nickolai just stared at her.

Angel sighed and turned away. "Oh, well. Nice knowing you, Kit."

"No," Nickolai said. "Stop."

Angel turned her head to look over her shoulder, her ears cocked to the side. "I'm listening."

"What happened to me isn't the same."

"Because you lived?"

"Because I had a choice."

Angel turned back around to face him. "Do tell."

"The church made rules that we both agreed to follow. But I had a choice about that. I was in a powerful family; I could have left the planet and the church if I had issue with their law. She never had that choice. And what choice did she have when I approached her to drag her into my sin."

"Sin? Were you denying anyone their will, their moral choice?"

"I was denying hers, and that of my unborn children." Nickolai shook his head. "The priests' power extends far beyond punishing *evil*. I knew that. I accepted it. I was part of it. I was complicit in her death and the death of my children."

"So, is it wrong the call upon God when they do this?"

"Yes. It's an obscenity."

Angel walked up to him. He was still on his hands and knees, so she crouched slightly so their faces were on the same level. The scar on her face pulled her mouth up in a smile that was almost cruel.

"Last question, Kit."

"Yes?"

"What is God?"

CHAPTER FORTY

Armageddon

"Nothing ends perfectly."
—*The Cynic's Book of Wisdom*

"And with the guts of the last priest, let us strangle
the last king."
—DENIS DIDEROT
(1713–1784)

Date: 2526.8.13 (Standard)
Bakunin–BD+50°1725

Adam's ships had become again a cloud of thinking matter. Not enough to form a ring around the planet, but He could content Himself with a slow invasion. Once on the surface, in contact with the mass of the planet, He would have enough resources to convert this land as He had every other planet He had set foot upon.

Adam rained down upon the atmosphere of Bakunin, unseen until His mass began coalescing into dropships aimed at the ten largest cities on the planet. He formed Himself and His chosen into glowing teardrops of living metal that sliced through the Bakunin atmosphere as, below them, Bakunin's single continent slowly rotated into view.

Toni II saw the flash of the plasma rifle, but in the fraction of a second that it took for her to realize what it was, she also realized that she shouldn't be alive to see it. They were firing at them ...

But over her and Toni, separating them from the PDC Mercenaries, there was a barely-tangible hemisphere rippling with reflected heat from the discharge of at least three plasma rifles. The hemisphere was only about five meters in diameter, and it was centered on Toni.

She looked at Toni and asked, "Are you doing that?"

Her other self practically growled, "*The bastards destroyed our ship.*" She glared at the men as they stopped firing their weapons. "*Do you know how many minds were in there?*"

One of the mercenaries called out, "Get an AM grenade—"

"*Too late!*" Toni yelled at them. The hemisphere fell, and beneath their feet the tarmac of the landing quad fractured and refractured, black faults rolling across its surface like fractal veins. Before they could bring their weapons to bear again, the veins pulled the surface out from under their feet. They fell down, and, for a moment, they all struggled like insects trapped in the web of a surprisingly geometric spider. The black web pulled them down, and the tarmac flowed back over the space where they had been standing.

"Oh, God," Toni II whispered, staring at the unbroken surface of the landing quad between them and the concourse. "Are they still alive under there?"

Toni said, "I couldn't care less."

"They tried to kill us—"

"Another mole, just like Colonel Xander."

"And we left Mallory with him."

Colonel Bartholomew pulled his sidearm and pointed it at Mallory. "So what side are you with, the living or the dead?"

Mallory shook his head. "There's still a chance to change your mind. You still own your soul."

The colonel laughed. "Damnation and Taxes, you *are* a priest, aren't you? What good is a soul, even if we had one? Adam is granting us—"

"Slavery," Mallory said. "That's what he grants you. An end to owning yourself."

"Sorry, Father. I'm not convinced."

"But one of his followers was, weren't they?"

"Pardon?"

"That was the coup," Mallory said. "Someone, probably one of Adam's spies, decided to purge the command of his agents. That's why there's only you left. None of his moles higher up in the PSDC survived. Am I right?"

The colonel walked up and pressed the slugthrower against Mallory's stomach. "Are you really trying to talk us into changing sides right before His final victory?"

"Don't you wonder, if he truly is omnipotent—if he is the god he claims to be—why does he need you?"

"Oh, to hell with this bullshit." The colonel pulled the trigger on the slugthrower. Mallory felt as if God himself had kicked him in the gut. He glanced down in response to the pain as his full weight fell on the guards holding him upright.

Lord, let this not be in vain.

The colonel fired again, and Mallory saw the flash, and the gases from the gunshot push out, shredding flesh and the fabric of his jumpsuit. The third shot hit him right under the sternum.

Lord, let me have done your will.

The guards let him collapse onto the floor in a pool of his own blood. Mallory heard the colonel say, "That man was a fool. Go and check to make sure his companions have been neutralized."

And, Lord, let those two women survive.

"Sir?"

"What?"

"All the comm channels are open. We've been broadcasting everything for the past five minutes."

Mallory was comforted in his final moments knowing his first prayer had been answered.

"Flynn?"

He didn't answer Tetsami. He seemed to have lapsed into unconsciousness. She didn't know why she was still aware enough to realize that. She would like to join him. It was dark, and silent, and the air was becoming hot and stale. She was pretty sure the wound in their gut had re-opened, but she wasn't able to move Flynn's arms to check.

It seemed an eternity she lay there, before she heard something.

It sounded like rocks moving in the darkness. Gravel raining down, earth shifting. She gathered what strength she could and tried to yell, "Help!" It only came out in a choked whisper.

Even so, whatever made the noise seemed to come closer.

"Help us!" Only slightly louder, the effort splitting Flynn's lip and leaking blood into their mouth.

Above them, the darkness parted like a curtain, the rock and earth flowing out from around them until they were prone on the floor of a softly glowing crystal chamber.

Just like the Protean had done to the outpost on Salmagundi.

The redheaded chick knelt down next to Flynn's body. Tetsami realized she still couldn't move anything below the neck, and it wasn't because Flynn had control. She could move his eyes and turn his head to face Tsoravitch as she knelt next to him.

Now that there was light, she could see the mess their body had become.

Oh, Flynn, you don't deserve this . . .

Whatever injury prevented her from moving had, as a blessing, prevented her from feeling the injuries. Below the waist, Flynn's body had been crushed to a pulp. Both arms were broken, and she saw the point of a rib sticking out a frothing hole in his chest.

Their chest.

Tsoravitch wasn't even dirty.

"That's not fair," Tetsami managed to wheeze.

"Flynn?" Tsoravitch said.

She wanted to shake her head no, but Flynn's injuries wouldn't permit it. "No. Tetsami."

Tetsami stared into Tsoravitch's face and realized the woman was crying. *Chicky, I'm touched.*

She also saw the corner of her face twitch in a way that was disturbingly familiar.

"Dom?" Her voice almost choked on the word.

"I'm sorry."

"You should be." She had to rest a moment before going on. "You let me think you were dead."

"I was," he said with Tsoravitch's mouth. "I'm just a copy."

"A copy?" *Like me* . . .

Dom placed Tsoravitch's hand gently on the side of Flynn's face. That, Tetsami could feel. She could feel tears building up, and she closed her eyes against them. "Dom, your timing sucks."

"I know."

"I'm dying here."

"You don't have to."

"I know." They could do to Flynn what the Protean had done to Nickolai. It was a leap of faith; she doubted they would be unchanged. And she had to trust Tsoravitch.

She had to trust Dom.

I told Flynn that I didn't want him to die.

"Flynn? Please, Flynn? Just tell me it's okay and I'll do it."

Flynn didn't answer, and she couldn't rouse him.

The more she thought of it, the more terrified she became. She needed Flynn to give her the strength . . .

But I don't want to die either.

"Do it," she snapped at him. "Do it before I change my mind."

Tsoravitch bent down, and kissed her.

Tetsami's eyes widened. She felt Tsoravitch's lips against Flynn's, against hers, and her skin burned with the contact. The warmth spread across Flynn's face, and across his skin, to places she shouldn't be able to feel anymore. Tetsami parted her own lips in response, and felt Tsoravitch's tongue enter her mouth. The warmth spread down inside her, as if Flynn's body was on fire.

She felt bones and organs knit back together and she could move her arms again . . .

"Gram?" came a groggy voice in the back of her head.

Flynn had awakened just as she was reaching up to embrace Tsoravitch. Tsoravitch/Dom sensed Tetsami's sudden hesitation and broke off from her healing kiss.

"Great timing, sonny."

"What's happening?"

"I didn't want y—I didn't want us to die."

"What do you—Oh."

She could feel Flynn staring at Tsoravitch through her eyes. Tsoravitch reached down and touched Flynn's face and whispered, "You're one of us now."

"Are you still there, Dom?"

Tsoravitch nodded. "Rebecca allowed me . . ."

"Flynn?"

"What are you asking me?"

"Can I?"

"I think you're asking, 'May I?' Gram."

"You know calling me that is making me even more uncomfortable."

"Not as uncomfortable as you're making both of us."

Tetsami realized that the ache she felt for her centuries-gone lover, whatever body he happened to inhabit right now, had become solidly physical.

Dom/Tsoravitch said, "You're blushing."

"Kiss her back, already."

Tetsami sat up with Flynn's repaired body, and kissed her back.

Colonel Bartholomew tried to raise any of the reunified PDC command, but none responded. Even the local units of the Eastern Division that were based with Proudhon didn't acknowledge the contact. He couldn't believe that things could have degraded like this. Adam had predicted the consolidation of power on Bakunin; he had placed him in a role that pushed him toward the top of that organization.

He was in command. He had to be.

One of the two soldiers left with him said flatly, "The orbital linac is firing."

"No!" Colonel Bartholomew slammed his fist into the console before him. The blockade was supposed to stand down during Adam's approach.

"Two definite contacts with incoming—"

"Don't tell me about it," he whispered. "We did all we could."

"Sir, Adam *will* come."

Colonel Bartholomew nodded and turned away from the communication console and faced the priest's body. "I'm sure he will. Nothing man can control will stop him."

"So why—" The man was interrupted by the sound of twisting metal. The door of the control room was bending, fracturing into facets interlaced with an angular web-work as dark as Bartholomew's thoughts.

He raised his sidearm and pointed it at the door. "He will come, but I doubt we'll be here to meet him."

The door folded inward and Colonel Bartholomew fired before he ever saw Toni Valentine.

As the first of Adam's dropships orbited into sight of Bakunin's one continent, the massive defensive array of the Proudhon Spaceport Development Corporation turned its fire on them.

The linear accelerators fired slugs of charged metal at the onrushing ships, an arc of projectiles approaching half the speed of light in velocity. Unlike the weaker projectiles that had vaporized the Xanadu but left the complexities of thinking mass intact, these projectiles carried enough energy that each hit not only exploded the physical structure of the dropships, but also released enough sterilizing radiation to lobotomize the web of thought contained within.

The defenders tore Adam apart seven times before the remaining dropships dispersed again, becoming a weak cloud that offered no resistance to the linac's projectiles.

The planet should have offered no resistance to Him. He had chosen His people to prepare the way.

His people had failed Him.

It didn't matter. He was vaster than His current incarnation. Whatever happened now, Adam knew He was spread throughout a dozen systems, soon a hundred. He had already sent parts of Himself abroad, carrying the knowledge of this planet's defiance.

If He failed this once—and even the word burned in His mind like a brand, a mark of fallibility that infuriated

Him—even if that came to pass, He would not fail. Adam would grace this world again, and again, and again; a thousand times, a million times, a billion—eventually He would claim Bakunin, or destroy it.

His cloud drifted into the orbit of the linacs, and He realized it would not come to that.

Toni II looked at her Protean self and swallowed. Toni was bent over Mallory, who looked old and frail where he had crumpled on the ground. She swallowed again before she asked, "Can you revive him?"

"No. It's too late."

"Not even—"

"*It's too late!*" she snapped and turned away from Mallory's corpse.

Toni II didn't press her. She felt the guilt herself, at not seeing a trap that seemed obvious in retrospect. She had seen her Protean self vent that guilt, and the anger, on Colonel Bartholomew and his two allies—all of whom were now little more than a thin smear on the wall and an uncomfortable smell. She had no desire to tempt any more of that forward, not unless there was a hostile target in the area.

She walked over to a still-active console, her boots sticking to atomized colonel on the floor. The holo showed a schematic of the linacs in orbit. They were firing, but their target wasn't visible in the schematic.

"Some good news," she whispered at Toni. "Mole or not, the blockade is trying to defend the surface."

"Oh?" Toni stepped up next to her. "What are they firing at?"

"Adam, I presume. It could be over the horiz—" The words caught in her throat as one of the linacs disappeared from the holo. Followed by another. And another.

"I don't believe this," Toni II said.

Toni sighed. "Believe it. We better get aboveground if I'm going to do anything to defend this city."

Above the planet, the orbital defenses disintegrated into Adam's being, more than making up for the mass of Himself lost to the seven dropships. He spared little thought to the loss, or to the occupants of those dropships that weren't as distributed as He was. All that mattered was the balm of erasing a prior failure. The threat was gone now, and He was as strong as He had been before, so it was not failure. He was not fallible.

He would not have to rely on His other selves to come back here.

He would claim His own victory here, and now.

In a dozen places, Adam burned His way through the atmosphere to claim all that was His.

Toni burst through outside in front of Toni II, stopping about three meters from the door. Toni II ran out, following. She stopped next to herself, standing on the edge of a rooftop lording over the concourse where they had landed. The strangely quiescent Proudhon skyline wrapped around them, still dominated by the damaged towers that had been the headquarters of the Proudhon Spaceport Development Corporation.

The sky was a cloudless desert blue, empty of aircraft.

That made the three fireballs plummeting toward the city all the more apparent.

"This is it," Toni said.

"Can you fight that?" Toni II asked. "By yourself?"

"Sure I can," Toni said. She turned toward the growing fireballs. "Just don't ask if I can win."

CHAPTER FORTY-ONE

Enlightenment

"If we had a perfect understanding of the consequences of our actions, we would never act."
—*The Cynic's Book of Wisdom*

"Pray as though everything depended on God. Work
as though everything depended on you."
—St. Augustine
(354–430)

Date: Unknown
Unknown

"What is God?"

Angel's words hung in the still air, a presence between
Nickolai and the almost comical rabbit-creature. He wasn't
certain he had even heard her correctly. He pushed himself
upright, staring at her, the lepine face. Could the Dolbrians
have chosen a more incongruous guardian for their secrets?

"Well?" she asked him.

"What are you asking me?"

She shook her head, and her long ears swayed slightly.
"You know what I'm asking, Kit. You need to explain God
to me."

"Why?"

"You said yourself, you're being tested. My boss has
some standards."

Nickolai stood and looked down at her. She was shorter

than a human, despite the muscled and oversized legs, and
when he stood, she seemed tiny.

"You must already know my mind. You read it clearly
enough during those visions."

"You're stalling."

"Maybe because I think you won't like the answer."

"Answer the question, Kit."

Nickolai closed his eyes. Quietly, he asked, "Is the Protean dead?"

"It knew the risk better than you did."

"I suppose so. It sent me here." If the Dolbrians truly
wanted to guard this place, they couldn't allow those who
failed the test to escape. Their test relied, he supposed, on
the subject having no preknowledge of what it entailed.
"Its people placed that barrier around you. They feared
what was in here."

"I won't speak for them."

"There was probably some wisdom in that. How many
did they send in before they closed you up?"

Angel shrugged. "Didn't close *me* up. I'm here specifically for you. I was just another memory, before you
stepped in here."

"Not my memory."

"No, not *your* memory. Answer my question."

"Answer mine."

"Two-thousand-three-hundred-and-sixty-four." Angel
folded her arms and said, "It's time, Nickolai."

He shook his head, knowing that there was little chance
his concept of God would ever sync with creatures that
had existed for aeons before the creators of his species had
even evolved. His understanding of the divine was at odds
with Brother Lazarus, and the canid monk was a contem-
porary of his, and when compared with the spans of time
involved, practically the same person.

But all he had left was his faith.

"God is the creator," he said quietly. "He is the first cause.
When I look out at the universe, the width and breadth of
it, and ask the void if there is a purpose to my existence,
God is the only answer I receive. God is the name I give to
my morality, the source of the first principles I use to define

right and wrong. God is the wall around the universe that reason cannot penetrate. God is the unprovable truth. God is the reason I am here."

He stared at Angel and waited for the Dolbrian avatar to declare him unworthy.

Instead, she unfolded her arms and gently clapped. "Kit, that was pretty damn good."

"I passed your test?"

Angel shrugged, "Well, you didn't fail. Kind of the same thing."

"The Dolbrians see God—"

"Oh, crap, Kit. Don't go there. You wouldn't understand. Just accept that you're close enough."

The small light that illuminated the two of them winked out, and for a moment Nickolai stood in complete darkness. Then, like the transitions into his visions, he was standing somewhere else.

A light wind rippled his fur, cold and smelling like the depths of the earth. He stood on a pentagonal platform suspended in a vast space. He couldn't see walls, ceiling, or floor in the darkness. What he could see of his immediate surroundings were illuminated by brightly glowing script tightly wrapping the pillar that pierced the center of the platform he stood upon.

The Dolbrian text scrolled upward, and he realized that the platform was descending into the darkness.

Angel still stood next to him.

"Another vision?" he asked her.

"Not the way you mean," she said.

"What you showed me earlier, the scientists, the battle, St. Rajasthan . . ."

"Your one-time lover?"

"Were they real?"

"As real as I am, Kit. But again, not in the sense you mean. My boss has a long and exact memory, and can bring out avatars like me to play things out for you."

"So you're some AI construct?"

"Again, not in the sense you mean. Creating something with true independent agency for something like this would be morally questionable."

"What are you, then?"

"A mask for my boss. A means to communicate."

"Who is your boss, then? Who am I talking to?"

Angel pointed over the edge of the platform and said, "The Hub, Kit."

He turned and sucked in a breath. Suspended below them, the Dolbrian script spilled across the face of the darkness, it twisted and spiraled below them, whorls wrapping around themselves as if he looked upon a galaxy from another dimension. As they descended, he saw depth to the writing, the lines of alien text spilling downward invisibly far, and spreading outward in all directions.

And the writing moved. It pulsed and twisted. Waves and ripples crested its surface like waves upon the ocean. And the more he stared at it, the farther he saw. Suddenly, the vastness of it all began sinking in as he descended.

"We're not under the surface of Bakunin anymore, are we?"

" '*Within*' the planet might be more accurate. I think 'beyond' might work, too."

Nickolai looked up from the swirling universe of Dolbrian writing, and saw that thousands, millions, of similar pillars shot up from the infinite sea of light below him. Pillars like the one he rode downward upon, themselves wrapped in glowing script and vanishing upward into the darkness above.

"And those are . . ."

"The other Hubs. Every planet they built, all are tied to the same . . . 'network' you'd probably call it." She waved a hand out at the light. "The Dolbrians weren't a single race, one species. They were, they are, millions of races, species, trillions of individuals, all contributing to building this consciousness."

"Why?"

"To come closer to understanding what you call God."

Nickolai was silent for a long time as they continued to descend. Finally, he asked, "Why did so many Proteans fail to reach this point?"

"They saw good and evil as clear as you. Problem is they couldn't ask *why*. It all boiled down to, 'because someone said so.' *This* is too damn powerful to trust to a creature who can't explain an external source for their moral compass." She looked up at him. "If you get to define good and evil all by your lonesome, the definition is arbitrary and you'll go ahead and move the goalposts whenever it's convenient. Just look at Adam."

"You know I came here to fight him?"

She pointed down at the swirling light. "My boss does."

Nickolai looked down into the maelstrom of light. They had almost reached the knot of light at the base of their pillar. "Will I be able to?"

Angel smiled and laughed. She patted his arm and said, "Kit, you have no fucking idea."

Date: 2526.8.13 (Standard)
Bakunin–BD+50°1725

The first fireball crashed into the heart of the tower complex that formed the center of Proudhon. The light from it turned the towers of the PSDC black before the buildings began to fold inward against the swirling light erupting from the impact site.

The other fireballs slammed into the ground to the east and west, in line with the one buried in Proudhon's heart. One burrowed into the abandoned graveyard that had been Mosasa Salvage, where acres of dead and half-dead aircraft began spilling into a swirling amorphous maw. The other slammed into the eastern desert, a pillar of fire burning before the would-be pharaohs of Bakunin.

The forces of the Eastern Division of the Proudhon Defense Corporation began unloading everything they had against the invaders. Because the vast portion of their forces were arrayed between Proudhon and the western mountains—guarding against a more conventional attack from more conventional forces—the bulk of their arsenal rained down upon the glowing vortex of Mosasa Salvage.

They understood the principle, *as much energy in as small a space as possible*. Lasers and plasma cannons superheated the air between the front line and Adam's vortex. The first missiles vanished into the swirling light, deconstructed without effect. However, the commanders compensated quickly, altering the timing of the fuses, and the second volley detonated before actually touching the swirling light.

A new sun rose in the west as antimatter bombs and more conventional nuclear weapons saturated a few square kilometers of ground, scouring the desert down to the bedrock, leaving a desolate, and lethally radioactive, crater of purple glass in their wake.

Within the city of Proudhon, the forces of the PDC were not as densely packed or heavily armed. Fighters streaked by the swirling mass framed by the twisting skyscrapers of the PSDC, but their bombs were not delivered closely or quickly enough to deter Adam's hand moving on the face of the city. Their missiles, and the fighters themselves, were torn free of the sky by whipping tendrils of light.

One of the in-folding towers of the Proudhon Spaceport Development Company was hit by a tac-nuke that detonated before Adam's hand could touch it. Light and heat broke upon Adam's presence like a wave, rippling his mass like a stone thrown into a pond. The effect on the surrounding city was much more drastic. Windows blew in as the closest towers imploded and collapsed, a firestorm erupted in the central city, the smoke and toxic gases from the flashover spilling upward to form the rolling underside of a hellish cloud, a crippled twin to the one forming to the west.

The blast broke around a hemisphere cloaking one of the many concourses to the south. Within the hemisphere, a woman's voice quietly spoke.

"My turn."

Within her, she only had one mind, one source for control, not the small legion she had taken embedded in the doomed dropship. Still, she had been bequeathed much of the knowledge of Proteus upon her conversion. That knowledge maintained the shield that protected her and her still human twin self. That knowledge also spread to her extended body, crystalline forms that grew where she had stepped within the sublevels of Proudhon, and the concourse below her.

Within the tunnels under Proudhon, Toni's self consumed ferrocrete, steel, and the earth itself, pushing its probes deeper under the firestorm that was Proudhon. The probes sped toward the center of the city as fast as the matter around them could be consumed.

She did not make Stefan's mistake of imperfectly reproducing herself. She knew she was not skilled enough to create anything completely autonomous. Instead, when black pillars shot up out of the burning wreckage of central Proudhon, they were as much her as the arms on the body standing on top of the concourse.

Adam's swirling hive was surrounded by Toni's skyscraper-tall fingers. The light struck out at them, extending itself to attack one of the black pillars, and four more of Toni's fingers shot up, impaling the probe, so its light turned gray and it lost its form, its outline disintegrating into the smoke and ash billowing up from the city below.

"*I got your attention, fucker!*"

But even as she defeated the single probe, the glowing mass sent out, at once, hundreds more. Even with a mind unrestricted by the limits of a fleshy brain, she was still only one mind versus thousands. She could not meet *every* threat everywhere.

Around the center of Proudhon, the grappling forces moved fast enough to be a blur. First black, then gray, then pulsing white as Toni's presence was painfully disassembled by the more powerful and numerous disciples of Adam.

On top of the concourse, beneath the shield, Toni's body dripped sweat and hyperventilated. She nearly collapsed to her knees, stopped only when her other self, her still human self, grabbed her shoulders and said, "Are you all right?"

Around them, the defensive shield flickered as Toni's mental energies began to fade in the face of the onslaught. Even so, she still managed a grim smile.

"*Suckers,*" she whispered as her frontal attack on Adam disintegrated.

She refocused all her attention on the shield as she withdrew her extended body away from thirty deeply buried power cores underneath central Proudhon. While she spent her energy attacking Adam's manifestation, part of her probing self had consumed and replaced the shielding bottling up the antimatter generators that had powered most

of the city for a century. The devices were heavily shielded
and protected by permanent superconducting magnets that
held their volatile power source safe.

But meter by meter, Toni's self quickly withdrew, opening wide holes in the fifty layers of shielding between the
surface and the naked cores, a kilometer down below the
site of the PSDC's now-absent central towers. For a fraction
of a second, there were thirty wormlike tunnels extending
from Adam's light-filled body down to the superconducting
heart containing the antimatter cores of the power plants.

Then the superconductors disintegrated at Toni's
touch, and the magnetic bottle—intended to be stable for
centuries—failed.

Beneath Adam, thirty power plants became thirty directed antimatter charges as their hearts became pure
radiation streaming up through the holes drilled in their
shielding. Toni's black skyscraper-fingers were replaced by
thirty fingers of sterilizing white light so bright that atoms
within the atmosphere fused at their touch, releasing a secondary nuclear blast that leveled much of the still burning
city.

The blast washed against the shield, and Toni II looked
up from her collapsing twin to the fading pillar of light that
now consumed the center of Proudhon.

The light gave way to fire and smoke, and Adam no longer writhed within. The shield around them faded, letting in
the smell of the burning city. "I don't believe it," she whispered to the now-unconscious Toni. "You beat him."

Toni II looked up, eyes watering, as the wind tore at the
smoking haze. Something glowed to the East.

She stared it as it took on a vaguely humanoid form,
standing at the eastern edge of Proudhon. The ground resonated with the volume of its voice.

*"You shall not defy your coming salvation. It is time
for all to choose."*

Toni II stared at the smoke-wrapped apparition and
whispered, "Oh, *hell,* no."

CHAPTER FORTY-TWO

Salvation

"In the end, you are the only answer to the question:
What to do?"

—The Cynic's Book of Wisdom

"The highest manifestation of life consists in this:
that a being governs its own actions."

—St. Thomas Aquinas
(1225–1274)

Date: 2526.8.13 (Standard)
Khamsin—Epsilon Eridani

In a darkened chamber on the night side of the planet once
known as Khamsin, a being that was once known as Mr.
Antonio contemplated its role in the universe. It still wore
the outward skin of a human being, the dark pigment of
African ancestry, the athletic musculature of someone with
a martial past, and the biological markers of a woman approaching middle age.

It all was a fraud, of course. The body of Ms. Columbia
was a convenient mask stolen from someone long dead,
just like its other masks; Mr. Antonio who had worked to
lay Adam's groundwork on Bakunin; Yousef Al-Hamadi,
the Caliphate intelligence chief who had maneuvered the
Caliphate into Adam's hands and turned the Caliphate into
a tool to spread Adam's promise to the worlds of men; and
dozens of others whose skin it had taken on since Adam
had raised it out of the dust of the Race homeworld.

It had so long played at being something other than what it was, that it had come to realize it had no identity of its own. Nothing it thought or felt came from itself. It had formed what it was with discarded scraps of the personas it had absorbed.

That, and its service to Adam, was all that it had.

Now that Adam had conquered, it existed in Adam's promised paradise, a world that had transcended flesh, transcended death. Now that its mission had been completed, it faced its eternal reward and realized there was nothing within itself to receive.

The thing within the skin of the long-dead Ms. Columbia sat in the center of the city that had once been named Al Meftah, and couldn't find joy, or even a sense of satisfaction within itself. It wondered how many of the billion souls left on this planet felt the same emptiness it did. How many felt guilt that they survived while two thirds of their neighbors had refused Adam's divinity and faced oblivion?

It couldn't even answer if it was guilty itself.

"I served Adam," it spoke in Ms. Columbia's voice. "I brought His light to this world."

The words carried little conviction, and he could not even go to his God for comfort. There was only one sin in Adam's theology, and that was any doubt of Him.

It considered the option anyway. If Adam erased its existence, then at least it would no longer face the emptiness its doubt left within itself.

Something moved within the chamber, and Ms. Columbia's head turned to look in that direction. The room was plain and ovoid in shape. It was not constructed with a human morphology in mind. It was patterned after the warrens of the long-dead Race; the species that created the AIs that had evolved into Adam. Khamsin may have been a human world once, but it pleased Adam that their buildings echoed His creators, and Adam's will was not to be questioned.

As it watched the curving wall, it seemed to ripple, bubbling almost as if it was molten. In the senses it had beyond Ms. Columbia's, it tried to feel the movement of the ubiquitous presence of Adam's nanomachines, the blanket of Himself that wrapped everything He made or touched.

It felt nothing, and that frightened it.

Mass began heaping up upon itself, pouring from the walls. The matter that pooled in front of it was organic, biological in origin. If anything, it seemed as if the bacteria in the walls, and even the air, had started coalescing and reproducing, evolving itself in front of Ms. Columbia's eyes.

The mound of flesh before it formed muscles, and skin, and fur.

It stood, towering over Ms. Columbia's body. The atavistic form, all striped fur, muscles, claws, and teeth. The tiger's eyes flashed a reflected green at it.

"How are *you* here?" it asked the tiger.

"For the moment, I am everywhere, Mr. Antonio."

When the tiger addressed it by that name, the being had to look down at Ms. Columbia's skin to confirm it had not somehow slipped into its prior identity, Mr. Antonio.

The tiger squatted on its digitigrade legs to look into Ms. Columbia's face. "I know you, whatever shell you're wearing now. You sold me into service of the thing that calls itself Adam."

"I served Him."

"You served evil," the tiger told it.

"No, He offers salvation to all life."

"And destroys all that do not accept it. Adam is the negation of moral choice."

"What are you?"

"The choice He did not give me." The tiger extended his hand. "Do you follow Adam's path, or your own?"

"I don't have a path," it told the tiger. "There is nothing within me but what Adam gave me."

"You own yourself," the tiger told him. "But only if you choose to accept it."

It stared at the tiger, and after a long moment's consideration, Ms. Columbia took Nickolai's hand.

Date: 2526.8.13 (Standard)
Bakunin–BD+50°1725
"It is time for all to choose."

Toni II tried to drag Toni's limp body away from the apparition, even if it made no sense. Adam's effigy stood

kilometers away from them, and stood as tall as Proudhon's now-missing skyscrapers. The few meters' movement
toward the doors back down into the concourse were not
going to make a difference.

She screamed at Toni, "Wake up. *Wake up!*"

Tears burned her eyes, and her pulse raced. Toni's body
was much heavier than she thought it should be. She was a
Protean, damn it, she had just single-handedly laid apocalyptic waste to Adam. She could do it again, if she would
just *wake up*.

Over and over, in Toni II's mind, she heard her own
voice, *"Don't ask me if I can win."*

"Damn it, damn it . . ."

The smoke swirled above the city, twisting into a fiery
pillar before the image of Adam. The effigy raised its arms
as if it was calling up the fiery tornado from the burning
firestorm below.

*"Worship He who shall deliver you from the tyranny
of the flesh."*

The wind gusted around her, and she fell to the ground
under Toni's body. The wind fed the swirling pillar of smoke
before Adam, and all around the flames in the city flared.

And went out.

Even as the wind intensified, the firestorm gripping
Proudhon died. Even the orange pillar in front of Adam
burned out and the twisting column became nothing but
smoke. The column became larger and thicker, as every
wisp of airborne particulate matter seemed drawn to it.
Even the body of the mushroom cloud above the city fed
the vast swirling cloud.

Toni II thought it was a manifestation of Adam's will,
until the towering effigy dropped its arms and took a step
back.

"Who defies me?"

The answer seemed to come from everywhere. **"YOU
ARE NOT GOD."**

The words shook the ground and vibrated the air so in-
tensely that Toni II's bones ached. In her arms, Toni groaned.

"Wake up," Toni II whispered, her voice lost in the tearing sound of the wind.

Adam's voice repeated, **"Who defies me?"** Somehow, by comparison, Adam sounded weaker.

The other voice slammed down like an asteroid from heaven. **"I DEFY YOU."** The pillar of smoke had consumed the mushroom cloud, and swirled thousands of kilometers into the stratosphere above Proudhon, dwarfing Adam's glowing effigy. The base of it split apart, the swirling dust and smoke forming three separate columns, which further refined their shape into two legs, *and a tail.*

Toni II's eyes widened in shock as she realized, *I know that voice.*

Toni groaned again, and over the roaring wind, Toni II could only understand one word slipping from her other self's lips.

"Nickolai?"

Adam's effigy screamed at the heavens, **"Who defies God?"**

The top of the pillar of smoke split apart into arms and a head. The right arm carried a flaming sword five hundred meters long. Nickolai's scowling face looked down at the mewling form of Adam below and said, **"YOU DO,"** as the sword came down.

Kugara blinked herself awake.

Must have passed out there.

She licked her lips and wondered how long she had blacked out. Her genetically engineered metabolism seemed to be working overtime to keep her from dying from shock. That meant dehydration would probably be what finished her off.

"I'm sorry," came a familiar voice from next to her.

She turned her head to see Nickolai. "Oh, so now I'm hallucinating." Strangely enough, though, the hallucinatory Nickolai had normal eyes, not the black holes the Protean had bequeathed him. These eyes were a deep green, that were richer and more expressive than even the artificial eyes he'd had when she had met him.

She smiled because she liked these eyes better.

"You aren't hallucinating."

"Of course, a hallucination would say that."

He bent and grabbed her shoulder, and it certainly didn't feel like a hallucination. She trembled at his touch, especially as he pulled her away from the rock pinning her down.

She gasped one word, "*Wait!*" as she felt her thigh tug free of the multi-ton rock. She squeezed her eyes shut, picturing fountains of arterial blood spraying the face of the rock as she bled out from a ragged stump.

"You're unhurt," Nickolai said, gently squeezing her shoulder.

"What?" She opened her eyes and looked down. Her leg was naked from the thigh down, but uninjured. She could even wriggle her toes. She looked over at Nickolai and said, "Tell me I am not hallucinating."

"I made it in," he said. "I met the Dolbrians."

She sat up and grabbed his shoulders. "You're kidding. This wild goose chase paid off? What the hell are you doing worrying about me? What about Adam? Can we—"

Nickolai placed the pad of a finger against Kugara's lips.

"You don't need to worry about Adam anymore."

The way he said it, a flat statement of fact, chilled her. She stared into his new eyes and, when he took his finger away, she asked, "Why were you apologizing, then?"

"Because I didn't take you with me."

"What?"

"I've gone somewhere . . . I don't think I can come back."

She placed a hand on his chest and shook her head. "You're here now. What do you mean?"

"The Dolbrians aren't dead," Nickolai said. "They aren't even sleeping. They're waiting for us."

"Us?"

"Any individual that can accept what the responsibility means. Who can accept the sovereignty of others." He looked down, away from her. "Me," he said.

"You?"

"I've returned for Adam. But I can't stay."

Kugara felt tears forming and she shook her head. "Why?"

"What is the sense of removing Adam, only to replace him?"

She embraced him and buried her face in the fur of his chest. "Damn it, I don't forgive you. We were supposed to face this crap together. You can't leave."

"I have to."

She shook her head.

"Kugara," he whispered.

"What?" She sobbed into his chest.

"I've opened up a tunnel to the surface. Dörner and Brody are already walking up that way. They'll meet up with Flynn and Parvi and the others soon enough." He pointed toward a crack in the massive fragment of the Milky Way that still pressed its glowing faux stars down on them. She blinked, and it seemed to go on forever. She had an escape route. "The war?"

"Adam is gone. But Bakunin is still Bakunin."

She laughed. If Adam was gone, a civil war seemed almost pleasant. He let her go, and she grabbed his arm. "Don't leave."

He gently removed her hand. "I'm sorry. You are the only thing I regret leaving."

"But—"

"Please, Kugara, if you care for us, just remember what's right, what's wrong ... and ask the right questions." He slipped out another crack in the fallen rock, directly opposite the path to the surface.

She looked at the path toward Dörner, and Brody, and everything else she knew. Then she looked off where Nickolai had disappeared.

What are you apologizing for?

Because I didn't take you with me.

What was there here that *she* would regret leaving?

She pushed herself up and followed Nickolai, wondering what he meant about asking the right questions.

LAST EPILOGUE

Apotheosis

"The human heart refuses to believe in a universe without a purpose."

—IMMANUEL KANT
(1724–1804)

CHAPTER FORTY-THREE

Eternity

"Things continue."
—*The Cynic's Book of Wisdom*

"Following the light of the sun, we left the Old World."
—CHRISTOPHER COLUMBUS
(1451–1506)

Date: 2526.8.15 (Standard)
Bakunin–BD+50°1725

Flynn Jorgenson emerged from underneath the Diderot Mountains holding Rebecca Tsoravitch's hand. He wasn't sure what Rebecca meant to him, but he knew what she meant to Tetsami—at least what one of the personalities within her meant to Tetsami. He held on to her as if the woman was *his* lover, and the way she pulled herself up and placed a hand on his shoulder for support, she was behaving likewise.

Behind them, the others crawled out of the Protean-reconstructed tunnel to stand on the frigid platform where Bleek Munitions' outpost once stood. Shane and Parvi, Brody and Dörner, a very disheveled-looking General Lubikov, and a random assortment of PDC mercenaries and nonhuman monks that they had accumulated in the ascent out of the ruined Dolbrian caverns.

"Godwin looks like hell," Parvi said in a puff of fog. Somehow she had survived, even when refusing Protean ministrations. Apparently, unlike Flynn, the tunnel hadn't collapsed *on* her.

The city below did look like hell. There were large sections leveled, and scars from fires that had consumed several city blocks. But even so, there was no sign of the devastation Flynn had only glimpsed on Salmagundi, or in the holo from Khamsin.

"I think we made it, Gram."

"Yeah, maybe we did."

Rebecca leaned against him, and he placed an arm around her waist.

He added, *"And your boyfriend's cute."*

There was an uncomfortable silence in his head, and he felt himself blushing. He almost laughed at the incongruity.

"Hey, there!" someone shouted, and all the military people moved suddenly to point weapons toward the sound.

Parvi shouted at them all to ease up.

Standing on a rise looking down at them was a pair of identical women.

"Guess the Valentine twins made it, too."

"Guess they did."

Rebecca called up to them, "Where's Mallory? Is he in charge of things?"

One of the Valentines shook her head as the pair started walking down the slope toward them. "No, he didn't make it."

"Who's in charge, then?" General Lubikov asked.

"It's Bakunin," the other Valentine said. "No one is."

Someone behind Flynn muttered, "Great."

The other Valentine continued. "What about Kugara and Nickolai?"

Dörner shook her head as Brody said, "They were down with us during the cave-in. We never saw them after that—they were almost certainly buried alive."

"Nickolai?" the first Valentine asked, "You're sure?"

"Why?" Dörner asked. "Did you see him?"

Date: Unknown
Unknown

"It's beautiful, Nickolai."

"You're beautiful."

"Why didn't you ask me to follow you?"

"It wouldn't have been fair to you."

"Why?"

"The risk, you could have died on the threshold."

"Do you know all the stupid things I've risked my life for?"

"It had to be your choice."

"You could have asked—"

"You had to come here on your own account, not mine."

"You are still annoying as all hell."

"But I'm glad you came."

"So answer me something."

"What?"

"Who is that annoying rabbit?"

Across all of human space, Adam and Adam's agents were met by Nickolai's avatar. Few as dramatically as on Bakunin, but many worlds saw the image of the final book in St. Rajasthan's scriptures—a tiger the height of a mountain, bearing a flaming sword to cut down the unrighteous. Perhaps the only failure of that particular prophecy was the fact that it did not mark the end of days.

It did not even mark the end of St. Rajasthan's faith. The sight of the prophet on so many worlds ignited the faith in a new congregation. Soon, the Church of St. Rajasthan found as many of its members within the Fallen as not. And as it spread, the Church found a thread of Christlike redemption in the fact that the world had not ended.

Likewise, those monks from Bakunin, who had survived the destruction of their monastery, founded a new faith based on the salvation brought by the Dolbrians. As apostles of a renewed faith, bearing testament of Adam's fate, they found fertile ground in the soil left raw by the assault by Adam on the core human worlds.

And, despite the fall of both Earth and Occisis to Adam, Father Mallory was proved wrong. He had not been witness to the last of his own faith. Once Adam had been removed from the worlds of men, their transhuman survivors were left themselves to face the guilt of their survival. The weight of their choice, against the billions that had chosen differently, was too great to bear alone. Many returned to what Adam had explicitly denied them, and one of the first of the ancient human structures those survivors rebuilt on Earth was the Vatican. The Kaaba followed, as did the foundations of Jerusalem, and the temples in Asia.

Beyond Earth, on dozens of worlds, Protean converts from the battle around Bakunin tached in to find that Adam's war was over. But despite their once-pariah status, the bans on heretical technology had collapsed in the face of Adam's destruction, and the Proteans' alliance with humanity. The Proteans found populations more welcoming than not, especially those on far-flung worlds who still worried about being unready for Adam's return. The Proteans suddenly found themselves given outposts all over human space.

And even Adam had worshipers. There were those remaining who still gave praise to the being that had lifted them out of the bonds of the flesh. But however many were among this number, there were twenty times more who condemned Adam as a false god.

All these, and more, now formed the people of mankind—humanity no longer quite exclusively human; all still sharing the need to understand, and to give themselves meaning.

And the expanding universe of humanity faced this diversity as it always had—painfully, inequitably, begrudgingly—with violence and joy, with denial and a near divine acceptance. Each of five hundred billion human hearts left to navigate its own path through the chaos of human belief.

Nothing had changed.

Everything had changed.

APPENDIX A:

Alphabetical listing of sources

Note: Dates are Terrestrial standard. Where the year is debatable due to interstellar travel, the Earth equivalent is used with an asterisk. Incomplete or uncertain biographical information is indicated by a question mark.

Lord Acton, John (1834–1902) English historian, statesman
Adams, John (1735–1826) American president.
Aristotle (384 BCE–322 BCE) Greek philosopher.
St. Thomas Aquinas (1225–1274) Italian theologian.
St. Augustine (354–430) Numidian Bishop of Hippo.
Marcus Aurelius Antoninus (121–180) Roman emperor, philosopher.
Bacon, Francis (1561–1626) English essayist, philosopher.
Bakunin, Mikhail A. (1814–1876) Russian political philosopher.
Browne, Thomas (1605–1682) English physician, writer.
Browning, Robert (1812–1889) English poet.
Carlyle, Thomas (1795–1881) Scottish historian, critic, writer.

Celine, Robert (1923–1996) American lawyer, anarchist.

Cheviot, Jean Honoré (2065–2128) United Nations secretary general.

Columbus, Christopher (1451–1506) Genoese explorer.

Darrow, Clarence S. (1857–1938) American lawyer, writer.

Debs, Eugene V. (1855–1926) American socialist.

de Maistre, Joseph (1753–1821) French diplomat.

Diderot, Denis (1713–1784) French philosopher.

Dostoevski, Fyodor (1821–1881) Russian novelist.

Emerson, Ralph Waldo (1803–1882) American essayist, poet, minister.

Engels, Friedrich (1820–1895) German socialist.

France, Anatole (1844–1924) French novelist, critic.

Galiani, August Benito (2019–*2105) European spaceship commander.

Godwin, William (1756–1836) English novelist, biographer, philosopher.

Gracián, Baltasar (1601–1658) Spanish writer, rector.

Hamilton, Alexander (1757–1804) American president, statesman.

Harper, Sylvia (2008–2081) American civil-rights activist, president.

Hazlitt, William (1778–1830) English essayist, critic.

Johnson, Samuel (1709–1784) English lexicographer, essayist, poet.

Kafka, Franz (1883–1924) Austrian writer.

Kalecsky, Boris (2103–2200) Terran Council president.

Kant, Immanuel (1724–1804) German philosopher.

Nietzsche, Friedrich (1844–1900) German philosopher.

Olmanov, Dimitri (2190–2350) Chairman of the Terran Executive Command.

Pascal, Blaise (1623–1662) French geometrician, philosopher, writer.

Phillips, Wendell (1811–1884) American orator, abolitionist.

St. Rajasthan 2075–2118) Tau Ceti nonhuman religious leader.

Shane, Marbury (2044–*2074) Occisian colonist, soldier.

Sun Tzu (ca. 500 BCE) Chinese army commander, strategist.

Lord Tennyson, Alfred (1809–1892) English poet.

Washington, George (1732–1799) American general, president, statesman.

Yeats, William Butler (1865–1939) Irish writer.

S. Andrew Swann
The Apotheosis Trilogy

It's been nearly two hundred years since the collapse of the Confederacy, the last government to claim humanity's colonies. So when signals come in revealing lost human colonies that could shift the power balance, the race is on between the Caliphate ships and a small team of scientists and mercenaries. But what awaits them all is a threat far beyond the scope of any human government.

PROPHETS
978-0-7564-0541-0

HERETICS
978-0-7564-0613-4

MESSIAH
978-0-7564-0657-8

To Order Call: 1-800-788-6262
www.dawbooks.com

DAW 160

S. Andrew Swann

CJ Cherryh
Complete Classic Novels in Omnibus Editions

To Order Call: 1-800-788-6262
www.dawbooks.com

Tanya Huff
The Confederation Novels

A CONFEDERATION OF VALOR
Omnibus Edition
(Valor's Choice, The Better Part of Valor)
978-0-7564-0399-7

THE HEART OF VALOR
978-0-7564-0481-9

VALOR'S TRIAL
978-0-7564-0557-1

THE TRUTH OF VALOR
978-0-7564-0620-2

To Order Call: 1-800-788-6262
www.dawbooks.com

RM Meluch

The Tour of the Merrimack

"An action-packed space opera. For readers who like romps through outer space, lots of battles with gooey horrific insects, and character sexplotation, *The Myriad* delivers..." —*SciFi.com*

"Like *The Myriad*, this one is grand space opera. You will enjoy it." —*Analog*

"This is grand old-fashioned space opera, so toss your disbelief out the nearest airlock and dive in."
  —*Publishers Weekly* (Starred Review)